# ADVENTURES

### O F

# RACE WILLIAMS

DIME DETECTIVE ™ PULP CLASSICS*

**THE ADVENTURES OF MAX LATIN by Norbert Davis**
**THE ADVENTURES OF SATAN HALL by Carroll John Daly**
**THE ADVENTURES OF MIKE BLAIR by Hank Searls**
**THE ADVENTURES OF CARDIGAN by Frederick Nebel**
**THE ADVENTURES OF RACE WILLIAMS by Carroll John Daly**

*Published by The Mysterious Press

# THE
# ADVENTURES
## OF
# RACE WILLIAMS

## A DIME DETECTIVE™ BOOK

■

## CARROLL JOHN DALY

### SERIES CONSULTANT: ROBERT WEINBERG

**THE MYSTERIOUS PRESS**
New York • London • Tokyo

"Some Die Hard," *Dime Detective Magazine*, September 1935. Copyright 1935 by Popular Publications, Inc. Copyright Renewed © 1963 and Assigned to Blazing Publications, Inc.

"Dead Hands Reaching," *Dime Detective Magazine*, November 1935. Copyright 1935 by Popular Publications, Inc. Copyright Renewed © 1963 and Assigned to Blazing Publications, Inc.

"Corpse & Co.," *Dime Detective Magazine*, February 1936. Copyright 1936 by Popular Publications, Inc. Copyright Renewed © 1964 and Assigned to Blazing Publications, Inc.

"Just Another Stiff," *Dime Detective Magazine*, April 1936. Copyright 1936 by Popular Publications, Inc. Copyright Renewed © 1964 and Assigned to Blazing Publications, Inc.

"City of Blood," *Dime Detective Magazine*, October 1936. Copyright 1936 by Popular Publications, Inc. Copyright Renewed © 1964 and Assigned to Blazing Publications, Inc.

DIME DETECTIVE and RACE WILLIAMS are exclusive trademarks of Blazing Publications, Inc.

The Mysterious Press, 129 West 56th Street, New York, N.Y. 10019
This Mysterious Press edition is published by arrangement with Blazing Publications, Inc., The Argosy Company, in cooperation with Mrs. Dorothy B. Nebel.

Printed in the United States of America
First Printing: January 1989
10  9  8  7  6  5  4  3  2  1

**Library of Congress Cataloging-in-Publication Data**

Daly, Carroll John, 1889–1958.
   The adventures of Race Williams : a Dime detective book / Carroll John Daly.
      p.   cm.
   ISBN 0-89296-959-8
   1. Williams, Race (Fictitious character)—Fiction. 2. Detective and mystery stories, American. I. Title.
PS3507.A4673A65   1989
813'.52—dc19
                                                                      88-15060
                                                                            CIP

# CONTENTS

■

RACE WILLIAMS by Robert Weinberg / 1

SOME DIE HARD / 5

DEAD HANDS REACHING / 83

CORPSE & CO. / 157

JUST ANOTHER STIFF / 213

CITY OF BLOOD / 279

# THE
# ADVENTURES
## OF
# RACE WILLIAMS

# RACE WILLIAMS

## BY ROBERT WEINBERG

The best-selling author of hardboiled detective fiction in the 1920s and 1930s was not Dashiell Hammett, Raymond Chandler, or Erle Stanley Gardner. Instead it was Carroll John Daly, a writer whose work has since faded into obscurity. Never a critical success, Daly pleased only the fans. Race Williams, his most famous creation, first appeared in "Knights of the Open Palm" in *Black Mask Magazine*, June 1, 1923. A tough, hardboiled detective, Williams believed in one kind of justice—the type delivered by two blazing forty-fives. He soon became the most popular character in the publication. A new Race Williams story in *Black Mask* guaranteed a 15 percent boost in sales for that issue. Those loyal readers made Daly king of the detective pulp writers.

In 1931, Popular Publications launched *Dime Detective* as an alternative to *Black Mask*. The new pulp featured the same hardboiled detective fiction that appeared in the other magazine, but with much more colorful cover illustrations and a better layout. However, the publishers of Popular also realized that big-name authors sold magazines. In a bold move, they offered the top writers for *Black Mask* the astonishing rate of four cents a word for stories featuring new characters created specifically for their magazine. Among those authors paid that top rate were Erle Stanley Gardner, Frederick Nebel, and Carroll John Daly.

One problem faced by the pulp was the editorial policy of Popular Publications not to feature serials. A number of different factors necessitated this strategy. Most important was that it ensured readers that all stories in the magazine were complete in the issue. During the height of the Depression, many publishers used serials as a hook to ensure continued sales of their pulps; however, many readers refused to buy magazines featuring such serials. In pleasing the fans, Popular lost ground with the authors.

The pulps served as the main market for detective and mystery fiction. However, secondary sales to hardcover often offered major rewards after that initial publication. A number of serials from *Black Mask* appeared in book form after their initial magazine serialization, including *The Maltese Falcon*. But *Dime Detective* refused to run serials and the hardcover market only wanted novels.

Daly, along with a number of other authors of the time, found a way around the problem. He wrote novels as a series of short stories. Each novelette worked independently but, at the same time, fit into the framework of the longer story. With minor rewriting and deletions, the book served as a series of short stories for magazine publication, and as a novel for hardcover reprint as well.

For the new magazine, Daly penned a series of long novelettes chronicling the adventures of Vee Brown, an Assistant District Attorney who composed hit songs in his spare time. Brown dealt out the same type of bullet justice as Race Williams and never hesitated to shoot first and ask questions later. The Vee Brown stories earned Daly over $500 each, and appeared frequently in *Dime Detective* during the early 1930s. Two sequences of adventures later appeared as hardcovers, *Murder Won't Wait* and *The Emperor of Evil*.

In 1934 Daly left *Black Mask* in a dispute with the editor. Late in 1935 he wrote a series of five stores featuring his most famous creation, Race Williams, for *Dime Detective*. This book collects those stories.

The adventures highlighted all of Daly's virtues as well as his faults as a writer. Unlike Chandler, Hammett, and Gardner, Carroll John Daly never escaped the pulps. The Race Williams adventures substituted action for believable plot and menacing masterminds for realistic villains. The stories never rose above the level of pulp thrillers, but, in that limited vein, they worked very well.

Take, for example, when the D.A. is asked to describe Race Williams in "City of Blood."

"I told him," said our D.A. rather stiffly, "that you were a man who was without fear, without heart, or without soul, and made a business of killing men."

Equally dramatic is Williams' deadly confrontation with Spats Willis, the flat-faced killer sent from the Orient with one mission—to kill Race Williams—featured in "Just Another Stiff." The same novelette also contains a furious gun battle as Race stands toe-to-toe with One Man Armin, the most feared killer in New York. The action never stopped.

And that essentially was what pulps were all about.

# SOME DIE HARD

■

*It was the first time in Williams' career that he'd ever had a corpse for a client but that didn't make him any less willing to earn his fee. Dead or alive, the one who'd hired him would get the same brand of blue-steel service he always put out for his customers, even though she could neither thank him nor hand him a bonus when the kill-job was done.*

# ONE

# THE CORPSE AND THE CLIENT

■

It was raw, foggy—and I didn't like the trip to begin with. But there was the house, lost in the thickness of trees. A little bungalow with light shining from behind yellow-white shades.

I parked my car on the deserted, muddy lane, switched a gun from shoulder holster to side pocket and plodded straight down the narrow stone path toward the light, just a glare in the fog.

No, I didn't like it. You see, I was there in answer to a letter. The end of it read—

> If you don't come or don't get this letter in time, then keep the money. I'll be dead.
>
> An Unfortunate Girl.

The money part consisted of just two hundred dollars. But there was a key in the envelope, too. And now I was there, on the porch, and pushing that key in the lock. Sure, I was careful! I've got enemies—plenty of them. Not that I mind a little gunplay on the other lad's part. But I want to play too.

One look into that lighted room and I knew that this was not any trap—for me, at least. The trap had been sprung before I entered, and what killers had been there had certainly departed. But being a cautious man I searched the place, then came back to the living room.

And there was the woman—a young woman. She was straight and stiff in a chair, held there by a thin, strong rope. Beautiful? Well, her eyes were sunk too far to tell. And the rest of her face—but why go into that? From the torn dress, exposing the bareness of her chest and shoulders, to the top of her head, it wasn't hard to conclude that she had met a horrible death; a slow one, before the knife was driven into her heart and left there, the dried blood caked around it. The hands still seemed to grip tightly the arms of the chair! The entire body, despite the strong rope that bit tightly into white flesh—dark flesh now—had twisted.

But business is business. Here was murder; here was I—and there were the police. No, I didn't like to drag them in with me. I'm a private operator who likes to work alone. Still, I can't chance trouble with the cops; that is, too much trouble—like finding a murdered body after receiving written directions how to reach the spot marked (X).

So I lifted the phone there on the table and called Sergeant O'Rourke—a right guy, a real guy, a cop who'd work with a lad, not against him. O'Rourke said he'd be up, but to expect someone from the nearest precinct ahead of him, muttered something about how I got around a lot and hung up.

I didn't look at the body much. The medical examiner could do that. It wouldn't be hard to tell how she died!

Then the police were at the door. I didn't know the sergeant from that uptown precinct, nor either of the two cops that came in with him. But the lad they stood aside to let enter, I did know.

Inspector Iron-Man Nelson! The hard-panned boy of the police system. He didn't need any department order to "muss them"— that was his stock-in-trade. They say that if he was in the mood, he'd beat a guy almost to death to get information about a dollar watch; and if he was convinced of a man's guilt, he'd plant a ton of coal in his cellar to pin the crime on him. A ton of coal! I say that because there's more than a mere rumor that he did exactly that once, on a case; only to find out later that the house was heated by oil. They say he went out that night and carried the coal away, bag by bag, himself. Anyway, that's the story; and true or not, it's a damn good one. Yep, they hung the title "One-Ton Nelson" on him, and he was ready to cut any man's heart out who threw it up at him now.

I didn't like Nelson and he didn't like me. Maybe he was honest—but certainly he was brutal, as unnecessarily brutal as the men he hunted. He saw the body and stared at it. If it jarred him he did not show it. But the sergeant rocked back on his heels, and the younger of the two harness bulls look as if he were going to be violently ill.

Nelson said to the sergeant: "All right, Bailey! Open a window"—and with a sneer—"and let that young squirt hang out it. You better detail him to a school crossing."

"He's a good man," said Sergeant Bailey. "A fine man. Open the window, Rogers, as the inspector says." A break for the boy there. Then to Nelson, "By God, sir, it's as brutal a bit of work as I've seen in twenty years on—"

Inspector Nelson turned his back on him, spoke to me. "Well, Race Williams. Come on! Spill it. What are you doing here?"

I shrugged my shoulders, lit a butt, saw the way he eyed me and put the burnt match in my pocket, then said: "Someone had to notify the police."

"Still a wise guy, eh?" There was nothing of the stage about Nelson's sneer. He had stuck it on his puss fifteen years ago and it came and went when he opened his mouth. "Well!" He jerked a thumb at the dead body. "How's your stomach?"

My shoulders went up and down. I said: "It was all right until you came in."

"Listen, smart guy." Nelson had a way of pounding a finger against your chest that I didn't like. "The girl's murdered. You found the body. No stalling! It's private dicks like you and the rest of those cheap vultures that mix up in things that don't concern them, who blackmail people into hiring you—then know exactly where to find your dead."

"Listen, sourpuss." I gave him back his own line. "If you want to exercise your facial muscles, try it on them. They're paid to listen—I'm not." And I added: "O'Rourke will be up to take charge in a few minutes."

"A sergeant, eh, to take charge—to tell me?" He paused, and

the sneer wasn't so hot. O'Rourke worked straight from the commissioner and, though he didn't bear any fancy title, he generally took complete charge of things—inspectors or no inspectors. What's more, Nelson knew that. His words of depreciation fell flat! He swung, tossed the phone into his hand, got headquarters and started shooting the baloney. I didn't get all of it, but enough to let me know that Nelson had just dropped in at the uptown precinct when O'Rourke's call came through, and rode up to the bungalow with Sergeant Bailey. I *would* get a break like that.

Inspector Iron-Man Nelson damn near broke the cradle when he flung the phone back. He gave orders quickly, sharply, and I have to admit they were good, intelligent orders. He knew his business all right, but he drove men with the fear of losing their rank, not with the hope of bettering it.

He sent the two cops to the cellar, Bailey to the attic. Then his hard, shrewd eyes stared at the girl's, as if he looked deep into her dead ones and tried to read what was there. After a bit he threw questions at me, as if I were a witness on the stand.

"What made you come here? Do you know the woman? Did anyone leave the house? Were you alone? Did a client come with you?" And when I told him I'd let O'Rourke in on the ground floor, he went sour entirely. He was yelling something about holding "guilty knowledge concerning a murder" when the two cops came up the cellar stairs, pounded over the kitchen floor and stepped into the room.

The young cop who had gulped air from the window spoke. "No one hiding in the cellar, sir." He half saluted.

"Now isn't that fine!" Nelson sneered. "With us tramping across the floor upstairs, you'd expect that? I want a report of that cellar."

"Well"—the officer scratched his head—"the furnace is out. Looks as if the ashes were quite cold."

"And what," said Nelson, "is peculiar about that?"

"Why," said the cop, "there's still coal in the bin. Just about one ton."

And I did it; I couldn't help it. That boy never knew the crack he'd made, had probably never heard the story. Sergeant Bailey had, though; you could see that by the way his face stiffened. But it was I who put the gag over.

"Just a ton!" I nodded at Nelson. "Something lucky or ominous in that, Inspector. Remember? One-Ton Nelson!" And I walked over to the mantel, found elbow room above the fireplace and took my laugh.

Nelson didn't lose his head exactly, but he was damn good and mad. He glared once at the young cop, shot orders through his teeth. Then he came to the mantel, gripped my shoulder and swung me around. "Smart guy. Fresh guy!" His head shot forward, his round little eyes blazed, the veins in his face glistened blue. Hard-panned was right. Hard fingers too!

I don't like guys laying hands on me; not even coppers. I shot up my right elbow and knocked his hand loose. He felt it too; his face went livid. He said: "A punk like you needs slapping around. It would do you good." He half raised his right hand.

"Try it!" I said simply. "It might do me good, but it wouldn't do you any."

Maybe Nelson would have smacked me. I'm not sure. But if he had started to slap me around, I'd have let him have it. He knew me and he knew that. I don't take it, lying down, from any guy.

But O'Rourke came. The medical examiner was right behind him, and a couple of other men. And there we stood like a couple of schoolboys, as O'Rourke said afterwards; though at the time I'd have bet a century he never noticed it.

I like to watch O'Rourke work; he has a way with him. He didn't give orders exactly—or if he did, you weren't conscious of them. It was as if he picked up suggestions, even from the stony silence of Iron-Man Nelson, and passed them along to the others.

He said: "Thanks a lot, Sergeant, for bringing the boys along and holding the fort. Lucky we had Inspector Nelson right on the job; we'll be sure of a good start. Much obliged for buzzing me, Race. Now, Doctor, it's a job for a man who has been around them for a long time."

Doctor Ritter's head bobbed up and down. He bent over the dead girl, sniffed a couple of times, shook his head as if he didn't find the job pleasant, then went to work as if it was the very corpse he had been looking forward to during his long career.

O'Rourke buzzed me in a corner while the boys set up their cameras and took their shots. He shook his head very seriously when I told him about the One-Ton Nelson crack, and didn't smile.

"I don't know what you got out of it, Race. After all, Nelson stands for something in the department. Brutal, forcible, efficient; and his dislikes are strong ones. Why pile up trouble?"

I couldn't answer that one so I shrugged my shoulders. Personally, I didn't think Nelson could dislike me more than he did. And I didn't like him. Also I still thought it was too good a crack to miss. I showed O'Rourke the note that brought me there.

He read it, handled it gingerly, looked at the postmark, said: "Ten o'clock the fourteenth! That's today. See?"

"Sure!" I nodded. The cancellation date, for once, was clear. "I received it in the mail this afternoon. It said to be here just before eleven."

O'Rourke looked at the postmark again, turned to the medical examiner. "Just off-hand, Doc, how long has she been dead?"

Doctor Ritter stroked his chin, looked at O'Rourke, said finally: "Long enough. Long enough!"

"Well"—O'Rourke grinned—"I don't want to pin you down. Was she alive at ten o'clock this morning?"

"No!" Emphatically. "Nor ten o'clock last night either. Further than that I won't go."

"I see." O'Rourke gave me that pleasant smile as he pocketed my letter. "The girl never wrote this letter to you, Race. That's odd."

"Odd? Sure!" I agreed with that. "There were two hundred-dollar bills in that letter. Someone wanted the body found!"

The doctor came over to us now. "Here's a note. She must have shoved it down her dress. It may mean a lot to you."

I read it over O'Rourke's shoulder.

Sweetheart:—

Will try to be there, but rather late. It was better we didn't see too much of each other for a few days. But you got my letter telling you that Blake can be bought off, despite his threats to you about us.

Kramer promised to have a talk with him, and did. And I think Kramer turned the trick. Don't wait too late for me.

Toby.

O'Rourke said to Ritter as Nelson stood grimly by: "Well, Doctor, what do you say?"

The medical examiner cleared his throat, said: "It was a brutal bit of work. I'd say—one of vengeance." And as O'Rourke smiled, "I'd also say that she was tortured in an endeavor to make her sign a document. Look here!" He walked over to the dead girl, lifted her right hand. "Plainly there are smears of ink on her fingers. A fountain pen, perhaps."

He was right, but it meant nothing to me. Whether she wrote or not couldn't be told by the ink.

Inspector Nelson, who hadn't opened his face, spoke just as I was leaving. "I suppose you are more or less in charge here, Sergeant. You're letting Williams go, eh?"

"Letting him go, Inspector!" O'Rourke seemed surprised. "Do I understand that you wish to hold him—Race Williams?" And with a chuckle, "Why—we'd have him locked up for murder half the time if we took him in every time we found him with a dead body."

"The circumstances are such—" Nelson started, stopped, glared at me. "You and I don't see eye to eye on Williams, Sergeant. Never did! Never will! To me, he's the cheapest sort of—"

This time I grinned, even tapped a finger against his chest. "Tut, tut." And as I stepped toward the door, "See you some more, O'Rourke. See you again, One-Ton!" And I was gone, whistling down the drive. Maybe it was bad politics and all that, but I'm a lad who has to get it out when he has it in.

Why did I walk off in such a hurry? No, it wasn't the anger in Nelson's face; something entirely different. I work for a living, and I had another job to do. Not much of a one. But I had made contact with a gem thief in a Newark hideout. Not high-class work, maybe; but there was half a grand in it for me and I only had to get the goods, deliver them to the rightful owner, and be done with it. The owner wanted the rocks, not newspaper excitement and police notoriety. The crook wanted the cash, and he knew I wouldn't turn him in.

So I spent the next couple of hours on that little jaunt, waiting and telephoning and being dragged around in a taxi—and arguing.

But finally getting the rocks, making the delivery and pocketing the half-grand from the grateful owner.

I was just going into my own apartment when a plainclothesman walked up and spoke to me. I knew his map but not his monicker. But he knew me.

"Hello, Race Williams!" He greeted me like a long-lost friend. "Going to hit the hay, eh? Well, you're lucky. I'll be around until— What time is it, anyway? My timepiece has gone screwy."

I don't know why. I didn't see the point in it then. But I hesitated, finally left my watch in my pocket and said as I left him: "You guys are lucky to have a watch even if it does go screwy. You're lucky, also, to work by the clock."

I was thoughtful as I went into the apartment. Of course there are a lot of plainclothesmen about the city, and plenty of them don't know what time it is. I didn't go to bed. I slipped into a robe, mixed myself a stiff drink, lay back in a chair and pretended to think.

O'Rourke pounded in later. He was full of conversation. "We've identified the woman, Race. A reporter spotted her. I just left her house. She's Mrs. Blake Southlow. Maiden name of Sarah Jane Adams. Inherited a lot of dough from her father, Vance Fairchild Adams."

"Doesn't mean a thing to me," I admitted. "How about Toby and Kramer?"

"All in the bag." O'Rourke rubbed his hands. "We'll clear this up quick. The servants know everything and suspect twice as much. It's just the regular triangle. Blake Southlow has been locked out of his house for months, sent his wife a few letters that might be called threatening."

"He didn't write anything about cutting her up?" I asked.

"Not exactly," said O'Rourke. "This dame, Mrs. Blake Southlow, went out a couple of nights ago and never did come back. The staying out was not unusual. She and her husband had not gotten along since Toby appeared on the scene. That's Major Toby Leighton. She wanted to divorce her husband and marry Toby, but said husband wouldn't stand for it. All that dope comes from the servants. A butler, two maids, a cook, and a chauffeur."

"Mrs. Southlow had money and her husband lived on her, eh?"

"He did not. He had plenty of dough of his own until lately. But he couldn't watch her and attend to business, so he chucked up business and started making drunken scenes every time he found his wife and Toby Leighton together. So the loving couple met elsewhere. Probably the little love nest where she was found tonight."

"And Blake Southlow was barred from the house."

"That's right. But once in a while he'd bust in and raise hell. It was over money. He needed a few thousand to protect his sliding business. Understand, Race! She was a rich woman in her own right, yet she spent his money; then turned him down flat unless he'd agree to a divorce. So it looks like he went haywire and butchered her. The net is out for him."

"And this Major Toby?"

O'Rourke poured himself a slug of whiskey, downed it. "We'll find him, or he'll pop up. The papers will give it a play. And here's something else! Mrs. Southlow made a will. It was in her desk. And it left every cent to her husband. They say she's worth a cool million, or will be some day."

"You think her husband would kill her and leave a trail like that? Was the will witnessed?"

"No. No! By God, Race! You think that was the document he tried to make her sign? The ink on her fingers! Then he slipped into the house and put it in her desk."

I shrugged my shoulders, asked: "And the Kramer in the note! Where does he fit?"

"That's Vincent Kramer, of Kramer and Beal—lawyers. An old, respected firm. The butler told me they handled Mrs. Southlow's business, and that of her dead father before her. See Kramer in the morning. He'll give you an earful."

"Me?" I took a laugh. "Someone who wanted that body found sent me the two hundred bucks. I haven't any client now."

"Wrong!" O'Rourke shook his head. "Someone who didn't want that body found sent you the letter. And you *have* a client."

"Yeah? Who?"

O'Rourke took a slip of paper from his pocket and gave it to me. "A note. An order to the butler, and written by Mrs. Blake Southlow." And when I just stared at it, "What—don't get it yet? Well, here's the letter the 'client' sent you. Compare the writing with Mrs. Southlow's memorandum to the butler. See, Race. You have a client. A dead one, maybe, but a client just the same. The handwriting is identical. You don't need an expert to show you that. Mrs. Sarah Jane Southlow sent you that note."

"Hell!" I gasped. "But how could she have mailed that letter to me after she was dead? A good twenty-four hours—more, even!"

O'Rourke shrugged his shoulders. "You haven't any information you didn't tell me?"

"No," I said, "I haven't."

"And you'll see Kramer tomorrow?"

"Sure. Sure, I'll see him."

"Didn't have a talk with Kramer tonight, did you?"

"Me? No!"

"Didn't work on the case since you left me?" And when my eyes just widened, "I'm laying my cards on the table, Race; giving it to you straight. You wouldn't hold out on me?"

"Hell, no!" I said. "I have nothing to hold out. Why?"

"Well"—O'Rourke stroked his chin—"you left the bungalow at ten minutes after eleven but didn't blow into your apartment until one-fifteen. Car trouble?"

I grinned. "So you had my homecoming watched, eh?"

"Not me!" O'Rourke shrugged, picked up his hat. "Your pal, One-Ton Nelson! He got a telephone call from a dick while he was still at the Southlow house. He's very suspicious, Race. Thinks you know something and that you are keeping it from him."

I laughed. "As a matter of fact," I told O'Rourke just before he left, "I went places to get the bad taste out of my mouth. The murder was pretty bad."

A lie, that? Sure it was. But my business was my business.

# TWO

# WILLED TO DIE

■

I got the papers late, at breakfast—more of them when I reached the office. They ran all kinds of heads. RICH BEAUTY SLAUGHTERED AT LONELY TRYST. HEIRESS TO ADAMS MILLIONS BRUTALLY SLAIN. And the early afternoon editions carried the account of the marriage of Sarah Jane Adams to Blake Southlow. There was the story of her mother's divorce from Vance Fairchild Adams, and of the mother's later marriage to a young painter, after which she had gone to live in Maine, taking her younger daughter with her. This daughter's handle was Anna May Adams, which showed that the Adams family had an old-fashioned way of dishing out names when the children were born. There were no other children.

There were harrowing, if imaginary descriptions of the painter-husband dying and leaving nothing but debts, and the mother living in poverty with her younger daughter. Then the mother died. After that, one guess was as good as another. Some papers had Anna May, the young sister of the dead woman, working as a secretary for a well known but unnamed executive at a huge salary; others had her practically starving in a cheap rooming house; still others stated that her father had created a trust fund and that she lived in idle luxury. You could take your choice. The papers agreed on just one thing—the slain Sarah Jane Southlow had been heiress to the Adams millions.

But I told myself in the elevator as it shot up to my office that there was nothing in this thing for me. Two hundred bucks! The police were in it, and— Hell! I owed the woman nothing. Look what I'd got already in the way of trouble for two hundred bucks! I'd simply drop from under and let the police handle the thing. To hell with Kramer! And with that thought I entered my office.

Jerry, my boy, jerked a thumb toward the inner room. "Vincent Kramer," he said. I pushed open the door and walked in on him.

He spoke at once. "Mr. Williams. I am here, of course, about the horrible tragedy that you discovered last night. This morning I had two visitors. One at a quarter to three and the other just as I was having breakfast. Inspector Nelson was the first, Sergeant O'Rourke the second. They hold different opinions of you." His smile was pleasant but slightly cynical. "I came to look at you myself."

"Well"—I don't much like talking with lawyers—"take a good look and pick your side."

"I want," he said slowly, "to know all about last night. All of it!"

He was entitled to know that.

"If O'Rourke talked out," I said, "you know all that I know. If he didn't, here's the story." And I gave it to him—all of it.

"It was Sarah Jane," he said. "Very much like her, to send you two hundred dollars. She was my client; her death was horrible and revolting. But she was not a very liberal woman. She was not all that a wife should be. She married some time before her father's death and was not at all sure just how she fitted into the financial end of the estate. When she found out she would inherit the estate and when her husband, Blake Southlow, lost his money, she turned from him."

"It seems an open-and-shut case," I told him. "The husband killed her. But he first forced her to make a will in his favor, which is queer, as it puts the finger squarely on him."

* * *

Kramer chewed on his lip, said: "Let me talk to you, Mr. Williams. Let me tell you that Blake Southlow was not so very much in love with his wife. And he wrote her those letters. Threatening letters, of course, which might have gotten her a divorce. But he knew about Major Toby Leighton. It would have been rather an ugly story if she started proceedings. Hardly 'coming into court with clean hands' as the law states. Besides, she had spent his money. The house she lived in was bought with his money and put in her name. She wouldn't raise a cent to help him!"

"There was something in a letter signed by this Toby about seeing you and the chances of buying Blake off. That referred to a divorce?"

"Yes. And Toby Leighton spoke to me about it. I even went so far as to speak to Blake Southlow. Not because of my client's interest but because I thought it would be best for Blake. The money offered would have put him back on his feet, provided, of course, he attended to his business."

"And how much was she to pay him?"

"She?" Kramer's glasses slid down his nose, bobbed back up again. "Major Leighton was to pay the price. It was fifty thousand dollars. God knows it was little enough; she had taken a great deal more from poor Blake. Damn it, sir, all his property was in her name and she wouldn't raise a penny to save him!"

"She wouldn't need to. There was her own fortune. Millions, eh?"

Kramer smiled as he saw through my attempt to get information out of him. "No, Mr. Williams." He took off his glasses, shook them at me. "She didn't have that much in cash or anywhere near it. Don't look surprised. The papers speak of millions so lightly!"

"Then she didn't have any money—left. Hasn't any now?"

"The estate of her father amounted to a little over four hundred thousand dollars."

"Even so, that's a pile of jack. But you mean she used only the income from it, never touched the principal at all?"

"She used only half the income from it. Her father, Vance Fairchild Adams, understood that things were going to get worse before they got better. His will stated that half the income was to go back, to bolster up the principal." His smile broadened. "You may well look surprised, Mr. Williams. There is more, that the papers don't know. She was to receive the principal of the estate if she reached the age of twenty-seven. Understand, Mr. Williams! I said *if*, not *when*. She would have been twenty-seven today." He looked toward the calendar on the wall.

"Then you mean that she didn't have the legal power to will the money; that it goes to someone else!"

"Yes. I mean exactly that. If she died before her twenty-seventh birthday, the entire estate was to be turned over to Anna May Adams, who lives in Portland, Maine. I have sent for her to come on at once."

"That," I thought aloud, "was a peculiar will."

The lawyer nodded. "Vance Fairchild Adams was a peculiar man. His older daughter, the dead Sarah Jane, was a peculiar woman. But there was a bond between them, something very strong. His first will left everything to Sarah Jane without reservation. I believe he hated his younger daughter, hated her as Sarah Jane hated her. Anna May chose the mother in the divorce. Yes, he hated her bitterly.

"I remember the day he came here to my office, just a few years ago and very shortly before he died. I remember the way he sat on the edge of the chair when he had me draw up the present will. He didn't explain it to me then, he was waiting for both his daughters to arrive. He sent for Anna May to come from Maine and for Sarah Jane to come from her beautiful home that had been deeded to her by her—well, drunken husband. He wouldn't listen to me when I suggested that something should be left outright to Anna May.

"And they both came. Sarah Jane, a very beautiful woman; but hard, calculating, and jittery with nerves. Anna May, still in her teens, with wondering, frightened blue eyes that kept avoiding the contemptuous glares of her older sister. Mr. Adams had me read that will aloud, in the presence of both girls. Then he leaned on the desk and explained it.

" 'Sarah Jane,' he said, looking straight at his older daughter as he jerked his head toward the silent younger one, 'there sits a girl we both hate. I have talked with my physician and yours. He has given me less than six months to live'—a long pause—'and he has given you less—far less than three years. That makes it quite impossible for you to survive your twenty-seventh birthday, and it defeats the purpose of both of us. It puts into the hands of that girl there, that girl we both hate, the Adams money—my money.'

"Sarah Jane jumped to her feet. Her eyes blazed. 'What do you mean—what do you mean?' She fairly screamed the words.

"Vance Fairchild Adams got up slowly and just as slowly walked to the door and put his hand on the knob. Then he turned and faced her. His words were slow and slightly vicious, I think. He said: 'You love me and you love money, and you hate that girl there. And you are doomed to death by drugs. Yes, yes—I know. You are a drug addict, far advanced; perhaps too far advanced. I'm playing a long shot. A cure for you is possible—just possible. But your hate of her and your love of money must be stronger than your desire, that insatiable craving.' He swung his head and pointed a finger at the wide-eyed Anna May. 'There she sits, the betrayer of her father. It is for you to decide if she spends my money—your money. I don't want to see either of you again.' The door swung open and closed. That was all. He died, Mr. Williams, without seeing either of them again."

"What happened afterward?"

"Sarah Jane disappeared for close to nine months. I don't know if it was willpower or not, but certainly she never touched drugs after that. Her hate was stronger than her craving. Old Adams knew it would be."

"And the younger daughter—Anna May?"

Kramer shook his head. "Her father had sent her money to come on but gave her nothing with which to return. I would not have known about it had I not asked her, and then she would take only the price of a ticket back to Portland. I don't believe the child had even eaten since the night before; I bought her lunch. She didn't want to talk about the will, about the hate. 'It doesn't matter much now,' she said, and she smiled. A plain sort of face that became almost beautiful when she smiled. 'I have a job. It starts Monday. Twelve dollars a week.' Imagine that, Mr. Williams! In a voice of pride, too; from a girl whose father was worth close to half a million dollars."

"Well"—and I got the point—"you mean that Sarah Jane's

husband could not inherit any of her money; therefore he would not— But did he know?"

"He must have known. But none knew of the little drama enacted in my office. Only you and I and our little heir, Anna May Adams. She will be a very rich girl indeed. Such a typewritten will as was found at the murdered Mrs. Southlow's house is ridiculous. Blake Southlow, drunk or sober, was not capable of such an act. Besides, there was no motive."

"Jealous rage—it looked like that sort of work."

"Maybe someone wanted it to look like that. Someone who—" He stopped, looked long and earnestly at me, finally said: "I am backing Sergeant O'Rourke's judgment now. But I have a will in my office, a will signed by Mrs. Sarah Jane Southlow, written in her own hand. A short will that leaves everything to Major Toby Leighton, who might have known nothing of her father's peculiar will."

"Good God!" I said. "You think Toby Leighton killed her, killed her like that, tortured her so—"

"So that it would look like her husband's threats, like the work of a distorted mind. Major Leighton is a clever man, Mr. Williams. I'm not stating facts, only suggesting possibilities. Toby Leighton will have covered himself well. But the shock of finding out the truth, that he killed her just a few days too soon, will be quite a blow to him. For now Anna May Adams, young, poor, discovers that a fortune, always rightfully hers but never intended for her by her father's will, is suddenly tossed into her lap by the will of God."

I shook my head. "You want me to look the ground over before you give any information to the police about Toby Leighton?"

He took out his watch and looked at it. "I want you to come to my office this afternoon at five. I think then that I will have a client for you. I think that she will wish murder to be punished and be willing to pay for it. Anna May Adams has no room in her heart for hate. She's flying down from Portland. It will be quite a thrill for a poor girl who is about to be a rich one."

"I'll be there. It looks as if, for once, out of vengeance and hate and murder will also come justice. I'll want to see the little girl who can take it on the chin and not—"

I frowned, reached for the receiver. The phone was buzzing.

Jerry said into my annoyed ear: "I'm sorry, boss. But it's O'Rourke, and he's got to speak to you."

I started to excuse myself when O'Rourke's voice shot in.

"Come over to the Ritz Terrace Apartments right away. I don't care what you're doing! Inspector Nelson has made quite a discovery. . . . Hell! It's about Toby. . . . Yeah! Major Toby Leighton has been shot dead."

# THREE

# MUSS-UP

∎

Over the dead body of Major Toby Leighton, Nelson and I had it out. Yep—you guessed it. Major Toby Leighton had been knocked over between twelve and one—at least, that was the medical guess—and Nelson wanted to question me about last night.

Nelson knew his business all right. He had already checked up my usual places and discovered I hadn't been there the night before. I was sorry I had lied to O'Rourke so I gave it to him straight. I said I was with a client, and it wasn't any police business; that I had given O'Rourke the run-around because it seemed simpler. And I wound up by telling Nelson to shut up or make a pinch.

A surprise there! You could have knocked me down with a case of gin. Nelson took it, and shut up! That was that. I took another look at the dead man. Then I walked out.

It was after three before I had a bite of lunch and trotted back to my office. Jerry's chest was like a pouter pigeon's. I had another visitor waiting inside.

She turned abruptly from the window, blew a bit of smoke

toward the ceiling and let her voice rise slightly as she spoke. "Mr. Williams? Race Williams?"

"That's right—both times."

Despite the front she put on, she was worried. She looked good—erect, rather tall. Her age? I'd say, twenty-five to thirty. She was nice to look at, though her lips were a trifle too thin and her eyebrows even thinner.

She dropped my hand as if it were a subway strap, and looked toward the curtain behind my desk. I walked to the curtain, pulled it aside and showed her the door.

"Another room, just a small one," I explained. "But a way out if you wish to leave without seeing anyone or anyone seeing you."

"Yes, I know. And I think I'll stand." This last as I motioned toward a chair. "You sit down. I can do better standing, Mr. Williams. I'm Ida Kranz."

She said it as if she expected me to hop over the desk, but I didn't. It didn't ring any bell with me. I just said: "Yes, Miss Kranz?"

She bit her lip and finally got it out. "I *was* a friend of the dead woman, Sarah Jane Southlow."

She got her rise that time. I guess I showed interest, but I didn't go fluttering about. I caught the inflection in her voice—I mean the word 'was.' She didn't say it as if it simply referred to the dear departed, so I tried: "Was! You mean—the friendship broke off before she died?"

"In a way, perhaps. Oh, I still saw her. But she resented my interference. It was about Blake. She treated him cruelly, horribly."

"And you liked Blake!" I did the 'heavy dick' as I put my glims on hers.

She wasn't startled, not even surprised. "Blake was all right," she said indifferently. "He just handled her wrong. But she'd never have found another man who would have taken so much from her."

"Not even Toby Leighton?"

"No!" she said, and I didn't jar her. "Not even Toby Leighton. You see, I was very fond of Sarah Jane. She was a devil at times, but she had lots of good in her; had willpower, too." She stopped. "I can't tell you about that."

"You don't mean about drugs, do you?"

"You know of that? Then she did come to see you; she told me she was going to. What did she tell you? What did she fear? What did she say?"

"How did you know she came to me?"

"I didn't know. I only guessed. You see, I advised her to come to you."

"Why? To protect her from her husband?"

She shook her head. "Not exactly. I don't really understand, myself. I don't know why. But I felt it and she felt it. Death lurking about her! Fear of him."

"Who? Blake, the husband? You think he killed her?"

"He must have. He must have! Who else could? But—like that! Why like that? It can't be like the papers say."

"Someone who wanted to put the blame on Blake Southlow, perhaps. Someone who knew about the threats of her husband."

"No. Why—who could it be?"

"Well," I said, "why do you come to me?"

"Because she appealed to you and because the murderer must be punished. But no one must know I came here," She moved closer to me now, looked at the door. "Lock it!" she said.

There was an earnestness in her eyes, something else too— either fear or horror. I couldn't lay a name on it. I locked the door, walked back to her, said simply: "Now, Miss Kranz, let me have it."

"Yes." She seemed anxious, even eager. "Remember you are to keep my name out of this. You will, won't you?"

"Sure!" I told her. "Just as long as it doesn't involve me with the police."

"Oh! I see. You report your clients to the police then?"

I grinned. I was thinking of One-Ton Nelson's ideas on that. "No. But you're not a client, are you?"

"Me? Me! No, I'm not." She came close to me then and gripped my shoulders. "I have had to work—had to work," she said. At first I thought she meant that was a disgrace, but she didn't, I guess. "I wasn't fitted for anything. I wasn't brought up to do anything. Just—just be a lady. We came out of school together—Sarah Jane and I. We made our début together. I—I—" The doorknob turned. Her face went white. Then a body pushed at the door.

"I must go," she said. "But I can't. I—" And a heavy body crashed against that door. I could hear the wood crack.

"Open the door, Williams," a voice called, "or we'll crash it in!" I thought I recognized that voice, but couldn't place it. The voice went on: "We want to see you. It's the cops!" I knew the voice then, knew the beef that butted against that door. It was Detective Dave Morse, one of Nelson's bruisers.

"I'll let you in in a minute," I called out. I led the woman to the curtain back of the desk, to the door behind it, said: "You can slip out the door and into the hall on the other side. What was it you had to tell me?" I was about to buzz her some more when the door groaned again.

"Get into that other room and wait there," I told her. "Or if you're afraid of the police, why—"

I dropped the curtain, swung quickly and hurried over to the office door. I could get that dick, Morse, in trouble—I could do a lot of things! But if he caved that door in, I'd never get the price of another one from the city. I knew that.

I spun the lock, said: "What the hell!"

The door burst open, three men pounded in. Morse first; then a dick with a broken nose and cauliflower ears, called Spinella; behind them, Iron-Man Nelson.

I slid close to my desk and took a grin as they went about their business. Morse turned and stood with his back against the closed door. Spinella moved slowly and stood against the wall, facing me. Iron-Man Nelson just walked over to the window sill and leaned on it. He stared at me a bit, let his sneer broaden, looked first to Dave Morse then to his other mauler, Sam Spinella; then he looked back at me again.

"Race Williams," he said slowly, chewing on each word, "I want to know who you visited between eleven and one last night. What I want to know, I find out."

"You don't want to know much then," I gave it to him straight, "if you find out everything you want to know."

He drew a paper from his jacket pocket, flipped it across so that it landed on the rug a foot or two in front of me. "Read that!" he said.

I wouldn't bend in such company. I simply said: "Tell me about it. I can find out if you lied later."

"It's a court order—nice words on it. You're to be held as a material witness. You know what happens to guys who don't talk downstairs at headquarters."

"So it's a pinch, and you bring a corporal's guard. You know I'll be out almost before I'm even booked."

"That's right. I know that." Nelson nodded, and I didn't like his nod. It was too grave. "But if you tell me where you were last night, you won't have to go at all. I don't have to use that paper."

"I told you that I was with a client. And I never divulge the name of a client."

"Williams"—Nelson shot his head forward—"this is murder. A double murder. I don't think you did it, but I think you know or suspect who did. And I think if the police knew where you were last night, we'd be a lot closer to the murderer. I don't like you. I don't like any flat-footed crooks and blackmailers who hide behind the name of private detective. You're going to talk and talk right here—now!"

Nelson looked at his two brutes; I looked at them too.

"You're not thinking of sicking those two punks on me!" I said. "Why that grease ball, Spinella—everyone knows he gouged the eye out of that East Side shyster you claimed resisted arrest."

Nelson's smile was a crooked grimace. "That East Side shyster finally talked and sent a man to the chair. Perhaps Sam's finger slipped when the shyster made the break."

"Let me get this right. You intend to have those two bums there manhandle me into talking? Have Sam shoot a finger—" I stopped, looked toward the phone.

"You'd never reach it," said Nelson, "and if you did, you'd never use it. Jerry ain't taking care of the switch outside any more."

"What happened to Jerry?"

Nelson's shoulders went up and down. "We were in a hurry and Jerry was in the way. Someone bumped into him and he fell down and stayed down. Eh, Sam?"

Spinella showed yellow teeth. "Sure, boss! Mr. B. Jack bumped into him."

Black-jacked, eh? I nodded to myself.

"So there it is," Nelson said. "You talk or you get it. You know the orders to bring them in 'mussed up.' Now, don't threaten, Williams. I know all about that gun stuff of yours. None of us are showing rods. You can't shoot cops, you know!" He looked toward Dave Morse. Dave rocked back on his heels, sort of looked out the window. I liked that. Dave wasn't so sure about my not shooting cops. But when I looked at Spinella, Sam smiled. I had made a monkey out of Spinella more than once, which wasn't such a hard job.

I did know what happened to guys who shot cops, all right, and I said: "Listen, Nelson, I'll go downtown with you if it's a pinch, nice and quiet. You've got no excuse."

It was honey-and-molasses stuff, and it didn't work. Nelson only said: "You talk or you take it. You won't shoot, and you know it. And when you can't shoot, you're just like any other common hood. Do you talk? Yes or no!"

My voice raised. "But listen, Nelson—" He gave sharp orders to the two men and those orders were: "Williams is resisting arrest. Get him!"

"No, Nelson. No!" I almost shouted. "Call them off. I can't— by God, Nelson, I won't take it!"

I saw Dave Morse hesitate, sort of trip and drop into line behind Spinella. Dave didn't like it. And I wasn't sure yet if it was bluff. I just stood there, my hands at my sides.

"All right Sam—let him have it." Nelson gave the order. And it wasn't simply a police order. There was triumph in it, hate and— yes, by God!—viciousness in it as he added: "Look! He don't dare even move his hands. Tough-guy Williams!"

I didn't move my hands. I just stood there. My future— everything—might depend on my action now. Right before me was that ugly face of Spinella. Glaring hateful eyes, mouth hanging open and yellow teeth showing. But most of all, those stretching hands; hands with long thick fingers—nails. I could see the dirt beneath the nails. Then Spinella sprang—fingers reaching, tearing toward my face.

Things blurred then. Cops disappeared from view. They became just men—just the thugs in the night I had fought so often. I thought of that lawyer who had lost the sight of one eye. I thought of another I had known, a crook all right, who would never— And I did it.

My right hand shot beneath my left armpit, shot in and out. I snapped the gun from its shoulder holster and crossed it back in one quick vicious movement—just as vicious as Nelson's words. I could have shot Sam dead, but I don't think that was in my mind at all then. He was too close to shoot.

His clawing fingers scraped my face as I let him have it. My gun, coming back and up, clipped him on the chin, rocked him, staggered him slightly. As he gave ground I struck again, pounded that gun down across his forehead, pounded him to the floor. He struck the rug like a steer in the stock yard, lay still.

Nelson shouted something about my "paying for this." I don't know just what he said; I only know that his voice shook with anger, that he yelled something to Dave about "letting me have it."

I saw Dave then, saw the gun he pulled from his hip, saw it starting up as I jerked mine down. And I knew that my career was over then. I was going to kill a cop. And as my finger started to tighten on that trigger, I had just one clear thought—better in his chest than in mine.

Dave must have read it in my eyes, for he dropped his gun, dropped it just as if I'd leaned forward and knocked it from his hand. I half swung as Iron-Man Nelson went for his rod.

I hated Nelson and he hated me. But he knew and I knew that one of us was going to die. And I knew too that, since I had the drop on him and since his hand was far around by his hip, it was going to be Nelson. I warned him. I cried out. But the thing had to be.

And then it didn't. A slight draft, the curtain behind my desk moved, and the girl was in the room, between myself and Nelson.

She said quickly: "I am Ida Kranz. I live at the Bradley Arms Hotel. Mr. Williams was with me last night. I was the client he visited."

Nelson opened his mouth to speak; I guess to say he didn't give a damn about that now. He glanced down to where the great carcass of the unconscious Sam decorated the rug. But Nelson didn't speak.

The girl said: "I was behind the curtain and heard everything."

I liked that *everything*, but I don't think Nelson did. He said: "Ida Kranz! Kranz, eh?" He thought for a moment. "Used to be in the big money, ran with the right people, and then—" He stopped, turned to me. "You could have said where you were, Williams."

He looked down at Spinella. "Assault!" he muttered, then smiled. "Sam Spinella isn't a man to forget."

"I hope he doesn't." I nodded. "How about Jerry, outside; and—" Ida Kranz looked at the man on the floor and hurried from the room. Nelson made no attempt to stop her. And me! I was grateful to her, for certainly she had interrupted the death of Nelson and—well, I've laughed off a lot of killings, but never one of a police inspector.

Jerry staggered into the office, announced: "No cop could knock me out for long. I buzzed O'Rourke, boss, and he'll be right over and—" Jerry stopped, his mouth hung open. Admiration shone in his eyes when he turned them from the big hunk of meat on the floor to me.

Nelson watched Jerry sidle out, said to me: "You would have killed me. Don't deny it! I saw it in your eyes."

"Nelson!"—I stared straight at him—"I'd be the last man in the world to deny that statement."

A moment of silence, then the outer door opened. Spinella stirred just as O'Rourke walked into the room.

I'll say this for O'Rourke. He didn't ask for any explanation, and he didn't get one. But he knew, and he gave quick, sharp orders. "Get some water!" he told Dave Morse, "and chuck it in his face."

I was near the cooler and, reaching for the glass, filled it. "Allow me!" I said politely, and chucked it in Spinella's face. His eyes were just opening, too. He was looking straight at me. Recollection and hate and vengeance were in his glare, curses starting on his lips. Maybe that's the reason I forgot to hold onto the glass when I chucked the water in his face. I stamped out of the office.

Jerry got me before I reached the elevator. "A letter, boss! A messenger boy brought it. I forgot, when the dame—"

I took the letter, broke open the long plain envelope and spotted a smaller one inside. I whistled softly. Written on the inner envelope in a bold hand were the words—*For Race Williams—The Message of Death.*

"Nut letter!" I grinned as I tore it open; then I didn't grin. My eyes popped.

Mr. Race Williams:—

First the unfaithful wife, second the unfaithful friend, third the woman who is to get the money. Leave town at once. My schedule did not include a fourth, but that schedule can easily be changed.

Blake Southlow.

I read it three times, I guess. Then I left it with Jerry to give O'Rourke so he could put an expert on it to be sure it was Blake Southlow's fist. Certainly he had enough of Southlow's letters for comparison.

There wasn't so much time before five o'clock, but I spent what there was in a newspaper morgue. I wanted to spot Ida Kranz. Nice people, our high society of the late Twenties! Ida Kranz's father had money—*had* it, understand. In Thirty it went. So he bought himself a bottle of poison and did his act. But Ida's name still meant something in society. She hied herself to one of our best hot spots and did a song and dance. Whether she was still doing it I couldn't find out, but I promised Leeds—the straight-shooting reporter who'd wangled me into the morgue—that I'd give him a break if he'd give me a hand with all I wanted to know about Ida Kranz.

After that I hopped a cab and drove straight to Vincent Kramer's office.

# FOUR

# THE OLD HOMESTEAD

■

Anna May Adams wasn't bad to look at and I don't think she was dumb. You wouldn't say she was beautiful; too many freckles for that, and a bit of a tilt to her nose. Yet you liked her. Her blue eyes didn't seem to register fear; more, nervous excitement—as if she were starting an adventure. It all added up to a sort of childlike appeal.

Kramer was a soft-spoken man, but when it came to telling the girl just what was what, he knew his stuff. She didn't want a bodyguard, told him flatly she wouldn't have one, and he put it to her direct—and how direct!

"Miss Adams," he said slowly, "the cold-blooded murderer of your sister is still free. And he has written a letter threatening your life. He signs that letter—Blake Southlow."

"I don't believe it!" she said. "He was so kind, so fine."

"You've got to believe it." I horned into the conversation. "I have just telephoned Sergeant O'Rourke. The handwriting experts identified the writing."

"Then he must be fooling."

Iron-Man Nelson, who'd got there just as I did, Vincent Kramer and myself all leaned forward, said together: "Fooling!"

"Oh! I don't mean that. I don't—I mean, he must be mad."

"That's just it," said Kramer. "Mad! Mad enough to kill two people—mad enough to kill more."

"No!" She came to her feet, her hands tightly clasped. "He couldn't do that. Not Blake!"

It was Iron-Man Nelson who tried now. "But his letters. His threatening letters to his wife, your sister! Then her death—well, it wasn't pleasant."

The girl half sobbed: "He was drinking. Don't you understand? He didn't know what he was writing."

I said: "It wouldn't hurt you any less, even if the thirst to kill came out of a bottle."

"Oh! He didn't kill—didn't kill anyone. Drink is like hypnotism. You can force the subject to say and threaten all sorts of terrible things, including murder; but he won't commit the act. He can't, if it isn't in his being—his soul—to do it. Blake might be mad with drink; mad enough even to write threats, but he couldn't kill."

"Made quite a study of it, eh?" Nelson shot the question.

"Oh, yes! I did—I did. Ever since—since—" She stopped. Wide blue eyes flashed to each of us. She put her hand across her mouth like a frightened child.

"Go on!" said Nelson. "Ever since you knew he was drinking." He was half out of his chair when I knocked down the arm he had stretched toward her, the accusing finger at the end of it.

Vincent Kramer said as he turned to Nelson: "I let you in against the advice of Mr. Williams. Miss Adams has nothing to hide. Now, Anna May, tell us everything. Why you don't think Blake Southlow did these things."

She came to the edge of her chair, began to cry a little. Then she straightened, said suddenly and rather proudly: "I was in love with him—very much in love with him. I was just a child. Sarah Jane took him from me, as she took everything from me. But he cared—he always cared. And she hated me for it. Later, I think she hated him. He sent me money too—for mother when she was so ill. He wanted me at their house after mother died, wanted my sister to provide for me. He even came to Portland to see me. Then he didn't have money any more."

"I see." Nelson's words rolled out—friendly, almost soothing. "He came to Portland to see you. He loved you, thought perhaps he'd get a divorce, then marry you."

Her blue eyes widened. "Oh, no. No!" she said. "He always spoke about her, spoke just as if I was his sister, too—his friend."

"But he loved you, didn't he? Didn't he tell you that?"

"No. No!" Her eyes looked frightened.

"And you loved him."

"I— No!"

"But you said you did."

"That was before—and it was different. I— Don't you see? Don't you understand? It's something I don't want to—can't talk about."

Nelson was ready to do his stuff again, saw my hand move, glared at me. Then he looked at Kramer, turned back and looked at me again, half winked. He came to his feet. "The girl's right. She won't need any bodyguard here in New York."

Kramer straightened. "After that letter! After—"

If Nelson winked at him or not, I don't know. But the girl horned in as Kramer stopped. "No. No, I don't." She clutched Nelson by the arm. "That's right! If Blake knows I'm in New York he'll look for me. Then I'll just have to look at him, talk to him, tell him I believe in him. He'll understand. He always has. That's why he used to come to Portland. Sarah Jane robbed him and deserted him when he needed her most. But Blake Southlow didn't kill her. He couldn't have."

"You've said that a dozen times." Kramer spoke softly. "Just as if you wanted to convince yourself of something you know is not true. But it's like this, Anna May. I have known you for a long time, known Blake, too. I didn't believe he did it either." He went across the room and lifted both hands. "And it wasn't Blake Southlow who killed Sarah Jane. It wasn't his real brain, but the madness in it. If he didn't kill her, why would he hide now?"

"Why? Why? Why?" She came to her feet. "With the papers printing their suspicions! With that man there!" She looked at Nelson. "He even suspects that I know something about it. Yes, I know! I'm young and very simple, but I'm not a fool. He means that Blake killed her so that he could marry me and get all that money. Well, he didn't kill her and he could never have married me. Yes, he came to me, said that he could get some of his money back from Sarah Jane if he gave her a divorce. He could save what was left of his business, if it was worth saving; or we could start again in some other place—some other country, even." The tears were rolling down her cheeks now. "And I told him, no—No—NO! I never could marry him. He understood; he had to understand. For I told him the truth. There! You got what you wanted to know, what you beat out of me with words and looks and—and—" She turned toward the door. "Please—let me rest in that other room a moment."

It was Nelson who opened the door for her. It was Nelson who spoke to her so low we couldn't even hear a whisper; just see his lips move. Then he returned and closed the door.

"You see the point," he said, directly to Kramer. "She's in love with Blake; and he, having lost his money to one sister, decided to get it back through the other sister. She loves him. It's in her every action, behind her every word. Maybe he planned the death of his wife carefully, maybe he planned to place the blame on Major Toby Leighton. Then he went to Portland and Anna May turned him down, told him why. Drink, perhaps! Things popped in his head. He discovered his wife's meetings with the major, saw every hope he ever held blasted, walked into the cottage and killed her."

"But the will! He made her sign that," Kramer exclaimed. "A document he must have known was useless."

Nelson shrugged. "We're talking about a madman now. And there's his letter to Williams that he intends to kill this girl." He jerked a thumb toward the door.

"Then certainly she needs all the protection she can get." Vincent Kramer nodded. "I'll see her alone and convince her that Mr. Williams is the man for the job."

Nelson let his huge mouth slip all over his face. "Williams is just a gunman; everybody knows that. Suppose there is some method behind this we don't know about! Why—the murderer would keep out of sight if Williams was with her everywhere. No. We want her alone—apparently alone. She may lead us to Blake Southlow."

"You'd— By God, Nelson! You mean you'd use that kid as bait to attract this vulture whose single wish seems to be to kill her?"

"Sure!" said Nelson. "Why not? Two murders, and the papers crying for blood. The department could keep her under surveillance day and night. Well—I'll be running along."

"Wait!" said Kramer. "We'll want—we'll demand police protection for this girl."

"Sure!" said Nelson, and the grin made more pronounced the sneer of his face. "Bring her in and tell her of your decision."

Vincent Kramer pressed a button on his desk. His secretary stuck her head in. Kramer said: "Miss Adams, in the anteroom! Ask her to return here, please."

"She's gone!" the secretary said. "She was crying. She seemed in a hurry."

I looked at Nelson, said: "You told her. I saw her nod. You told her to slip out."

"Me?" Nelson's eyes widened as he pointed a finger against his own chest. "What right have I to tell her? She's over twenty-one, isn't she?"

"And just because you want to double-cross me, you let me risk being shot to death—even on the street before the building!"

"Listen, cheap dick." The cloak of even outwardly working together, which Nelson had put on for Kramer's benefit when he horned in on our talk, slipped away now. "Once I put the finger on a man or a woman, the finger stays put." And when Kramer would have talked, "As for you, Mr. Kramer, if you'd put your confidence in the police instead of in this gun-toting heel, Williams, you'd be better off. Now, don't squawk. I'll crack this case wide open in a few days."

He turned and tramped out. Kramer looked at me and I looked at him, but we didn't speak. Then I too was gone.

Out on the street—and no Anna May, of course. I didn't run up and down and I didn't follow Inspector Iron-Man Nelson. I saw him cross the street and climb leisurely into a small car and drive off. He was a tough bird and no mistake—heartless, cruel, cold.

I did a bit of telephoning, got Leeds, the reporter, and found out this much: Ida Kranz was still singing at a night spot—more of a restaurant.

"Who do you think runs it?" Leeds ran on. And when I didn't answer—I'm no good at riddles—"Joseph G. Patton!"

"What's the G for?" I said sarcastically.

"Giovoni. . . . Don't get it, Race? Well, be ready to drop the receiver. He's Joe Patton. Don't you remember?"

"Joe Patton. Joe Patton!" Sure the name was familiar. Then I got it. "Not Joe Patton, the lad who was supposed to do all the thinking for the big shot in the days of the beer racket! The brains of Jimmy Kester!"

"That's the guy. When you see his dump you won't think he's such a hot number. You'd hardly know him. And don't laugh! He's studying to be a lawyer."

"Why—" I thought back and tried to get those thoughts into words. "Didn't Joe blow up years ago? Didn't he drag Jimmy Kester down with him? He went to dope or something."

"That's right! Just dope—not 'something.' And that's what broke him down, made him talk when the cops wouldn't give him a sniff. Sure! He disappeared for a long time, then showed up again. I understand he doesn't smoke, drink or sniff. As for being crooked! They say he's so straight he bends backwards, and—"

"My God!" I told Leeds, "I'm not interested in the virtues of a former beer runner. It's a dive, eh?"

"Hell, no!" Leeds said sharply. "Just cheap. Family trade, even." And he gave me the name and address of Patton's place. It was called the Old Homestead.

I spent the rest of the day with Jerry covering all the big hotels and some of the smaller ones, looking for Anna May Adams, under any name. No luck! And that night, along about eleven, I hit the Old Homestead. Some name for a side-street restaurant! Though the stone steps down to it were worn, the place inside was clean enough. It wasn't a gay spot and it wasn't a tough spot. They had an orchestra—or at least, lads who played musical instruments. A dance floor was in the center of the room, and a spot light for the "entertainers."

I was looking the crowd over—even going to ask for Miss Kranz—when I saw her. Saw her, not because she was prominently located but because she ducked back into a booth. It was her disappearing act caught my attention. I slid by the tables, saw she was alone and dropped into the seat opposite her.

She looked at me; looked out across the room, spoke almost at once. "You shouldn't have come—not here." And in almost the same breath, "I tried to get you this afternoon! No one answered."

"You tried to get me. Yet you don't want to see me, eh?" I

smiled. "You did me a good turn today. I know some of the boys in the better spots. I might fix you up."

My attempt to put her at her ease was not so good. She was fidgety. The color ran in and out of her face; which was some job considering the makeup she had on. But she did better when she started to talk.

"I don't want to give you the impression that I am ashamed of being here—that's not true." She put emphasis on that. "But I do not meet people—not even in a business way—during working hours."

"Did you know Anna May Adams very well?" I asked.

"Yes, of course. I knew all the Adamses well."

"Fine!" I gave it to her flat. "Anna May came to New York today, and she's disappeared."

Her hand went to her mouth. "She's not—not murdered."

"That's right!" I nodded. "She's not murdered—yet. And don't look so worried, Miss Kranz." I leaned over the table and gripped her wrist. "I wouldn't do you any harm. You gave me an alibi for the other night, an alibi I was beginning to need. Nelson could have made it nasty."

"Why the nice speech?" Her voice was more friendly now. "I know. You want my help. I know Blake Southlow couldn't have—"

"But Blake did!" I told her. Then I went into the details of the letter threatening my life as well as the girl's.

She looked at me for a long time. "He did then. He did!" she said. "I have been afraid of that. You see, he didn't drink like you or I or the other fellow, and—it snapped all right; the tiny thread in his brain. He must be insane. Mr. Williams, they can't—they won't give a death sentence to a madman."

"Of course not. But it's about the girl, I want to know. And—" I saw the look in her face before I felt the hand on my shoulder.

I heard the voice, too. Low, threatening; something even ominous about it, that didn't mix in with the name Old Homestead, nor the simplicity of the surroundings. The voice said: "Mister, we do not permit unaccompanied gentlemen to sit with ladies who are our artists." And, the voice coming closer to my ear, "You'd better go—very fast."

I wasn't unduly excited. I had been threatened with being tossed to the street in pretty tough spots, and had even gone out of one or two with a gun smoking in my hand. Now I took an inward chuckle, turned slowly and looked at the speaker, the threatening face. But was the face threatening? Maybe it had been before I saw it. But, after a quick surprised look, it smiled. Pleasant, rather handsome, I suppose, from a female point of view. And its owner beat me to the punch.

"If it isn't my old friend—or was it my old enemy in those days—Race Williams? Pardon my rough speech. It is of the past, and I keep it for those who hurt my business."

I didn't speak as he slid in beside me. Back went the years, and I knew. Partly from my own recollection and partly from what Leeds had told me over the phone. "Why," I said, "you're Joe Patton."

"No. *Sh!*" He put a finger to his lips, looked about the room, but his laugh was rather pleasant. "I am Joseph G. Patton—Joe Patton is dead as the headlines of five years ago. And I am glad."

"I bet a lot of others are, too."

"But I am glad because very soon now I plan to sell out, go to Italy and practice law."

"Then what?"

"Well—" He looked at me then, said to Ida Kranz: "Go and dance for them, for us, for me." And as she came to her feet, watching us closely, "After I have settled in Italy, I will send for Miss Kranz. Ah, no widening of the eyes, Williams! I have changed in many ways. We are to be married."

The girl looked at him, smiled and left the table. A few minutes later she busted into song. I half nodded. Certainly Joe Patton must have been in love with her! But he was talking.

"Mr. Williams, I am going to talk to you in great confidence. Not because I trust, admire and respect our laws, but because you are investigating this Southlow murder case and can give me unwanted publicity. You see, I have had much experience in crime and with the professional criminal and his dominating motive. You know that motive, of course."

"Sure!" I told him. "Greed."

"Correct! So we may be assured, to start with, that Mrs. Sarah Jane Southlow died by the hand of an amateur. Vengeance—hate—madness. No one could profit by the woman's death but her sister, Anna May Adams. I understand that, with Miss Adams, the thought of such an act and such a brutal slaying is out of the question. The one who stood to gain could not have done it. We have nothing left then but jealousy, hate, madness—and from what I know, I favor jealousy and hate."

My eyes widened. "Not madness!"

"No. No! That may be true, but I will not believe it. I would hate to kill a madman."

"You would hate to kill a madman! What do you mean?"

"Just this." He leaned forward now and his bright eyes flashed. "Sarah Jane Southlow may have been cruel, wicked, rotten through and through. But she, and she alone, put me where I am today. She lifted me out of the depths of hell, and if I can find this man, Blake Southlow—mad or sane—I'll force the truth from him, then kill him with my bare hands." He extended those hands now.

"You've got me," I admitted. "Want to talk some more?"

"Yes. You know I was an addict. Just for pleasure, I thought— as many have thought before. I could take it or leave it alone! It stimulated my mind, made me capable of giving that good advice to Jimmy Kester." He paused, rubbed at his chin. "Various reasons are given for the cause of crime. Heredity, environment, poverty—drugs. Well, I had the environment for it, I had the poverty for it, but I never did a crooked act until the drugs came into the picture."

"You kept hopped up when you worked for Kester, eh?"

He shook his head. "I was hopped up only when I couldn't stand the thing any longer, the deadly brutality of it, the—well, just the things my fertile brain thought up and which brought me thousands of dollars from Kester. Then I'd hit the stuff, hit it hard, and Kester always sent me away for the cure. A cure I always believed impossible." He leaned forward now. "But I made arrangements for that. I had the stuff smuggled in to me and petered off slowly, until I hit my regular stride—and then came back apparently cured."

I didn't know if I believed him or not and didn't care much. I half hid a yawn as he continued. "I tell you because of the sanitarium I went to. The biggest in the country, the best. Doctor Von Jurgon! The one on Long Island."

"So—what?"

"So—what! You don't know then! That is where Sarah Jane Southlow was, and that is where I met her, and that is where we sat in the sun together. I saw her go through hell. I saw her, crazed with the desire that she kept even from the doctor, knock the powder I offered her from my hand. I saw her battle and win, and I heard her say to me just before she left, 'The big brain that's cracking for want of guts!'"

That got me, all right. I didn't yawn then. I sat up straight and stared at him.

He smiled at me, and it wasn't a bad smile. He was still smiling when he said: "And so—there is your bedtime story. If you doubt it, look it up on the records of Doctor Von Jurgon's Sanitarium. Yes, Doctor Von Jurgon is taking them in, sending them out cured, and taking them back to cure again. But he's got at least two on his records who will never come back."

"One, anyway." I leaned over and slapped him on the back. "I guess you've done something, boy."

His shoulders shrugged. "I haven't made much money, but I saved what I made. Now—a small legacy in Italy! An amount I'd have laughed at a few years ago. But today"—his hands spread far apart—"well, there are the hills and a blue sea and sky above it. Yes, and a little inn. And"—he looked out on the floor—"and Ida, who will run that inn after her husband becomes a recognized barrister."

"By God!" I wiped away an imaginary tear. "You oughta send that story to the Society for the Prevention of Cruelty to Criminals."

He leaned back and laughed pleasantly. "I don't blame you for enjoying it as a joke. I haven't got used to it myself yet." And suddenly, more practical, "Besides, the government has made it very difficult for the big business of crime." And as Ida Kranz approached the table, "Poor kid. She liked this Blake Southlow. See that I'm saved the trouble of killing him."

He got up, took Ida in his arms, and just before they whirled away across the dance floor, said: "I always do this. We have regular customers, and they expect it after their favorite number."

The girl, Ida Kranz, came to me afterwards out there in the dimly lit hall. "I am going to marry him someday." She looked straight at me. "He's been so—he's told me most of his past. What do you think of him?"

"Well," I told her, "it's your marriage. I hope you like it."

"Yes, yes." She spoke quickly. "You see, I—I love him very much."

"I guess he loves you too. Now—about Anna May! Can't you help?"

"She should have come to me—and she will. I know she will! I'll let you know, Mr. Williams. Please don't bring me into it."

"Nelson hasn't looked you up?" My eyebrows went up, I guess.

"No!" she said. "Why should he?"

I shrugged my shoulders. "Not simply because of his dislike for me. He's sure to find out you knew the dead woman."

She bit at her lip. For a moment her face seemed very hard and determined. She waved a hand about the room. "Do you think I like this—this way of making a living? Remember! Once I had everything I wanted. I went to the best places, met the best people, wore the best clothes." And after a bit, "Don't worry too much about Anna May. She'll come to me finally—or I'll find Blake Southlow for you."

"Kid," I told her at parting, "if you know where Blake Southlow is, if for some reason you're hiding that knowledge—don't do it. Nelson is"—and I gulped when I got this out—"well, not the thickest cop on the force. He hasn't looked you up! The reason for that is either stupidity or shrewdness; it can't be indifference." And after a long pause, to let my words sink in, "He isn't stupid."

# FIVE

# DOUBLE ALIBI

■

I went to see O'Rourke then. It was late. I caught him at his home and watched him pace the library. He didn't seem over glad to see me, but he answered my questions straight enough. That is, about Joe Patton. My complaint about Nelson's action in Vincent Kramer's office, he ignored.

O'Rourke said: "Few criminals like Joe go straight. I guess I sneered a bit when he opened the Old Homestead and stuck the fancy title, Joseph G. Patton, on himself. We watched him like a hawk for a long time too. We check up on him occasionally yet. But in the best crime circles he's forgotten; in the smaller crime circles he never was known. Nelson has just gone through his records again. He's got a clean slate. Now, what else do you want, that any law-abiding citizen is entitled to know?"

"Law-abiding citizen, eh? That's a nice title to wish on me."

O'Rourke cut loose. "Williams, eh? The great Race Williams comes here tonight to squawk all over his face about being abused by Nelson! He stole your client on you, right from under your nose; got her to slip out so he could follow and watch her, and see

where she went. Why, I had to come to your office today to protect
you from Iron-Man Nelson. One-Ton Nelson!" he added, throwing heavy sarcasm into the "One-Ton."

"Protect me!" I took a laugh. "Yeah. Protect me from blowing
the top of Nelson's brilliant head off." And suddenly, "What's the
real grouch?"

O'Rourke swung on me, his eyes blazed. "The grouch is this.
Inspector Nelson has been given full swing to work on this case.
Full swing, understand! That means no orders from me, direct or
indirect. Oh, I can still work it; alone or with the great Race
Williams, if I wish." Now the heavy sarcasm was doing its stuff
again. "But I am not to interfere with the activities of Nelson. No,
not if he decided to mop up the avenue with you."

I dismissed the added attraction of the street-mopping, asked:
"And the reason?"

O'Rourke laughed. "Because Nelson was at the scene of the
crime first. At least, that's the official reason. The real reason is—
that he's turning up stuff that I lost by believing in you."

"And when did you discover all this?"

"Twenty minutes ago. Nelson is going to beat me to it because
of you. Yes—you! I laid my cards on the table; I came straight
from the dead woman's house to give you what information I had.
But did you tell me whom you saw last night between eleven and
one? No. Did you even hint that the client you visited between
those hours was very close to the dead woman; went to school with
her, came out in society with her; had been close to her for years?
No! Nor did you tell me that the client you visited was directly
interested in this case and hired you. Well, why did she hire you?"

"Hell, man!" I told him. "The truth is, I never met the girl that
night. It was a different client, in no way connected with this case.
The girl, Ida Kranz, visited me at my office only a few minutes
before Nelson and his storm troops busted in. She slipped behind
the curtain leading to the next room, heard the row when Nelson
said I would talk or take a beating. All she knew was that I needed
an alibi for that night, and she stepped out and gave it to me."

"So she handed you an alibi for the hours between eleven and
one, when Major Toby Leighton was shot! Mighty decent of her."

"Yes, it was. Guess it's my personal charm." I tried to kid
O'Rourke out of it. But his face was hard, stony.

"I guess that's all," he said, leading the way to the front door.

He wanted to say a lot more, but he didn't. It must have griped him like the devil to have Nelson grab the case from him.

"That's not quite all," I told him, halfway out the door. "I made you a promise, O'Rourke, that I'd deal you in at the finish."

"Sure. Sure! And it'll be a pleasure to see Nelson make a monkey out of you. Good-night!"

"Good-night!" I said. My voice was light but my thoughts weren't. "Make a monkey" was my own line. That was what I'd told myself I'd do to Nelson. And the realization didn't make me feel any better.

I left O'Rourke feeling downright sorry for myself. Then I went straight home, mixed a drink and began to think how, after all, there was nothing in this for me. I didn't really have any client. Then a thought I liked even less. I had let down O'Rourke. Yes, and let him down for a man who was as brutal and unscrupulous as the very murderers he hunted—

The phone rang, and it was Ida Kranz. She seemed excited.

"Race, Race!" A little familiar, of course—but then, interesting, very interesting. "Come to my apartment now—at once!" And she gave me the address, adding: "Apartment 5-C. That's the top floor. I live with a girl friend."

I was going to chirp something about not having to tell me she was a good woman, but I didn't. There were more things I wanted to verify. "Is it about Anna May Adams?"

"Yes, yes! I can't talk any longer. Come right away! She's in great danger. But there's no danger here—none for you. Don't let anyone know where you're coming. Just hurry!"

"Well—" But that was that. It was a long time since a woman had hung up on me, but she had.

In the taxi I didn't think of Anna May Adams so much, or of the woman who was dead. I was thinking of Iron-Man Nelson and that he had lost the girl; and I was thinking of O'Rourke and how I might break the case ahead of Nelson.

I leaned back and killed a couple of butts. Things began to look better. I had a soft spot in my heart for Ida Kranz—she was certainly giving me the breaks. She thought quick too. A smart gal and a swell one. I smoothed down my coat lapels. Oh, I can take dames or leave them alone. But Ida Kranz was a friend of the dead girl and she must have known she would be questioned about the killing of Sarah Jane Southlow. Yet she had walked out right in front of the cops and given me an alibi. Why? She might have been dragged into a dirty mess just by alibiing me that way. O'Rourke had wondered why she'd done it, too. Probably simply because she thought I—I—

I leaned forward and ordered the taxi to stop. The cab squealed to the curb. I paid off the driver, saw a friendly bar and walked in, leaned against it. I took my drink straight and took it quick. Then I stared at myself in the mirror—and didn't like the dumb look that stared back. The dumb look went. A surprised one took its place, to fade to an angry one. I gulped, slapped a coin down on the bar, turned and walked out.

It had suddenly come to me why Ida Kranz alibied me between the hours of eleven and one the night Major Toby Leighton was killed. When Ida Kranz alibied me that night, she also alibied someone else—and that someone else was Ida Kranz herself. Certainly if she had been with me, she could not have been at the Ritz Terrace Apartments when Toby Leighton was killed. And, me—yes, she had simply made a sucker out of me.

But she had forgotten one thing, and so had I until the minute the volcanic eruption bubbled out of that keen brain of mine. She had said we were in her room at the fairly swanky Bradley Arms Hotel. Now she gave me an apartment number to come to, and spoke about a girl friend she shared it with. And this present address didn't jibe with the previous one she had given to Nelson.

I strode heavily, determinedly, down the street. I knew my stuff now. No more floundering in darkness, trying to be the dilly-dallying, pipe-smoking, deep-thinking detective. I was out for blood.

Mad? Sure! I was mad. But I'd hear what she had to say before I cut loose and told her what was on my chest. I'd be nice, and smile, and—

I turned into the doorway of the apartment next to the number she had given me. There were three on the block, all walk-ups; all built close together, bricked together. Ida Kranz had told me there would be no danger. No reason to tell me that unless there was danger and plenty of it. And where would it come from? Maybe the blast of a tommy gun working on the stairs—maybe from behind tightly drawn curtains in the room where she met me—

maybe right through a window. Well—not me! If a bit of killing was to be done—

I pressed a wall button in the adjoining apartment house, pushed open the door when the latch clicked and started up the stairs. I knew this kind of apartment house. There would be a regular flight of stairs to the roof and a door to go through, then a mess of clotheslines and aerials.

I cooled down a bit as I climbed the stairs of the adjoining apartment house. Maybe the girl was just trying to protect Blake Southlow. But—hell! She was in love with another man. Joe Patton, alias Joseph G. Patton. And no matter what a fine life he had led for years, with his past he couldn't afford to get mixed up in a murder.

Yet he had said he would kill Blake Southlow or whoever killed Sarah Jane. Still, that might be the ex-gunman's bull. Guys with records, guys who know their stuff, don't talk about murders they're going to commit.

My plan, when I reached the roof, was simply to cross to the next roof, hop down the iron ladder that led to the fire-escape by apartment 5-C, take a look-see through the window and decide from what I found if I'd drop in with a gun in each hand, or just tap and be let in.

There was just a knee-high wall between the two buildings. I crouched, looked over the wall, saw the outline of a man.

I moved quickly, eased over onto the adjoining roof, nearly tore my head off on a neglected clothesline but made the shadows of the chimney behind him; made it because his back was to me as he leaned over the coping and looked down.

A radio made faint sounds in the distance but must have been plenty loud in some room below, to reach me. But I heard the man plainly. He said, evidently speaking to someone below, for he still leaned over the roof: "He's there, eh? Yeah. I got your signal. Don't let him have it until I come down."

If the guy answered below or if he had some set of signals, I don't know. I heard nothing but the radio, which I guess was turned up to drown outside sounds. And that was that. Not much in the conversation to make me think that two honest citizens were talking.

I walked across the roof, saw the man putting one foot over the

little wall. I saw him hesitate, draw back his leg—and then, like
Dempsey in his famous bout with Tunney, "forget to duck."

He was swinging around all right. I could even see the whiteness
of his profile beneath the cap he wore, when I struck him with my
gun. It was half a downward blow and half a side swipe. But it had
power behind it, and I struck only once. I know my business; I
knew it then. He gave slightly at the knees, started to pitch
forward, and I stuck out my arms and let him ease into them.

I rolled him close against the wall, looked pleasantly at the nose
of my gun that had landed such a pretty blow, and made a decision.
I thrust my slouch hat into my pocket, grabbed the cap from the
unconscious man's head and pulled it down over my own forehead.
Then turning up my coat collar, which was just as dark as his, I
stuck a foot over that coping.

A nice moment that. I didn't dare come down the ladder facing
out. The man below might spot my map, note the difference even
in the darkness—for certainly, without being conceited, I didn't
look much like the flat-faced punk I'd crashed. But I wasn't
worrying about his coming to and shooting me from above. That
lad would be out for a long time.

I found the iron ladder, and with my face to the wall I put both feet
on it. I took time out to look down and saw the whiteness of the
face below me as I shaded my own face with my arm. I saw, too,
the man wave for me to come on, and I saw the gun in his hand and
damn near let go a pot-shot at him.

Then he struck a finger to his lips, turned, and kneeling gave his
attention to the window. The radio grew louder as I went lower,
climbing slowly down that ladder, pushing my body out every step
or so to glance below. But he wasn't watching me now. He was
looking into the room beyond that window, from which a glare of
light shone against the outer blackness.

I landed, stepped over the dark hole that led to the fire-escape
stairs and was just above him when he looked up, muttered:
"Hello! Hel— Oh!"

With one knee on the fire-escape, his other foot planted squarely
on the rusty iron, he looked right into my face.

His gun hand moved, and I let him have it. He pitched forward
instead of backward, which was bad timing on my part. But I got
an elbow under his chin before he did a nose dive down the open

space to the fire-escape landing below. Then I pushed his limp body far over against the iron railing. I didn't want him bumping down and annoying the other tenants; at least, until my interview with the young lady was over.

I remembered the words of the man on the roof about someone having arrived in that room, the room where I was expected. Did he mean me? But I hadn't arrived—yet. Did he mean Blake Southlow? I shook my head. Southlow couldn't be controlling a gang—or could he?

I crouched down on the fire-escape, lay almost flat, and looking under the waving curtain—for the window was slightly raised— peered straight into the room. And almost the very moment I spotted the occupants of that room the radio stopped—and a gruff voice spoke.

"There! We can't talk with that damn thing exploding. Now let me have it!"

The woman said: "I don't understand you, Inspector Nelson. And why this intrusion?"

# SIX

# THE IRON MAN

■

Ida Kranz stood close to a small piano and leaned against it. There was a curve to her thin lips and a cigarette hung from one corner of her mouth. I saw her half glance toward the window. That was when Iron-Man Nelson looked about the room, walked to a door, flung it open, closed it again and came back to the girl.

"I work fast," he said. He stood, his legs spread far apart, hands on his hips, that perpetual sneer on his face. "And like Race Williams, I work alone—sometimes. But unlike Williams, I don't let a dame walk in and make a fool of me. I knew the alibi was a fake the moment I heard it. It was to alibi you, not Williams. That's why I never went to the Old Homestead and asked questions about you. I didn't want any suspicions aroused. And I know why you wanted that alibi."

"Why?" was all she said.

"Because," Nelson told her, "you were in Toby Leighton's apartment the night Blake Southlow killed him. I'm not saying you fired the shot. But you were there and saw Leighton take the dose."

Ida Kranz said, as she copped another look at the window: "I don't know what you are talking about. Get out of my rooms!"

"Your rooms!" Nelson sneered. "You hired this dump furnished. You've been living elegant in that swell hotel where you alibied Williams and made a sucker out of him. Now—listen!" Nelson leaned over, rather close to the girl, shot that ugly face forward. "Listen!" he said again. "That girl—that dumb cluck from Portland, Anna May Adams—came here, entered this apartment house. And she didn't come out the front way. Dumb dicks out front, asleep on their feet, finally discovered that she left by the back and disappeared in a black car with yellow wheels."

"Yes, yes," said Ida Kranz. "She was here, said she was being followed—and I let her go. She went through the back."

"A man was with her!" Nelson said sharply. "Who was he? Blake Southlow?"

"No, no. No man was— I don't have to answer questions; I know my rights." She tried to straighten up, but Nelson was so close to her that she only succeeded in moving the upper part of her body further along the piano.

"So you know your rights." Nelson's grin was more vicious than his usual sneer. "Well, there are just two questions I'm going to ask you and two questions I'm going to get an answer to. Don't shake your head—I know! Know how I'll get those answers and you don't. The two questions are: One—where will I find the girl, Anna May Adams? Two—where will I find Blake Southlow?"

The girl shook her head again. "If I did know, I wouldn't answer you. And I—"

"Think!" Nelson's words bit like a knife now. "Two people were murdered. One, a woman—tortured to death. The papers are blazing it all over the front page. It's an important case! I turned a girl loose on the city streets as bait to catch the murderer, and I may have sent her to her death. Now—with so much importance, such a big case—and with nineteen thousand cops, any one or any hundred of whom I could bring up here—I come alone. Why?"

The woman's lips parted, curved at the ends. "I suppose, because you wanted to ask me riddles."

"Yeah?" Nelson's words were nasty, foul as they spewed from his thick lips. "It's because some of the boys don't like the way I get information from a man, and most of them can't stomach the way I get it from a woman. That's why I'm here alone. That's why

I'm going through with this case alone, not bothered by weak-stomached cops and a set of police regulations."

Nelson acted suddenly. He brought his right hand up and smacked it across her face. Not the palm of it, but the back. The curtain must have blown in my face when he struck the real blow for I didn't see it. I just heard her squeal, heard her body hit the floor. But I saw Nelson nearly rip her dress off as he dragged her to her feet.

"I wouldn't talk if you—"

Ida Kranz started to speak and stopped. I saw the blow plainly this time, saw his right fist do a short jab—a short, quick jab as his left hand released her, so that she was staggering when his fist landed straight against her mouth.

I could have shot him; I damn near did. I was drawing a bead on his shoulder when he bellowed: "That's only the beginning." He had leaned over to drag her erect again as he snarled the words. "The next blow will crush your nose to a pulp. All right, take it!"

Ida Kranz cried out. "I'll tell! I'll tell!"

Maybe if he had struck her again I would have been fool enough to put a bullet in him. As it was, for the moment only my finger started to close on the trigger. I didn't fire. I didn't even dash into that room. I was sticking my ear to the crack below the window, to get every word the woman spoke. After all, it may have made me shudder, but it didn't make me deaf, or dumb either—at least, dumb enough to dash into that room and bust up the party.

The girl's words came in gasps at first, then rang with a clearness and sincerity as she got going, as if she wanted to get it off her chest.

"Blake Southlow was to get money to divorce his wife," she said. "She talked to me, Major Toby Leighton talked to me and Blake talked to me. He agreed to take the fifty thousand for one reason only. Because I told him he could do something with it he had always wanted to do. He could lay off liquor and reestablish his business; and he could go to Portland, find Anna May and make her happy. Yes—he spoke of her all the time, sent her money and pretended it came from some little fund her father had created when she was a child. I told him what I believed to be the truth—that Anna May had always loved him.

"Blake Southlow went to Portland and came back a changed

man. Anna May had refused to marry him. His hopes were shattered. He may have been drinking. But if so, it had not affected his head—only his nerves.

"He came to me and said, 'Sarah Jane has always taken everything from me—everything I wanted. I gave up drink—I knew I was the type who could not drink. She drove me to it again—encouraged it. She has broken my health and broken my business. Now—somehow her shadow stands between me and Anna May.' After that, he thought a long time. 'If I killed her—killed her at once,' he said, 'the world would be well rid of her. Anna May will receive money that may repay her somewhat for all she has suffered. If I killed her it would be the best thing I ever did—the only fine act of my life.' "

Inspector Nelson was the efficient officer then. He asked abruptly: "Were there any other witnesses to that statement of Blake Southlow's?"

"No!" the woman said. "There weren't. There weren't apt to be." Then she sobbed a little.

"I didn't ask you what was 'apt' to be. Have you any proof of that statement?"

The woman hesitated. "Not proof, perhaps—but proof that I didn't make it up just now. I wrote down his words, sealed the paper in an envelope and left it with a lawyer."

"Who the hell told you to do that?"

"No one." Ida Kranz was emphatic. "I've knocked around enough to know. I—I simply asked this lawyer to keep it. Oh, don't look at me like that! It was Mr. Kramer. Of course he had no idea what was in the envelope, but you can have it now."

"Kramer, eh? Vincent Kramer. You told him about the statement, and being a lawyer, he advised you to write it out, sign it and put it in his safe."

"No, no!" she said. "He didn't know."

"No?" Nelson seemed to be thinking aloud. "Kramer! A motive there. He—" And suddenly, to the girl. "Did the dead Mrs. Southlow ever question Kramer's accounts, ever tell you—"

"No. That is, I don't think so. She wanted more money, of course, but she never—"

"So the statement is in Kramer's safe," Nelson sneered in. "And he didn't know what it was when he put it there. The honest, fatherly, high-class—" He stopped, said abruptly: "Yet you shielded Blake Southlow, even after you heard how your dear friend, Mrs. Southlow, died. You shielded him after he had told you what he was going to do." And gripping her wrist, "And you killed Toby Leighton. Why?"

"No, no! I didn't," she cried out. "God! Don't—you're breaking my arm! Yes, I came to his apartment that night. Sarah Jane was missing. And—and Toby Leighton was there on the floor, dead. Blake was there. I didn't know of Sarah Jane's death then. Oh, can't you see? Can't you understand? Blake had killed the man who had taken his wife from him. I just—just told him where he could hide. He was—well, dazed. Drunk! If you must have it that way."

"And you helped him from the scene of the murder. Is that right?"

"No, no! I told him where to hide, where to go. Then when I learned the whole truth, I didn't know what to do. I just—"

"Ah!" Nelson was elated. "That's it! I don't care what you thought, what you did. Where did he go? Or I'll— Where is Blake Southlow now?"

Ida Kranz hesitated, screamed once. Nelson must have struck her again for I heard the dull thud. But I was straining to catch her answer—the address where Blake Southlow was hiding. Then I'd dash down that fire-escape, find the missing man and, perhaps, even Anna May Adams before Nelson did. Then a call to O'Rourke—

Things don't always go, in life, as you plan them. I didn't hear that address. But I knew she gave it, for Nelson straightened up after stooping over the girl. She still crouched there on the floor, her mouth smeared with red, blood running from between the fingers she held across it.

Nelson looked around that room quickly, nodded as if in satisfaction as his eyes rested on a long pipe—the riser from the floor to the ceiling.

"Guess they don't give you much heat this time of year," he said to the girl. "That's right, sister. I'm going to handcuff you to that piece of pipe. I'm working alone tonight, and I'm going to get every bit of evidence there is, if I have to beat it out of Blake Southlow—or even Kramer." He looked at the flat desk where a phone stood. "I don't think you can reach it but I won't take chances tonight. You've got no worry. Not a cop will bother you until I come back."

"But you'll come back and set me free; let me go, as you promised when you first came in?"

"I'll come back!" Nelson said emphatically. "Drag you in and let twelve men see what they think of your behavior. They may let you go if you look pretty enough. And you'll look beautiful all right, I bet, unless"—he raised his great fist and laughed—"unless you've lied to me about that address."

He leaned down, caught her roughly by her torn dress, started to drag her to her feet. Then he let her crash back, swung quickly and faced me. That's right. I just shot up the window and stepped into the room. He didn't go for his gun; he saw mine hanging in my hand.

I said: "I'm going to join you, Nelson. I didn't catch the address where Blake Southlow is hiding." And when his surprise was over and his sneer doing double work again, "I wasn't quite a fool all along the line. I got that alibi racket of Ida Kranz just in time to—"

"To what?" He shot the words through closed teeth.

"To save your life," I told him. "Come! Take a look on the fire-escape." And when he walked uncertainly across the room and looked out at the silent unconscious figure, "There's another man on the roof. But they both would have been in that window and one of them would have killed you."

Nelson looked at me a long moment. There was nothing grateful in his eyes, in his glance, in the hard granite of his face. He said: "And what do you want?"

"I want the address the girl gave you. I want to go there with you. I'm not asking to beat you to the pinch, but I want you to deal me in—and someone else."

"Yeah? Who are you working for, anyway?"

"I'm not—" I began. Then I grinned. "I'm working for a grand guy, Nelson. I'm working for Sergeant O'Rourke. He's the one I want to deal in."

"And you didn't hear the address the girl gave me?"

"No," I said, "I didn't."

He looked toward the window, half down at my gun. Then he walked across to the phone. He lifted it, gave a sudden jerk, ripped the wires loose, then hurled the instrument across the room. The girl ducked her blood-stained head, but the phone passed so close that I saw the cord catch in her hair and jar her head back as the instrument crashed against the wall. Then Nelson turned to me.

"All right, Race." He gripped my hand, and I guess it was the first time in his life he'd done that. "Maybe you didn't mean to do it, but I suppose you did save my life. I'll take you with me. Yes— by God! I'll show you I can play the game and— What's that?" He clutched my arm suddenly, stretched out a hand and pressed the light button. The single dome light went out. Complete darkness! Nelson was forcing me slightly back; his voice was a whisper.

"Someone in the hall. Listen!" He gripped my arm tightly. The fool! It was the arm of the hand in which I held my gun.

I didn't hear anything—and then I did. The swish of air! It seemed just above me. And after that, a thud. A terrible blasting inside my head! My knees gave; I tried to grasp Nelson's arm. A thousand lights danced before my eyes. Then a sinking, a nausea.

I thought that I heard a laugh—followed by the sound of a door closing. But whether it just closed inside my head or not, I didn't know. Then blackness!

# SEVEN

# THE KEY

■

My head throbbed when my eyes opened and I blinked in the sudden light. I tried to cover the room with my glance. What of Nelson? Had they gotten him too? Then I knew the truth, for I saw the girl on her knees, staggering erect, opening one of the cupboards in the desk table. I saw her hand go up and wipe the blood from her face. And I saw that hand reach into the cupboard and reapppear holding a French phone. Nelson had not been so damn clever after all.

Plainly I heard Ida Kranz call a number—the name of the exchange and the figures ran through my head, pounded so loudly that I could not hear what the girl was saying. Then a period of blackness—a deathly silence—and the words, as if the girl were repeating something back, some message that she'd heard over the wire.

"You'll handle Nelson," she was saying. "And Williams is here, unconscious. . . . I understand. There is no other way."

Then more blackness. How long it lasted, I don't know. Maybe just a split second, maybe a minute or many minutes; but it could not have been hours, for the girl was still on the phone. Whether she had talked to several people or just one, I didn't know.

At last I heard the phone crash into its cradle. But the girl just stood there, holding the instrument, looking vacantly at a blank wall.

And I was doing a bit of thinking now, in a dazed sort of way. Just the girl and myself in that room! Where was Nelson! Inspector Nelson, who had shaken my hand and— It flashed to me as I stared at the smooth white-plastered ceiling. My lips tightened. Sure! There could be no other explanation. The two-timing, double-crossing rat! He'd gripped my hand in pretended friendship after I'd saved his life; then crashed me over the head, left me there— maybe to be killed by—

Ida Kranz moved. I closed my eyes, closed them just as I thought of getting to my feet, lifting my gun. But I didn't lift my gun. I lay very still. For I saw the gun I had thought of lifting and it was in the girl's hand, gripped tightly there as she walked across the floor toward me. Through lowered lids I watched her reach my side, move to where she could look straight down into my face. She raised the gun, drew a bead directly on the center of my forehead. Then she turned her head slightly, closed her eyes and tightened her finger on the trigger.

I swung my body as the gun exploded and the lead pounded into the floor. I gripped her ankles as she fired again, grabbed both those beautifully formed and slender ankles and sent her spinning with every bit of strength that was in me.

Even above that second shot I heard her body crash and her head hit the floor with what's usually called a sickening thud. But I didn't have any feeling of nausea, any stomach weakness about a brute of a man striking a woman then. Not me! The crash of her body was like an eight-course dinner to me.

I staggered to my feet. The room spun, straightened somewhat, and I jumped for the woman who lay on her back, arms stretched out, the gun still in her right hand. I tore the gun—my own gun— from her grasp. On my knees I gripped her throat and shouted: "The address! Where Nelson went. Where? Where!"

Then I quit shaking her head, let it rest on the floor again—for she was out—cold. That was all of that. The shots would have

been heard unless the apartment below were vacant. People would
be coming up to investigate.

It's funny what a knock on the head will do to a guy. I actually
forgot the boy I had crashed on the fire-escape until my foot
slipped off the side of his face, and I gripped the rusty iron rail just
in time to keep from falling. And that recalled the lad on the roof
above, though he didn't need any recalling. I took those flights in
running jumps, slipped through the rear court of the apartment
house, climbed a fence, crossed another court and finally reached
the street behind. After three or four blocks, I found an all-night
drugstore with a phone and called a number—the one I'd heard Ida
Kranz call back in that room.

I wanted to find out if it was Vincent Kramer, and I had it all
planned just what to say. I'd whisper very low, so that the lad who
answered the phone couldn't tell if it was a man or a woman. And
I'd try and see if I could recognize the voice that came over the
wire to me. I had it planned swell; a quick line to find out just
where that number was— A voice answered my ring—a loud voice
free from any attempt at secrecy—a voice that seemed to expect
the call or at least take it as a matter of routine. And that voice said:
"Good evening! This is the Old Homestead. How can we best
serve you?"

I replaced the receiver on the hook, wondering if I had just
wasted a nickel or if it was the best one I had ever spent. But I did
jump a taxi and drive straight to the Old Homestead. I didn't know
if Ida Kranz had made one, two, or even three calls. I didn't know
if she spoke to Joe Patton, or Kramer, or Blake Southlow—or all
three of them for that matter. Hell! I couldn't figure it. Certainly
Ida Kranz had helped hide Blake Southlow and certainly she had
called that telephone number; and certainly she had wanted to
speak to Joe, her boy friend. Maybe she was hoping he'd help her
out of her trouble, or—

The cab pulled up before the Old Homestead. I hopped out and
walked in. The first guy I spotted, leaning against the cigar counter
by the hat-check girl, was Joe himself. I clamped a hand on his
shoulder. He swung slowly and faced me.

"Oh! Williams." And then, the smile leaving his lips and his
eyes tightening, "Trouble, eh? Not just a social call!"

"It's about Ida Kranz!" I told him flat. "She's mixed up in the Southlow and Leighton murders. Nelson put the finger on her tonight."

His eyes widened but he didn't speak and didn't change color. He just looked around to see if anyone had heard me, then screwed up his mouth.

"Is it bad?" His right hand clutched my left arm. That was all right by me; my gun was in my right pocket. And when I just stared at him and didn't speak, he jerked his head over his shoulder. "It's that bad, eh? Want to talk in my office?"

I didn't like that. Joe had a reputation back in the old days. I never made a move.

"So that's how it is!" He bobbed his head up and down. "You've got funny ideas, Race. It was Nelson, eh? One-Ton Nelson!' He smiled with his lips. "But Nelson hasn't got your idea, he hasn't come to me yet."

"Nelson," I said, "went straight to the hideout of Blake Southlow. He'll be looking for you later."

"Yeah?" Joe watched me very carefully.

"Yeah!" I said. "What are you going to do?"

"I'll do what I always did." Joe nodded his head slowly. "I'll sit tight. I'll telephone a good mouthpiece for myself and let the state go to work." He shrugged his shoulders. "I don't like spreading my map across the papers again, and I'm ready to pull out for the Bay of Naples any day." And suddenly, "Look here, Race. This Ida Kranz! I thought she was the real stuff. New York's best people! No crook, no crime, no dope."

"She called you a little while ago, didn't she?" I demanded.

He hesitated for a long time, finally said: "Yes, she did. She seemed hysterical, seemed—" He stopped. "I'll spill my guts, such as they are, if you'll keep my name out of it. I mean, if you like my talk."

"O.K.! If I like your talk."

He pulled me to one side. "I've quit the racket." He spoke quickly. "I've gone straight. I've saved money and I'm going across the pond. Then this dame, Ida Kranz. She had everything but money. Represented everything I always wanted to be but never could. Sarah Jane Southlow brought her here to this restaurant. I gave her a job. I was going to marry her. Now— Of course she acted funny after her friend's murder, but that was to be expected. And, to tell you the truth, she thought Blake Southlow did it. She jabbered about sticking to a friend, helping him. And I told her I'd kill him with my own hands if he was the lad who murdered the Southlow woman. Tonight, well, less than half an hour before you rushed in here, she buzzed me. A lot of wild talk about the police, Nelson—even talk about you! She wanted me to come to her, and she knows where Blake Southlow is hiding! She wanted me to turn him loose and then come to her!"

"And what did you do?"

Joe Patton's grin was evil. "I sat tight," he said simply.

"And that's all you did for the woman you love!"

"There are other women, but only one Joseph G. Patton. I hung up the receiver and sat down in my own dining room. I even visited different tables, spoke to people, noted the time."

"So you got yourself an alibi—at least, for tonight."

"At least for tonight!" Joe nodded.

"And you won't help her?"

He closed his eyes for a few seconds before he spoke, then said: "I won't raise a finger until I see how far she's in the mess. I'll think of myself first, then of her."

"Did she tell you where Blake Southlow is hiding out?"

"No!" Joe shook his head. "No, she didn't." He looked at me a long time. "But for a promise—a single promise, Race—I'll make a pretty good guess at it."

"And the promise?"

"To forget you talked to me tonight. To forget you know she called me on the phone tonight. To make your pinch, if there is any, without my name coming into it. And for that I'll give you the address where I'm sure Blake Southlow is hiding out."

I said: "It's a bargain. Now—the place! And how do you know?"

"Well"—Joe pulled me further along the dimly lit hallway— "it's like this. Sarah Jane Southlow was broad-minded. She owned a house—or rather, her estate owned it—right on the block behind this one. It wasn't rented. She let Ida Kranz and me make use of it. If you're at all romantic, you might call it a love nest." He put his hand in his pocket and pulled out a key. "The house is easy to find.

Almost in the middle of the block and next to a vacant one. That key will let you in the back door of that house. If Blake Southlow pulled these murders, I'd advise your going in that way."

I juggled the key in my hand. "What makes you think it's that house?"

He shrugged his shoulders. "Ida told me almost as soon as Mrs. Southlow's body was found that Vincent Kramer asked her for the key back. It seemed natural then, but not so hot now. Kramer must have had other things on his mind. That's the key. I didn't have it handy then."

"Oh!" I said. "Kramer knew about the key then?" I looked down at the bit of metal.

"I didn't think so when Sarah Jane Southlow first passed it over. But it looks like it now."

"Kramer, eh?" I thought a long time. "Did you ever think that he and Ida Kranz might have been—"

"Nix!" Joe shook his head. "He was too old, too stuffy for her. That dame was goofy about me."

"I don't mean that," I told him. "I mean that Kramer might have robbed the estate and worked some— Hell! I don't know."

Joe's eyes widened. He opened his mouth to speak, closed it with a snap.

"Well, what do you think?" I tried.

"I don't think, dick," he said. "I don't even give it a thought. It's your racket. I only ask for a break—just half as good a one as I'm giving you with that key." And as I turned to leave him, "Listen, Race! Bring the cops with you."

"And get a laugh if your dope is wrong?"

"O'Rourke's your pal," Joe told me. "Get him. There's a phone here." He jerked his thumb toward a telephone booth. "You can wait here for him. Remember—two people have been killed, and now—"

"No!" I shook my head. "I'll get in alone, then buzz the cops if Nelson hasn't got the place surrounded."

"Nelson!" he said. "Don't tell me he's beat you to it."

"Beat me to what?" I asked him. For the moment I was seeing red. I'd held in as long as I could.

"Beat you to the capture of Blake Southlow, or whoever murdered those two people."

And I laughed—it struck me so funny. "Hell, Joe! I'm no cop tonight. I'm not looking for the murderer Nelson is looking for. I'm just looking for Nelson."

"Nelson! Why?"

"Why? To drive his head right down through his shoulders. Even if the whole police force is there."

# EIGHT

# THE FACE OF EVIL

■

I left the Old Homestead, footed it down the block and around the corner, started up to where that house was. There was, of course, a car or two parked along the block, but none before where I figured that house number to be. And if any cops were on that block, they were doing comic-strip stuff and hiding in ash cans.

So Nelson had gone without the cops. He knew that the men hated him and that they liked O'Rourke. He'd go alone, afraid of a leak which would find O'Rourke on the ground almost as soon as he got there.

But Nelson would park his car down the block and certainly not in front of the house. Another thought—and a pleasant one. Ida Kranz may have lied to him. I believed, though, that in her fear, perhaps actual terror of Nelson, she had told him the truth. Still, as I say, she might have lied to him and I'd beat Nelson to the pinch. On the other hand, Iron-Man Nelson might already have gone to the house, surprised Blake Southlow, and grabbing him off without a struggle, be even now gurgling to the news hounds how he had done it.

I reached the vacant house next to the one I wanted and swung into the far alley along the side of it. If Blake Southlow were a maddened, desperate killer and had done for Nelson, he'd be watching those front and back doors. It didn't take me long to bust a window and enter that house.

I had my gun and my pocket flash in my hands and was looking over the ghostly room. If you wanted atmosphere for an eerie setting, it was there. White sheets covered all the furniture. I shook my head and pocketed my gun. It was spooky all right, and I guess my head was a bit jumpy yet, for I damn near shot the top off a china closet. Well, Joe had not lied to me about the house being vacant. Not only the sheets told me that a careful householder was away, but my entrance had not been entirely quiet.

I moved fast, straight up to the attic. I was going from one roof to the other. But this was no apartment house and the roofs were slanting, and a lad didn't just step lightly from one to another. However, I knew the lay of those old-fashioned houses. There was a trap door far above me, slanting with the slope of the roof. And leading up to that trap door was a ladder.

It may all sound simple and easy to you—that is, if you happen to be a house painter. But though I had done it before and hoped to do it again, it was tricky. I had to get the ladder through the trap, twist it, slide it down the roof, and then slip down alongside of it. After that, the worst was yet to come. There was a gutter to brace my foot against as I slid that ladder across, but it wasn't much to blow about.

I did have one break. Right below that roof across from me, perhaps twenty feet from where I placed the ladder, was a window—wide open, curtains blowing in the breeze. Did that mean that Blake Southlow used that room to sleep in—or that it was just forgotten when the love nest was abandoned so suddenly?

I hopped over the ladder onto that roof, then inched sideways along the roof, my rubber heels helping and my palms flat upon the shingles. Then I turned, lay on my stomach, and half crawled, half slid—like a lizard—down the slope.

I was directly above that window. A little more manipulating and I did my "young man on the flying trapeze" act. I let myself down on that sill, gripped the upraised window with one hand, let go of the gutter above, gripped the window with both hands and slid

quietly into that room. And as I landed, my hands ducked in and
out of both jacket pockets. My right hand held my gun, my left my
flash.

A woman screamed! Well, not screamed exactly. The beginning
of a scream, like those you hear off stage. As if someone had
grabbed her by the throat or placed a hand over her mouth. It was
my light that stopped her scream as it hit straight upon her white
terror-stricken face. And it was my hand across her mouth that
prevented that scream from coming again, and my soothing words
might have helped too. "What the hell are you doing here?" I said.

It was a fair enough question, you'll admit, but I got no answer.
Yes, you guessed it. It was Anna May Adams. She sat straight up
in bed, one hand clutching at her breast, the other tightly gripping
the sheets.

I moved the flash from her face to mine, back again. The terror
had gone out of her eyes but fear was still there. I took my hand
from her mouth, held it close, waiting for a squawk—but none
came.

She said: "Mr. Williams. Race Williams! I saw the shadow—I
thought it was he."

"Who?" And when she didn't answer at once, "Blake Southlow?"

"Yes. Yes!" She nodded. "That's why I didn't quite scream.
How did you get in the window?"

"Never mind that," I cut her off. "You're over twenty-one,
Miss Adams—you must have some sense. You've come here to
meet Blake Southlow, yet you went to bed."

"Oh!" The flash was between us now but I could see the natural
white of her face redden. "I wasn't to meet him until morning."

"Kid"—I sat down on the side of the bed—"I'm going to talk
to you like a Dutch uncle." And when she started to talk about
Blake being the soul of honesty and having a heart of gold, and not
harming a fly—or words that were just as silly, I cut in: "I don't
want that line. Blake Southlow wrote a letter threatening your life.
The letter was proved genuine by handwriting experts. I have
reason to believe he's in this house now and that he'll—" But I let
that ride. "Who sent you here?"

"I can't tell that," she said. "Oh I can't!" And she started in to
cry. "I love him. I love him! I told him I didn't. I lied to him. I

want to see him once, have him hold me just once, know the truth just once."

I didn't tell her then that when he held her she'd better have a police guard to keep him from sticking a knife in her back. She was frightened, she was bewildered. No two ways about that! And it was a cinch—so far—she was the only one in the whole mix-up that you could be sure was on the level. That is, everything level about her but her head. She wanted to spoon with a homicidal maniac.

"Did Ida Kranz send you?"

She wiped at her eyes, pulled the sheets higher, said: "Yes."

"Who brought you?"

She hesitated over that one, finally said: "It sounds stupid, but—I don't know. I was afraid, but he was quite a gentleman."

"I'll bet he was!" And I think the heavy crack fell dead. Then she grabbed my arms, started to turn on the water works, stopped almost at once and sat up straight and stiff.

"I'm rich, Mr. Williams, very rich indeed. I don't know how rich. I'll pay you what you ask. I ran away from Mr. Kramer's office today, telephoned Ida where she works. She arranged for me to meet her and see Blake. But I had to stay here—hide here from you, from the police—or Blake wouldn't dare come. Please go away. I must see him. I must talk to him before he is arrested."

What did I make of that? Nothing. Nothing more than that Ida Kranz had sent this child straight to her death, straight to Blake Southlow, who might be lurking in the hall outside now, to kill her—who had written a note that he would kill her. And another nice thought! That he would kill both of us. And here we were, waiting for him to strike.

But why hadn't he struck? Why hadn't he killed the girl? Was it possible that he hadn't arrived at the house yet? Was it possible that he had waited for Nelson, even for me? But he had help—the gunmen I had conquered, the man who had brought the girl to that house. But then Ida Kranz might have furnished that aid.

I went to work on the girl, in earnest. I talked to her like a father—straight from the shoulder. The show-down was that she was to get herself dressed, stay in that room until I had searched the house and then come with me. The alternative, that I'd drag in the police, who would carry her from the house, wait for Blake Southlow and probably make him look like a sieve.

"There you are!" I finished. "If he's innocent he'll have nothing to fear. If he's guilty, you'll have nothing to fear. Right?" And when she agreed, "You lock the door now, and don't open it until I come back."

"But the door is locked on the outside." She started to raise her voice but I cautioned her to whisper. Hell! She was there in that room, trapped like an animal, locked in, waiting to be butchered. And she actually expected a lad who had brutally slain one woman, then shot a man to death, to come in, toss down his books, say he was sorry for playing hooky from school and promise not to do it again.

Dumb? Maybe. But she never struck me that way. Just innocent and honest and real. A child who had suddenly been tossed into this maelstrom of money and murder. I almost asked her if she believed in fairies, but I didn't.

I went to the door instead, put the flash on it. There was no key on the other side and the lock was an ordinary one, the kind found in almost every house—on inside doors, of course. There was nothing to that. I slipped my master key from my pocket, spun the lock a couple of times, then went back to the bed.

"Listen, Anna May"—you'd no more think of calling her Miss Adams than you would of calling her "Toots"—"lock that door as soon as I leave and get yourself dressed—in the dark, of course. Here's a rod—a gun," I explained. "Don't be afraid of it. If anyone tries to get in that door or that window, just stand by the window and shoot the gun out into the night. You know how to shoot it? Good!" And as I saw her dim figure getting up from the bed, "Remember! No matter if you hear guns blasting downstairs or not, that's not the point. Don't fire that gun unless you're in personal danger—then fire it out the window." And one final word as she followed me to the door. "Remember I'm with you, I'm your friend. Your life may—and mine certainly will—depend on your trusting me tonight."

I snapped out the flash, jerked my other gun into my hand and, swinging around, opened the door, half backed into the hall. Why backed? I don't know. I knew the girl was fine, knew she was straight, knew there wasn't a crooked bone in her body nor an evil thought in her head. Yet—well, she had a gun in her hand—my gun. I'm just— Hell! I probably wouldn't trust my own reflection in the mirror.

The door closed, the lock clicked behind me. I stood in darkness and in silence.

I've got good ears, damn good ones, but I couldn't pick up a sound there in the blackness. That is, any sound below in the house. That might have been because there wasn't any sound, or because the girl was moving across the room.

Bad, that! That was my first thought. My second—not so bad! Certainly she was known to be in that room above. If there was anyone in the house, her moving around would seem natural even at that time of night—or rather, morning. I had another pleasant thought. Nelson had not been there and done his stuff. Certainly the girl would have heard him and certainly she would have mentioned it to me.

I've hunted men in the darkness before. I thought of that as I touched the banister, ran my left hand along it and felt the curve that led to the stairs. I made the first flight, and listened. Silence on that floor. I made another flight. Silence there too. One more flight to go and I'd reach the ground floor. So—what? So I sat down on the top step above the main floor, and waited. I didn't stop to think, understand! I just waited—for a break.

But nothing happened, not a thing. Dead silence. And—I came to my feet. Somewhere far below in the darkness a door closed. Plainly I heard the dull click of the latch. And I was on my way. I was sure of my direction when I reached the main floor and heard the steps, steps that trod softly but not too softly on wood. Wood—cellar steps! For the fall of those feet came from below.

A quick flash of my light now and then, and I passed through the dining room, made the pantry. Another swing door and I was in the kitchen, at the open door that led straight down to the cellar.

At the top of that flight of stairs I had a bit of listening. And the temptation was strong to show a light. A false move forward, a missing step on the stairs—meant death. A light, a clear view to the cellar, would probably mean a bellyful of lead after I got that view. So I decided to chance the missing step. Sticking each foot down and testing each step below me, I started on the journey.

If I had the right guy cornered in that cellar, well and good; if I didn't, then Anna May might have her throat cut upstairs while I was pussy-footing it around that cellar. And the guy was there. Plainly I heard the scraping of a foot, then a sound like metal, as if a shovel scraped across hard cement. I wondered if Blake Southlow had trapped Nelson, killed him and was disposing of his body.

I took my chance, stretched my gun out in my right hand, my flash in my left, and let the flash go. A pencil of light, a small open door, a sudden half-jumping, half-running-crouching dive—and I was down those steps and into that cellar.

I saw the man—at least, something lying there in the corner—close to a coal bin. The figure turned. A white face, smeared with blood and dirt—and I put out the light. It looked like the face of a maniac. Blake Southlow? I'd had too quick a glimpse to tell then. I could have shot the man to death but I didn't. I leaned against the wall close to that door, ran my hand along it, felt the protruding button, hesitated a moment, then flooded the room with light.

The man was there all right. He was lying with his face buried in dirty matting, talking incoherently to himself. There was a bottle of whiskey close to his body, a couple of others on their sides. The place reeked with the fumes, for the room was small. Just a heavily boarded space, with the coal bin at the end.

My gun still covered that figure that lay so still and groaned so lightly. I didn't want him to suddenly twist around, sit up and do a knife-throwing act. There was no place anyone else could be hiding, except the coal bin. The other walls ran right up to the ceiling; but the coal bin, at the end, had a break two or three feet below the ceiling. There was a door in the center of the bin and the white boards which held in the coal were smeared and black. Tiny bits of coal slipped from under the large crack beneath that door.

I moved quickly across, half circling the room, spotted a convenient if broken chair, stepped up on it and took a quick look-see into that coal bin. Satisfied—yes, more than satisfied—I jumped back to the floor.

The man on the matting spoke without turning his head. "I can't find the bottle," he said. "Just one little drink—just one drink." A hand that was smeared with the coal dust upon the floor waved out and back, groped about the wall, never touching the bottle. "Another drink!" the voice said again. "That's what you want. To keep me drunk! Well—well." And the voice raised. "That's what I want too."

My eyes widened as I moved toward that man. If it was Blake Southlow, he was— And I was looking at the thick chain about his ankle; the padlock that held it there; the iron staple driven into the cement wall, to which the other end of that chain was attached. Well, if it was Blake Southlow, certainly he had nothing to do with those crimes. Or else someone was keeping him there to prevent him from committing another.

I walked straight to him, turned him over, recognized him by his pictures now, in the full glare of the light. The next moment he had me. Both his hands had caught at my knees. His free leg, suddenly shot up like a piston rod, and I was lying on the floor, struggling frantically with a wild man.

I could have shot him, could have placed a bullet right between his eyes. Even before his hands had gripped my knees or his foot had more than started up. Why didn't I? In the first place, I would have had to kill him, for his forehead almost cracked against the nose of my gun. In the second place, I didn't think it would be much of a struggle. And it wasn't.

A half-minute, a minute at the most, and I had chucked my elbow so hard beneath his chin that the fight went out of him. He collapsed like a wet rag, let me hold his head and look straight into his eyes. Eyes that didn't seem mad then, eyes that suddenly seemed just hopeless and then—yes—took on a look of actual hope.

"You're Williams. Race Williams!" he cried. "You've come to— Oh, God! Look out!"

I saw the change in his eyes, even saw the shadow on the wall behind him. I swung, jerked up my gun, but I didn't fire. All hell broke loose. A gun exploded in my face. And I passed out, passed out with a single face implanted in my roaring head—an evil, sinister face that I knew—a face that others had known years before, and feared. Yes, the face I had seen in the fraction of a split second before I did the nose dive was the face of Joe Patton.

But it didn't make any difference to me. A gun had exploded in my face—and I was dead.

# NINE

# SOME DIE HARD

■

Death was not the easy passing to a better world that lads tell you about. Men were there, many of them—cursing, snarling men. I joined into the party and cursed with them. It was good cursing. I could hear it ringing in my ears.

And a voice told me to *"s-sh"* and something was wet against my forehead. It ran down my face, burned in my eyes, choked me in my mouth—and I sat up. I reached out my hand, grabbed the bottle, took one good swig—and I wasn't dead any more. I was alive—and I had left that girl upstairs to be murdered.

I forgot that a hand held that bottle to my lips, forgot that I no longer held a gun in my hand, forgot that the room was in darkness. I just sprang forward, made a leap toward the place where the door should be and landed on my face. And I knew then. My ankle was chained to the wall. The low whisper that told me so in words wasn't necessary.

The voice said: "He's chained you as he chained me. He tortured me here with the newspaper accounts of how, maddened with liquor, I had brutally killed my wife and shot Toby Leighton dead. Yes, I'm Blake Southlow. Will the police come? Are they to follow you?" And when I didn't answer that one, for I knew Joe Patton had very nicely had me tell him that I wasn't bringing the police into it, he added: "Better take another drink."

"Not me!" I shook my head, stopped it quickly. The gesture tore my head loose. "You try it, Southlow. It's there on the floor."

"God!" he said. "I wouldn't touch it if it would save my life. It was liquor that made me marry Sarah Jane. It was the liquor she encouraged me to take that let her get my fortune from me and ruin my business. It was liquor that—well—sent me away from Anna May when I went to Portland. It was—"

I wasn't going to spend my last few minutes on earth listening to a temperance lecture, so I cut in as I felt of my head. "I thought he shot me through the head."

"No," he told me. "The bullet just creased your forehead. I saw the hole it made in the wood before he put the light out. It was my fault, grabbing you. But I thought you were—"

"And I thought you were drunk."

"That was pretense," he said. "I hoped to get my hands on him, just as I did on you. I had to drink some liquor, of course. But I was sober when he picked me up and brought me here, and I have been just as sober ever since."

I tried: "If you didn't do the killing, who did? What is the racket?"

He gave it to me and gave it to me straight, and certainly he was sober enough. "Joseph G. Patton!" he said. "He came to see Sarah Jane, told her that she was responsible for his cure and that talks with her would help him go straight. I think he simply amused and interested her. But she helped him in starting his restaurant and he gave Ida a job. Ida got queer after her father killed himself and I never trusted her. But Patton certainly seemed devoted to my wife.

"Sarah Jane milked me dry and cast me off. She said I always wanted her sister anyway, and finally I consented to the divorce. Fifty thousand dollars would start me off in business again. I knew that Anna May— Well, I thought—and she was alone, so innocent. I wanted the money for her."

"Yes, yes. I know your family troubles. But this Patton! Where did he fit?"

"Only to the extent that Sarah Jane told me once that she thought some day Patton was going to kill her. No reason, except that she read it in his eyes—saw it there often, so she said. I advised her seeing a doctor—and later, seeing you. She seemed to consider seeing you. I returned from Portland, found Ida Kranz waiting for me. She said that Major Toby Leighton was ready to make the payment. I came with her and have been here as you see me ever since. Chained like this! Told of what I am supposed to have done, been read to about the man-hunt from the papers and advised of the end."

"And that end?"

"A 'suicide' leap from the George Washington Bridge late at night—just tossed to death, I suppose. From what the newspapers say about me, my suicide would not be hard to believe."

"A very neat little plan," I admitted.

"Yes." His voice had seemed very calm but grew excited now. "I didn't mind before. I was glad to die that she might live. But now that you are here, who is watching over her? What of her?"

There was an earnestness in his voice, maybe a real love. But he had written a note threatening to kill her. Perhaps torture forced him to do that, but I thought—if he loved the girl—he would have stuck it out.

He spoke again. "Then I sent that message to you." He grew eager. "That was clever. I knew you would understand, find me some way." And sadly, "Which you did. But my stupidity and his fiendish cleverness, waiting there in the recess beside the door while you entered the room, spoiled that. But I knew you would understand my message."

"What message?" I couldn't keep that question back.

"I mean the letter, of course. I couldn't get any message to you—at least, any other way. You see, I begged for more whiskey as if I didn't think they'd bring it to me anyway. Then I'd spill it on the floor. I said I'd even kill you or Anna May for drink, and it put the thought in their heads. I think it was Ida Kranz who thought of it first—that was why they left me alive a little longer. But when it came to writing the letter I was filled with pretended remorse. Then I wrote it. You were clever to understand! But even if you didn't, I knew you would recognize Anna May's danger and protect her."

I didn't have the heart to tell Southlow about the girl upstairs.

For certainly if she had to die to make things complete, she'd have to die before Blake Southlow's body was discovered. They couldn't kill her afterward and then blame him for it. Yes, it was a good set-up and—

Southlow broke in on my thoughts. "Is there any chance? I don't mind dying so much—but I feel now, after these dreadful days and nights, that—well—that I could live to be worthy of her. Any chance?"

I started to say "no" and stopped. The girl upstairs was armed. If Joe Patton for any reason went in her room, went to bring her down here, was afraid of leaving her there alone any longer— Well, if she obeyed my instructions and blasted that gun out the window, there would be a chance that a cop would hear it, though a slim one that the police would arrive in time.

But I only said: "If it's in the cards!" And then, "There's just one thing I can't understand. Where does Joe Patton stand to profit by this?"

The lights snapped on and Joe Patton stood in the doorway. "I'm afraid that is one thing you cannot understand." He smiled pleasantly at me. "But the little lady above might enlighten you, if she wished. What I can't understand is—that thick skull of yours. I'll swear the bullet bounced right off it."

And Blake Southlow screamed. It was a cry of agony, torn from someplace inside of him. "Who—who is the lady upstairs?"

I gripped his arm as Joe Patton spoke. "Anna May Adams is the name, if that helps any. And you may shout as loud as you wish. This little room was prepared for you many months ago. In fact, death was prepared for you over a year ago. Your wife hated and despised you; yet, with all her coldness and hardness she shuddered at the thought of murder, though I hinted at it. I've felt ever since that she read the truth—that I would kill her some day. That's right, Blake Southlow. Though your wife hated you, she preferred you to me. I thought of that when I killed her. The ink on her fingers and the will which Ida Kranz put in Sarah Jane's house were touches of color. Your madness was the idea, Blake Southlow."

"And you are going to kill Miss Adams?" It was peculiar the way Blake brought out the *Miss*—seemed silly at a time like that—

but I don't think I ever heard any word spoken more naturally and with a greater insult to the man to whom it was spoken.

Patton's lips twisted, his eyes narrowed. "I kill only for money," he said. "And vengeance! Be careful, *Mister* Blake Southlow, that I don't think of this vengeance when you come to die." And the smile returning and his voice growing light, "Just one thing more to attend to." He stretched his hand and arm out the open door, leaned forward, finally straightened with a phone in his hand. "Ida Kranz, poor soul"—he didn't lift the receiver yet— "never fully understood what she was getting into until she stood there beside me when I shot Toby Leighton. You hated him, Southlow. His death was to implicate you further. And besides, he had Sarah Jane's confidence, perhaps even knew of her fear of me. His death also brought Ida directly into the crimes. It cemented love so much stronger. I mean her love of life, of course."

He lifted the receiver and called a number, waited, clicked again, and then, with relief on his face: "You say you're quite safe, my dear. I'm sorry, Ida." A long pause. "I mean—it's too late. Williams has let me call you in return for giving him a full confession. Yes, Race Williams. The irons are on me now. No, there is no chance for you to escape in this world, Ida. But I kept my promise—to give you the way out. I love you. I—I—" He seemed to listen, smiled slightly.

He shook his head, laid down the phone. His mouth was a twisted gash of purple.

"That leaves me alone—standing alone. The women who pull themselves up from the gutter are far above those who start at the top and drop themselves into that gutter. She squealed all over her face the first time she was smacked around, then wanted me to straighten things out. Well, I did—I will. I was a bit foolish to think you knew a lot—that Sarah Jane had told you too much. I doubt now that she ever even visited you. But I did know that she left a letter with one of her servants to mail to you if she did not return home by a certain time. She had an idea she might be held prisoner in that bungalow. Not a dead prisoner, of course."

I understood about the delayed delivery of the letter then.

Joe Patton replaced the phone, turned suddenly, jerked up his gun and fairly snarled: "Now—you first, Blake Southlow."

"But your plans!" I tried to make my voice natural. "You know,

Patton. To toss him from the bridge and make it look like suicide."
Anything to keep us alive for a bit!

"My plans have changed," he said. "The story will be—that
you hunted Blake Southlow. You found him and you shot it out,
and both of you died. Stand in front of him if you wish, Williams.
I'm really not particular who takes the dose first."

"You're clever, all right." I sparred for time. "But the money,
man! How do you profit there? How would you ever get the Adams
money?"

He laughed, and I couldn't see then how I had believed in him
for a minute—a second, even. His words were just slurred out as
his finger started to close on the trigger.

"You see it in the movies, eh? Villain confesses all while police
rush to the rescue! Well, if death is all knowledge, you'll find out
soon. You have the lives of a cat, Williams. You have been hated
and feared for years by the biggest boys on the Avenue. They've
had you and talked themselves out of it—talked themselves to
death. Now—" His eyes narrowed and his finger tightened on the
trigger.

I straightened slightly. I'd rather take it that way. It might help
Blake Southlow when it came his turn.

And the girl rushed through that door into the room! I saw the
flash of her coat, the color of her hair, the little hat on the side of
her head, even the big purse she had hooked over her arm. And I
saw her hands too—white empty hands.

Anna May said, and her voice held more of excitement than of
fear: "I thought I heard a cry, and—and—"

The gun roared. She crashed against Patton's arm and a piece of
ice seared my side—ice that burned.

It was then for the first time that the girl saw us. Bewildered,
frightened, finally terror-stricken, she started toward Blake Southlow, swung back almost as quickly and tossed both her arms
around the killer's neck.

"Frank, Frank!" she cried over and over. "What is this? These
men! They are my friends. I—"

And he struck her cruelly, viciously with the back of his hand.
Almost as Nelson had first struck Ida Kranz. Her arms came from
his neck, flung out suddenly like a bird taking flight. She was
knocked to the left of me. Her bag flew off her arm, striking the

floor almost at my feet—a bag that thudded and snapped open—a bag that held something that stuck out of it.

I think Patton suspected the truth as I dove for it and got it. I think he saw my fingers close about the gun—the gun I had given the girl and that popped out of that bag. I think he knew as he pressed the trigger and saw his bullet jar me back. After that, curtains—at least, the beginning of curtains. I didn't jerk the gun up high enough to put the bullet in his head. He was a crack shot, had had years of practice—but maybe he had gotten a little rusty in the long lay-off, or maybe a little yellow.

His gun was on me when I squeezed lead. It took him in the belly and doubled him up like a camp chair. He tried to swing slightly and fire again. I never changed the position of my gun—I didn't need to. I let him have it, one right after the other—all in the stomach. He must have had a dozen lives. Three or four times he spun as he staggered. I lifted my eyes slightly, let the nose of the gun follow them, then planted a forty-four through the side of his head that took all those twelve lives and laid them out neatly on the floor in a single pile.

Then I had to grab the girl. She was breathing heavily and leaning against me. "That lad," I said to her, "that lad you call Frank! Who do you think he is?"

"Why"—her big eyes widened—"he's Frank Passerelo. He's my husband."

With that she fainted—and I damn near did too.

The curse of drink may be a terrible thing and whiskey may be the downfall of man. But I'm here to tell you that right then it was the uplift of one man and one woman too. If Anna May Adams, or Mrs. Passerelo, or whatever her name was, had not come to pretty fast, she would have had a jag on.

But the kid could take it—to a certain extent. She came around and was willing to talk. Even willing to go up in that big silent house, which must have been a house of terror to her now, to fetch water to fix my scratches—one of which needed a handkerchief tourniquet to keep it from breaking loose.

But she wouldn't go near the dead man. She wouldn't go into his pockets and get the key to the padlocks that held the chains—and certainly he had it on him. She was brave and stayed on her feet, but that act she couldn't pull no matter how I coaxed her. I couldn't really blame her! I've killed guys in my day and some of them had died hard, but I don't think I ever saw anyone die harder than Mr. Joe Patton, alias Joseph G. Patton, and now alias Frank Passerelo. I had certainly ripped hell out of him, and no mistake.

She was able to get the phone, though. And damn near tearing my leg off, I was able to talk to O'Rourke. I told him the whole mess was cleaned up and to get over with a few of the boys.

"Make it snappy!" I advised. "And you'll beat Inspector Nelson to the pinch."

"Nelson!" he said. "I don't even know where Nelson is." And when I laughed, "Do you?"

"You'd be surprised!" I hung up the receiver then kept my promise to Leeds, the reporter, and buzzed him too. My back was nearly broken from the position I was in.

The girl was held tightly in Blake Southlow's arms—which was fast work for a widow, you've got to admit. Especially, a widow whose husband had just had his guts spilled all over the place.

I got the story from her—not all of it, of course. That was to come later, put together piece by piece by O'Rourke. But I'll toss it all in here anyway.

She had met Joe in Portland and he got her a job. He gave her a line, too, that he was on a diplomatic mission for the Italian government and of course working hand in hand with the dear old U.S.A. Sure! He even waved the flag. Poor kid! She was starved for love, for romance, had spent her life thinking of Blake Southlow and telling herself it was wrong to do that. Ida Kranz was in on the racket. Whether Joe needed her to help put over the marriage, or if he did really love her will never be known. But she did visit the girl and did influence her to marry Joe by telling her that all Blake's trouble with Sarah Jane was the still-alive jealousy of her younger sister. After the husband had completed his mission they could announce their marriage to the world.

After that, your guess is as good as mine. They'd be living in Italy. He could squeeze the money out of her or lose her in a catacomb, or maybe just cut her throat, inherit her money and start moving around with the Kranz girl again. But any way you look at it, Joe had figured things out. His real name *was* Frank Passerelo, and that was the name he was married under. No one in the racket knew his right moniker. He had just walked into New York years back, stuck the name Joe Patton on himself and forgot his past, which was the only good thing he had.

"I was going to tell you this in Portland when you came there." Anna May was telling most of the story to Blake Southlow and I had to horn in to get anything. "I loved you, Blake—I always loved you. Maybe I thought I loved him—maybe he was just very kind to me. And then that day I knew I had lost you forever! The world just dropped from under. You know I always believed him innocent, Mr. Williams."

"And so did Race Williams." Blake patted my shoulder.

"But—" The girl started and stopped. Then suddenly, "What was that?"

"Oh! just the coal moving in the bin," I explained.

O'Rourke crashed the house then, with half the cops in town. Leeds was on O'Rourke's heels. O'Rourke wanted to know this and that. But he did get the key out of the dead Patton's pocket and let Southlow and me loose. Then I had to tell him to get a line on Ida Kranz. Not that I thought he'd find her—at least, alive. And he called headquarters.

Anna May talked and I talked and Blake talked. And the coal rattled in the bin—and I talked louder. Then headquarters called back just as O'Rourke sent a couple of men to take a look-see into the coal bin.

O'Rourke turned from the phone, moved his shoulders. "The Kranz girl is dead all right, and it looks like suicide." And as I nodded and guessed it was, O'Rourke exclaimed: "What the hell have you fellows got there?"

He strode across the room, jerked off the catch, pulled open the coal-bin door. Coal came out, of course, but a man came with the coal. A man whose hands and feet were tied and who had a gag in his mouth. His face and hair were black.

O'Rourke turned to me. "This guy in it? And who the—" He stopped, looked down, took a handkerchief from his pocket, spat on it, rubbed it over the grimy face. His eyes flashed anger as he looked at me. I looked innocently back.

"By God!" I said, in great surprise, as I winked at O'Rourke, "it's One-Ton Nelson. Now—whatever do you think possessed him to tie himself up like that and hide in there?"

# DEAD HANDS
# REACHING

■

*It all began with a slug of bad rye and a ten-grand bribe-offer that was supposed to keep that easy-to-dumbfound dick off a case he hadn't even heard about. Of course he refused, but ten minutes later he was in it up to his neck, and startled to find himself putting up an equal amount of his own money for the highly dubious privilege of gunning out a covey of human vultures.*

# BLOND GUNMAN

■

They were doing a poor business at the bar of the Royal Hotel—just a couple of customers up front. I walked down the length of it, stood at the far end. When the bartender, who didn't have any drinkers to serve, kept wiping glasses, I tapped on the mahogany with a two-bit piece.

He looked annoyed, glared at me, then, wiping his hands on his apron, came slowly down. He didn't say in so many words that I should have come up, but he meant it when he mumbled: "What'll it be?"

"Rye—straight." And when he started carrying the sour puss away with him, I added: "And not the kind of whiskey that tosses you for a loss."

He walked leisurely back with the glass, pounded it on the bar, and stood watching me as I ran the liquor below my nose, made a face and let it roll. Then I spun him a quarter.

He stopped it by planting his index finger on the edge, held it so, said: "Thirty-five cents, mister. You asked for good stuff."

"Sure," I agreed. "I asked for it, but I didn't get it. The two bits stands."

He flipped the quarter into the air, caught it in the palm of his hand, leaned both his hands on the bar, said: "You're looking for trouble, eh?"

"I'm always looking for trouble. Name of Williams—Race Williams. Now what?"

The ugly sneer went off his face as if you'd grabbed up the bar rag and rubbed it away. His hands came off the bar and he rocked back slightly. The ruddy complexion wasn't so good either. And I liked it—damned if I didn't. Conceited? Maybe. But it's nice to know you've built up a name along the old Avenue that saves you a lot of back-room brawls.

The bartender said—and a sweetness had crept into his voice, a sweetness that you'd never suspect from that hole in his face: "I didn't recognize you, Williams. On the level, Race, I didn't place you." And after a gulp, "The boss said you'd give me the tip-off. Go through the door there, down the hall to the right, and up the stairs." He shot the quarter along the bar to me. "On the house, Race. It's an honor to have you drop in."

I picked up the quarter. It was as good in my pocket as in his, and the liquor was lousy.

The hall was rather dark but there was enough light at the top of the stairs. A figure moved in the darkness, came into the light on the floor above. I knew him all right. His name was Armin Loring, but that didn't tag him for the kind of a gent he actually was.

Armin had been around the rackets for a long time—not of them, understand, just around them—a lad who appeared here and there for a price. Armin was a lad you could talk to. He didn't play at being a tough guy, he didn't need to. You just naturally knew he was dynamite. He had both his hands in the side pockets of his dinner jacket now and I said as I reached the top step and faced him: "Is that the way it's going to be?"

He looked at my right hand in my coat pocket and laughed, pulled both his hands into view and made use of them. One ran his oily hair straight back. The other pulled at his collar. His shoulders moved and he shrugged. I followed him along the hall.

"I've got nothing to tell you, Race," Armin said pleasantly

enough. "I'm just here to announce you. You know who sent for you?"

"Sure," I said, "Gentle Jim Corrigan—who used to be big things in politics."

"That's right"—he nodded—"Gentle Jim, always doing someone a favor, never thinking of himself. That's what put him down; and out of the state for awhile. You remember him, of course."

"Of course," I nodded. "Dear old Jim, who got his start in life by poisoning his own mother."

Armin Loring stopped dead in that hallway. His eyes narrowed, his lips tightened. "You know me, Race," he said abruptly. "One Man Armin. I work for one man—myself. And I haven't any special interest in you. But I'm telling you this. Don't take that attitude with Gentle Jim. You got some cash coming to you—the easiest you ever made."

Voices came in a mumbled, hushed monotone from behind a heavy door.

"That's the door, Race." Armin's voice was somewhat sulky now. "I'd take your word and all that, but I got orders to search you for weapons—and relieve you of them."

I leaned against the wall and took a laugh. "No joking, Armin," I said to him. "Certainly you didn't believe I'd trot in on the boys without a gun."

"You got a gun then?" He didn't speak about a search now.

"Two of them, boy," I told him. "Two of them—and the will to use them."

His shoulders shrugged. He turned his back on me and walked to the door, tapped—three long and two short. A bit of wood slid open almost at once. Armin spoke. "Williams is here and sporting a couple of rods. What's the answer?"

The slit closed—a long moment of silence—then a whisper from inside I didn't hear. But I heard Armin Loring's answer, and I liked it. He said: "No, I didn't try to take them from him. Hell, ain't I still alive to talk to you?" And after another pause, "And I didn't sign any suicide pact either. He's in or out as he stands. Take your choice."

Heavy feet lumbered across thick carpet behind that door. A latch clicked, a chain clanked, and the door came open. For the first time in over two years I got a look at Gentle Jim Corrigan.

\* \* \*

He hadn't changed any. Perhaps he had added a chin or two, but his face wasn't any older—it couldn't be. There was no way to tell. He had a face that was always in motion. The wrinkles ran in and out of it while he talked. Blue veins became tiny flowing rivers that disappeared entirely, someplace up in his forehead.

He reached out both hands to grasp mine, but he only got one—the left one, as I half swung my body so as to be facing both Armin and him. But Armin had already started back down the hall. He called over his shoulder: "Stop at the bar on the way out and have a drink with me, Race." And he was gone. As for me, it was just as if I gripped a bag full of loose clams and the bag had split—moist and slippery and rolling. Gentle Jim still held my hand.

"Race Williams! Good old Race, the pride of the Avenue," Jim was saying in that soft, gentle voice of his. "I never expected to see you again. Never expected a fellow like you to live so long. You know, Race, when I went away for my health, I said to myself, 'There's one name I can scratch off the books if I ever come back to New York.'" He laughed then, a birdlike laugh. "Well, you did get in my hair then"—he touched the baldness of his roof—"what hair there was. But I never hold grudges. I never—" He backed into the room ahead of me, closed the door and snapped on the chain.

I was expecting almost anything. That's why I kept his huge body between me and the rest of the room. But I got a look-see just the same. I'll admit I was surprised.

The other two men in that room did not have the courteous manner of Gentle Jim, and maybe for that reason alone they were not as dangerous. But if Jim wasn't there you'd easily say that one of the other two was the most dangerous man in the country today.

Albert Swartz was tall, slightly graying at the temples, and his face was hard and straight and intelligent. Albert had been the beer king in better days. He had also seen repeal coming, had sold out at a good price, evaded the government's investigation of his income tax, and disappeared from view.

But Albert was not a talker. He just looked at me and nodded unpleasantly. The other man was like him, perhaps a little younger—say around twenty-five, the time when the public enemy becomes ripe, most dangerous because he's fully aware of his own power. The swaggering type of racketeer who has just reached the top and doesn't know how to settle on it.

You don't see many of them in the racket today. They don't live long enough. While they last they're just killers. I didn't know his name, and no one gave it to me. But he came to his feet, swaggered forward and looked me over contemptuously.

"So this is the dick we pay good money to buy off. If I had my way, I'd—"

But Jim Corrigan was talking—low, gentle. "Williams is a fine fellow—really one of the boys. One of the boys who, through a peculiar quirk of fate, is on the wrong side of the fence. One of the boys who—"

But I wasn't listening then, and I didn't have to keep an eye on the big blond bad man, for he had turned and was looking at a picture on the wall—his back to me.

I was looking at the other figure in that room. The figure in black— all in black. A black cassock like a monk's and a hooded cowl like a monk's but, unlike a monk—at least the pictures of monks I have seen—that cowl was pulled down completely over the figure's head. If there were holes for eyes, I could not see them. If there was a slit to breathe through, I could not see that. Nothing to see but that all-enveloping black cassock, and the toes of two shoes. Man, woman or child—take your choice. The figure seemed to double into itself so you couldn't tell.

"So you've gone in for the heavy melodrama, eh?" I said to Jim as I ignored the seat he offered me and pulled a chair up with its back to the wall and sat down.

"Just a touch of color." Gentle Jim rubbed his huge hands together and let that smile run up and down his face as his little blue eyes popped in and out.

The blond stranger went to the long table, flopped down in a chair, and banged his hand upon the table. "Damn it to hell, Jim," he said abruptly, "you've got a Hooded Menace here—and now this flat foot, Williams. Why, Williams was simply to come in and sit down at the table, take the cash, and go and buy himself a trip— all friendly and sociable. Now what? He sits with his back to a wall, tucks his thumbs beneath his vest, and almost has two guns falling into his hands."

"Tut, tut, Bertie." Gentle Jim went over and laid a hand on the other's shoulder. "Race Williams sits with his back to the wall because he is most susceptible to drafts. That's right, isn't it, Race?" He smiled pleasantly at me.

"Correct," I agreed. "Especially drafts let in by bullet holes." And I added so the boys might as well know from the beginning where I stood: "If that big, yellow-haired punk thinks he's so handy with a rod, he's perfectly welcome to jerk one out and show what he can do with it."

The yellow-haired punk swung. Corrigan grabbed his gun-arm; spoke to me. His voice was still soft, but the gentleness had gone out of it. "Why make trouble, Race?" He tried to keep the threat out of his voice. "You had my word that you'd be safe here."

"I know, Jim." I didn't try to keep the sneer out of my voice. "But I'm willing to release you from that word if the bad boy whose puss I can't place feels like showing off."

No one spoke after that. All looked at the black figure in the big chair in the corner. The black figure had stamped a foot—just once.

Gentle Jim arranged things. He pushed the long table closer to me. I had only to rock forward, jerk the chair up a bit, and I was at the end of it.

Jim's words were coaxing. "Come, come, Race. Make things easy for me. I'm simply going to offer you a business proposition. Now boys"—as he sat down closest to me—"hands on the table—all of us. Honest and aboveboard, eh, Race?"

I watched the three pairs of hands come onto that table—white empty hands. I jarred my chair to the table, sat there with my thumbs in the armholes of my vest.

"Well—" Gentle Jim even honeyed that soft voice of his up a bit. "We got to talk, Race, honest and friendly. How about spreading out your paws? You're pretty good aren't you—not going soft?"

"Or yellow," said Bertie.

Albert Swartz smiled lazily. I simply jerked my head toward the Masked Marvel, said: "I'd like to see some white hands shining over there and—"

Black moved—black arms that were like the huge wings of a bird—and two delicate, well shaped hands came into view and folded on black knees.

"All set." Gentle Jim leaned forward.

"All set—but for one thing." I put both my hands on the table now. "This punk, Bertie—I don't know him. I can't place him. But he knows me or you've told him about me and he still thinks he's good. Maybe he is. So—just a warning. I'll do him the honor of believing he's as good as he thinks he is, and if his hands leave the table—either of them—I'll shoot him to death. Fair enough?"

All of us, including the Masked Marvel, looked at Bertie. He grinned, twisted up his mouth, narrowed his eyes and I guess thought that he was smiling.

"You may be hot stuff in this town, Williams, but you're just a laugh to me. You're to be offered a proposition, and you'd better take it." He paused and did his big act. You could see it was big by the contortions he put his face through. "If I want a gun—your hands won't be off the table before I'm making use of it. Remember that!"

"I'll remember that," I said very seriously, and we got down to business. The proposition was not entirely new. Gentle Jim Corrigan put it a little better, that was all.

"It's like this, Race," he said. "Me and my friend"—he jerked a finger toward the silent, dark figure—"and the boys here are back in the city and we're going into business. We're offering you ten thousand dollars to take a cruise around the world. If you wish, you only have to leave the city for a few weeks, and if things go wrong, turn down a client later—a client it's a hundred-to-one shot you'd never get anyway. It's a lot of money, Race—and it's the top price. You know me. I don't bargain."

"And you know me," I told him. "I don't take a run-out powder at a price."

"But it isn't that, Race. It's simply—we're engaging your services."

I shook my head. "You've given me straight talk, Jim, and I'll give you straight talk. There's a case coming my way. I might not have taken it. Now it'll have to smell to high heaven to get me to turn it down. I hope you don't get burnt, Jim."

"That's enough." It was friend Bertie speaking and his voice was ugly. "I was against this from the beginning. I'd have taken half that dough you offered Race Williams—and seen he didn't take the case, or any other. Now—"

And when Jim would have interrupted him, "You did a flop,

Jim. I'll talk now. I'll talk the kind of language this bird will understand."

He killed me and cut my body up in little pieces, at least with his eyes. Then, "It's like this, Williams. You take the cash now. You get out of the city now. You keep your word that Jim thinks is worth something—or in twelve hours I'll blast you right out."

I laughed. That's right. It wasn't a fake either. This boy really meant it. I hadn't had a lad talk like that to me in years. Then I didn't laugh. I looked him over good—said: "Buddy, I can't place you and that face. But you're playing the big time now. You've got something, of course, or the boys wouldn't have you here. But keep it for rainy nights, dark alleys—and staggering drunks. Enough?"

He blew up higher than a kite—his face, his eyes, and even the words that spewed out of his mouth. Despite his two-hundred-dollar suit, the seven-fifty necktie, and the tiny point of the handkerchief that showed from that breast pocket, he was talking from the gutter he came out of.

Cutting out the filth, he said: "Why do you figure you came here? Why do you figure you got one grand mailed you for just ten minutes' talk? Why do you suppose I'm here—me who's popped them off like flies and never got a jolt. You either knuckle down, take the jack, and beat it—or you'll never leave this room alive."

I half glanced at Gentle Jim. "So that's your word, eh?"

Great shoulders moved. "That's the way it looks, Race. I never for a moment thought you'd back down on me. I hate to see a guy like you, whom I've known for years, go out like that. But the room's padded and—"

"You took the thousand bucks and came here didn't you?" Bertie was at it again. "It wasn't all curiosity, then. You found out something—maybe got in touch with the client and came here to see what you could learn. Don't tell me you ever suspected we knew. You thought you'd see just one man—and could handle things. You never suspected a trap—a death trap. You just pocketed the single grand Jim sent you and came."

"I've known Jim for a number of years"—I came slowly to my feet, both my hands in plain view on the table—"and I certainly suspected almost anything. Yes, even the death trap."

"Aw"—Bertie was talking through his teeth now, the old trick of the gunman, working up to the kill—"you can't make me believe that."

I nodded slowly as I leaned heavily on my left hand. Where my right hand rested on the table and seemingly helped to support my body, it actually did not. But the leaning position did flip open my jacket a bit wider, and did throw a shoulder holster into a rather nice position.

Bertie went on talking. He liked his own voice, his own words. He was pretty loud. He was one tough guy. He knew it, admitted it. He liked it and in a way so did I. But he said: "So you suspected more than one person, and you came. You suspected even a death trap, and you came. Why?"

"Why?" I said quietly. "I sized up the situation at the door. But I came in because I didn't think you could make good. And I don't think you can now."

Despite his talk this lad, Bertie, was good. Gentle Jim thought he was good, for he sat quietly by. Albert Swartz thought he was good, for his hands still stayed on the table. I saw the whole play, and it was a tough one. Bertie was there to start the fireworks.

Gentle Jim Corrigan said sharply: "Let it go, Bertie boy. You can't bluff Race. All right, Race. You had my word, beat it along. No one will bother you."

Yes, I was sure of the play then. I started a glance toward Gentle Jim—just started it, mind you. Then I threw my eyes sharply back to the Boy Wonder, Bertie. And I was right. One of his hands had gone—or at least was going—

Fair is fair. You'll have to admit it was every man for himself after that. Bertie's glaring eyes weren't five feet away now. Then his gun flashed almost in my face. There was a single shot. But it wasn't from Bertie's gun. I had jerked up my right hand and damn near shot his head off.

I know Swartz and I know Gentle Jim, and I know that it wasn't fear of me that made them drop their hands back empty upon the table. It was Bertie, the horribly dead gunman. It was good shooting—damn good shooting on my part. But there was nothing artistic about it.

Albert Swartz got up from the table—walked to the window that was heavily padded. He was trying to remove the pad.

I said simply: "Don't do that, Albert." And when he turned

back and was nearly crashed by the hooded figure who was disappearing through a door in the rear of the room, I added: "The cops aren't going to like it."

"No, no," said Corrigan. "But they don't need to know, Race. We can take care of our own dead." Gentle Jim even gulped. "You heard me tell Bertie to let you go. I had no intention—" He stuck a cigar so suddenly into his mouth that I nearly killed him. Then he said: "God! Bertie was a dead shot. He said he was the fastest shot in Philly."

"You mustn't let guys kid you like that, Jim."

Swartz coughed, said: "He was off balance, Race—when you gave him the dose."

"Sure, sure," I agreed. "You want to remember that, Albert."

"Remember it. Me? Why?"

"Oh"—I stuck my gun indifferently against his stomach—"You might get off balance yourself some day. Don't forget to sit up with your dead."

# THE GIRL AT THE BAR

■

Armin Loring was leaning against the bar talking to a dame when I swaggered in. She was sitting on the edge of the mahogany, swinging her legs against the side, but she dropped so suddenly to the floor, and turned toward the bar, that I didn't get a chance to see her face.

I never cut in with gunmen and their women, and I didn't now. I just said, "Hello Armin," and moved to the front end of the bar, not far from the big plate-glass window that gave onto the street.

And the tough-pussed bartender was there. But he wasn't so tough then. His arms trembled, though he laid his hands flat on that bar for support. His voice shook when he spoke. I nodded and smiled. Maybe he wasn't in on the thing. But it was a cinch he'd never expected to see me alive again.

I liked that. I gave it to him hard. Here was a guy who didn't want to play rough any more. I said simply: "Rye—bonded stuff. And don't make a mistake this time."

Armin Loring moved down the bar leaving the girl at the rear end. He asked calmly: "Well—which one was it, Race?"

I grinned my appreciation. "So you didn't expect me back either."

His shoulders moved. He said simply: "It can't be Jim or they'd need me. It can't be Albert Swartz, for he's got too much of a head. It"—he grabbed my arm—"it wasn't— Not—"

When he paused I gave it to him.

"It was a lad who rather fancied himself with a gun. Boys had kidded him into thinking he was fast. Went by the name of Bertie and—"

Armin's fingers closed on my arm, his lips grew tight, his eyes brightened. "So." He hardly muttered the words then. "It was Bertie Logan, the fastest, the quickest—"

"Sure," I broke in. And letting the liquor burn added: "That's what Bertie thought, too. Hell—what was that?"

I turned. The girl was slim and wiry. You couldn't tell much from her face. It was painted like a camouflaged cruiser in war time. But the picture at least had plenty of action.

She had been standing right at the end of the bar—around the side of it. A man stepped out of a little side door, held it open with his foot and made two quick motions with his hands. One hand shot over her mouth—the other around her neck. Just a quick jerk and she would have disappeared through that doorway. You can see it in the movies any time.

But his dame knew tricks that the movie men didn't. When he lifted her off the floor, she kicked back with both feet, closed her teeth into his hand and when I turned and looked, it was the man who was making a squawk, not the girl. Armin turned toward her, cursed softly. As he ran up and gripped her arm the girl shrieked; shrieked straight at me.

"Don't go, mister. Give me a break. Get me out of here!"

I was pretty close to Armin then—not too far from the girl either. At least I got a good look at her. You couldn't tell if she was young or not, the way she was painted.

"You did your trick." Armin turned to me. "I like the girl but she wants to swallow the whole bar. Better beat it along. I'll handle her."

I turned and started toward the door. I had had my fun and was well paid for it—a thousand just to call on Gentle Jim. And the girl shrieked again.

"Race—Race Williams," she cried. "I need you now—if you dare chance it. If you don't dare now, try later and—"

It wasn't the word "dare" that got me, and maybe it wasn't the direct appeal to me by name, for most of the boys and girls along the Avenue who know anything know my mug and my moniker. I think it was the thing in her voice—the sudden change in her voice. It was not only sober, but it didn't belong in the Royal Bar.

Anyway, I swung back in time to see the lad in the doorway slam his hand across her mouth again, and Armin sink his fingers into the white flesh of her shoulder above the low evening gown.

I only swung, understand. Nothing in my mind exactly. Then I stepped closer. There was something in the girl's eyes—blue eyes, deep blue, no film over them, no doe-like, soused look. They were proud too, but I didn't see much of that, for they changed so quickly—changed as the hand that belonged to that thick arm started to drag her through the doorway.

I said: "I want to talk to the girl."

He was a big bruiser, but nothing to be alarmed over. Oh, hot stuff to beat up a woman or kick a few drunks around. But as real tough boys go in my line, I couldn't see him at all. Yet he still held the girl.

I said again, and this time put pressure into my voice: "Take your hand off her mouth, fellow." And when he didn't move, I added simply: "If you've got any desire to live at all."

His hand dropped as if you'd hit it with a crowbar. Armin spoke to the girl before she could say a word. "You stay here." His strong fingers bit into her flesh. "You must know what will happen if you talk now."

The girl's lips set tightly, grimly. She winced under the pain.

I looked at her a long moment. The make-up was certainly on thick; too thick even for a real tough moll. She wasn't of the night, that was a cinch. I said to her: "If you want out I'll take you out. Come! Yes or no."

"Yes. Oh yes, yes!" She wasn't doing so good now. Her knees were beginning to give.

Armin Loring said: "Take it easy, Race. Don't cross me like this; not with a woman."

The girl trembled. Teeth bit into her lip. Blue showed on her shoulder as Armin's fingers tightened. But she didn't scream. I rather liked that. I said: "Take your hand off her shoulder, Armin." And when he sneered I flipped my fingers up under my left shoulder. A gun slid easily into my right hand. No one but Armin could see it. His black eyes grew wide—more with surprise than fear, but he held her shoulder just the same.

I said: "You've got five seconds to remove your hand, then I'll shoot it off at the wrist."

Armin spent three of those seconds looking from my gun to my eyes. Then he said: "No fooling, Race?"

I didn't laugh, just told him the truth: "No fooling, Armin. At the wrist."

His hand fell from her shoulder to his side. He said simply: "You're making a big mistake, Race. I don't like what you're trying to do. No, I don't like it."

"We can't have everything we want in this world, Armin." I shed a tear with him. And to the girl, "All right, kid—get moving."

"You're not going!" Armin did the Trilby act with his eyes.

The girl spoke to me, and she had hard work getting the words out. "He's right. I'm not going." And after a moment's hesitation, "Besides—I—you. You couldn't get me out—with safety to yourself."

"This is no time for funny cracks." I smiled at her.

"The girl says she's not going." Armin's face was livid, but his hands were directly in front of him. He had will power, all right. Another man with a temper like his would have pulled a gun and—well, he wouldn't have had that temper to bother him any more.

The girl also started to say she wasn't going. But I was through playing guessing games. I jerked her quickly, sent her half staggering toward the door, said: "The thing's out of your hands now—and yours too, Armin. The girl goes out."

And out she went, with a frightened look over her shoulder, but still anxious to get through that door. I closed it behind us and we were in the dimly lighted hall.

I clutched the girl's arm, stood still. There was a slight rustle on the stairs. A woman came down. Her face was hard, determined, the face of a woman who had lived. Yet, I knew that face could be young and soft and beautiful. That's right—I knew the woman. It was the Flame—Florence Drummond—the Girl with the Criminal Mind. A woman of good—a woman of evil. Take your choice. There was a time when I could see only the good side of her.

Sergeant O'Rourke—my real friend among the cops—had said I was in love with her. I don't know. But I don't ever remember O'Rourke lying to me.

How did I feel about her then? I don't know. But I do know that I called out her name there in the dimness of that hall; called it as she turned beneath the light. I saw her face, just for a split second, and it didn't seem hard or cold. It was young and the sparkle of youth was in her eyes. But it was the thing she carried that got me—a black garment. Plainly I saw the hood which hung over her arm.

Then she was gone.

Maybe I stood there dumbfounded or maybe just dumb, with my left arm caught under the girl's right—half supporting her. Then I snapped out of it and dragged the girl down the hall and out the front door.

And the coincidence of no one else being in that bar was no longer a coincidence. The door was locked on the inside. When I made the street I saw the sign—*Royal Bar Closed for Alterations*. Alterations was right!

I saw something else, too. I saw the Flame swing out the main entrance of the hotel and grab herself a taxi. By the time I got another one, she was gone.

Since I didn't have any special directions from the girl, and wanted to get moving, I called to the driver: "Hit it for Central Park."

He nodded; the car jumped forward. The girl leaned close to me and whispered hoarsely: "But if they follow us! Central Park—it'll be dark and they'll—why they'll catch up to us!"

I looked down at the little face in the darkness; smeared as if she had cried a lot, dug her knuckles into her eyes, and made a grinning clown out of her face. Mascara was running wild and no mistake.

My answer will show you the kind of humor I was in. "If they follow us and catch us," I told her flat, "I'll mess up that park so that the city will need to hire a dozen new street cleaners before morning."

Of course, it was the Flame who had put me in that state of

mind. Was it possible that she, the Flame, could sit beneath that black outfit and see me shot to death? And the answer apparently was—she could. Yet I didn't believe it. At least I told myself I didn't believe it. Sure, I'd have gotten a kick in shooting it out with the boys right smack in Central Park.

The girl leaned on my shoulder. Little hands clutched mine. She was sobbing softly. And suddenly my lust to kill was gone. She was warm and soft and young and—yes, and clean.

"They'll kill me. They'll kill me!" she cried over and over, and when I patted her head as if she were just a child, she added a humorous thought—"And they'll kill you too."

"Don't you believe it, kid." I gave it to her straight. "The boys aren't really bad." And when she turned those blue, tear-dimmed eyes up at me I said simply: "I'd pop them off—one, two, three. Now, why do they want to—to—" I swallowed once, took out the word "kill" and tried: "Why do they wish to harm you?" I put it all light and gay and happy.

And she said: "They want to kill me because I saw a man murdered."

Light and gay and happy did I say? The kid had dumped over a trunk full of words in that single sentence. I must have put black-and-blue marks on her arm, I gripped it so tightly.

"Kid," I told her, "that's bad—real bad. Do you mean you can stand up in court and send someone straight to the chair?"

"Yes," she said. "I could do exactly that. I try to tell myself that I must do it. Yet I don't do it." She wrung her hands now. "I can't. I can't! You'll help me—save me—won't you?"

You've got to admit that things looked tough—real tough—for me. It's one thing to do the noble "unhand that woman" act, and drag the girl from the villain's grasp. But it's quite another thing to have the unhappy maiden anchored on you. Racketeers, gunmen, even yellow rats will take a chance on putting a bit of lead in a girl's back if it keeps them from sitting down at eleven o'clock some night and later being lifted off fried.

Somehow the girl didn't seem such a knock-out now; she didn't seem so soft and warm. But if I make a play I finish it. There were just two things to do. Give her a few twenties and let her skip, or call up Sergeant O'Rourke who'd give her protection while she spilled her story. But she broke in just as I was about to offer her those alternatives.

"Of course, Mr. Williams," she said, "you've done so much for me already, and what you will do I can never repay with money. But I am going to ask you to work for me. I'm going to offer you nine thousand dollars—now or when it's all over."

Funny how things change. She seemed warm and soft again, and certainly attractive. But I'm a cautious man. "How old are you?" I asked.

"Twenty," she told me.

"Oh—who's to put up the dough?" I know it sounds brutal, but you don't give things away in your business—and you don't extend credit to minors either.

"I will, but you mustn't tell, because I saved the money out of my allowance. You must say you are working for nothing. Because—well"—she did a bit of nose-rubbing on my shoulder—"because I am a woman in trouble and you like me."

The "like" part wouldn't be hard at any price—at nine grand it was downright infatuation. But I said: "Why exactly nine thousand dollars?"

"First," she demanded, "will you take my case? Protect me and save someone's life?"

Nine thousand sounded like a lot of jack, but I gave her a fair answer.

"You're under age, but I'll take your case. If it doesn't fit in with my ethics I'll drop it, shoot eight grand right back to you, keeping one for my trouble."

"Ethics?" She shuddered slightly. "I'm afraid I'll lose you then, Mr. Williams. I'm afraid it is not entirely—maybe far from—ethical."

I gave her a smile and a pat on the back. "You put up the money, kid," I told her. "You'd be surprised what I can do with a bunch of ethics." But I didn't add, "For nine grand." I said: "Now why—just nine?"

"Well"—I think she bit her lip for she talked indistinctly for a couple of words—"I was told that you would be offered ten thousand dollars to turn me down and that I should offer you eleven to take the case." She paused a moment and then, "I had heard about you, read about you, and I didn't believe—couldn't believe—that. So I'm offering you a little less. It will make you seem more like the man I've pictured. Like the man I'd like to have helping me."

Hot stuff, eh? Some compliment! Sure it was. For a moment I nearly broke down and offered to save her for nothing. But something protected me from that noble act. Maybe it was the excitement of actually believing for the first time that I'd get the money. Yes—it looked like this was the client. The client that I'd been offered ten grand to turn down.

So what! Could she take me to her home and talk to me? I'll say she could!

# THREE

# FAMILY SKELETON

■

It was a dignified brownstone family front on a good street, even if she did take me in the back way, up some stairs and right smack into her bedroom. She closed the door. Then, damn it, if she didn't enter a bathroom, close that door and take a shower. Said something about feeling dirty, which might have meant the boys at the Royal Bar.

I took a look-see around that bedroom. A small cupboard caught my eye. It struck me that it might contain good liquor, so I got up and gave the tiny knob a whirl—locked. I grinned, pulled out my nail file, snapped the lock back and opened the door. Nothing there but a white bit of folded paper. I looked at the bathroom door, still heard water splashing and unfolded the paper. White powder, known to some people as "happy dust." Sure! It was dope.

I folded it up, found an envelope in my pocket, put it carefully away, pressed the heel of my hand hard against the door and the cupboard clicked locked again.

I felt like a real detective. A clue! I took another look under the bed, but neither the Chinese Ambassador nor a Malay strangler was lurking there. The breaks were against me. I sat down, lit a butt and the girl came out.

If she had wanted to make a hit, she sure did. No woman of the night now—young, clean-faced, clear-eyed. She wore a negligee which in love stories is supposed to be hot stuff in anybody's bedroom. In her case, it was just a swell bathrobe that hid her slim young body like a tent. She curled up on a chair and gave me an earful. Her first crack was a beaut.

"You like me, don't you?" And there was nothing of the dame on the make in her voice or eyes as she said: "I like you too."

And there's a love scene that should knock you flat on your back. It did me. There was nothing funny about it either.

"I'm Mary Morse." She went into her act before I could even mention the money. "You know Morse and Lee, of course. The jewelers." There was a touch of pride in her voice. "My grandfather, Frederick Morse, headed that firm, and some day it will be mine—all of it. You know all about the business, and how I happen to own it?"

There was no use to lie to a client, so I shook my head, and she rattled the bones of the family skeleton.

"My grandfather had two sons. One, Joseph, my father; the other, Frank, my uncle. My father went into the firm. My uncle"—she shrugged her shoulders—"well, there was some trouble there. I'm not sure but—well, Grandfather was very narrow, and I think it was about Uncle Frank wishing to marry an actress. Anyway Uncle Frank went away.

"My father married, and I don't think my grandfather was overpleased when I was born. He expected a boy to carry on the family name." She smiled. "I guess he always hoped for a male Morse until Father died and my mother married again."

I said: "That must have hit your grandfather between the eyes. Busted the line of Morses higher than a kite, eh?" Hell, a lad had to show an interest when she was so serious about it.

"No"—she shook her head—"Grandfather was rather pleased at Mother's second marriage. You see, she married Conklyn Lee—Grandfather's manager."

I didn't say: "So what?" I just waited. And she proceeded to give me a little more of the family tree.

"Then Grandfather died and Uncle Frank came back for the

funeral. Oh, that's ten years ago. And well, I guess I coaxed Father to take him in the shop where a Morse really belonged and—"

"Young lady"—I shook a finger at her—"I've been following your family better than you think. You said your father died, and your mother married the manager of your grandfather's jewelry business—Conklyn Lee."

"She did," Mary Morse hurried on, "but he's a real father to me. He made Mother very happy and he made me very happy, and since Mother died he's been everything to me. I call him Lee."

I said I thought that was nice and waited. Affectionate stepfathers are not in my line.

"Uncle Frank is just on a small salary, though I'll give him an interest in the firm some day. That will be a surprise. If Uncle Frank ever led a fast life he certainly has changed. Never takes any drink but port wine, reads the most tiresome books and is just about the model man. Grandfather was rather peculiar."

I had gathered that, but I didn't crack wise. I asked Uncle Frank's salary.

"Ten thousand a year and the house here to live in. It's mine, but I'm going to give it to Uncle Frank when I'm twenty-one. That's a surprise, too."

She was as full of surprises as a pair of dice. But I stuck to business. "And your stepfather, Conklyn Lee. What is his salary?"

"Oh, he receives fifty thousand a year. Grandfather fixed that when Lee married Mother—a wedding present. Lee is president of the company, but he's really holding down the position for me. I'm to be Morse some day."

"You will own the entire business?" I guess my eyebrows did theatrical tricks.

"Yes, I will, when I'm of age."

Things get around. I said: "I heard the business wasn't so hot." She simply smiled. "All business has been bad—and especially the high-class gem trade like ours. But nothing could happen to Morse and Lee."

"That's what you think," was on my lips, but didn't get out. I wasn't there to lay crape all over the place. "I heard"—and I gave it to her straight—"that Morse money was being dumped into the business by the tens of thousands to keep the doors open. Was that your dough?"

"Some of it," she admitted. "Lee had to get an order from the court. He's my guardian, you know." I didn't know, but it sounded interesting. Then she threw another. "Lee has put every penny of his fifty-thousand-dollar salary back into the business for the past few years."

"Did you see him put it back?" I asked. "Did you see the books?"

"Why no, he just told me once when I wanted him to use more of my money. But only this week he was to go before the court with me."

"And he didn't go with you?"

"No." She paused, leaned forward. "That's the trouble. He disappeared."

That's a woman for you. Lets me sit there and try to figure out family relations, and then smacks out suddenly that her stepfather has disappeared. I simply said as I leaned back and lit a butt: "Let's have it, kid."

And she did—smack in the face. "That's it," she said. "If I tell what I know, they'll tell the federal men about Lee. That's why I was made up tonight. That's why I followed a man to the Royal Hotel—the man who brought me the threat. Then I was recognized and you—"

"Just a minute. Federal men?" I could see that nine grand going. "Is this stepfather of yours, Conklyn Lee, in trouble, or is someone trying to frame him?"

She looked at me a long time; looked at the door, found a key and opened the little cupboard I had searched. A board creaked and she turned with a stack of bills in her hand.

"Nine thousand dollars." She slapped it right into my hand. "That's for your help and your confidence—and your word never to tell."

It was a lot of jack. Innocent she may have been, but she knew how to hold a lad on a spot just as he was ready to jump off it. Oh, I'll take a chance at anything. But it's different with G-men. The best lawyer, the finest mouthpiece on the Avenue will always tell you: "Sorry, boy—no can fix."

I guess a dozen times I said to myself: "Get thee behind me, Satan." Then the bills would sort of crinkle and slip between my fingers. And Satan won—at least for the time being. I was simply protecting an innocent and fine girl. With that happy and noble thought I buried the wad and told her to shoot the works—with the understanding there were strings.

She finally said, simple and direct: "I don't think the government suspects, but Lee has been smuggling in narcotics. He has always been very close to the steamship people. With his knowledge it might be easy for him."

I looked at that innocent young face, gulped the words: "Did he tell you that? How in God's name do you know?"

"He didn't tell me—that is, not until after he was gone. I was told over the phone; asked to search his private study, burn everything I found there that might be incriminating."

"His study! Where?"

"I lived with Lee. After he disappeared, Uncle Frank brought me here. He seemed very much disturbed. But if he knew, he told me nothing. But then he wouldn't. He knows how much I love Lee. He was afraid it would hurt me."

"This Lee, your stepfather—he telephoned you?"

"No, someone phoned for him. It was a disguised voice, but it wasn't his. I think it was a woman."

A woman! My mind rushed to the Flame. But I said: "Then what?"

"I burnt or destroyed everything I found in the study. Letters—strangely worded letters. Some tins too, and a paper I brought here to the house to have analyzed. It's"—she turned to the cabinet, swung back white-faced—"it's gone," she said. "But how? Uncle Frank never visits my apartments when I'm staying here. I have a separate staircase."

"I have the paper," I told her. Then tried: "Did you know what you destroyed? Know what it meant? The personal danger to you?"

"Yes, I knew." She nodded. "But I did it for Lee."

"You thought someone was framing him?" I tried to get some reason out of her.

"No, I didn't think that. He had been nervous for days. Talked to me funny—about the Morse name, and how I was to buck up." And suddenly, with a bang, for I guess I was staring at her, "Don't look at me like that! What he did was to save the house—the name of Morse. He was straight and honest and kind. He did it for me. I

know—I know about the government. Well, I chanced the government. I'll chance it again. He's my father, and I love him!''

It was a nice speech and if I'd just met her casually I would have
patted her on the back and let it go at that. She went on.

"When I was a little girl I liked wild flowers. I wanted them in a
wreath, and he'd go off into the country—" She stopped, looked at
the ceiling and smiled rather sadly. "Sometimes he'd forget his
gloves and his fingers would be torn and cut. He does it yet. He—
You can't understand. He's everything to me. And now he's in
trouble. Every cent of the money he made that way went back in
the firm for me.''

I had to admire the kid. Yet I had to set her straight. I dare say the
dirty crook would make her a wreath today, and if there was
anything in it for him he'd lay it on her chest—her dead chest. But
there was no use to up and tell her he was playing her for a sucker.
A guy has to be slick in my game. So I went to work on her.

It's not easy to break down the love of a woman, and such a
woman. But I got out the old tear towel and cried all over the
place. I pictured what happened when dope was smuggled into the
country. I pictured little children going to school—drugs put into
their candies. Then I had the children grow up—creeping shadows
in the night, with a knife in their hands and murder in their hearts.

I put on a great show, but believe me it wasn't all show. I would
have preferred to have taken that nine grand and laid a gun-full of
lead in dear old stepfather's middle. At the end I hit my stride. By
God, you'll have to admit I'm good. I had the tears rolling down
her face with the grand finale.

"This man you love even better than your own father. Would he
disgrace the name of Morse? Wouldn't he rather see you dead than
have you live to know that because of you thousands of helpless,
drug-crazed men, women, and children slink through the city
streets?" Yep, I laid it on with a shovel.

I stopped. I had her. I came to my feet and held her in my arms.
She sobbed so pitifully. Sure, I felt sorry for her. Why, I had
damned near broken my own heart.

"You're right, Mr. Williams—you're right," she sobbed. "And
you make me feel so ashamed of myself. To think that I could
believe that of Lee for a single moment. Of course, he never could

have shipped in those narcotics. He couldn't have done it. You must save him."

So my fine words bounced back and hit me smack on the chin. Yep, the nine grand flapped its wings and tried desperately to get out of my pockets, but I held it tightly—for a bit yet. You'd put up a fight for that amount in these days, too. Besides I liked the girl. And I did make a deal with her. I agreed that he was probably innocent, but that if he wasn't why he'd have to take the rap. How did I do it? By getting her to laugh—laugh at the very idea of his being guilty.

Now if I got mixed up with the G-men I could recall our conversation, and be working both for the girl and the law.

She felt better too, showed me Lee's picture, pointed out all the good features in his face. To me, he was just an ordinary little runt, with his eyes set too closely together.

Mary Morse, pepped up considerably, flopped on the side of the chair, half put an arm about my shoulder and talked.

"I won't be afraid any more. You understand now. These men framed Lee, put that stuff in his room, maybe threatened to do terrible things to him or to me. Then they kidnapped him. Maybe the narcotics came through our firm, and Lee found out. Some unfaithful employee—"

She had a thousand reasons and a thousand excuses for Lee's innocence, and not one moment of doubt. I took a sigh and let that angle hang, tried the other. "You say you saw a man murdered. Who? And how?"

"I don't know who." She shook her head. "It was the night I went back to our home and searched Lee's study—after the phone call. I was just going to leave, was at the front door, when the man came up the steps. He was bent and was carrying heavy books— like ledgers. Then I saw the other man, saw him pass directly beneath the light, run easily up those steps and"—she held her face in her hands—"he raised the knife. I saw it flash. Oh God, I thought I heard it drive in! I'm not sure if I cried out. When I looked again another man was helping the first to put the dead man in a car." She shuddered.

"But you saw the man who did the killing?"

"Yes, yes—and I saw him again tonight at the Royal Hotel. I don't know his name. Someone called him Albert." And she gave me a description of friend Albert Swartz that was as finely drawn as a police identification.

"And you threatened to—" I started and stopped. Mary Morse stiffened and came to her feet. I, too, was standing now. The house was old; boards creaked in the hall. Feet were doing their stuff. I grinned—just one pair of feet.

The girl whispered hoarsely: "No one ever enters this wing of the house. They've come to kill me!"

"Nonsense," I whispered. "The party's mine now. Stay there."

# FOUR

# PORT WINE AND HAPPY DUST

■

I took up a position close to that door. But I twisted my shoulder slightly. If it was crashed open I wasn't going to take it on the head. I waited.

Feet came—stopped. Silence—then another creak. The knob turned noiselessly; then it clicked. The door opened slowly.

A big moment that. A hair-raising thrill! Well, maybe, if you're a lad who doesn't get around, but it was nothing to me. If any guy thought he could slip into a lighted room and take a pot shot at me, he was welcome to try.

The door moved further. I watched it as my gun dropped into my hand. My eyes widened. The door stayed about a foot ajar. A white hand came through—a white hand that held something black. Yep, a .38 automatic was gripped by thick fingers. There was hair on the back of the man's hand, part of his wrist.

I stepped forward quickly, reached out with my gun and rapped Mr. Hairy Hand a crack on the knuckles that crashed his gun to the floor. Then I grabbed that wrist, pulled open the door, twirled our visitor in and closed the door behind him.

I didn't laugh. The villain in the piece didn't seem to be such a villain after all. He was a little lad who should have been safe in a girl's boarding school. His hair was gray with streaks of black in it. He had a tiny mustache, a hooked nose, and glasses that should have been on that nose, but were now dangling from a black ribbon. His get-up was a knock-out. Bathrobe, slippers, and a slight shiver.

The girl said: "Why, Uncle Frank! Your asthma, and the draft in that hall!"

That was no surprise to me, except maybe the draft. Uncle Frank was straight and stiff now like a toy soldier. He was trying to get back his dignity which finally came when he got the glasses on his nose. So I leaned against the wall and waited for his explanation—an explanation that did not come. Instead, he started in to bawl me out—me and the girl. It was rich—at least in the beginning.

"Mary!" He said the name like someone else had buried it in a load of dirt and he had dug it out himself. "So that's why you always wished your own apartments. A male visitor, and you—like that."

The girl tried to get in a word, and did actually start a sentence. "Uncle Frank, this man is—"

But Uncle Frank turned on me. His words started off to be dignified and scathing, but my grin must have touched off what dynamite the old boy had yet—and it was plenty. There was talk of the police and the scandal in the same voice.

"It's men like you"—he pointed a finger at me—"gaining this young girl's confidence." Then he threw in some pretty mean words at which I moved my head to let go by to hit the wall. And finally his masterpiece, which I didn't like worth a damn.

"You feel safe because the Morse name won't permit a scandal. She is young and innocent, then you come along. A man your age—"

Perhaps "your age" is what got me. Maybe it was the chin-sticking act, for he did push his face close to mine. Anyway I just popped up a thumb and sent his teeth clicking against his tongue right in the middle of a word. Then I threw it at him.

"I'm a businessman. I'm here to protect your niece, and you walk in and try to make a bedroom farce out of it."

"Protect—" he started, and I clicked his chin again. I had the floor.

"Yes, protect her. But I didn't have any idea it would be from old codgers running around in bathrobes and talking like a dirty book. I'm a detective, if that will help you any."

"A detective, but why—" And after a burp that ruined his dignity and laid it on the floor with his gun, "The girl—Mary—she knows."

My eyebrows went up. It looked as if he knew something. But, of course, he must.

I jumped in with, "She knows enough to get herself in a pile of trouble, and you too. My name is Williams." I grinned down at his hand. "Race Williams."

His smile was not unpleasant. It wasn't rich in the vitamins of brotherly love either. He touched his chin, looked at his hand and said: "Perhaps, Mr. Williams, you and I should go below and talk." He walked over to the girl. "I'm sorry, Mary. I am sorry you did not place more confidence in me." And after a moment while he held her hand, "But I am doubly sorry, and entirely to blame, that I did not give my confidence to you. Be sure, child, that it was to save you pain. Mr. Williams and I will talk in the library. I may be able to help him."

I looked at the girl. She nodded, came to the door, patted Uncle on the back, kissed his cheek. He looked at her rather sternly, but finally he smiled, put an arm about her shoulders and said: "That's her way with us all, Williams. She does just as she pleases with herself, and just as she pleases with Conklyn and me." His face hardened. "Maybe you'd better come down and join us, Mary. I don't know what you have learned. There may be some great danger hanging over your head."

"Not with Mr. Williams in the house," the girl laughed. "Things are all locked up, every door snapped behind me. Besides I—" And as he shook his head, "All right, I'll get dressed and join you. But I believe, Uncle Frank, you simply want an excuse for an extra port." And to me, "I always humor him despite what he says."

The door closed. I followed Uncle Frank down the dimly lit hall, through a heavy door and into what must have been the main part of the house.

"It's the first time that I have broken in on her privacy, Mr. Williams," he told me as we descended the steps to the ground floor. "I was worried for her safety. By God, I should go to the police, but I can't. I can't! Should I send her away?"

He went across to a couch before heavy curtains, stood looking at his trembling fingers, tried to steady them before he lit a cigarette.

I noticed the rawness of his knuckles and did the high-class gentlemanly stuff. "I suppose I owe you an apology," I said.

"Maybe we both do. I don't think I have ever before been irritable with the child, for we look on her as a child. I have been worried—frightfully worried—and with good cause."

I watched him half collapse on the couch, point to a small closet door and mutter something about port.

"You'd better have something yourself," he added as I poured him a drink and set the bottle on the mantel beside an old urn of some kind.

His thought about my guzzling a drink was noble, but the contents of that closet were not for me. Port is, no doubt, damn good for some, maybe for him. But I'm no invalid, and I like my liquor to burn me. He made his apologies, and despite his trembling hand managed to sip the wine.

"All these things"—he moved his head and his left hand as he tried to take in the entire room—vases, urns, pots of different periods—"they were priceless years ago, and are beginning to sell again now. I'm sorry there is nothing stronger than port in the house. I am not a heavy drinking man. Yet things are coming back." And when I thought he was referring to a little real liquor, I found out it was just the business he was talking about.

"Yes, we go in for the Chinese on a rather large scale. Conklyn Lee was strong for it. You see, many of his *objets d'art* and certainly those in our establishment are too rare to be stolen. Any collector would recognize the piece and its value at once. Really, the port won't hurt you."

I said, by way of intelligently butting into a monologue that jumped from port to vases: "This Chinese business with vases, Mr. Morse, does that fit in at all with the family trouble?"

His eyes widened. "She suspects then?"

"I'm not talking about her," I told him flat. "I'm talking about

Conklyn Lee. He's been running in happy dust. You know. Narcotics, if you want to be fancy. Where do you stand?"

"Me? I—" He stuttered and spluttered.

"Hell," I said. "Let's get down to business. To what extent are you involved?"

"I—" He straightened slightly, brushed his shoulders against the huge curtain behind him and sent it wavering, almost lifted himself from the couch. "Really, Mr. Williams, I must say you are an outspoken man."

"Right smack from the shoulder." I nodded my head. "The girl's life is in danger. More immediate than you think. It's up to you to talk out or come under suspicion. Truth is truth. I'm damn near ready to go right to the G-men myself. Now, what's on your chest?"

"Good God! You can't think—" He stopped and I jerked a thumb toward the urns, vases, junk, or what have you.

I said without beating about the dictionary: "You spoke of China. You do heavy business with the Orient then. Have you or this Conklyn Lee been using the Morse name to pick up a piece of change in the drug market?" Then I thought of Albert Swartz, Gentle Jim Corrigan, the Flame, and even Armin Loring and whistled softly. "Hell," I finished, "it looks as if someone is in with a gang who want to do big business."

His face turned ashen, fingers gripped into the soft cushions of the couch. He said: "I am offering you ten thousand dollars to work for me. Now—a check at once. I need a man like you, Williams."

I could believe that. But I said: "I'm working for Miss Morse— Mary Morse. If you're looking for justice, her interest should be your interest."

"Mary? Mary! Why, she had no money to engage you."

"I like her and I'm working for nothing." I damned near choked over the words, but I got them out anyway. After all, she was my boss.

"Race Williams! That doesn't seem like you—the things I've heard about you."

"No, it doesn't." I had to admit he was right there, so I added: "I have no explanation to give."

"In plain words—you won't work for me."

"That's right. I won't."

"But if my interest is her interest, and the Morse interest and the firm's—"

"That's too much interest." I shrugged my shoulders. "If you want to talk before she comes down—talk. If you don't, then I'm simply warning you that I may run into things that will embarrass you." He licked at his lips, seemed about to speak and hesitated as I leaned on the low mantel. "It won't embarrass me," I finished.

He was a sharp-eyed little runt. Knew his way about, too. You could see him measuring things behind those green eyes of his. Finally he said: "What would you like to know?"

I gave it to him straight. I said: "Conklyn Lee was bringing in dope. Did you know that?"

"Yes," he nodded. "I knew that."

"Were you connected with it?"

"No." He paused a long time. "I don't think I can be connected with it."

"Don't think," I gasped. "Hell man, don't you know!"

And Uncle Frank gargled a cheek full of port. He started: "It is quite possible that I may be in serious trouble—the house of Morse in serious trouble. Mary, who idolizes Conklyn—" He coughed once, moved slightly on the couch. The curtains wavered behind him.

"Yes, I did know. Conklyn Lee was doing a rather heavy business with China—cheap stuff compared with what our house used to send for. It was not hard for him to get things through, and I did wonder about the money. Then one night I found him there below the shop. There were other men, but I waited—waited until they left. Opium, I believe it was. Conklyn Lee broke down, and—and—he was doing it for the Morse name."

"You aided and abetted in his crime? You let it continue?"

"No, no!" He almost cried out the words. "He swore to me that it would never happen again, but that he was only doing it for Mary, for the house. God, Mr. Williams, I couldn't send him to jail."

"You believed him, eh?"

"I had to believe him. For a long time he was putting back every cent of his salary—fifty thousand dollars a year—into the business. It kept the business alive."

"So," I asked him, "how did you know he wasn't drawing half a million out of the dope racket? Did you watch him after that?"

"I did, yes. That is, I popped in at times. But he wasn't about the shop so much—never at night. And his shipments of urns stopped coming to the shop."

"To the shop," I cut in with. "Do you know that they didn't keep on coming to his home—elsewhere?"

But he was talking of the Morse name, of his friendship with Lee over the years, of Lee wanting to take him into partnership, of Mary. He talked on. I got a word here and there. And I got something else. I moved and stood almost directly in front of Morse, the full width of the room between us. The curtains were moving behind him, just back of his head. He wasn't jumping around then. He was sitting straight, rather stiffly erect. I tried to spot what did move, couldn't place it, couldn't be sure. There was a slit in the curtains just to the right of his head. That slit seemed to be moving, maybe moving toward the back of Uncle Frank's head—or maybe it was moving toward—

And by God I knew the truth! Death was behind that curtain.

# FIVE

# BEHIND THAT CURTAIN

■

A man was behind those curtains. A man who held a gun—a gun that was trained either on the back of Uncle Frank's head or on me. One thing was certain—a killer was taking his time. A killer was getting ready. A killer who never hurried but always did a clean job, was arranging to do a clean job now. And I couldn't shoot without putting lead through Uncle Frank's head first.

I guessed or tried to guess just who that lad would be. Not another Bertie Logan; not a wild coked-up boy of the night who'd come straight to his feet shooting, but a calm, quiet killer. I thought I knew who he was—a lad who would wait until he was sure, until my back was turned.

I turned my back for a split second, swung quickly, dropped to one knee and was facing the curtain again.

The shot came just as I hit the floor. From between those curtains blue flame flashed into a vivid yellow. The urn on the mantel rang like a gong in a shooting gallery and crashed to the floor.

Did lead follow me to my kneeling position? It did not. The black nose of a gun did. And a white hand did. And perhaps also a keen pair of eyes through the now widening slit in the curtain. But the hand and gun were dropping as the man ducked quickly behind Uncle Frank—that is, partly behind him. He never quite made it. I slapped three bullets just above that white hand, even inside it. Three shots that must have been close enough for Uncle Frank to feel the heat.

Those bullets didn't flatten the killer. Funny that! They brought him to his feet, erect. I could see the outline of his tottering body, his left hand outside the curtain clutching at it, the gun hanging in his right hand. A gun that didn't point at me, but dropped forward directly over Uncle Frank's head, just as the whiteness of a forehead showed between the slit.

I closed a finger once and put a blue hole in the white. The killer didn't cry out. He just twisted like a cork screw, clutched the curtains and crashed to the floor dragging them down upon him. Yep, Mr. Would-Be-Killer rolled himself into a knot and dropped out of sight behind the sofa.

What did I do then? Jump forward, lean over the couch and hold a gun on him? Not me. There was only room for one man behind that couch and that one was there. I slid my gun back beneath my arm, got Uncle Frank a port and held it while he drank it. That is, half drank and half spouted it out on my three-dollar tie.

It was Uncle Frank who spoke first. "There may be others. He—they— Someone would have killed me. I—" And he came to his feet dumping the port altogether. "Who could it be? God, man, look. Find out!"

I shrugged my shoulders. "The lad's name is Albert Swartz," I told him. "I don't need a look. Swartz is a slow worker, likes to shoot at a guy's back, especially a guy like me. That's the reason I made myself a target for him." I grinned slightly. "But I warned him about being off balance."

Uncle Frank clutched my arm, said: "You saved my life. I owe my life to your being here tonight. How could he get in?"

"Albert Swartz?" I shrugged. "Oh, lads like him get in when they want in. And don't stew so much about things. I saved your life, yes, but I had to save mine first."

"But Mary, my niece!"

\* \* \*

He staggered across the room and went to work on the port himself now as he held his left hand against his heart. "She didn't tell you about any such person, did she?" And without waiting for an answer, "I—I never heard the name. Why should he want to kill you?"

"Never mind that," I told him while he played with his heart as if he were tuning up a harp. "He had his reasons—plenty."

I walked to the couch, looked behind it, reached over, jerked the twisted curtains slightly. "It is Swartz," I told Uncle Frank. Then I walked to the flat desk and started to lift the phone.

"What are you doing?" He grabbed at my hand and when I told him I was calling the cops he shook me off. That is he tried to shake me off before I shoved him back on the couch with enough force to drive the furniture against the body. Uncle Frank bounced back from that couch like an acrobat as I buzzed Sergeant O'Rourke. And while I waited for my connection, Uncle Frank spouted how impossible it was to have the police in, spouted about the good name of Morse, the firm—and what have you.

"Listen, Mr. Morse." I gave him straight talk. "I don't know exactly what your method is for moving undesirable bodies. It may be excellent. But this is my corpse and . . .

"Hello, O'Rourke? I've got a stiff for you up at Frank Morse's house. . . . Sure, Morse and Lee." And after giving him the address, "Of course he's dead. He died from being over-cautious. . . . Hell, no. Not a bit of trouble. You'll be glad to take a look at him. It's your old pal, Albert Swartz. I hope you like it."

"Wait. Listen, Race!" O'Rourke's eagerness kept me from hanging up. "We just identified a dead body found in Brooklyn. His name is Boise. Andrew Boise, accountant for Morse and Lee—been with them for years. He was stabbed in the back. Do you think—"

"Hell, I never think," I cut in. "But the guy who killed him is lying here waiting for you—Albert Swartz. He's hiding behind a couch. 'Night." And I dropped the receiver into his ear.

I turned and faced Frank Morse. Inwardly he seemed calm enough. There wasn't much back behind his eyes that looked like the jitters, but outside he was not so good. He kept running his hand back and forth over his mouth like the kids do when they change faces. No, I didn't think it was the time to tell him about Boise's murder.

Finally he spoke. "You're the most cold-blooded man I ever met, Mr. Williams. I hope you'll help me—help us—help Mary. Help, if possible"—he choked slightly there, but got it out—"yes, help Conklyn Lee."

"Help Lee?" I put the eye on him. "Help him down to the federal prison at Atlanta. That's twice tonight Lee tried to lay the finger on me. He's lucky if he meets up with the G-men, instead of finding himself carting around a belly full of lead. Oh, I try not to be fussy, Mr. Morse"—I laid the sarcasm on thick—"but I have peculiar ideas. Little oddities that I try to hide. Being shot in the back is one of them."

I turned, walked to the door, flung it open. "Mary," I said. "She must have heard the shots and—"

God! My feet sank into the floor as if it were soft cement. At least that's the way they felt. Somewhere—just above me in that house—a woman screamed. And then a slamming door and above it all a single word—a single name.

"Race!"

I have heard women scream. I have heard their screams cut off with a hand across their mouth or fingers biting into warm flesh, and I've heard them cut off with the thunder of a gun. But this time—that single name, "Race," was dragged out as if—as if—well, as if it had died in her throat. Why I thought of a knife, I don't know. But I did think of a knife. And I was on the run, out into the hall, up the stairs.

Right here I'll give Uncle Frank credit for having the guts when the time came. He was still trembling. But he did follow me just the same as I made those steps two and three at a time. As I ran I was loading my gun. Not dropping my eyes, understand. I've done it enough to keep my eyes ahead and not slip.

Loring, Corrigan, the Flame—called for two guns; two fully loaded ones. Believe me, that idea was not nerves, it was just good sense. Never undervalue your opponent or you'll wake up, the late lamented, with some guy tossing dirt in your face.

I made the hall and reached Mary's apartment door, threw my

body against it. Then the patter of feet behind me, the wheezing breath and frightened words of Uncle Frank. He was saying, and his voice trembled: "Is she safe? Do you hear her? I've got a key someplace. You can't break that door in. Heavy wood. Strong lock. Mary's idea that—"

I watched him fumbling in his pocket, watched him for a single second—and took another leap at that door. Maybe one more—maybe two more.

Maybe the door wasn't as strong as he thought. Maybe I'm built for a strong man at a circus. Maybe the wood the lock ran into didn't have the stuff. But I like to think it was the kid, Mary, and the child-like faith she had in me. Anyway the door went in. Yes, by God, my hundred and ninety pounds damned near tore the wall apart with it. And I was through, guns raised, blazing death along the narrow strip of darkness.

Letting bullets go? Sure, why not? If the girl was there she'd scream. If she was so that she couldn't scream, she'd be flat on the floor. If Armin Loring, or any of the crowd that Gentle Jim would pick were waiting, they'd be motionless figures in the darkness. Hell, no one but a fool stands in the light and lets the boys who are used to shooting take turns trying to knock him over.

There were no running feet, no cries of pain, no falling bodies. And I was down the hall, had reached the girl's door, thrown it open and snapped on the light.

I looked under the bed, in the closet, in the bathroom, across the hall in a living room she used. It was then that I knew the truth. There was no dead body for me to find, no blood to show that she was murdered.

Living or dead, Mary Morse had been carried away.

Poor Uncle Frank! He tried so to help but only got in the way. He suggested so many places to look—impossible ones. I guess he wasn't used to taking his thoughts on murder and putting them together properly.

By the time we reached the door at the bottom of the stairway, I knew it was a useless job. Certainly the kidnapers or killers were gone in the night.

We had light now and I swung suddenly and faced Uncle Frank. You could have knocked me down with a ton of brick. There was a gun in his hand, and—yes, viciousness in his eyes, in the twist of his mouth.

I said quickly: "Lower that gun. You might shoot me in the back."

He didn't speak. He just stood there, looked at me. I pushed his gun down. I said in actual admiration: "By God, Morse, you'd have killed them yourself if you had come across them."

The viciousness left his face almost at once. His eyes regarded me peculiarly—puzzled. His smile was not much of a one. He staggered slightly, dropped the gun from his hand. We can't all take sudden and violent death followed by a kidnaping as I can. After all it's my business. But Uncle Frank had good stuff in him. I half pushed him, half helped him up the stairs. I didn't speak, I couldn't. It wasn't simply that the kid had dumped nine grand into my hand. I liked her. Yes, liked her a hell of a lot, and I had just let a load of gunmen snatch her from under my nose.

Uncle Frank said, and his voice didn't have much to it: "The police—the government—all should have been told. And now"—he straightened—"I'll tell them at once."

I clutched his arm, said: "Forget about Mary being kidnaped. Forget about the dope and Lee." And as I shook him, "Don't you see, man! They took her alive—or why take her? Conklyn Lee will want to protect himself through Mary Morse, keep you silent through her."

"But the law—the police you sent for."

"The girl was safe when I sent for the police." I bit my lip, realized the chance I was taking and plunged right into it. "We'll beat it along now. Right down those stairs and out. God, man! It may mean your life. Don't you see, you're the last to know—the last alive to know. Mary dead, you dead—and Conklyn Lee is safe."

He stared at me, looked toward the stairs—at his bathrobe. He didn't fully understand, but I got him to his room and into his clothes. O'Rourke would be there any minute. Twice I started to tell Uncle Frank about Andrew Boise, the Morse and Lee accountant, but I didn't. Hell, I didn't want him to collapse right then.

I did leave him for a minute, though. I ducked down the front stairs, back into the library, and after scribbling a message on a card, planted it smack in the center of the table.

O'Rourke—

Frank Morse's life is in danger. He left for the night.
You'll find the stiff behind the couch. Don't do anything
until you hear from me.

Race.

That last line ought to get him. When he'd hear from me, I
didn't know—if ever. But I had plans for the night which carried
death—death for someone.

When I got back upstairs Uncle Frank asked: "What of the
police? What can I tell them?"

"I'll tell them." I was hustling him toward those rear stairs
again, there wasn't much time to waste. "I'll buzz O'Rourke, tell
him there's a threat against your life, and that I advised you to
leave the house and stay at a hotel. You're the only living man who
can put the finger on Conklyn Lee, on the crowd of tough boys he's
in with. Come on."

I didn't take any chances on O'Rourke being ahead of us. I'll bet it
was the first fence he had hopped in years. Sure, that's right. I took
him through the yard behind, half lifted, half pushed him over the
high wooden boards. We reached the street beyond, and I pounded
along the pavement after my tottering charge.

I tried to pump Uncle Frank after I had shoved him into a taxi.
He seemed in a cold sweat. No one could tell me the port wine he
had downed could have made him wobbly. And there was no
reason for him to keep silent if he knew anything more. So I told
him about Andrew Boise getting knocked off. It didn't matter if he
passed out now.

"Andrew Boise." His words sounded like a man about to break
up. "He must have known something or suspected something.
And he's dead." A long moment of silence. "My niece learned too
much and she has been taken away." He suddenly grabbed my
arm, held it tightly. "You understand, Mr. Williams! You must
understand! I know—I know just as they knew. And I'm alive and
free." His voice went a little shrill. "You must protect me, Mr.
Williams. You must protect me!"

I said: "A few minutes ago you were all for saving the girl. Now
it's yourself." And feeling the man shaking violently there beside

me in the cab, "Of course you'll be safe. You think Conklyn Lee is planning your death and the girl's?"

"No, no. I can't think that. It must be those he works with. He can't be doing it alone. Not after tonight and the dead man who tried to kill me. Conklyn Lee thought a lot of Mary and of me. We were like brothers."

I let the sentiment slip by, said simply: "And he knew the Chinese market well?"

"Yes, very well indeed. There is no doubt of that. You ask your own price, Mr. Williams. Any amount you name." His eyes blazed in the darkness now. "You know the underworld of the city. I have read about you often. Do something—anything. Pay for Mary's freedom. Get her safely away. There is enough money for her to live comfortably on. Maybe even enough to save the firm if the court permits it."

"And then?"

"Then I'll talk—to the police, to the government. Ten thousand dollars a year is all I have in life. But if I must, I'll let the house of Morse face it. Let the crumbling walls of a great name come tumbling down upon me. Mary must be saved. In the morning I shall go straight to the police."

It sounded as if he talked right out of a book, but he looked the kind who would. Yet, he was right about the house of Morse. It was common gossip in the jewelry trade that it was tottering, and of course, I'm more or less informed about the gem business.

I said: "Could Andrew Boise possibly have discovered what was going on? I mean about the drugs."

"Hardly." And after resting his chin upon his chest, "Yes, he could have. I sent him down to the shop several nights. I thought his being there might prevent Lee from continuing with his—his evil practice. . . . It is probably the truth, Mr. Williams, that I sent Andrew Boise to his death."

I thought of that too, but it was rather late to bring it up and toss it in his face. It wouldn't make Andrew Boise, the good and faithful servant, any less dead. So I let it slide.

I gave Uncle Frank straight talk. "You go to a hotel and register under another name. I'm going to play a long shot. Mary is still alive. They have her so that she can't talk. Now"—I pounded a finger against his chest because it isn't often that my brain turns out a Sherlock Holmes—"you know more than any of them. You've kept silent to save the name of Morse. If you talk, the show is over. If they harm Mary you will talk and the government will hop in. Mary has to live as long as—well, as long as you can talk."

After he digested that one, I gave him the fruit of my brilliant mind.

"They'll want to do business with you. Don't see anyone. Don't talk to anyone. I'll be your agent and see what can be done. They'll want silence for Mary's life. I'll figure it out."

I didn't want to figure it out for him then. He didn't look like a lad who could take much more, and death alone brings silence.

The taxi reached the Nicholas Hotel. I picked it myself. It was not big and flashy, just small, and fairly respectable. Uncle Frank disappeared in the lobby.

I gave him a few minutes then followed him in, took a look-see at the register and handed myself a grin. Damn it, he had signed his name John H. Smith. Deep thinker, Uncle Frank. But I'll give him what credit was due him. The "H" was original.

So on my way, and ready for work. I had a feeling that I was going to meet the boys again tonight and that Armin Loring was going to lead me to those boys. A nice lad, Armin! He was fond of money; other people's money.

# SIX

# THE FLAME

■

Of course, I knew where to find Armin Loring. He had been in the Royal Hotel and must have guessed, if not actually known, that Albert Swartz had been sent to the Morse residence to kill Morse or me. And he himself might have been in on the kidnaping of the girl.

I knew he would be alone. One Man Armin was his name, and One Man Armin was his business. So I couldn't see Loring mixed up with this outfit. He worked for no gang and every gang. He took a single job, collected for it and was through. That's why he was still walking the streets a free man. He seldom made mistakes of his own, and he wouldn't get himself mixed up in the mistakes of others. At least that's what he thought.

So I was sure where I could find Armin. In the attempted killing and kidnaping at Uncle Frank's, or not, he'd be fixing himself up a nice alibi. So I went straight to that well-known supper club, the Colonial Blue Grass.

I'll admit I didn't like it when a captain of waiters spotted me, gave one of those half-bows which tempt you to pull up a right and keep it moving until he takes his chin away—and the rest of his body with the chin. But it was his words that got me then.

"You are looking for Mr. Loring, Mr. Williams?" And when I just stared at him, "Mr. Loring is keeping a place at his table for you if you came particularly to join him."

All right. There was nothing sarcastic about the captain's remarks. I can take it. I let it go as score number one for Armin Loring, and hinted to Boiled Front that a seat at Mr. Loring's table was the greatest desire of my life.

Loring was using a booth almost directly opposite the center of the dance floor which had about as much privacy as a fish bowl. But I guess he wasn't looking for privacy at that time. He didn't rise as I laid a hand on his shoulder. He simply said: "Sit down, Williams. I've been expecting you."

The captain left. I slid into the seat opposite Armin, faced him squarely and said: "So you expected me? You know why I'm here then?"

Loring's eyes were steady, not sneering and certainly not smiling. "I can make a guess at it," he said. "Something went wrong and you intend to threaten me if I don't right it." He blew smoke from the cigarette he held in his left hand. His right was below the table. "It's rather public for any melodrama, isn't it, Race?"

"If anything happens to the girl you'll ride with the others." It was best not to kid around with Armin. He liked to hear straight talk, and I liked to give it.

"So they took her away from you." And as I held my gun tightly below the table, a steady finger ready, "I know you, Race. Know that time and place doesn't matter when you're on the kill. You're on the kill tonight. I'm covering you below the table, too. Neither shot would be fatal. We'd both make ourselves ridiculous."

Armin beckoned the waiter, ordered champagne, then continued easily: "Now Race, I was paid to see that you came nice and easy to meet Gentle Jim. I was paid to see that the girl was protected. That's straight, Race. I was paid to see that she didn't leave the hotel. You took her. Now, outside of threatening to kill me what else have you to offer?"

\* \* \*

He paused, came suddenly to his feet. He was an easy shot for me then with his hand still below the table, and his gun certainly pointing downward.

"You have met," he said, "Miss Florence Drummond. Will you slide in and let her sit beside you, or do you prefer to step out and let her have the inside? As you see, her wraps are beside me and there is no room."

I hesitated. If I stepped out I'd have to park the gun. If I stayed in, it would be clearly visible in my hand to the Flame. If I shot him to death—and the temptation was certainly there to do it—well, what good would that do Mary Morse? It would just raise a lot of hell around the dance floor.

The Flame took over the conversation as she slid in beside me. "You know I wouldn't kid you along, Race. I was watching from another table. It was my cue to come to this one as soon as you sat down."

"Make it look like I killed him over a woman, eh? Well—" I stopped and looked at brown eyes; soft, alluring eyes that could be so cold and cruel.

"So." She looked straight at me. "You won't say it out loud, but to yourself you are thinking I am very beautiful. And you are remembering that once I—well, hinted that I liked you." She patted Armin's hand, said: "There, you won't mind about Race."

"Not me." Armin looked at her and there was admiration in his eyes. "If Race can take it." His hand closed about hers.

Maybe my eyes did widen. Why not? One Man Armin—the man without a weakness. And now he was taking Florence into our conversation.

I said: "I came here to talk business and you have a woman in on it." I let him glimpse my gun going back in its shoulder holster. There didn't seem much sense in putting a bullet in him, and I wasn't out for a pleasant evening. I put it to him this way. "I'd like to find a certain girl, Armin. The one you would have kept from me tonight. There will be a good price paid for her return."

Armin Loring just said: "What do you mean, a good price? And who will pay it? Certainly not you."

"The girl's uncle will pay it. He—" And Armin laughed, finally said: "Frank Morse, eh? I keep my ears open. The house of Morse can't pay its bills." And leaning closer, and twisting his face at my jerking head that indicated the Flame's presence was not exactly desirable, "Florence has got more brains than either one of us. She thought you'd come tonight. And she thought it would be about the girl. She—"

"I'm not interested in the Flame's psychic powers," I told him flat. "Talk real talk."

Shoulders moved. He said: "You know me and I know you. We've both lived a long time. We don't kid. I know every rat and every big shot. Maybe I give a guy information once in a while. Maybe I do a little clean work. But I'm a one-man worker. I did my work tonight—I'm through with it. I've got an alibi if this Mary Morse was snatched."

"By God!" I leaned even closer now. "If anything happens to the girl—bing—like that. You go out."

"That," said Armin slowly, "is a threat. I can neither protect nor harm the girl. I don't like threats. I could get a hundred guys to knock you over for half a grand."

"To try to knock me over, you mean."

"Well, try then," he admitted. "You cost me a piece of change tonight, Race. I'm not exactly your best friend."

The Flame said: "The Conklyn Lee racket is washed up, Armin. No one can stick a finger on you. Why not—" She hesitated, looked at me. "Armin might make a damn good guess where the girl is for a price. Cash on the line, Race."

"How much?" I looked at Armin.

He did tricks with his tongue in his mouth, finally said: "Ten grand now—and forty grand more if she comes out of it safe."

I looked him straight in the eye. "I shoot straight," I finally told him. "You know that. I can't promise that Frank Morse can lay his hands on that amount."

"I can promise he can't," Armin laughed. "Listen, Race, there isn't a big guy from the millionaire to the picker throwing a front that I can't put a price on. Morse and Lee are bouncing on and off of the rocks."

"So they ran drugs and—"

"I don't want to know anything about it," Armin cut in quickly. Then, "I know it's a stiff price, Race." And suddenly, "Look here, rustle up ten grand and I'll tell you where they have her, how to get in and"—he paused, shrugged his shoulders—"how to get out will have to be your business. Hell, the girl's got money in her own name. If she's grateful you might shake her down for twenty-five grand—twenty anyway. Want to gamble ten of your own money?"

That nine thousand dollars the girl gave me burnt hell out of my pockets. I damned near agreed to put up the jack when a new angle came up. Armin wanted the ten thousand before he talked.

We were at what's known in the best circles as an *impasse*. Which means we were raising hell back and forth across the table, when the Flame spoke.

"It's our music, Race. Remember?" She hummed with the orchestra. "You can't have forgotten that night."

If there was such a night, I had. But I didn't say so. My mind was blank on the subject.

The Flame said: "Let's dance." And she was on her feet, dragging me from the booth. Now there were only two things to do. One was to smack her down right before all those people. The other was to dance with her. And as far as I knew Armin still had his gun in his lap.

Oh, you might say that common sense would teach me he wouldn't shoot there. But you can't tell me that common sense would take the lead out of me if he did.

Anyway I found myself dancing with the Flame. Her hair was against my cheek. Her eyes were young, the sparkle was there now. Perfect red lips—slender white neck. Yes, an armful of beauty.

And me? Hell, I was trying to keep an eye on Armin Loring and the gun beneath the table.

"You're so romantic, Race," the Flame laughed. "Why not twist around so that any bullets would strike me in the back?"

"Not a bad idea." I swung her quickly and kept her back to One Man Armin, then asked: "How did you get mixed up with that punk, Florence?"

She didn't flare into abusive language—not the Flame—that was her great strength. Her laugh was even pleasant. "I take what men I wish," she told me. "The 'punk,' as you call him, reminded me of you—and our love."

"Our love—" I grunted a bit, but she was a nice armful. I mean on another occasion. "No, Florence, I'm one man you never got."

She nodded very slowly. "I spared you, Race. I don't know why. Unless it was that I really loved you. But there were times, my boy, when I could have led you to your death. Times when you trusted me. Times like tonight."

"Tonight?"

"Yes, tonight. You want to save Mary Morse. She'll be dead by sunrise."

"She can't die," I told her. "Frank Morse would talk then."

"She's a good girl, Race," was all she answered. "Pay Armin Loring the ten grand now—tonight. Or the girl will be dead by morning. That's a fact."

I looked at the Flame's eyes now. They were deadly serious, peculiar eyes, as if they opened up almost smack in the center of the pupil and let you look inside for a second—to learn exactly nothing; except perhaps to sense the reason why men smacked down hard for her. The Flame. Her name had come from the many "moths" she had destroyed. For it was written in the book of the night that to love the Flame was to die.

I said: "Look here, Florence. Suppose I had the money or could get it. Why, Armin would simply send me to a trap—to death. I wouldn't be out the door before he'd have Gentle Jim or this lad, Conklyn Lee, or some of the boys on the phone and preparing them to mow me down."

The Flame laughed. "That's why I loved you, Race. That's why I still—well, like you. You're dumb—so terribly dumb except when you have a gun in your hand and death in your heart and a human target to shoot at."

"All right—give me the answer to that one."

And the Flame gave me the answer. She said: "You pay him the ten thousand, then he tells you where the girl is. I'd tell you myself, Race, if I knew and—"

"Yeah. After he gets the ten, then what?"

White shoulders rose and fell. "Then put Mr. Armin Loring in a position where he won't be able to tell. Must I advise you how to do that?"

Good? Of course it was good. The Flame was always good. But if she was good for one lad, she was naturally bad for the other. Now which lad was I?

She went on: "You don't trust me, Race. That's it, isn't it?" And she made the words soft.

"And what the hell is queer about that?" I gave it to her straight.

"You're mixed up with a guy who makes murder a business. You have looks. You have poise. You have courage. You have everything. Yet there are times when I actually believe you don't know the difference between right and wrong. I fell for it once—"

"Race"—she raised her hands, placed both of them squarely on my shoulders—"you're not suggesting the little home in the country—the slippers and newspaper?"

"Not unless I expect a bullet to go through that newspaper. This queer criminal mind of yours, Florence, may be swell stuff to you, but not to a lad who wouldn't care to find a knife in his back when he leaned over to pick up the slippers."

Her laugh was pleasant. "Armin has a lot of you in him, Race, except that he has more ambition and is more careful. But in an emergency he'll go out, just like you, and use his own gun. I wouldn't cross him again as you did tonight. It took me some time to talk him out of knocking you over."

"Huh," I told her. "In plain words you didn't think he'd look nice on a slab." And suddenly as we swung back near the table, "Hell, Florence, several times you've gotten away from the rotten criminal world only to drop back in it again. Why?"

She said without emphasis or regret: "I like to eat well, dress well, and I like excitement." And suddenly, "Are you afraid to save the girl? She'll die, Race."

"Yeah—" I looked steadily into those now child-like eyes. "How do I know if you're the beautiful young girl tonight or the Flame with the criminal mind?"

She threw back her head and laughed. "That's what makes it sporting, Race. That's what makes me the delightful woman I am. And you the man I loved—maybe could love again."

"And maybe could hate," I said as we swung back to the table.

"Maybe!" And she wasn't smiling now. Her eyes were very grave—very cold. "That's for you to figure out. I won't promise you your life tonight, but I'll promise you the girl's life whether I love or hate you."

So romance entered our peaceful little kidnaping and murder, if you can see lead in the belly and a beautiful woman in your arms at the same time.

We were at the table when the Flame spoke again, gave it right out to Loring. "I've been talking to Race, Armin." She leaned slender arms on the table. "He'll lay ten grand right here on the line. You'll tell him where the girl is—and he'll forget us entirely." And when Armin just looked at her, "Well, I've put money in your pocket before, Armin. Race is a right guy, at least for tonight. He won't talk if it's a bust, and won't squawk for the ten back if you've given him the break—an honest break."

Armin took a small sip of wine, said to me: "You'll pay, eh? And keep your trap shut."

"I'll pay and I'll shoot you to death tomorrow if you've given me a wrong steer."

"That's your idea." Armin leaned back, gazed at the ceiling. "If I give you a wrong steer you won't be alive to shoot me to death. Maybe you won't even be alive with the right one. I can only tell you where Mary Morse is. You'll have to handle things uptown your own way. I wouldn't want to go there tonight, but if I did, I'd walk in with a gun in each hand—and begin shooting the first time I saw a figure."

"As bad as that?"

"Just as bad," he told me. "Maybe worse. You and I never crossed until tonight. If you start shooting they'll kill the girl; if you don't, they'll kill you. I'm not especially anxious to play with you on this."

But enough of all that. It was a ticklish job all around, and where I can use my head, I can use my hands a damn sight better. We finally agreed to his taking five grand right then, and another five grand within an hour—neither of us to leave the table during the time.

I let him think I had to send for the rest of the money. Get it? I had a note I wanted to reach Uncle Frank Morse. Armin didn't mind my having to send for the second five but he wanted the whole ten before he spoke. It was the Flame who fixed it up.

"We'll play Race's way, Armin. Ten grand is ten grand. You owe the boys nothing. Gentle Jim ceased being gentle when he found out the girl, Mary, had gone with Race. Jim's a big shot, Armin. The big shot you're going to be. The big shot I'm going to make you."

Armin's eyes were slits when he looked at her. "I'll be big, kid," he said to her. "And I'll drag you along with me. I never toss over a friend."

"Hell," I said, "you never had one. Well, are you still going to beef around?"

And he wasn't.

I slipped the five grand to him under the table. He counted it without a visible movement of his hands, folded the bills and put them in his pocket.

He didn't waste time then. He said directly: "The place is in Mount Vernon. It's a big house with plenty of ground. The street number is—" And he finished by tracing out the road right to the house.

"Are you sure?"

"Sure. I covered the car that took them there." He grinned. "No, I'm not double-crossing them. They hired me to see that they reached the place safe. They didn't pay me any ten grand to see that you didn't come later." And turning to the Flame, "News to you, too, sweetheart. Well"—his shoulders shrugged—"you couldn't talk if you didn't know. Now, Race, dish up the rest of the money."

The waiter plugged in a phone and I called to my home. Jerry, the boy I had picked up in the underworld, answered almost at once. "The Colonial Blue Grass, Jerry," I told him. "I want you right away."

Silence after that as I jerked a page from my notebook and wrote, my hand shielding the writing from both the Flame and Armin. Armin sipped wine slowly. The Flame stared at the top of my head as if she would read the message I was writing. But the message had nothing to do with money though Armin thought it had. It was directed to John H. Smith at the Nicholas Hotel— simple and direct.

> I'm making a bid for Mary's freedom tonight. If you
> don't hear from me by eight o'clock in the morning, I'll
> be dead. Give O'Rourke a ring. Spill your guts.

I hesitated there thinking of Uncle Frank's dignity, and crossing out the last three words, wrote instead—

> Tell O'Rourke everything. Your life depends on it.

When I signed my name there was plenty of room left on the paper. I chewed on the pencil a second or two, finally wrote—

Jerry—

> Deliver this note above in person. Say nothing. Return and wait outside in the car. When I bring a guest out, hit him on the head with a wrench.

Not very elegant, but it was the Flame's suggestion. She might do it in a more refined manner, but me, I like a wrench.

# SEVEN

# THE CAR BEHIND

■

Armin didn't like the note business. He wanted to know why I couldn't telephone to the friend who'd lend me the cash.

I said simply: "Someone might listen in. He wouldn't want it to be known that Race Williams could hit him for five grand at one in the morning. O.K.?"

"O.K." he said.

Things went according to schedule. Jerry came and took the note. The Flame put her hand on Armin's arm as he half came to his feet. I said as he sat down again: "Don't come in with the money, Jerry. Wait outside."

Armin kicked a bit, but Jerry was gone. There was nothing to do but wait, and convince Armin that I wouldn't leave him, that he could come out with me for the money.

"And the Flame, too," I added.

"No—not her." Armin shook his head. "I rather fancy Florence. She'll stay inside. I don't want her to get hurt." His look at her was suggestive of the very thing of which I was afraid. That Armin would give me the right house, but that he would also advise them of my coming—of my coming alone. And now I wondered if he was leaving the Flame behind for that very purpose. Perhaps it isn't gallant to admit it, but truth is truth. I was wondering just then if a wrench on the Flame's head would be very much out of place.

The waiter came at last to tell us the car was outside. Armin and I got to our feet. Again he looked at the Flame, then he turned his back on her. For a moment her face was sideways to me. If she gave him a reassuring look or not, I don't know. Then he turned, and for a moment the Flame and I faced each other. Her brown eyes held a dull luster; a silken film came and went before them. Brown and good and honest and—

It was on my tongue to insist that the Flame come with us—but I didn't. Maybe it was her mouth forming words, words that seemed to say: "I can't promise you your life, but I promise you the girl's." Words that seemed to mock me, mock my courage. Yet her eyes didn't mock. They were beautiful. They—they—

Hell, I don't know. Maybe I'm a sap, but I left her there standing alone by the table, and followed Armin Loring from the room.

We went out the door, were on the street, when he got cagey—a little talkative. "Look here, Race, I'm playing the game with you and—"

I said: "There's my car—and here's the money."

That got him. He swung around to face me when he saw the money in my hand. He must have known then that I had had the money with me all the time. But greed got the better of him. He backed slightly from me as I stretched out my hand. He hardly gave a glance at Jerry standing there by the side of the car.

Armin was quick—Armin was clever. There was a gun that I didn't see appear, nestling in the palm of his right hand. A small toy pistol—but death if a man knows how to use it and where to put the bullet.

But greed got him. He watched my left hand as I gave him the money with my right. He started to shove the money into his pocket then decided to take one quick look at the bills.

Something warned him then, but his natural instinct got the better of him. He ignored the warning. Though he raised his gun-hand he stuffed the cash away in his pocket. Certainly instinct told him of danger or maybe just the shadow behind him—the slight push I gave him as my extended hand fell only lightly on his chest.

But I don't think he was ever fully aware of the real danger. Then Jerry struck. A soft thudding sound as the wrench crashed and Armin's dapper gray hat bounced slightly on his head.

Two men were passing then, but I'd lay ten to one that neither one knew what was happening. Jerry pulled and I heaved. Armin just left the sidewalk and disappeared inside the car—legs and all. Sure, it was a neat job. But, of course, it wasn't the first time we'd done it. Not by a damn sight.

One good look in the car and I closed the door. "Nice work, Jerry." I patted his back. "Drive him around; he'll need the air. But after you get him a few blocks put the cuffs on him and tie him up. He's too valuable to lose. He's got ten grand of mine in his pocket. If you don't hear from me by eight o'clock, why that ten grand belongs to you. Pocket it."

"To me—you mean to you."

"No, Jerry"—I shook my head—"to you. I won't be alive then."

"So that's how it is." Jerry knew the ways of the night. "If you don't show up at eight, how about—" Jerry tapped his hip pocket. I never could get him to go in for a shoulder harness. "How about giving him the dose?"

I gave that one a little thought. "Sure. He'll have it coming to him. Just—" And then, "No, Jerry. Don't you understand? That would be murder." One must teach the young the correct way to live—and die.

I watched Jerry drive off. Then I walked toward the corner, hopped a taxi for a few blocks, reached the garage where I kept my own car, and was on my way. I drove up Broadway, turned at Van Cortlandt Park, up the hill above the golf links, then alongside Woodlawn Cemetery.

I felt pretty good—rather noble if you're at all sentimental. Mary Morse had given me exactly nine thousand dollars to take care of her. With that and the one grand I was about even on the deal. Not only that, but I was taking a ride that might end with death. But it wasn't sure death by any means—at least not for me. Shooting is like swimming. It's hard to get started, but once you're in, things go along all right.

Alone in the night. Bright moon. Girl to be saved. What more could you want? Besides, you might as well die now as forty years from now with cramps in the stomach.

Alone in the night. And I quit looking into the mirror, cut my speed again and looked back through the rear window. I couldn't tell on Broadway, but I did have a feeling that a car might have followed me up the lonely Van Cortlandt Park hill and along by the cemetery.

Now I was sure. Twin curb lights went dark as I looked at them, leaving a small black blur in the road—a black blur that slowed down to my speed. I recognized the type of car in the moonlight. A little devil that will jump you so fast it could hop on the roof before you even knew it.

It's useless to try to beat it away from a car that will catch you and open fire with machine guns. There was just one thing to do— and I did it. I jammed on my brakes, tossed open the door nearest the curb, hopped out and crouched beside the car. If some boys felt like a little loose lead, why I'd give it to them, and give it to them first.

The boys behind evidently didn't want to play that game. The car stopped, lights flashed on and off a couple of times, then the brights stayed put. A figure climbed from the car, walked directly in front of that light, and came down the road toward me. Yep, you guessed it. It was the Flame, the Girl with the Criminal Mind, and which way it was working now is anybody's guess.

"All right," I called out. "If you're alone—let me have what's on your chest."

She didn't laugh this time. She said: "I've known you long enough, Race, to know the way you work. So I didn't drive up, I walked. Here's the lay. You want to save the girl. Well, I want to help you. Take me with you, and I'll get you safely in the house."

"Yeah," I told her. "Why didn't you have that pretty thought before I laid out my ten grand?"

"Because," she said, "I didn't know where Mary Morse was until you spent the ten grand. One Man Armin doesn't give me his entire trust. I don't ask for it. I'll have that later. If you go alone to that house—you'll die before you get in."

"All right." I shrugged. "How do we start? No use trying to change your plans, Florence."

She tried to look at me, then nodded. "I'll ride with you. Wait while I pull the little car to the curb."

"You'll have hard work explaining its being there in the morning if anything happens tonight."

"Why?" She laughed as she left me. "It's not my car. Don't look at me like that. It was handy and I took it."

She was back in three minutes, in beside me. She nudged my arm, said: "I left a ten-spot on the seat to pay for the gas and the trouble."

"To ease your conscience."

"Not mine—yours," she told me as I knocked the big purse she carried to the floor and started to drive on. Then, "There's a lot of the boy in you, Race—the bad boy. But I wasn't going to shoot you, and I'm not going to be dropped out on the Parkway and told to walk home. Don't look at me like that. That's what you intended to do, of course."

I had, but I didn't say anything. I let her go on. Let her do exactly what she intended to do; talk me into taking her with me. But it wasn't the past that got me. It was the damned common sense of her argument.

"I'm not saying you should trust me, Race. I'm not saying that you ever actually loved me. But I loved you once, and could have brought you right to my feet as I will Armin. Maybe I didn't because I loved you. Tonight, if I had wanted to trap you to your death, I had only to lift the phone and warn them you were coming. So, why go with you to a death I could so easily have arranged?"

There wasn't much of an answer to that. I only said—and I couldn't help my words: "You've got everything it takes, Florence. You even admit it. What keeps you in the racket? You have risked your life for society—for the government—for—well, perhaps for me. Now, you're in with crime again. Hell, I was willing to stake you any time you wanted it."

"That's right." She was emphatic now and not laughing either. "But maybe it isn't furs and cars and money I want. Maybe it's the excitement, the thrill of it. Tonight for instance—you and I and the moon, with sudden death perhaps, at the end of the trail. I can love you at times like this, Race. I can! You're so sure, so confident. A guy who thinks he's good and doesn't care who knows it. I—"

"All right—all right." I switched off the Parkway at Mount

Vernon. "Now—just how to get in this house where Mary Morse is held."

"Right in by the front door," she said. "They'll let me in. They'll be sure Armin gave me directions and they'll be expecting Armin. You'll have your chance. Only Gentle Jim Corrigan, a couple of tough boys, and the guy under the hood."

That rocked me. I put it to her straight. "It's a guy in the hood—not a woman?"

"Yes, it's a guy in the hood, not a woman," was all she said.

"I'll chance it," I said. Then we shot up the grade between high trees to the big old house standing on the hill.

She was matter-of-fact as she stepped out, picked up her purse, pointed out a good place for me to park the car. She looked at the gun in my hand, nodded, gripped my arm and whispered hoarsely: "You've got to trust me, Race, or chuck the thing. I'm promising you Mary's life—and, I hope, your own. I know what's in your mind. To crack me down here and go it alone. Don't do it, Race. Walk straight up that narrow path there with me. They'll take you for Armin. Come on and be a sport." And when I took a laugh, she threw both her arms about my neck and kissed me—full on the lips. Even there in the darkness I saw the thing in her eyes; bright, exciting, and—damn it—honest.

I shook my head as she let me go. It was like a strong drink. But I said: "All right, Florence. Let's go." And as we started I added: "Just remember that there is no sex in crime."

Up that path we went. We reached the house, mounted the front steps. Silently—or fairly silently—we crossed the porch, my eyes darting left and right. Then we passed right into the dark vestibule which gave to the inner door.

The Flame whispered: "I wouldn't double-cross you, Race. The door will be unlocked, but to ease your suspicion I'll go first. Then they'll have to kill me to get you."

And that got me—got me more than you think. I held my right hand close against my hip, gripped the knob of the door with my left hand, turned it slowly—and pushed it.

I stepped into that house—into blackness—a blackness that didn't last but was suddenly illuminated. Just the click of a button, the glare in my eyes, and I was facing a man across the hall. A man who held a tommy gun that was directed straight at my chest. And the man was Gunner Slade, the meanest, dirtiest murderer in the entire city.

I don't know if he spoke. I don't know if his finger started to close on the trigger. I only know that I saw the gun, the hands, the glaring hateful eyes that meant death. And my own finger closed three times. And three bullets pounded into Gunner Slade. I won't say all three went into his heart. I wasn't out to make any record for fine marksmanship. But I will say as I dropped back in the shadows of the vestibule that Mr. Slade of the fancy fingers and hateful eyes was stiffer than a mackerel even before he followed his tommy gun to the floor.

Trap, eh? Maybe yes—maybe no. Certainly when Slade saw my face there in the doorway he intended to blast it out of sight. But my shots would echo through the house and—I was ready now. Standing in darkness, looking into light, I waited for things to get hot.

Get the picture? They had expected Armin, but they were ready. And then, I mowed down the Gunner, stood outside the fire of anyone who entered that hall. Of course, I felt cocky. I felt—I felt—

Yep, that's right. I felt the gun in my back, the hard nose of it smack against my spine. The hand that held it didn't tremble. The words that came were cold as dry ice.

The Flame said: "There is no sex in crime, Race. Drop your rods. You've been played for a sucker. Drop them!"

# EIGHT

# ROPE'S END

■

Though I expect to die by lead some day, I'd like that lead to be found in my chest and not my back. I held my guns. Not that I didn't think the Flame would shoot. Just that if I was going to die anyway, I might as well go down with a gun in each hand.

Two other round, hard, pipe-like objects pounded against my back. I heard the Flame say: "Don't shoot yet. This man, Williams, may have something to say. Don't shoot."

A rough voice or maybe two, and my guns crashed to the floor. There were others beside the Flame there now. Lads with voices that sounded as if they wanted to kill. Plain common sense told me that I wouldn't be worth a hell of a lot to Mary Morse dead; or to myself either, for that matter.

Guys held guns against my back. One was a cheap hood called Louis. I didn't know his last name—if he ever had one. The other was a new one on me.

Out of a side room walked Gentle Jim Corrigan. His voice was soft—the ripples rolled steadily up his face. "Dear me, Race—dear me. You have such atrocious manners." And to the Flame,

"Nice mess. Slade was so valuable. You assured me on the phone that there would be no trouble."

And the Flame swung by me. I started to speak to her and didn't. The word "rat" died on my lips. By God, you wouldn't know her. Nothing of the slim, cultured girl, now. Her beauty was still there, but a sinister sort of beauty—hard and cold—as she looked into the suspicious little eyes of Gentle Jim.

She swung a contemptuous look at me. "Can't you trust anyone, Jim? I called you up and blew the show. Walked Race right into the trap. And there was to be no shooting. If this thick dick, Williams, had made me go first, I'd have been treated like a sieve." And before Jim would speak, "Anyway, you can get a hundred guys better than Slade. You hadn't paid him, had you?"

"No, no—" Gentle Jim seemed pleased as he walked toward me, said: "Put a gun in his back, Louie." And when the gun planted itself hard against me again, he frisked me for a third gun, ran his hands along my legs and arms.

"You've been looking at the funny sheets," I told him. "Now what?"

"Now what?" He bobbed his head up and down. "You turned down ten thousand dollars early tonight. You picked death instead." And going over to the Flame and putting his arm about her shoulders, "I really didn't think any woman could put it over on Race. Besides, I wasn't sure you'd go through with it." He squeezed her arm. "You're a wonder, Miss Flame—quite a wonder. If it wasn't for Armin I might risk"—he patted her cheek—"death myself, for the Flame."

The Flame said in that rough, low voice I hadn't heard in years: "You'd have to get rid of thirty or forty pounds first, Jim." And looking straight at him, "But you're coming along—coming along big in the racket."

"Flattery, flattery. I'm far too old and far too careful." And with a laugh, "And perhaps as you suggest, a little too hefty to sprout wings and become a moth. But this is business tonight. So get along. Good-night."

The Flame turned, passed out the front door and closed it behind her.

We went up two flights of stairs. Not one gun, but two were against my spine now.

* * *

Lights went on ahead of us and we entered a pleasant room. There was a door at the other end of it—bookcases, couch, and a large chair something like the one the hooded figure had been in at the Royal Hotel. There were four of us. Myself, Jim Corrigan, and the two gunmen. The one I didn't know carried the tommy gun. Plainly I saw red on it. Slade had been careless in death.

They made a monkey out of me then, tying my hands before me, running the strong cord from my wrist to my feet. Then I was pushed onto the couch. I struggled to gain a sitting position.

Gentle Jim Corrigan began to grin. "You'll excuse me, Race, but I've never seen anything quite so funny. And a woman, too. Pitiable, my boy, with a career like yours. But they say the Flame has her way with men." He shivered slightly—sarcastically. "I hope she doesn't go after me. Are you prepared to listen?"

I just nodded.

"Very well." He got up from behind the small table and walked across the room, opened the opposite door. A small figure slid in— same black outfit, same cowl pulled over the face. White, slender hands seemed to fold upon the knees as he sat down. He? I wondered. The hands were very slender, rather beautiful. I remembered that the Flame wore two rings. These hands were stripped of jewelry. If there were marks where rings might have been, the light where the figure sat was too dim to tell.

I did get the idea that the hands were not those of a man and— and—hell, the fingers didn't even move. They might have been dead hands except that they were very beautiful, very much like a woman's—a beautiful woman's.

Gentle Jim was back at the table. He leaned on his elbows and talked very slowly and very distinctly, choosing his words very carefully. Occasionally he lowered his hand and his fingers played with a piece of paper before him.

"You have no cards, Race Williams, to lay on this table. But I am laying mine. No matter how you arrange them or rearrange them they'll always be the winning hand. Certain people had a prosperous business smuggling narcotics into this city. Morse and Lee were the agents. Unforeseen circumstances interrupted that business. Interrupted it I say, for it is intended that it be resumed. Andrew Boise, the faithful accountant, discovered the little plan, and was removed. Mary Morse discovered the little plan, and is now awaiting her removal." And raising his voice, "If you please, Joe. Our first scene. And be careful you don't strangle her. Joe," he explained, "is our head prop man. Look up, Race. You'll be surprised."

I did look up—and I was surprised. A trap door had opened above me, slid noiselessly back in the ceiling. And being lowered through that trap door was a woman. She spun slightly as her body came slowly down. Rope was wrapped about her body, holding her hands tightly by her sides, and the rope that lowered her was caught under her arms.

I would have come to my feet if I could have. It was not a pleasant sight. There was something fiendish about it. I saw her face—her white, pale childish face. It was Mary Morse. And I saw something else too. I saw the red trickle of blood coming from her lower lip—coming as white upper teeth bit tightly to prevent her from screaming.

There was fear, horror, everything in that girl's face—yet a determination not to cry out. A determination that was broken the moment her eyes rested full on mine.

"Race—Race!" she cried. "You've come! I knew you'd come."

God, the hell of it! She didn't know, didn't realize, that I too was a prisoner as the huge bulk of Corrigan moved quickly across the room, caught at her feet and sent her spinning around. She was jerked up then. I lowered my eyes so as not to see. But I heard the thud of her head, the moan—a short moan as if her head hitting the ceiling had knocked her unconscious. The trap remained open.

Gentle Jim was speaking. "That is her first appearance. Her next"—Jim was back at the table now—"the rope will be about her neck. The ceiling is rather high. She will drop so that the bones in her neck will snap almost before your face. You can prevent that."

"How?" My lips set tightly.

"Oh, you can't save her life or yours," Gentle Jim said softly. "You know that. She knows too much and you know too much. But you can determine the nature of her death—your death—the violence of it"—he leaned far forward—"the horror of it. Whether you're to sit there and watch the twisting of a young body—the body of a girl who trusted and believed in you."

And I cut in. Fear, horror, all left me suddenly. I had a trump

card—and I had forgotten it. Now I played it. "If I am not alive—
if the girl is not alive by eight o'clock tomorrow morning, each one
of your names will be turned over to the police."

"Each one," Gentle Jim said. "How?"

"I wrote a note—sent my boy with a note." And when he just
smiled, and the lad with the tommy gun eased himself against the
wall, and Louie leaned on the mantel to light a butt, I added: "Ask
the Flame. She and Armin thought the note was for money."

"Did they really?" Jim picked up the paper he had been
fingering and deftly shot it across to me. "You're not referring to
that?"

The paper hit my hands and my fingers were free to open it. But
it was as much of a shock merely to recognize it, know exactly
what it meant. It was the note of warning I had sent to Uncle
Frank, under the name John H. Smith, at the Nicholas Hotel.

Gentle Jim answered my question before I asked it. "We don't
need to worry about him." he said. "He'll never talk about it."

"So you killed Morse." I guess there was a helplessness in my
voice. "What's the game then? Who else could know—who else
could I tell?"

"There's your friend, O'Rourke." And suddenly, "By God, you
didn't tell him! It's on your face. It's death now, Race."

I might have tried—intended to try. That was what they feared.
O'Rourke was my friend. It would have been easy to have left a
note for him at headquarters, but I hadn't. I couldn't see how they
could have gotten Frank Morse—poor nervous Uncle Frank. Jerry,
the clever Jerry—product of the underworld—must have been
followed.

"It's death now!" Gentle Jim almost cried the words out this
time. And I heard the sound above me. I looked up. There was
Mary. She was going to die like that—now. Vengeance—simply
vengeance against me for killing Bertie earlier that evening, and
putting it over on Gentle Jim Corrigan.

I saw Mary's face. Was she coming down head first? Then I saw
an arm—a bare, slender arm. Her hands were free then, her— And
I saw the thing in that hand, saw it drop, moved my body quickly
to receive it.

Of course I knew what it was and of course I knew what to do
with it. I didn't care what had gone on up above. I didn't care about

the dull, blurred face behind Mary. Somehow the kid must have gotten a gun and was dropping it to me.

Hands tied? Sure—but only at the wrist. Legs tied? Sure—but I didn't expect to use my feet.

The gun turned twice in the air. I slid slightly on the couch and it pounded down. Pounded right into the palm of my hand as the lad Louie swung, cursed, jerked up his gun, and parted my hair. The rod, a thirty-eight, dropped into my hand, turned over once, and I placed a bullet in the wide-open mouth of the lad Louie.

# DEAD HANDS REACHING

∎

Luck? Sure, it was luck. A break? Sure? Wasn't I entitled to a break by this time? The others? They were knocked cock-eyed. There's nothing like a stiff or two about a room to throw fear into the hearts—rather, stomachs—of killers. They just turned and looked at Louie. And I had them.

"Rats," I said as they turned back, "make a move and I'll open you up—one, two, three—and see what you had for supper."

They looked in my eyes, the hooded figure through the black slits. Gentle Jim's eyes widened as he knew fear. I don't know what he saw in my eyes, but it was there. I knew it was there. The lust to kill.

I guess it was my face as much as it was the gun in my hand that held them. It must have been, for I was trussed up like a chicken. Mad? I was damn near a raving maniac. Have you ever been that close to death yourself? Do you know the feeling of getting a gun in your hand, and a chunk of meat like Gentle Jim to shoot at?

Did Gentle Jim know it? Why, his hands went into the air so high that his vest and trousers parted company.

The lad with the machine gun whom I couldn't place went panicky. Anyway, he suddenly opened up with that tommy gun, opened up while it was directed at the floor. I stopped it before he ever raised it an inch.

He just looked sort of dazed and surprised as he slid slowly to the floor and sat there. There was a single hole right in the center of his forehead. I wasn't wasting lead.

I kept my eyes on Gentle Jim and the Hooded Silence. Jim's eyes met mine. Then I turned to that figure. Hands still crossed upon black covered knees.

I said: "Put them up or I'll—"

And the shot came. Cripes, it tore a piece clean out of my shoulder. I was dumbfounded more than stunned—or maybe just dumb. For the shot had come from the hooded figure; the figure that sat there with hands folded—white hands—empty hands.

I threw myself across the couch as the second shot came. This time I saw the yellow-blue flame—and felt it too. I was almost hidden by Jim then, yet the shot burned my cheek.

Gentle Jim had never read the line about giving up your life for your friend. He jumped six feet when my first shot flashed across his front. The figure in the chair jarred. You know the kind of jar— the jar that comes with the soft thud of a bullet smack into a body.

Flame flashed again from the figure. Plaster fell ten feet from me and I put two more slugs into the Hooded Wonder. The figure started to fall forward then didn't. It seemed to sort of change its mind and slumped in the chair. A gun fell to the floor.

After I fired—after I saw the body jerk—I wondered if it was the—well, the Flame. But it couldn't be. The Flame didn't have three arms. But then no one else did either.

I snapped out of it, shook my head. Three-armed people, eh? I must have been shot worse than I thought.

I straightened on the couch. Blood was warm and wet on me. "Jim," I said, "get a knife. Come over and cut me loose." And before he could get the words out, "If you haven't got a knife, I'll fire."

Would I have fired? To be honest I think I would have. There was a dizzy feeling in my head. If I had to pass out, why I'd sleep more comfortably knowing Jim was there on the floor.

* * *

Jim cut the ropes. It wasn't pleasant having his huge body leaning over me, the long sharp knife in his hand. But I wanted it that way. For my gun was pressed hard against his stomach while he set me free. And I whispered sweet predictions of intestinal troubles if he made a slip with the knife.

Then Jim was talking. He was a good talker, too. "We don't want this thing public, Race—bad for your client. Certainly you cleaned things up. Now, if I were arrested I'd have to talk, and that would be very bad for the Morse firm. You're puzzled about the shooting, eh boy? The hands on the lap."

He walked over to the slumped black figure, jerked off the two hands and tossed them across the room. "Just fake arms and hands," he said. "Ingenious I'll admit, but quite simple. Pickpockets work it now and then in the subway and on trains. Their hands are apparently visible while their real hands, from beneath their coats, explore their fellow passengers' pockets. Damn it, Race, that was some nice shooting. How the girl got loose I don't know. Must have bought Joe over and—"

And I stopped him. Jim was alive. The others were dead, and I— Hell, I felt lousy. I called out, "Mary," and she answered me. What's more she was able to crawl to the trap and—damn it—I made Gentle Jim catch her when she landed. It was funny to watch him. Gentle isn't strong enough for the way he handled her—and spoke, too.

"There, there—poor child." He untied her very carefully. "A most unfortunate circumstance that brought you into this. I would have protected you, my dear. My whole idea was—" She shrank away from him, suddenly saw the bodies and placed her hands over her eyes.

That was the moment. That was when she must know. That was when she had to be convinced that Conklyn Lee, her loving stepfather, was the murderer behind the whole rotten show.

"Mary," I said, "you've got to take it. "Look"—I lifted her head—"he murdered people. He shot me. He would have had you horribly murdered. You might as well face it now. He's dead there."

"Who—who are you talking about?" Her little hands clung to my arms.

"Who? Why, Conklyn Lee, your stepfather, of course. And—and—what are you glaring at?"

She *was* glaring too. She finally swallowed and said: "You've been hurt. You've been hurt! My stepfather, Conklyn Lee, is in that room above the trap. I must get to him." And Gentle Jim was lifting a ladder from a corner and putting it up for her.

I turned toward the dead body beneath the hood. I had never really thought—never really believed it was the Flame. Now—now—I staggered back, gulped the words: "The Flame—so it was the Flame."

"The Flame?" Mary Morse looked at me queerly as she mounted the ladder. "I don't know what you mean."

I turned toward the dead body beneath the black hood. Slender, frail it must have been in life. I'll admit the Flame had double-crossed me, triple-crossed me. She—she— But it's hell to kill a woman—and such a woman. I stooped, grabbed at the hood.

Gentle Jim spoke. "You're in for the surprise of your life, Race."

I hesitated, then lifted that hood, swept it off. I stared a long time at that dead white face. Then I laughed—leaned against the wall and laughed. For the face beneath that hood was Uncle Frank's; dear old Uncle Frank himself in person. I was never so glad to see anyone before.

After that Mary came down and fixed my arm, Gentle Jim hopping back and forth with water. Part of the truth I got from Mary, part from Gentle Jim, but the bulk of it came from Conklyn Lee himself. It was the same story Mary had told me, but with reverse English. Frank Morse pulled all the stunts his partner, Conklyn Lee, was supposed to have pulled.

"Yes, I caught Frank at it," Conklyn Lee explained. "And I was desperate. The firm was shaky enough anyway. I don't know why I kept silent at first. Perhaps for Mary—certainly not for my job. The books will prove that. Then I found Frank had broken his word, and was still bringing in the drugs from China. It was he and not I who handled all the Oriental trade. I was determined then to go straight to the government men.

"That's how I was fooled. This man here"—he pointed to Gentle Jim—"and another came to see me. They represented themselves as Department of Justice men. They said Frank Morse had brought them a full confession. They wanted me to go with them. I went—and have been a prisoner ever since."

"That is correct," Gentle Jim said easily. "What you didn't know, Mr. Lee, was that Frank Morse served ten years in jail. That was why he was not admitted to the firm, and not because of any simple romance with an actress. No one knew this but his father. The black gown was to hide his identity from others. I was simply a sort of agent."

But enough of that. As I said, Gentle Jim was a good talker. I wasn't anxious to explain all that shooting. Conklyn Lee would find it tough telling why he had not gone immediately to the authorities. And Mary Morse would have the jewelry firm dumped over into her lap.

Gentle Jim made things simple and plain. He was a fair-minded man. He was willing to forget if we were willing to forget. And what's more he'd cart the body of Frank Morse off and hide it away so that it wouldn't be found for a week—or ten years if we wished. As for the dead in that house—just another gunmen's battle.

So that's the way it was when we left. I got my guns back, and damn near shot Gentle Jim's hand off when he had the nerve to pat Mary playfully on the back. Yep, he acted as if we were all mixed up in a pleasant conspiracy to defeat the law. And hell, in a way I suppose he was right.

Oh, I'll admit that he had a fat front that even a guy with his first hunting license couldn't miss—and I was tempted to put four or five slugs in his middle. Why didn't I then? I don't know. But I had a feeling that someday I— But hell, you've got to admit that at that moment at least, Gentle Jim was better to the girl alive than dead.

And the Flame. What of her?

In the car, I asked Mary how she got the gun.

She looked blankly at me. "Why, your assistant dropped that— the young lady who was above there with us. Just after she had stuck that same gun in the back of the man called Joe, forced him down the ladder out the window, saying something about orders from Armin. She left right after she pushed me to the opening and we were safe."

Conklyn Lee insisted I come to his house, and he explained just how Frank Morse had planted the evidence, had someone telephone Mary it was there, and fixed things so if anything went wrong, Lee would be the suspected one. And, being dead, would be unable to defend himself.

Then the phone rang. It was for me—the Flame. Her voice was low and pleasant. You'd think we had just parted at an afternoon tea.

"I'll clear up a few things for you, Race, to save you from racking that master brain of yours. It was I who first telephoned Mary Morse and told her to get you for the job. Of course, she didn't know. I pretended the message came through her stepfather, Conklyn Lee. And it was I who told her to clean the evidence out of his house. Of course, after the girl saw the murder, her life wasn't worth much.

"There, don't thank me for tonight, Race. Things went wrong. You damn near took the dose. And don't worry about Jerry. I paid him a little visit, took Armin home, and you'll find the car in Doran's Garage on Fifty-eighth Street. I'm mailing you the parking ticket."

I got a word in at last. "What—what was the point of your telephoning Jim, and then helping me? A change of that criminal mind?"

"Oh, I don't know. I've got a horror of killing people, I guess. Maybe I was brought up better than you were. But you see, Frank Morse knew something about me that would have hurt me with Armin if he'd told him; something that was enough to make me carry his black kimono in and out of places for him. Since Armin is going to be the big shot, why I didn't like that." A long pause and then, "So you really did me a nice turn. Thank you for killing Mr. Frank Morse."

I hung up after a few seconds. There's not much satisfaction in talking to yourself. Then I decided to go home. Mary clung to me, her hair brushed my cheek. But she didn't speak.

"Not bad news, I hope." Conklyn Lee was plainly interested.

I pushed the kid's arm down, looked at the tears in her eyes—tears of happiness. "In a way." I shrugged my shoulders. "I just lost ten thousand dollars. Take care of yourself."

So I went down the steps to the street. Just a sucker? Sure. What's so damned funny about that?

# CORPSE & CO.

■

*It was only a penciled scrawl on cheap notepaper—that offer from the Smart Guy to cut Race in on a five-grand block of reward money. But that big dick jumped at it as though it had been an engraved invitation. How could he guess it was going to lead him to open a one-man kill factory running under the slogan—"When better corpses are made, Race Williams will make them"?*

# ONE

# MURDER BOOMERANG

■

I read the note a couple of times, chucked it on the desk and looked at the advertisement that had been clipped to it. A big company wanted some stolen securities back and were willing to pay cash on the line to the tune of five thousand dollars for them. There was something in the ad about the arrest and conviction of the thief, but I let that go as a bit of baloney for the public to sap up. What that company wanted were the bonds. The ad was on the level; I checked it by phone. Then I read the letter again.

It was scrawled in pencil on a smudged sheet of five-and-dime-store paper—

Dear Race Williams—

I picked up this hot paper through a pal who took a dose of lead. I can't handle the reward deal as the cops could easy use me for a fall guy.

I'll split that five grand two ways with you if you'll handle the company and see that they're satisfied with getting the paper back without squawking all over their face afterwards.

Give it a thought and I'll buzz you at four and slip you my hide-out. But you got to act now. I've got the bonds on me and they're burning my coat.

A Smart Guy.

It looked good and I can use twenty-five hundred dollars any time. I know it isn't nice clean work, but it's legitimate business. The company would want those bonds. They'd hedge a bit but finally agree to cough up the five grand and call the "incident" closed. Yep, it looked like an easy way to make twenty-five hundred bucks—about two hours' work. Of course I wouldn't go to see the company until I had the bonds. If I yapped about returning them, then didn't come across, they'd have half the cops in New York crowding into my office. So there was nothing to do but wait until four o'clock. I was good at waiting; I'd done a lot of it lately.

Jerry, my office boy, who knows more about crooks than they know about themselves, breezed in with the same old story. "Miss Morse was in," he said. "She looked worried. I told her you were still out of town. On the level, boss, she acts like a regular dame."

"Jerry," I said, "Miss Morse is not a dame. She is the sole owner of the largest and oldest jewelry business on Fifth Avenue."

"Yeah, and ain't got a nickel."

"How do you know that? Did she tell you?"

Jerry shook his head. "You don't run a charitable institution. If she had any jack we'd be doing business."

I got up, leaned over the desk. "Miss Morse's case is closed," I said, and then added a little bitterly, "and it cost me exactly ten grand."

"She cried a little," Jerry told me as he backed toward the door. "And she has got a case—a case on you. . . . Yeah—I'm going."

I pushed a butt into my face, rolled smoke up at the ceiling. Sure, Mary Morse was a swell kid—and she had gotten me into a swell jam. Her dear Uncle Frank Morse—who returned to New York after her grandfather had died—had been using her jewelry firm as a blind to ship opium into the country. Mary had paid me nine thousand dollars to help her out, and I'd picked up an extra single grand from Gentle Jim Corrigan, who was deep in the dirt. Then Uncle Frank Morse and Gentle Jim and a couple of gunmen had snatched Mary and her stepfather, Conklyn Lee, and were about to kill them when I busted up their show by shooting to death Uncle Frank and the two guns. Only Gentle Jim remained alive.

To save Mary Morse and the jewelry business, which was damned near on the rocks, and avoid bringing in the feds, I didn't call in the police. Gentle Jim promised to get rid of the bodies, which he did, for one hood turned up in the East River, another in Brooklyn, and Uncle Frank's not at all. It was a good job on Gentle Jim's part, seeing the shooting took place in Mount Vernon. But then Corrigan and his boys had had plenty of experience with bodies before, and knew how to drop them promiscuously about to the surprise of the law-abiding people who first stumbled over them.

As for the ten grand, I had paid that out of my own pocket to get the information where the girl was kept. Paid it to Armin Loring— One Man Armin—a lad who worked for just one person—himself. Lately he'd taken up with Florence Drummond, the Flame. It was she who had given me the gun which saved my life that night. Whether she'd done it to save me or to have me kill Frank Morse who knew something she wanted hidden, I don't know. Maybe I hadn't actually lost any money on the deal. Maybe I did pay out only the ten grand I'd just received. But I'm no amateur detective. I don't go around shooting people to death just for the pleasure of it—

The phone rang. Exactly four P.M.!

The lad on the other end of the wire talked as if he were at the bottom of a thirty-foot ditch. "Williams?" He dug the hole three feet deeper. "Will you split the five grand?"

I gave it to him straight. "If it can be fixed, I'll fix it. But I'll have to have the bonds first, sink them, then see the president of the company and either deliver the goods and split the cash with you—or dump back the bonds to you." And when no answer came right away, "Well, it's your play. That's mine."

After a minute he spoke. "You're a white guy, Williams. You've always treated the boys right. A halfway house between us and the saps. You're a real guy—"

"Do you want to make a speech or do business?" I cut in on him. "Come on—yap!"

And he yapped, fast but clear. His hideout was on the East Side. It was a four-story wooden fire-trap. I was to go to the third floor and through the last door in the back on the right. The time was to be two A.M. I spilled it back to him over the wire. It fitted and I dropped the phone.

Back down the block a clock struck two and I stood smack in front of the damnedest-looking building you ever set eyes on. Not even habitable you'd say; not even fit for a human being to hide out in. Dark and deserted.

I turned up my collar, pulled down my hat, stuck both my hands in my overcoat pockets and walked toward the front door. It was hanging open, half off its hinges. The inside door was closed but wasn't locked; probably hadn't sported a lock that would work in years. With my left hand I gripped the knob, pulled it open, closed it behind me.

Complete blackness now except for the dim glow from the street lights through cracks in the wood of the door. I waited, listened. Somewhere far above me in that blackness a board creaked—then again, this time more distant. I shrugged, buried my hands deeper in my pockets. There wouldn't be anyone on the floor above. The old house was simply giving up its dead.

I had a flash, of course, but I didn't want to use it yet. I took a step forward, saw the light. It was on the floor above and after a second step it threw the dusty, dirt-covered, broken stairs into dull relief. I stepped forward again, saw the banister that wavered as if it would topple over, and reached out with my left hand to grip it.

Then I saw it—not the figure at first—just the thing that flashed in the air. Shiny glittering steel that cut through the murky darkness as if that darkness actually had substance. Yes, I saw it rise and fall; saw the whiteness of the hand that held the knife; the dull outline of that arm, and the body. No face, mind you—just a body without a face; without a head.

Ghostly—terrifying? Sure, I suppose it was all that. But as I saw the glimmering, flaying knife shooting straight at my throat, I saw too the outline, even the bulk of a body.

The knife was at my throat when I closed the index finger of my right hand; closed it three times. Burnt powder cut through the dampness and into my nostrils. Yellow-blue flame spit three flashes that looked like one. Steel clanked on wood, and a heavy body crashed to the floor.

I stepped back, gripped the knob of the door and waited; listened too. Listened to see if any doors opened in that silent house. They didn't. It was deserted all right. As to the shots being heard outside—well, there was no shrill blast of a police whistle, no screeching siren of a radio car.

I could see, faintly, both the white hands of the dead man upon the floor. Dead? Well, his hands didn't move and I work rather heavy artillery.

I was a little mad. My suit had set me back seventy-five bucks, and I had burnt a hole in the pocket. I couldn't figure out any reason for the attack. I've got lots of enemies, of course. But I hadn't had a threat of violence that was worth a damn in a couple of months.

Could it be the lad who telephoned me? Could he have thought I'd brought the five grand with me and wanted the dough and the bonds both? I shook my head. If he knew me he wouldn't be that dumb. Then what? Things were still silent inside and out so I decided to have a look at the would-be murderer.

I chanced the light that might flicker through the cracks in the door, jerked out my flash and ran the ray up over the holes in the stiff's chest to where his face should have been. The headless part was easily explained. He had a cap pulled down far over his face, must have bent his head forward. Now the whiteness of a chin showed, thick lips, yellow teeth. I reached down, jerked off his cap and got a good look at his map; at his eyes that were open, staring sightlessly up at me.

I took a whistle and a nod. Few guys in the city did it with a knife today. And the nerve of this one pulling the knife trick on me. Hell, it was almost insulting—would have been except he was so dead.

I knew him. Tony Lassario he was called, and a knife was his stock-in-trade—he liked silence. I grinned. He'd get plenty of it from now on.

I was bothered—not worried, understand. This lad and I had never crossed. He was a killer, a hired killer, and hell—who had enough interest to hire a lad to knock me over?

It wasn't pleasant, but I went through Tony, emptied out his pockets, and got nothing but small change until I drew from the torn lining of his jacket a crisp wad of bills. Crisp and new. Ten of them—ten one-hundred-dollar bills right straight from the bank. Not a wrinkle in them.

So I knew how things stood. Tony had been paid exactly one grand to knock me over. Me—imagine it! One grand. I stuck the bills in my pocket, dropped the small change, turned, carefully opened the door and walked out onto the silent and deserted street. I made my way toward the corner, went up a block and stepped briskly toward the subway. I felt better. No amateur work this time—I had been paid well for the job. Most any hood would have knocked Tony Lassario over for a century note and blown about the pay. I didn't worry about taking that money. Tony had been paid one grand to do a certain job. He hadn't done it and he wasn't entitled to the money—what's more he couldn't use it now anyway.

One grand—one lousy grand to knock me over! Now who could want me dead and yet not be willing to pay a good price for a death car?

I was walking down my own block—not three doors away from my apartment house—and still thinking that a guy who really wanted me dead would go into the thing in a big way and use the death car. And the car came; came down the block behind me. None of this sneaking up on a guy; this was a speeding car. I didn't see the car, only heard it. I was completely taken off my guard. I always say the unexpected never happens, but who'd ever think of two attempts on my life within the hour when I didn't even know one man who wanted me dead. I won't put it down to cleverness that saved my life this time. I won't put it down to luck either. Just call it instinct. I've lived close to death, but never closer perhaps than at that very moment when brakes screeched and I pitched myself straight out across that sidewalk on my chest and stomach. You old-timers will know if you ever saw the great ball players of the past who disdained spiked shoes and went for the bases head first. Sure—I hit the sidewalk, skidded across it, avoided the iron fence and, bouncing down stone steps on my chest and stomach, landed in an areaway. Landed in it the very moment that lead from at least two machine guns split the night.

It wasn't pleasant going down those steps, but despite the wear and tear I was turning my body and before I reached the bottom I was gripping two guns in my hands.

Chips of rock, glass from windows, and even splinters of wood from windowsills dropped around me like hail. I swung over, pressed my body close against the wall, set my eyes and guns, straightened up toward the sidewalk and waited. If the boys meant business, and it sounded as if they did, then they'd have to come and get me. What's more they'd have to poke a gun over that iron railing, and look down. And I'm telling you flat that anyone who did that would be taking his last look-see in this world.

Mad? Of course I was mad. You'd be too. But what could I do? Just lie there—nothing more—hoping that someone with a tommy gun would stick a face over that railing. Hoping—

And then I heard it. Single shots; spaced shots here and there that seemed to punctuate the steady staccato notes of the heavy artillery. The tommy guns stopped dead, but the other shots continued; single quick blasts of heavy revolvers. Then the grind of too quickly meshed gears, the roar of a powerful engine, and I knew that a big car shot away and went down the street.

Silence a moment; then opening windows, shrieking females, calling men. Running feet, too, from the row of apartments. The danger over, the good citizens were coming to the relief of their fellow man.

I came to my feet, walked up the steps to the street, and damn near shoved a gun through the stomach of Inspector Iron-Man Nelson. Nelson, the meanest, the roughest, the hardest man by a long shot, who had ever worn a policeman's uniform. And what's more, he didn't like me. Not that I liked him either but he was out to get me.

I parked both my guns by simply crossing my arms, lit a butt and tried to act like the advertisements. But it was Inspector Nelson's show and he took advantage of it.

"Race Williams. The great Race Williams," he sneered. "The killer that all men fear. And a bunch of hoodlums chase him up a back alley"—even if my death was planned right smack in front of a house—"where he lies down on his stomach and crawls into a hole."

A voice behind Nelson spoke. There was a chuckle in it, but there was no sarcasm. It was my friend, Sergeant O'Rourke, a square-shooting cop. He said: "Hardly crawl, Nelson. Williams could get a job on the Giants." And to me, "I don't know how you made it, Race."

"Me either," was all I said as I tried to brush myself off. Half an hour ago I had been worrying about that suit. Now I might as well send it to some amateur theatrical group that was putting on *Oliver Twist*.

A patrol car come up; then another. Nelson turned and gave some orders. Something about a license number, and the chances that it would be changed or the car abandoned around the corner. Then he and O'Rourke decided to have a talk with me in my apartment. When we got there I squawked a bit and my squawk wiped the grin off Nelson's face.

"It's a hell of a note for you cops to ride a guy who's just missed being bumped off. I was hurrying home to call you, O'Rourke. That's the second attempt on my life tonight. I want to make a complaint."

"The second," said Nelson. "What happened in the other one?"

Here was my chance. There could be no doubt even in Nelson's mind now that someone wanted me dead. So I said: "A lad telephoned me he was in trouble—" And when Nelson glared, "Well, my business is getting people out of trouble. So I went downtown. A guy tried to knife me and—"

"You shot him to death." Nelson and O'Rourke spoke together. Good guessers those boys.

"That's right." I gave them the East Side address. "His name is—was—Tony Lassario."

Nelson didn't like me. Never had; never would. But he had hard work not showing his appreciation then. Tony Lassario was no favorite with the cops.

I said: "Now—about you boys. How come you're here?"

Nelson wanted to keep questioning me, but O'Rourke said: "Inspector Nelson got a call to go down to the morgue where he'd find your body. The call came just before two o'clock. I was there at the time. We phoned the morgue. You weren't there. We decided to come up to your apartment and warn you."

"I thought we'd find you dead," Nelson said gruffly. "So don't thank me for coming."

"I can thank you for shooting, though." I was willing to get that out.

Nelson said: "I never drew a rod until after you sneaked down those steps."

"And never hit anyone with it when you did, eh?" I wasn't questioning Nelson's honesty, or efficiency either, for that matter. But I'd rather have been found with a couple of hundred slugs in my chest than owe my life to that big chunk of baloney.

O'Rourke said: "No, we didn't help you, Race. You think fast. You were well fortified before we knew what was happening. Never even thought of the car until you did a nose dive."

"About this guy downtown." Nelson did a bit of glaring. "Are you sure, Williams, that you just didn't fancy him, went down and popped him over and his friends followed you and tried for the blast-out? Sure it wasn't murder downtown?"

"Oh, it wasn't murder—just suicide, Nelson," I told him. "Tony must have been sure of that dose of lead when he laid the trap."

"O.K., O.K." O'Rourke took Nelson by the arm, for although O'Rourke only sported the title of sergeant, he was the big shot in the police department. He could have been an inspector long ago, but as he told the commissioner—a sergeant is closer to the men, and the men are closer to crime. To me he said: "The D.A. will want a statement from you sometime tomorrow, Race."

Before they left Nelson said: "The next time I get an invitation to the morgue, I'll accept it—and maybe have more luck."

"That's the only place you'll ever find a stiff," I told him, and cut the conversation with the slamming door.

**T W O**

# CASH ON THE LINE

■

I reached my office next morning without even being hit with a stick of dynamite, which you'll have to admit was a rather dull way to begin the day after the preceding night's activities.

Jerry grabbed my arm as I started to open the door to my private office. "Clients, boss—an old man and a boy."

I didn't say anything but as I reached for the knob I paused. I pulled a gun from my shoulder holster, pushed it into my right jacket pocket and let my hand stay with it.

Jerry laughed. "No trouble, boss. Respectable old party. Boy just a kid—and from what I heard going to be worth millions."

Millions—I liked the sound of the word. I straightened somewhat, pushed open the door, but still kept my hand in my pocket. Nerves? I don't admit having nerves. After the early-morning celebrations it was just damn good common sense.

An old gray-haired, quiet, dignified gent with a gold-headed cane came to his feet the moment I entered the room. He was class. The kindly, fatherly sort of the movies—a little too perfect for real life maybe, but then the movies have nothing on the oddities I meet in my business. I took my hand out of my pocket, left the gun there.

My eyes drifted to the boy—just a slim kid who stood with his back to me looking down at the street below. From thirteen to sixteen I'd say, for although he sported long trousers, he wore a cap; it was still stuck on his head. Bad manners, but then I suppose his money had taught him that good manners are things other people had toward him.

The old man was talking. He squeaked like a music box we had when I was a kid. "Mr. Williams, Mr. Race Williams!" He came across to me and played with my hand like you'd pump a well. "I'm not going to stay. I'm not going to talk until afterwards. The boy came of his own free will. You may have trouble getting the truth out of him. But he's promised, and I'm certain you'll be interested. There, there, it's hard for him to remember the horror of it all—so I'll run along."

And that was that. The boy still stood by the window as the old man passed out the door, gave me a final bow, jerked at his gray mustaches, and was gone like a two-line actor trying to steal the show at a Broadway opening.

"Well, son"—I put on a light, easy air—"maybe the old gent can't take it, but I've heard plenty in my day. Let me have it."

The kid murmured something about not talking and I went into my act. I walked over to the window, put an arm about the kid's shoulders and said: "So you won't talk, eh?"

And the kid turned, threw both arms about my neck and cried: "Race, Race—how could you be so cruel to me!"

Stunned? Sure I was stunned. And so would you be. For it wasn't a boy, it was a girl—Mary Morse, my headache of a few months before. The girl whose uncle I'd popped out right through his black bathrobe while he was playing the Masked Marvel.

"I'm so glad you're back," she said when I grabbed her shoulders, broke the stranglehold she had on me and set her feet on the floor. She was still working the sex interest. She pulled off her cap, let the hair run wild, and put those fine blue eyes on me.

I didn't go into the old baloney, pretend I had really been away, and that I was glad to see her. I said: "Sit down, Miss Morse, and I'll give it to you straight." Then I went around the desk, flopped into my own chair and watched her pull up another and squat on the end of it. She was eager; anxious. Her eyes were bright, but there were dark ridges under them, little lines creeping up from her mouth, a slight quiver to her lips. She had changed a bit from the happy kid I'd first met and made a happy kid again. Hell, I didn't like it.

"Miss Morse—" I started and stopped.

"If you call me that again I'll scream," she told me. "We went through hell together, Race. I don't know, maybe you'd been there before—but it was my first trip. Now, now—why don't you want to see me?"

I stiffened, said: "You were a client of mine and I did for you what I'd do for any other client. Now it's over and—and— Don't you understand? Your head is turned—you think you're in love with me."

Her eyes grew wide, her mouth opened, white teeth gleamed. She laughed, but though it wasn't forced, it was hollow—as if she hadn't laughed much lately. "Whatever," she said, "put such an idea into your head?"

"Well—you—the things you said. Your coming here to see me."

"Why, I like you. You like me. You're my friend. I need—want more advice from you. I need you terribly."

"There's nothing I can do for you. I told you then and I tell you now the case is closed. You'll simply have to try to stop thinking about it as you would a terrible nightmare."

"But"—she leaned forward—"I saw men killed. I know that my Uncle Frank used the Morse name, the Morse shop, to smuggle in drugs—and I said nothing—nothing. They could send me to prison for that."

I shook my head. "If the skeletons that rattle in the closets of thousands of our most self-respecting citizens were brought out for an airing the prisons would be crowded. That's why blackmail is such a nice easy racket. You did what you thought right—forget it. The only man who knows, besides your stepfather and myself, is Gentle Jim Corrigan. We won't talk. He can't—without involving himself. You're lucky there isn't someone else in on the know and that you're not being blackmailed."

"But I am," she said. "And that's what's breaking the House of Morse. Five thousand a month of my allowance goes to this man."

I was on my feet, leaning heavily on the desk. "You gave some man money. Who is he? Not Corrigan."

"Not Corrigan," she said. "I don't know him. He telephoned me. I've met him at night in Central Park and—"

"You're a fool!" I slammed down a hand. "Why didn't you tell—tell—" And I stopped. She couldn't have told me. I hadn't given her a chance.

I was alarmed at first and then I wasn't. I questioned her closely. She had never seen him before. He talked vaguely of the house in Mount Vernon, of the knowledge she hid—and then collected. Did I know the racket? Of course. This lad knew nothing. He was just a messenger from Gentle Jim Corrigan. Corrigan couldn't use his name in it because the girl would know, her stepfather would know, and I'd know he would never dare squawk.

The girl finished. "I threatened this man, said I'd go to you, but he only laughed. He said he knew exactly what my allowance was, and that there wouldn't be enough left to hire you. That you wouldn't save your best friend unless you were paid—and paid well for it. I knew that wasn't true, of course."

"But it is true," I told her brutally, and tried to look straight at her and couldn't. "You don't let people you know walk into your jewelry store and help themselves, do you? This business is just the same. I sell my services, meet danger for money. The more danger the more money." And when her eyes grew wider and her mouth opened, "Besides, you don't need anyone. Corrigan is blackmailing you himself. He can't talk. Just don't pay."

"But I told the man money wouldn't make any difference to you. You see—"

"You told him wrong. Money makes all the difference."

And she laughed. Yes, laughed at me. "Race," she said, "you could never make me believe you'd let me down." And when I started to throw a hard face, she beat me to it. "Besides," she chirped, "I told this man you were already working for me. I told him I had just talked to you, and that you told me I was not to give him another nickel. And that if he knew anything about killing why—why—you'd teach him some more—and his boss too, who sent him. He said another, a powerful man, sent him."

I just leaned back and gasped. I think I said: "What made you tell him that?"

"Because I knew it was true. I know it's true now no matter what you say. Besides"—she hesitated, lowered her head, raised it again, looked directly at me—"the House of Morse is being pushed to the wall. Every penny I get is needed to—keep it away from that wall. Oh, I know what you are going to say—that I'll be twenty-one soon, that I'll inherit a great fortune. I can't go before the court anymore. They have said that—have more than hinted that the business should be sold to satisfy creditors. But—but—don't you see? It's Morse, it's mine, it's the name! I'm living in a small apartment now. I—"

She talked more, but I didn't listen. Thoughts were actually forming in that thick skull of mine. Corrigan, of course, was shaking her down for this money and—I asked her suddenly: "When did you last see this man. When did you tell him this?"

"Just a day or two ago. I said you'd been away and had come back."

I knew the truth. Gentle Jim Corrigan wanted to collect five thousand dollars a month. And Gentle Jim Corrigan now felt that I would interfere with that collecting. And Gentle Jim Corrigan knew that I could not interfere with it if I were dead. So the knife in the hallway and the death car on the street—

I looked at the girl. Had she told that lie because she believed in me or because she wanted to put the dough in the jewelry firm? Certainly, she hadn't said a word about money. She looked at me now, said innocently, and I wondered if too innocently: "Did I do wrong?"

"Oh no, not a bit. Your clever little idea to save the jack nearly chucked a few shovels full of dirt in my face. I went through that last racket for you, Miss Morse. I laid wide open for an ending to my career. Oh, the killings were in self-defense, and to save you from death. But I never reported it to the police and I never peeped to the federals about the dope. What's more, there are some officials in this city—some powerful police officers, too—who'd like to get me. And now you play me for a sucker."

She seemed surprised, uncertain. She said: "Would money have made a difference then? I could buy your services?"

"There's no use in going into that. You've got nothing but debts."

"I will be twenty-one very shortly. I could pay you well then. You'll take my case?"

"No!" I slapped out the word. "And you haven't any case. Just don't pay."

"I see." She moved back slowly toward the door. "I am confused, Race—very much confused. I didn't know where else to turn. I never had a doubt of you." She raised her head, looked at me. "I—it's hard to doubt you now. It's even hard for me to think clearly."

"Think clearly, huh." I took a villain's laugh. "You should be running the Morse shop with that head of yours."

"I am." She still faced me squarely. "And it hasn't been easy pacing the floor at night, trying to appear in the store by day. My name—people have respected the name of Morse for so many years. And then my assurance to the creditors that the firm will weather the storm. They're businessmen like you, Race, but most of them would take my word, my promise of the money when I'm twenty-one. It's just that they can't. They need the money so badly now."

I set my lips tightly and followed her through the outer office and into the hall. She didn't speak—just took out a card and a pencil and scribbled something on it.

"That's my phone number and my address. I think you'll use it. You may think I'm a fool, but I can't help still believing in you." She gripped my hand. Hers was small, cold; her tired eyes were lifeless.

I opened my mouth to speak—but I don't know what the hell I was going to tell her. I just stood there as the elevator door opened and shut and she was gone.

"Well—" Jerry started as I stormed back into the office.

"I guess that dame won't bother me anymore," I told him as I went into my private office. But she did bother me, bother me a lot as I picked up my hat, then passed back through the office, slamming the outer door behind me.

Imagine a kid—a twenty-year-old kid—putting me on the spot for Gentle Jim Corrigan. She sure had one first-class nerve. I was well rid of her and told myself I felt pretty good about the way I'd handled her. But truth is truth. I felt lousy.

# THREE

# THE FLAME

■

Gentle Jim Corrigan had anything but impressive offices in the Cutting Building on Lower Broadway. Jim did most of his business in his suite of rooms in the Royal Hotel further uptown. But he had to have a business of some kind and since the legitimate real estate firms weren't doing much in these times, Jim wasn't bothered. Certainly, the killing of Frank Morse must have hurt the dope racket, though I never believed that Mary's uncle was actually running it. Gentle Jim was the man for that job—soft, easy-going, and a killer.

I turned the knob of the office door and walked in, paused as the door clicked shut behind me. The outer office was empty, but I heard footsteps cross from the room beyond, saw the door open and saw the man come out. His lips parted, his eyes narrowed.

He was six feet two, weighed close to two hundred pounds. His face was a perfect example of modern art—all shoved around as if a horse with a taste for the latest in sculpture had kicked him carefully in the kisser. He'd come from the lighted room beyond into the dimness of the outer office and didn't get a good look at me at first. When he spoke it was tough, side-of-the-mouth stuff.

"There's a sign on the door says knock." He walked slowly toward me—menacing, threatening—or at least his interpretation of such theatricals. It was a cinch that here was one real-estate firm that wasn't used to clients and didn't wish any, at least at this time.

I slipped sideways closer to the wall and deeper dimness, said: "I want to see Jim Corrigan, and I don't want any of your lip."

"You do, eh?" He tried to get a look under my hat, couldn't make out my face. "What do you want to see Mister Corrigan about." And he laid the "Mister" on thick.

"I was thinking," I said slowly, "of knocking all his teeth down his throat."

Both his hands were empty and so were mine. He glanced down at them before he took that final step and swung his right hand. Real bad, real tough—fancied himself with his fists. Well, my business is rough and it don't matter a damn to me if it's chairs and bottles in a back room, fists in an open yard, or guns in a dark alley.

I could have shot the lad to death, but I didn't. I did what I intended to do, what I'd trapped him into. I stepped inside that flaying ham of a fist, crossed my right hand over my chest and snapped up my gun with a little jerk. Little—I mean it only traveled a little ways. It caught Flat Pan under the chin and made a little thumping sound against bone. He didn't cry out. He just gave a grunt, rocked back on his heels, dropped both his hands to his sides. I smacked him a clout on the side of the head that would have driven an ordinary guy's skull in.

Good work? Of course it was good work. I know my business. But the hard part came after he started to go. You see, that clout on the head had to knock him toward me—not away from me. And I had to catch his weight as he started to fall—not after he was near the ground. He was too big and heavy for that.

It wasn't the knocking around I was so proud of. It was the direction I got. Yep, I caught him right in my arms, let his body sink with mine, and holding my hand beneath his head eased him to the floor. I had a little trouble shoving his huge body beneath a flat desk.

I sprung the lock on the door, walked through the office Flat

Face had come out of and strode softly across it to Gentle Jim's private office. I knew the lay.

This thickly carpeted office was better, but not much better than the dilapidated one outside. There were lots of chairs, a couple of desks and a heavy wooden door marked *Private* at the far end of the room. Alongside this door a straight-backed office chair with a black leather seat was tilted against the wall. It was a cinch that Gentle Jim was in that room labeled *Private*. It didn't take a hell of a good detective three guesses to reach the conclusion that Flat Face had come off that tilted chair when I entered the outer office.

So far so good. This was as much as I knew of the lay. I gripped the knob of that door, turned it as slowly and as carefully as any burglar might. I lifted my gun, got set and jerked open the door.

Surprised? Sure, I was surprised. For there was a hall, perhaps six or seven feet long—no longer—and at the end of that hall was another door.

I took a couple of steps, wrapped my hand around the knob of this second door, then dropped it as if it were red hot. Dropped it and stepped back. The knob had turned suddenly in my hand.

I was down that hall, through the other door, with no chance to close it behind me, and sitting in that tilted chair. Was Gentle Jim coming out or did he have a visitor?

And he had a visitor; a visitor who was not coming out just yet but whose voice brought me out of that chair, listening by that partly open door. It was the voice of the Flame.

She was saying: "I like you, Jim—I could like you a lot more."

Then the soft voice of Jim Corrigan. "That's right, Florence. That's fine. But what of Loring? Armin Loring?"

"What of him?" she demanded almost sharply. "You're afraid of him, you mean? That's a laugh, Jim. I know there isn't a man in the city you're afraid of. But Armin Loring *is* Armin Loring. He obeys nobody's orders, is responsible to no man."

"I'm not so sure of that," Jim said as I looked along that hall and saw the inner door half open, the Flame standing by it, her back to me, her hand behind her still on that knob.

"Well, I am," the girl told him. "Look, Jim, I'll drop Armin like that." Her fingers must have snapped from the sound. "I'll drop him if I can be sure of you. You know me, know what they say about me—have said for years. One Man Loring—I've helped build him up. You want my brains, Jim.''

"I want more than just your brains," Jim Corrigan said and his voice dripped honey now. "Hell, Florence, what do you want me to do?''

"I want to know who gives you orders—who's behind you— who's behind this dope racket. Oh, don't put that front on for me, Jim. I worked close to Frank Morse. I know you didn't head it. I know he didn't. Come on, Jim—come on. You're playing with thousands when you might be playing with hundreds of thousands—millions even.''

"Millions even." Gentle Jim echoed her words. "It was set for that, Florence; all set for that when Race Williams busted in and shot Morse to death. The big lad behind it is very careful now."

"The big lad—the big lad." The Flame's voice burned with excitement. "That's it, Jim. That's it. Who is he?" It wasn't hard to tell now which side of the fence the Flame was on. She wasn't the young girl with the brown eyes and the sparkle of youth in them now. She was the woman of the night—cruel, sinister, dangerous to all honest men.

Gentle Jim said: "I don't know, Florence, I wish I did. You were in. You can be in again. You—''

The woman stamped her foot, and her words this time made me wince—which is some job. I don't wince easy. "Didn't I show you how to cash in on the Morse girl?" she said. "Didn't I show you how to plant the stuff again? Jim—Jim, I want money. Lots of it. I'll make you rich. I'll get everything out of this lad who gives you orders—everything.''

She moved from the door then and I backed away, but not before I heard her say: "Jim—Jim, tell me who this man is—the big lad. You need me, Jim—I need you. You want me, Jim—and—''

I remembered the day when the Flame's arms had gone around my neck and she had whispered such words to me, and—and— yes, I had believed them, too.

Would Jim believe her? Would Jim give her the name? I thought he would, for the Flame's lips would be very close and her brown eyes burning like glowing coals.

Jim's voice was hoarse when he spoke. "Florence, God's truth,

I'd tell you if I could! But I don't know his name. You—you—Hell, Florence, don't look at me like that—after—"

I closed the door softly, pussy-footed across the big office, passed into the outer one, clicked the latch of the main entrance, and was out in the hall lighting a butt. This time I held my hand on the knob of the door when the Flame clutched it on the other side. And this time I gripped it tightly and turned it against her turn.

I was the surprised one, not the Flame, when I pushed the door open and we stood face to face. At least I pretended to be surprised. And the Flame—well, it was pretty hard to read anything in her face that she didn't want you to read.

"Hi, Race." Her long quick fingers moved suddenly and the cigarette went from my lips to hers. "Going to see Gentle Jim?"

"If he's in." I hesitated and then, "I want to thank you for that night—the gun—when you saved my life."

She smiled. "The pleasure was all mine. I rather fancied Frank Morse more dead than alive. I want to compliment you on your efficiency."

She was the woman of the night then all right—hard, cold, cruel. There was no understanding her. "I'd stay away from Jim, Race," she continued. "I'd drop out of the thing. You intended to do that. It was rather a massacre in that Mount Vernon house, I understand. Imagine what would have happened if your hands hadn't been tied together."

"I wonder," I said, "if Gentle Jim can imagine that. They're not tied now."

She looked at me a long time. "You have something on Jim, and Jim has something on you. It's stuff that neither one of you would be apt to write in a diary or confide to a friend. I suppose it would simplify matters for you—and Miss Morse"—her lips twisted at the left corner of her mouth—"if you eliminated Gentle Jim Corrigan. But—" And after watching me closely, "I see you've thought of that."

"I have—but it isn't original with me. Jim thought of it first—of killing me I mean."

"It's that damn girl," the Flame told me. "I thought you were a businessman, Race. That you figured danger and death in dollars and cents—not in big eyes and small talk. Stay away from Jim."

I took a laugh. "And let half the gunmen in the city take pot shots at me?"

"Not half, Race—all of them." Her shoulders shrugged. "The law of averages will be sure to get you. Listen. Breeze in on Jim, give him the office that you're out of the mess. He'll take your word for it." She leaned forward. "There might even be a few grand in it—so you can take a trip. Not the ten grand he promised you before, but enough. You see, Jim isn't dough-heavy right now."

"But the man behind him is."

The Flame's eyes widened. She looked at me curiously, then she nodded.

"You'd guess that, of course."

"You know who he is?"

"No," she said, "nor do you." Though her lips smiled, her eyes were very serious. "Remember, Race, you can't shoot what you can't see. That not only applies to the man behind this racket, but to every man who may be hired to kill you. Think of it—and even your conceit will vanish. A single man with a tommy gun in an alley. The death car on a vacant street. A man with a rifle in the window of an apartment. A gun in the back even on crowded Broadway. The stranger beside you in the subway rush. The theater, the movies, the park. Your car at a traffic signal. It's a matter of time—maybe one or two days, maybe only an hour or two. But it's sure and certain to come—your death by violence."

I shrugged. "If it's in the cards." And before she could answer, "And that goes whether the cards are stacked or not. Whether Jim deals from the bottom or top."

The Flame leaned forward, put both her hands on my shoulders. "A warning, Race. This is a new racket to you. Not just thugs threatening to toss bombs through a window, or gangsters shooting down honest businessmen who don't pay tribute. It's big—halted only for the moment by the death of Frank Morse, halted only to grow bigger again. Brains are what are needed against this racket. And brains are something you haven't got."

I just stood there and stared at her. The thing was almost uncanny. For a moment there was no evil in her face or in her voice. She was strangely beautiful. It was as if she were a crusader; a crusader for good, instead of for evil. But it went almost at once.

She turned toward the stairs, said just before she darted down them: "Miss Morse is in it up to her neck—a neck that someone might twist so that it would face the other way if she tries to get out. Go in and have your talk with Gentle Jim, then find yourself sprawled on the sidewalk within the hour. Good-bye."

"See you some more." I leaned over the railing by the stairs as she hurried down.

"Not if Gentle Jim lives," she flung back over her shoulder.

# FOUR

# FIVE SHOTS IN THE STOMACH

∎

If Gentle Jim Corrigan was surprised to see me he hid it well. He looked up when I busted in the door and caught him flat-seated behind a broad desk. The annoyance left his face almost at once. His mouth opened, his eyes shone, the great layers of loose skin on his face started to wave up and down, and the veins along his cheeks and even on his nose became little pulsing streams of shimmering blue.

"Williams! Race Williams of all people! I was just thinking of you." Blue eyes narrowed a moment, he rolled words around inside his mouth before he spoke them—figuring whether I had met the Flame, and figuring correctly. "I just had a visit from a very charming woman, an old friend of yours—more than a friend, eh? We were talking about you. Sit down."

When I remained standing, keeping hard eyes on him, his own blue ones fell to my empty hands, then jumped to my face again. His voice when he spoke now was still soft, but it carried a message of warning despite his pleasant smile.

"Circumstances make strange bed-fellows, Williams. We share

**181**

something that our friend, John Law, would hardly understand. We share the secret of the dead—to protect the living. We must take care of each other, Race."

"That's what I'm here to talk to you about. You're taking a little too good care of Miss Morse—and myself."

"I'm afraid," he said, "I don't understand." His great head shook. "And I always felt, always said, you were a straight-speaking man."

So I gave it to him straight. "It's blackmail, Jim, but as far as the girl's concerned that's off. I simply told her not to pay. It's that secret of the dead, Jim—to protect the living that interests me— and at present you're one of the living."

I didn't get excited, didn't get mad. I just explained to him very carefully that someone was shaking Mary Morse down. And I listened to him just as carefully as he went through being shocked, surprised, and amazed—and at the end just a little fearful of the results.

"My dear boy. My dear boy, Race"—wrinkles kept forming and disappearing and rising almost to his forehead—"you alarm me greatly. Can there be someone else who knows? You wouldn't talk, of course. Nor her stepfather, nor the girl, and I—I certainly would not talk."

"No, you certainly would not. And you have nothing to worry you, Jim. Not a thing. If the blackmailer is a fake, just guessing, why, it doesn't matter. Miss Morse won't pay any more."

"Fine, fine." Gentle Jim rubbed his hands. "Thanks for warning me, Race—thanks. You did alarm me, but he can't know, of course. Now I wonder who could make a guess—a guess that would frighten the girl. And who could have sent this unknown man to collect."

I looked squarely at Gentle Jim. I could have laughed, but I didn't. The stage had lost quite an actor—a comedian maybe. He looked so concerned, so interested. I said: "I'm still in business, Jim, if you want to find out who meets her, and if you want to find out who sends him. I'll beat his face in with the butt of my gun to find out."

"No, no. It really doesn't matter—does it?" I saw Jim look down at the partly open drawer of his desk, even feel of his coat, push it back quickly, eye me, then jerk the jacket back over his big front again.

I said: "I have another warning for you, Jim. There have been a couple of attempts on my life. Oh, nothing to be alarmed about— that is for me to be alarmed about. It's just you that must worry."

"What do you mean?" He drew back in his chair now. I had crossed to his desk, leaned on it, shot my face forward.

"I mean," I said, "the price for my dead body is off."

Jim looked puzzled. "I don't know what you're talking about." And when I told him about those two attempts on my life, "Yes, yes, I heard of it, Race. I'm pretty well informed on such things." He pointed a pencil at me. "Now listen. I was unfortunate or perhaps fortunate enough to be connected indirectly with a little business that might make a certain person rich, might even make me rich. You understand it—and I understand it. Neither you nor I are in a position to talk about the other. Without mentioning any names, I'll say this. There is a certain young lady who for reasons of her own is paying a certain man five thousand dollars a month. That's quite a bit of money. It could go on until she was twenty-one—then a lump sum might free the young lady from all worry. Have I your attention?" Blue eyes had film over them now, but the pupils bored through that film like darting points of steel.

"All my attention, Jim," I told him. "Even to knowing that the man is you."

"Let us pretend, Race, for our own amusement"—he smiled slightly—"or perhaps just for my amusement, that the man is me, and that the man who eventually may interfere with a million-dollar project is you. Now what would I do? Just what this man you fear might do. I'd see that you were killed. At first I would give the job to one man to do. Have another or several others ready if he failed." And with a shrug, "Then, having a bit of Scotch blood in me, I'd decide to pay only for success, not failure. In plain words, if I were this man I'd put a price on your head—a good price. The money to go to the man who wiped you out."

"So that's what you'd do?"

"That," said Jim, "is exactly what I'd do."

"And what do you think I would do?"

"If you were a sensible man, Race, you'd come to this man— this man who, for the sake of argument, you are pretending to be me." He let his teeth show and clapped a hand down on his knee. "And that's just what you've done. My advice to you, Race, would be—this lad isn't a bad chap. He knows you. He would take your word not to see Mary Morse again, and let you live."

"And what does that man think I'd answer?" There was a sneer in my voice. "Well—I'll tell him. I'd see Mary Morse any time I damn well pleased. I'd offer to help her in any way I could—see her every day, or twice a day if it was necessary to—"

I stopped, tossed back my head and laughed. For some time past I had spent my days dodging Mary Morse. Only an hour or so I told her where she got off and that I was through with her. Now—well, the Flame's warning that I didn't fit into this racket, didn't have the brains for it, had started me, I guess. Now—Jim's threat, and my answer. Funny? Sure it was funny. I guess it's just that I won't let anyone tell me where I get off. I can't be coaxed, cajoled or pushed into anything by sentiment. But what's more I can't be scared out of anything by threats.

"Well"—Jim started to rise—"I've given you some advice. It's up to you from now on. I imagine from what you say about this man that you won't live very long." He dropped back in his seat then and began to talk. The softness went out of his voice. A loudness took its place.

What he said didn't matter. The sounds that came out of his throat didn't matter. It was what those words and sounds hid—or tried to hide. But I heard it—just the single creak of an opening door, behind me, partly to my right. And Jim had given himself away by the shrill, loud words he was speaking. I wouldn't have noticed that single creak otherwise. The change in his voice had made me listen for it.

My right hand slipped up, a heavy forty-four-caliber revolver slipped from a shoulder holster and dropped into my hand. I didn't swing. One man, two, three or even four might be in that doorway. And Gentle Jim would be behind me if I turned. Gentle Jim, whose right hand moved along the desk to rest partly above a half-open drawer, whose eyes dropped to that drawer just as a voice spoke behind me.

"Don't move, Williams. Don't move your hands at all. If you'll recall the night you had me covered and copped off the Morse girl and the Morse case, you'll understand how easy it would be for me to squeeze lead. Feel that." Something round and hard dug into my back, and if I'd had some tea leaves handy, I might have seen a gun in the cup.

\* \* \*

I didn't need the reminders of the girl and the gun to tell me who the man behind me was. He was the greatest single danger in the city of New York. I say single danger, because he didn't hire others to do his dirty work—he let others hire him for just one single job. That's right. It was One Man Armin. Was this the single job?

Knowing Armin, I didn't move hand or arm. And what's more I didn't need to. My gun was pointing straight at Gentle Jim Corrigan's stomach. And it was a stomach that a beginner, with a gun in his hand for the first time in his life, wouldn't be apt to miss.

"I'm going to let you have it, Race," Armin said. "I'm not fussy about where I shoot a guy and—"

I didn't speak. I just closed my trigger finger and let the hammer of my gun slip up and down—up and down. Hard to do that? Right! Damned hard, if you give the hammer plenty of play. Dangerous too? Well—yes. Dangerous to the guy who happens to be watching the trick at the other end of the gun.

And Jim Corrigan was watching. You'd think a breeze of hurricane proportions had swept over his face, the way the skin rolled and the rivers of blue veins went whipping up and bulging until you thought they'd burst.

I didn't speak. Jim Corrigan did the talking. And this time, though his voice was loud and shrill, it wasn't to hide anything. No, not even fear, for the terror was plain in his popping eyes. You see, Jim knew guns, and knew that if my little exhibition failed he'd never live to sneer about it.

"Don't—don't shoot, Armin," Jim cried out. "Williams has a gun on me, he's— For God's sake, Race, stop! He—Armin isn't going to hurt you."

"No," I said, "I didn't really think he would. Charming chap, Armin."

Armin spoke. "He'd be dead, Jim, before his finger closed up on the trigger. Right in the spine." And with a harsh laugh, "I've made a study of anatomy, Race."

I steadied my hand, let my thumb slip up to the hammer, drew that hammer back and waited. My death wouldn't save Jim now. I said: "So you studied anatomy, eh, Armin? Then make your kill, and you can dig a hand inside the hole in Jim's middle and take a post-graduate course. A forty-four and two feet—you might even crawl in and look around. Jim's roomy."

"The hammer's back, Armin!" Jim almost screeched the words. "His thumb's on it. It'll slip off when he dies and—and—"

I said: "It's getting to be cheap stuff, Armin. Make your play or drop your gun. I know, I know. It all depends how much is in it for you. If Jim pays you to knock me over, I know it's a big figure. If Jim's dead you may have trouble collecting it from his estate. Courts are funny about murder contracts. Most of them don't recognize them as legal."

Armin finally spoke. "If I drop the gun—what do you do then?"

My shoulders moved slightly. "I got some advice for Jim. I'll give him some and leave."

"Only words, Race?"

"Only words," I repeated.

"After that what?"

"Whatever you or Jim want to make it."

"You'll drop the Morse case—this five-grand angle of it?"

I half sneered. "Blackmail and One Man Armin. You'll be picking pockets yet."

Armin dug his gun deeper into my spine. "To hell with that." I remembered his temper, remembered also the control he had over it. I stiffened. For a moment I thought it was coming, and so did Jim. He screeched again: "Don't, don't—"

But Armin only said: "Will you drop the Morse case—yes or no."

"No," I said. "Not a chance." Hell, I didn't want the Morse case. I didn't want any part of something that would finally be mixed up with the federal government. So why did I say no? The answer is simple—maybe unreasonable, but simple just the same. I couldn't say yes. I couldn't have said it if the trigger closed. I'm built that way.

"You couldn't help Mary Morse if you were dead."

"Nor could Jim harm her. I don't know how deep you're into this thing, Armin. But it's dope—government stuff. Press Mary Morse or her stepfather and they'll blow up. Go straight to the Department of Justice and the G-men will come straight to you."

"You're an off-trail guy, Race. You've been seeing too many movies." There was sarcasm in Armin's words, but it seemed as if he were talking just to gain time. Was there someone else coming?

I said: "I'll count thirty—then blow a hole in Jim's middle. One—"

"You mean that?" Armin sort of gasped.

"My word on it," I told him.

"All right," Armin said as I ran the count up to ten. "Put your gun away, and I'll give you my word to park mine."

"Sixteen, seventeen, eighteen—" I counted. "Drop your gun, Armin or put it away, and come around by Jim. My word I won't shoot—just talk."

"But why should I take your word when you won't—"

"Twenty-one, twenty-two— Because you know my word's good, and I know yours isn't. Twenty-three, twenty-four, twenty-five—"

"Damn it to hell!"—the sweat was pouring down Jim's face—"get rid of your gun. Come around, Armin. I think—I know—I—"

"Twenty-nine—"

And Armin passed around the desk—his hands empty. "You're a fool, Williams," he said. And after looking at my face, "By God, I think you'd have done it!"

"By God, I would!" I told him.

Jim was wiping a handkerchief across his forehead. Armin rubbed a hand, the fingers of which were steady, through his black, oily hair.

I parked my gun. I didn't like to do it, standing with two men as quick as Gentle Jim, and the fastest-drawing man in the underworld, Armin Loring. No, it wasn't bravado that made me do it, nor conceit either. It's just that I won't let anyone know—or any two, for that matter—that I think a rod can be pulled on me. Pulled and used, I mean. It was just good business, that's all.

If the time ever came when one of them alone had the yen to draw, that one would remember that I'd faced the two of them, and that my hands hung by my sides—and hung empty. It's fear that makes man's hand slow, and his fingers thumbs when he has to draw to make his kill. And the creating of fear is my stock in trade.

I didn't intend to hang around longer than I had to, so I made the speech I came to make. I said: "We're still pretending this man who wants me dead is you, Jim. You told me what you'd do—and what I should do. Now—I'll tell you what I will do. You have

orders out to kill me. If I knock over ten of the boys you send to
kill me or even twenty, you can still sit here and get more to try the
job. So here's my advice. I'm giving you one more chance at my
life—just one more. Get the best guy you can or the best ten guys.
But be sure they get me on the first try."

"Yeah?" Jim was getting back his courage—at least the veins
were not so prominent, not so turbulent. "And if he or they don't
kill you the first time—what?"

"Then"—I leaned across the desk and pounded a finger against
that fat middle of his—"I'll empty one of my guns right smack in
your stomach. Any place, any time I see you. Remember, Jim.
Your office here—in Times Square—in the dining room of the Ritz
Hotel. The first time I find you—five shots, five heavy slugs right
smack in your stomach. You've got one more chance to kill me.
Make it sure, Jim, or take the dose."

I backed toward the door, opened it, passed out and slammed it
behind me. But it didn't click closed, it jarred open just a part of an
inch. Gentle Jim was talking, and as no one followed me I
stopped, listened. His voice was puzzled.

"A bad actor, Williams—damned bad. Why do you suppose he
put it that way—smack in the stomach? Bluff!"

Armin said: "Race is like I am, Jim—not like you. He never
bluffs."

"Huh!" I heard Jim dialing a telephone number. And a moment
later, "You, Carey? Listen. Call off that blow-off tonight. . . .
Yes, yes, that's what I said. . . . To hell with that. Leave
Williams alone until further orders." He hung up.

I smiled, started to move along. And Jim spoke again. "But
why the stomach?"

I was moving down that narrow hall when I heard Armin's final
words. "Because, Jim," he said slowly, "Race Williams doesn't
like you. And it hurts like hell in the stomach."

# FIVE

# GUN GIRL

■

I felt pretty cocky when I left that office, taking a look at Flat Face who was still listening to the chirp of birds. I had laid down the law—the law of death by violence—the only law Gentle Jim Corrigan, Armin Loring, and their kind knew.

As for Mary Morse, she wouldn't need me now. She had nothing to do but—just not pay.

I didn't feel so good when I popped into my office and saw Sergeant O'Rourke sitting there. He didn't give me his usual good-natured grin, the clap on the back. He came right down to business—and what he said was true.

"Race," he said, "you and I have to have a talk. I'll talk first." He put his face in a notebook he had. "First, the night you called me up and told me you had shot a man to death at Frank Morse's house. That man was Albert Swartz. Oh, I was glad to get Swartz dead and all that. But I came to Frank Morse's home on your call. Swartz was there dead—just as you said. And the D.A. believed your story that Swartz had made an attempt on Frank Morse's life.

But Frank Morse disappeared." He coughed. "So far so good. Your pal, Inspector Nelson, didn't believe that closed the case."

"He wouldn't." I tried to appear indifferent. "He'd like to see me in trouble." And I was thinking that he could see me in plenty if Gentle Jim ever opened his face.

"Well," O'Rourke went on, "that might be it. Did you know when you went to Frank Morse's house in answer to an urgent call that his life was threatened—and I'm quoting what you told me— did you know that Morse had served a term in jail, that his own father kept it secret from everyone, and that he served his term under another name?"

"No." I saw an opening, a chance to get from under. "I didn't know it then. I found it out later. I guess he was being blackmailed by someone."

"You guess. Don't you know?"

I ducked that one good. "You're treading on my ethics now, O'Rourke." I tried to be stiff.

"Ethics." He laughed. "Hell, Race, I'm here as your friend. I hope to leave this office as your friend—not as a police officer doing his duty. Why did Frank Morse disappear?"

That was the opening. I took it—talked fast, talked well. But it was hard to tell if O'Rourke believed me. I said: "I understood Frank Morse disappeared because his past was discovered. Mary Morse didn't know why her grandfather left the business to her instead of his son and her uncle, Frank Morse. It was a great blow to her. She had made this uncle partner in the firm with her stepfather. You know—her mother's second husband. He's general manager and the same as a real father to Mary and—"

"God in Heaven!" said O'Rourke. "You talk like my wife's sister with her relatives. So he left through fear of something coming up in his past or just a feeling that if the truth came out about him it would hurt the jewelry firm of Morse."

I shrugged my shoulders. "He just left."

"Well," O'Rourke said, "from his record under his different aliases that Nelson has been tracing back, he left through fear— and left suddenly. Damn suddenly! Was it Gentle Jim Corrigan who was blackmailing him?"

I jumped inside—not out—my face was steady, but O'Rourke was getting hot. And so was I, but in a different way.

"Why Jim?"

"Why, you ask me. Nelson was on to that for some time. He knew that Frank Morse went to the Royal Hotel and visited Corrigan." O'Rourke leaned toward me. "I'm not Nelson, Race. I'm not trying to trap you. If anything is wrong I'm giving you a chance to get from under. You see, Nelson and I both know you visited Gentle Jim Corrigan today."

I smiled, or rather went through the contortions that were supposed to register a smile. But I thought back to that night when I could have shot Corrigan for kidnapping Mary Morse—and didn't. Not because I coudn't have found a hundred or more excuses for knocking him over, but because of his suggestion that he'd take care of the bodies—especially the body of Frank Morse. Yep, I did it for a client and now—

O'Rourke waited. I held the smile, said: "I'm not fussy, O'Rourke. I've visited guys worse than Jim."

"Not much." O'Rourke shook his head. "I spent a good many years of my life driving Jim Corrigan out of the city. It took the deaths of three men, the indictment of five public officials, and the change of an entire administration before it was done. Now he's back. If you've got anything on him, let me have it before he rolls into dough once again and buys his way even to murder."

I didn't say anything at first—and then just a stupid remark that worried me as soon as I'd made it. I said: "Does Inspector Iron-Man Nelson know as much as you do?"

"He knows more." O'Rourke came to his feet. "So Nelson hasn't been in to see you?" And when I shook my head, "You know, Race, it's not like Nelson not to come around and try to bully you. Oh, I know, you won't take it, but does that help any? The other night in front of your apartment—well, I went with Nelson because I was sure he— Damn it, Race, he thinks you're mixed up in something outside the law. Don't grin. Remember you've been unnecessarily rough with Nelson on some deals. He never forgets—never forgives. He knows as well as I do that you play the game outside the law. He plays inside it. Look out he doesn't drag you from outside in."

"I'll look out," I half gulped. Mary Morse, her stepfather, myself—even the Flame—were all in real trouble if Jim got dragged in for dope and talked. The Flame—well, I wasn't sure about her. She had dropped me the gun, of course, but then Gentle Jim couldn't have known that. Who would he think dropped it to me? But O'Rourke was talking.

"Remember, Race, whether you like Nelson or not he's a determined manhunter—efficient, intelligent. He thinks Gentle Jim can talk something about Frank Morse. And he thinks also that that talk will not be to your advantage."

"Fine." I shrugged my shoulders with an indifference I did not feel. "And just how will Mr. Inspector Nelson get Jim Corrigan to talk? Jim Corrigan who had his own way for so many years; Corrigan, whose murders you know of—yet can't prove."

"Like this." O'Rourke was very serious. "We tried for years to hang well known crimes on Gentle Jim. But he was too well protected. Alibis, witnesses, political friends—it was impossible to touch him. But Nelson's clever. He forgot those crimes and has spent months going into Jim's past—his youth. And I think he's dug up something, something he hopes to have absolute proof of some day soon. Nelson is hot on something and it concerns you. Iron-Man Nelson doesn't laugh often. He's been chuckling, Race. He has a card up his sleeve that I don't know about."

I said as he left: "I've got nothing to worry about for myself. My only interest is the interest of my client."

"Well—if that client should happen to be Mary Morse—you'd better show some interest in her. She looks as if she'd gone through hell, and is making the trip again."

Perhaps O'Rourke was right, I thought, when he closed the door. I'd give the poor kid a buzz, or better still I'd go up and see her. There was her address still on my desk. But it was an hour or so later that I went whistling out of my office and called to Jerry: "The car, James. We are calling on a lady." And when his mouth split open and his eyes brightened, "That's right, Jerry—the girl you rang in on me. Miss Mary Morse."

No bomb exploded in that hallway. No one cut the cable of the elevator, and tommy guns were silent on dear old Broadway. Not even one sinister figure crept up to me, asked me for the time and shot me to death while I was looking for my watch. Gentle Jim was cured. I guess I'm bad medicine and it looked like bad medicine was good medicine this time.

Jerry drove the car and I had him stop it just around the corner from the apartment—I don't often park before doors. I told him to wait, but I knew that he followed me down to the corner. I just grinned and let him slip around it. If I wasn't in love with the girl, Jerry was. If she got in my hair, she certainly didn't get in Jerry's. I saw him sliding down along the buildings of the mostly deserted side street, hoping perhaps he'd get a look at her if I brought her out.

I stopped dead, leaned against the building, pressed back close. A man had come from the apartment house just before me. A man who hurried and was heavy on his feet. He didn't see me. There was no question about who he was; no question either that he was angry—damn near in a rage. Even at that distance I saw the rolling skin of his face was slightly red, lined now with bulging blue veins. He was Gentle Jim Corrigan.

Swinging quickly I jerked a thumb from Jerry to the car, then held my ground until the doorman had opened the door of the long expensive coupe. Gentle Jim slid in behind the wheel. The doorman, waiting for his tip, was lucky he didn't lose his fingers in the door that Jim slammed so viciously.

The car jumped from the curb and Jerry and I acted together. Jerry dashed along the sidewalk, came on the car sideways from the curb to avoid being seen in the mirror above Jim's head. For a moment I didn't think he'd make it, the car gathered speed so quickly. Jerry grabbed the spare tire on the rear. His feet dragged along the pavement, then swung up and he was crouched securely in the very center of that tire.

For a moment the doorman was stunned. Then he grabbed at his whistle, raised it to his mouth just as I gripped his hand, opened his fingers and slipped a ten-dollar bill into his palm.

"All right, General," I said to the buttoned and braided front. "Divorce evidence—forget it. The big bum."

The doorman looked at his fingers that might have been caught in that door, looked also at the ten-spot. Then he simply echoed my words. "The big bum."

The car had turned the corner. Could Jerry stick? I knew that he'd tie himself up into a knot, pull his hair down over his face, and do everything to make the curious think he was just a kid hitching a ride.

I looked at the number of the apartment house and went inside. It was Mary Morse's place, all right, and you can have just one guess who Gentle Jim Corrigan was visiting. And I remembered how his face had been contorted with anger not fear. I gulped. Had something happened to Mary Morse?

I reached for the bell of Mary Morse's apartment, drew back and gripped the doorknob. I had seen the tiny crack in the door where the latch had not caught. Inside the hall was dark, but down at the end of it light crept in from another room.

Not a sound in that apartment after I let the door slip closed and heard the lock click. I didn't want anyone following me in. I didn't call out. If Mary Morse was in that apartment she'd hear me and call. If someone else was there, they'd hear me but wouldn't call out. So why waste breath?

There were curtains at the end of the hall—partly open; then a living room. No place to hide there. I found the kitchen—empty. Then I located the dumbwaiter, opened the door, took a look. Dumbwaiter far below—dull light above. I went back through the living-room, stopped at the bathroom. A quick look there was enough. The shower sheet was folded, no one could get behind that. And then the final room—the bedroom.

Like the old maid, I looked under the bed—still nothing. I walked to the closed closet door. It was locked. There was no key in the lock. Natural that? Well—Mary might have a maid, might have clothes she only wanted to wear herself.

I gave the knob a jerk, listened, even called, "Mary." No answer. I shook my head, gave the door another jerk that nearly tore the latch out, then stepped back and stood by the window.

What would Gentle Jim want with Mary Morse? I went back through the rooms again, took a few seconds' thought. If Gentle Jim had been in that apartment looking for something he was an unusually orderly man. No sign of a struggle; everything just so; nothing disturbed.

I started back toward the hall, stopped. It was a big apartment house. Gentle Jim Corrigan might have been visiting someone else in that place. That would be a coincidence, of course and— Hell, I've always said I don't like coincidences.

I went back to the bedroom. The only place I hadn't looked was in that closet. I walked across the room, gripped the knob of the door and damn near tore it apart on my first yank. I put my foot against the wall and tugged again. Two dollars and ninety cents' worth of damage that time. O.K., I'd pay it myself. I was getting used to paying.

The door was ripe, the lock ready to do its stuff. I gripped the knob with one hand, forced in a nail file with the other, used a snapping jerk. The door opened. I stepped back slightly, then stepped forward again—and caught the body of Mary Morse as it pitched out and into my arms just like a movie corpse.

She was bound and gagged and very white. Not a movement, not a sound as I tore the towel from her face, cut loose the ropes. I thought she was dead as I jumped to my feet, ran to the bathroom, back with water. But the girl wasn't dead. She was alive. The movies had played me false.

I had a bad five minutes, though—maybe more—before she sat up suddenly, cried: "Race, Race—you—I knew you'd come."

I said that was fine, or something about as brilliant, let on I didn't know her arms were about my neck as I carted her into the living room, parked her on the sofa. Then I sat down beside her and started questions.

"Was Corrigan here?"

"That's the fat man—the one—you let go that night?" She drank more water.

"Yes—what did he want? What did he say?"

"He told me that you had been to see him and that if I kept you in the case you would die. He talked as if it were another man collecting this money from me—threatening you—"

"He would," I said. "What else?"

"I was afraid," she said. "Afraid for you, Race. I told him that you wouldn't take my case."

"You did? Did you tell him why?"

"I—" She stopped, red ran into the white of her cheeks. "I told him I didn't have money to pay you." She ran on quickly then. "I think he believed me. He seemed pleased. Said he guessed you just came to see him to protect yourself; that you were ashamed to admit you wouldn't help me after I had saved your life."

"You—saved my life?" I was surprised and showed it.

"Oh, I knew I didn't, but he thought I did. Don't you remember, Race? You couldn't forget. You sat below that trap door, your hands and feet tied, and then you suddenly had a gun—the gun your assistant dropped down to you."

I remembered. It was the Flame who had dropped that gun. And the Flame had told Mary she was my assistant. I nodded and Mary Morse said: "This Corrigan saw a woman's hand and arm push down through that trap. He thought I dropped the gun. He said that I cost the lives of his friends, and he thought I was lying about your refusing to work for me for nothing. And I told him I didn't drop that gun. Why, Race—what's the matter?"

"Go on," I said. I didn't know just what was the matter, but I did know something terrible was.

"His face changed just like yours," Mary Morse said. "He was standing before me so quietly, speaking so softly before that. Then his face changed—you know how it moves. He looked like a beast. His great hairy hands shot out, gripped me by the throat. I tried to scream—couldn't. He forced me to my knees. God!" She turned her head. "I thought he was going to kill me—strangle me to death. He kept demanding, 'Who dropped that gun? Who dropped that gun?'"

"And you told him?"

"I—I—Race, it wasn't fear of death. It wasn't the pain. I'm not a coward—I didn't want to die, but I thought no one would dare harm your—assistant." She kept looking at me when I didn't speak. "Yes, I told him it was your assistant and—"

"And he made you describe her—helped you describe her." For a moment I damn near took the girl by the throat myself—but I didn't. She was so helpless in a thing like this. Guarded and pampered and watched over for years and then this. It was my fault. I should have told her, should have warned her—should have guarded her.

She was crying softly. I stretched out a hand and took hers. "Let me have it, kid," I said. "All of it."

\* \* \*

It was bad, couldn't have been worse—what I got through her tears. Jim had been so surprised that he had blurted out the truth to the girl, at least some of it. And now she was quoting Jim's words between sobs.

"He said, 'It was the Flame pretending to work in with me—in with Frank Morse whom she had Williams murder. By God, she wanted Frank out! She tried to get the name from me today of the lad who ran things. If she got that name, I'd be dead too, and—and—' His face went livid, Race. I never saw anything like it. He acted as if he didn't know I was in the room. He said, 'I'd be dead and One Man Armin would take my place.' Who is the Flame, Race?"

"Never mind." I tried to hurry her. "And after that—"

"After that he struck me. The next thing I remember he was staggering to the bedroom with me. I pleaded with him not to put me in the closet—not to put the towel in my mouth—that I would smother to death. He laughed, Race—a horrible laugh. It was a narrow, shallow closet, and I had just room to stand erect in it. 'No, you won't die,' this Corrigan man said. 'Armin Loring has said you are too valuable to die—and I think he added too beautiful. No, no, I will come back. Someone else will die tonight, though. A woman, too—a lovely woman. Then you and I will go away together, Mary. You will be my alibi if someone should suspect—or you will remain—dead in that closet.' "

I came to my feet, said: "You have a good memory, Mary."

"A good memory! Why every syllable is cut deep in my brain. You didn't see his face, Race—you didn't— It was horrible, fiendish." And coming to her feet and following me across the room, "You're not—not leaving me? He'll be back tonight."

"No, Mary," I told her and meant it. "He won't be back tonight. If he kills the Flame he won't ever be back." And as she gripped at my sleeve, "Remember, if he dies—you are free."

She threw her arms about my neck, clung to me. "It isn't that. It's you, Race. Don't go. He'll kill you! I know it."

"Me?" I took a laugh. "I hope he gets a chance to try it. I hope I get a chance to give him a try." And when she still held on, "The Flame saved my life, Mary. She also saved yours, and by dropping that gun she saved the name of Morse. Now—let me go. She needs me."

"Yes—yes," she said. "You must go." She dropped her hands to her side, looked straight at me, said: "Race, I lied to you in your office today. I want to tell you the truth now."

"Sure—let me have it." I was moving toward the door. "What was the lie?"

She spoke very slowly. "I said that I didn't love you, Race. I—I—" She paused, took my arm, followed me to the door. "That was the lie," she finished, and closing the door behind me put on the chain.

# SIX

# HOUSE OF DEATH

■

Conceited? Sure, I'm conceited. So are you. But whether I liked it or not, I don't know. I couldn't think about it. I could think only of one thing—five things. Yep, I should have buried five slugs of lead in Gentle Jim's middle and not just talked about it. Action is my strength, not conversation.

But I didn't run about the city looking for the Flame. I didn't know where to find her. And Jim would kill her—kill her within the next few hours—just as soon as he could locate her and call her to her death.

I couldn't find the Flame, but I might find out where Gentle Jim was before the Flame met him. And the place I would find out would be at my own apartment. Jerry would telephone me there. It was far too late for me to be at the office.

In my own living-room I paced the floor, killed butt after butt and waited for that damn phone to ring. Oh, I know—I was down on the Flame—she was playing a rotten game, a game I couldn't understand her being mixed up in. Was I in love with her? No—emphatically—no. Did I care if she lived or died? Well—I told myself I must save her because she had saved my life, the life of my client, Mary Morse.

Twice I picked up the phone and asked Central if someone had called. Then I walked some more. The truth is, I wasn't thinking then that the Flame had saved my life, I was simply thinking that hers was in danger. And I could do nothing. I couldn't telephone around trying to locate the Flame for I didn't know where to start—and besides I didn't dare use the phone.

Where was Jerry? Had someone discovered him on the back of that car. A cop at a red light? But if that happened he'd be back by now, and certainly would have telephoned unless—unless— And I knew the answer to that one—unless Gentle Jim had driven out to some lonely road, parked the car and shot Jerry to death.

All right. I'd go out looking for Armin Loring. He'd know where the Flame was. I crossed my arms over my chest, felt of both guns, grabbed up my hat, turned the doorknob—and stopped. The phone was ringing.

A few quick steps and I had the phone. Yep, it was Jerry.

"Listen, boss, it's like this. This fat bird who drove the car didn't go a hell of a way before he stopped at a cigar store across town and went in. I seen then who he was. I dropped off and waited. He must have been particular about what he smoked, for he spent a long time in there and—"

"I'm not interested in what he smokes. Where are you now?"

"I'm in a saloon up in Mount Vernon that some guy's named a 'Tavern.' The beer is lousy and a lad was in the telephone booth so—"

"Cripes, Jerry," I slammed in, "are you a detective or a public lecturer? Did you find out where Corrigan went?"

"Well, no, boss. I had a bad break."

I damned near slammed the phone up—then I said: "All right, Jerry. Let me have it."

"Well"—Jerry didn't like it any more than I did, he was the best shadow in the entire city—"I stuck right on the spare up through Van Cortlandt Park, by Woodlawn Cemetery, straight up the Bronx River Parkway and into Mount Vernon. I had to drop off on a hill. A cop on a motorcycle saw me, followed the car and I—"

"Jerry, Jerry! Did you turn right to go up the hill? Was there an old-fashioned house, a big white one near the top—where the hill curved to the right and—"

"Sure, boss. That's right."

Of course it was right. Van Cortlandt Park. Woodlawn Cemetery. Bronx River Parkway. That was the trip I'd taken before with the Flame; taken to the house in Mount Vernon where so many had died and from which Gentle Jim Corrigan had the bodies removed. It was isolated. No one had heard the shots. There'd been no police investigation because there was no complaint. What better place could Jim use? It wasn't likely that I'd go there again. And it wasn't likely that I'd think Jim would. As far as Corrigan knew there was no reason why I should even suspect he intended to kill the Flame.

"Did anyone know you were on the back of that car?"

Jerry laughed. "Half the city of New York. Everybody but the fat lad who drove. I played the kid, boss. I grinned and stuck my finger to my mouth for silence when other motorists were near. It's a panic what swell sports the citizens think they are. Why, I might have stood up, smacked a gun against that rear window and knocked the fat driver stiffer than a mackerel."

"You might have! You should have." I guess I thought aloud into the phone. "But the motor cop in Mount Vernon. Did he stop the car and tell Corrigan that someone was on the back?"

"Not him. He chased me through a couple of backyards, over a few fences. I damn near doubled back on him and swiped his motorcycle. Tough break, boss."

"Not so tough, Jerry," I said. "Unless you mean tough for Jim Corrigan. You did a swell job. Now get out of Mount Vernon. Come right back to New York. Strangers in that town tonight may get into trouble. If things break right, Gentle Jim Corrigan won't be able to hide undesirable bodies this time. At least one undesirable body."

Downstairs, out on the street, and into my car. This was action—and that's what I like. Was I going to kill Jim Corrigan? That's a tough question to answer. I've never started out to murder, but I could see right then how easily a lad could.

On the death of Jim Corrigan hung a lot of things. Mary Morse would be free of blackmail. For that matter so would I. Perhaps he wasn't actually blackmailing me, but he knew enough to put me on a spot. That he would put himself on one also, was the only thing that protected me. But suppose he got a different spot entirely. He had enemies. Suppose one popped him over—and as he lay dying in the hospital he decided to clear his conscience, or just take it out on me.

Of course it would be better for a lot of people if Jim were dead. Can you think of a worse danger to the city—to the state—to the entire nation, for that matter—than the drug traffic suddenly taking on enormous proportions?

Oh, all right. Maybe I was trying to talk myself into knocking Jim over for the good of my fellow men.

Yes, I know. The right thing to do would be to blow off my face, tell the truth about Gentle Jim Corrigan, let the Flame go to jail, let Mary Morse close up her jewelry business, and go off to prison myself with head held high, knowing that I had served my country. But the truth is, I don't like jails any better than you do. Let the cops run their business. I'll run mine.

More thoughts as I turned up the hill in Mount Vernon. What would Corrigan do? Why did he go to that house in Mount Vernon? And the answers seemed simple. He'd telephone the Flame, get her to come up—and kill her. Three motives for his crime. Hate of the woman who had doubled on him by dropping the gun to me. Vengeance for that act. And most of all—fear of her knowledge, fear of what she might tell me, fear of what she might tell Armin Loring. Fear, perhaps, that she had planned his death that night and would plan it again.

Would she come? Why not? She wouldn't know he suspected. Besides, he could lure her there by telling her he had discovered the name of the big man who controlled the racket.

I backed off the lonely road, turned out my lights and parked my car. Just a jump behind the wheel, a foot on the starter, and I'd be ready for the getaway.

I felt I had plenty of time, and didn't hurry my approach to the house. Jim had arrived there and telephoned the Flame. Jerry had buzzed me—and I had burnt up the road. At last I came close to the house and spotted the light. It was hardly noticeable there on that second floor. I didn't like it. It made me feel funny down in my stomach. For the light was in the very room where I had been tied in a chair, and where the gun had dropped into my hands and I had shot men to death. I listened beneath that window. No sound came—but then it couldn't. Shutters were closed tightly over it.

There is only one way to enter a house—and that is from above, not below. The last time I'd entered this house from below and met a man with a machine gun. I told myself now that the Flame couldn't have gotten there yet. And my cue was to be there in the attic above the room of death, where the open trap door would let me in on the whole show when she did come.

Far above me I made out the oblong of the window that gave ventilation to the attic. No way to reach it—yet the Flame had left that way before; she must have. A ladder was the only answer, and the garage behind would be the place to find it.

Five minutes later I was in and out of that garage and I had the ladder. It didn't seem long enough, but it must be. Or was it? It rested on a slanting bit of roof that led to that attic window. I ran up, found that the copper drain was new and strong, braced my foot a single second, made the sprawl, and gripping the windowsill above, pulled myself up.

Why did I take it all on the run? That's easy. It takes one fourth the time—which means one fourth the chance of someone coming along and plugging you. Besides, slow-moving figures are easy to shoot at—and what's more, easy to hit.

The attic window pushed in easily, and I followed it—stepping softly to the floor. There was light there. It came from the open trap door, and something else came through it—the voice of Gentle Jim Corrigan.

I crossed over, crouched beside that bright oblong hole in the floor through which only a few months before Gentle Jim was going to hang Mary Morse.

And I saw the Flame, understood, too, how she got there so quickly. When Jerry thought Jim Corrigan was taking a long time to pick his smokes, Corrigan was actually telephoning the Flame—telephoning her to come to her death.

# BETTER CORPSES

■

The Flame was leaning against the very couch I had occupied when she dropped the gun into my hands. There was blood on her lips, a welt on her cheek. I couldn't see Gentle Jim, couldn't get in a position to see him yet. I knew from his voice that he faced the girl. I knew it also for another reason. For as I looked down a pat pudgy hand flicked out and tore a gash in her face. She flinched, but stood her ground. I held my gun ready—waited. I was looking from darkness into light. In another moment I might be shooting under the same conditions. If I couldn't see Jim, how could I shoot? Well I had seen the moving hand—the thick wrist. I might see it again or—

But Jim was talking and I like to listen.

"I got it straight from the blue-eyed baby, Mary Morse." Jim's voice was still low, but it wasn't soft any more. There was a hollow sort of hardness in it, and hate. "It's the same as it was that night when you ratted on the boys, ratted on me," he went on. "The trap door is still open—just as it was open then. And the eyes of the dead look down—those you sent to their death when you dropped the gun to Race Williams. You wanted Frank Morse dead. You wanted me dead. You wanted Armin to take my place with the big lad in the racket—the racket you nearly ruined with the death of Frank Morse." He paused. "You shake your head. What was it then? You simply wanted to save Williams' life? Ah, you were working for Race Williams then?"

"You're crazy, Jim," the girl was pleading. "It was Morse I wanted dead. He threatened me. I—I— Don't! Armin will kill you for this."

"He won't kill me if he wasn't in it. He'll thank me. And he'll kill Williams—kill him without wanting a cent. The Flame, eh? The Girl with the Criminal Mind. Do you know what Williams said to me today? He threatened to shoot me five times—five times in the stomach. Did you hear what I said? Five times in the stomach. And that's the way they'll find you—right in the stomach."

I came to my feet and stood on the edge of the lighted pit. It was a chance—a big chance. I'd have to jump down between Jim and the Flame. Jim who must have a gun in his hand, a finger on the trigger. And I'd have to reach the floor before I could shoot with any assurance. I'm damned handy with a gun, but I'm no miracle man. Yet I had to jump and hope to God that the surprise would throw Jim.

Gun in my right hand, I crouched low, got ready to spring, and Jim's hand flicked out again. His voice was husky. "Right in the stomach—and now."

My finger closed on the trigger—my gun roared, and I jumped.

I didn't know when I dropped into space if my single shot hit Jim's hand or not. It should have—would have if I'd watched and waited. And it had. For I was hardly in the air when I heard Jim cry out with pain. Then I struck the floor, raised my gun and hesitated—just a second too long.

Jim had jumped back with the sudden pain, I guess, for his right hand clutched at the fingers of his left, and blood dripped on the floor. That's why I hesitated, because the gun in Jim's right hand was not facing me. Its nose covered the floor. As I came to my feet I got a look at the Flame's face—swollen and bruised. The flesh was torn as if an animal had clawed at it.

Gentle Jim Corrigan's eyes were misty. They rolled and settled on me. Then they grew small, the pupils bright little twin points.

There wasn't terror in his face then—just a sort of confused wonder. He simply stared. His gun stayed pointed at the floor. Blood dripped from his fingers.

"You've got a gun, Jim." I straightened and moved toward him. "Better use it—I'm on the kill. Five times right smack in the stomach. Come on, Jim. Lift it. Take a chance. Remember what Armin said. It hurts like hell in the stomach."

The dazed look went out of his eyes and fear crept in. His right hand moved slightly and his eyes changed again. Cunning showed in them now. He opened his right hand and let the gun drop to the floor.

"We're all mixed up in this thing together, Race." He backed from me, staggering. "I'm not armed now. You can't kill an unarmed man—not a wounded man. Not—not—" And Gentle Jim put his right hand over his eyes, let his knees go and slipped slowly down in a huddle against the wall below the window.

Mad? Of course I was mad. You'd be, too. He wasn't hurt that bad. Gentle Jim Corrigan who had shot plenty of helpless men to death; who would kill me if our positions were reversed. And now he half sat, half lay there, moaning. And he knew that I couldn't shoot a helpless wounded man.

No man had it coming to him more than Jim. He held all our futures in his rotten evil brain. And there he lay and—and— "Can't—can't—the hell I can't!" I guess I must have shouted the words as I crossed the room and stood above him. "Five times, Jim—in the stomach—hurts like hell."

Jim's eyes opened. Fear. Terror. It was all in his eyes now as I slowly—very slowly—tightened my finger upon the trigger of my gun.

Feet beat rapidly across wood. A hand clutched my wrist, raised it. It was the Flame.

"It means more to me to have him dead than it does to you, Race," she said and her voice for a moment was the old voice— not the voice of the woman of the night, but the voice of the young girl O'Rourke had said I loved. Would I have killed Jim? I don't know so you can't know. But the Flame went on talking, holding my wrist, a hand on my shoulder, her swollen face close to mine.

"I can't see you do it, Race. I don't ever want to picture you like that. Maybe—maybe I could do it. Maybe it would seem right if I did it. But you—to kill a helpless man. I know he's a coward. I know he isn't hurt. But it's you—not him. I've always seen you facing guns, standing with your feet apart, drawing and firing in the face of odds—"

She stopped at the crash from below, breaking wood, falling glass.

"The window, Florence." I reached out, tore aside the heavy iron inner shutters that were meant to keep light out and keep sound in. Then I flung up the window, said quickly: "It's only a short drop to the ground—a terrace on this side. Go to it!"

Men were in the house now, feet on the stairs. I stooped quickly, ran careful hands over the whining Jim's person, spotted another gun and came to my feet as the knob turned and a heavy fist beat on the door.

I called out: "Try shaking that door again, fellow, and a bullet will carry splinters from it into your chest."

"It's the law," said a voice I thought I recognized, and then came a voice that I knew was familiar.

"By God, it's you, Race!" That was Sergeant O'Rourke.

Hell! Things were bad—damned bad. The first voice then had been Nelson's. I motioned the Flame toward the window, said: "Get out—the cops."

I saw her turn, throw a leg over the sill. Then I looked down at Gentle Jim. Had they come for him? Did they have something on him, and would he talk—talk to save his own hide? The answer was simple enough. He'd talk all over his face.

Gentle Jim alive and nothing accomplished. Gentle Jim dead—I raised my gun. Yep, the temptation to turn on the heat was strong. I wished Jim had a gun in his hand. I wished—

I dropped my gun to my side. It's the weakness in the best of us, I guess. No, I didn't think of it as murder. I just didn't have the guts to kill a helpless man. If he could only shoot once I'd be glad to take a dose of lead. But he couldn't. I had his guns.

The Flame was back in the room, gripping my wrist again. The wood of the door cracked and groaned as a heavy body swung against it.

I said to the Flame just before I crossed the room to the door: "Jim Corrigan sent for you to come here, tried to blackmail you into working for him. But you're honest now and wouldn't." The

door damn near gave. I flung over my shoulder to the Flame:
"That's your story, so stick to it." And I called just before I spun
the key in the lock: "O.K., O'Rourke."

Then I stepped back and let the cops fall in. O'Rourke was a
stickler for form and a local lieutenant of police and a couple of
harness boys were with Nelson and him.

Iron-Man Nelson nodded to me, crossed to the Flame, jerked up
her head roughly, said: "So—Florence Drummond—the Flame.
Back in business, eh? Ah, and Corrigan—Gentle Jim Corrigan.
The bad boy of Broadway. Had his chance when he slipped out of
the city a few years ago, but came back again. Hurt badly, Jim? I
may have words that will interest you—if you're a sensible man."

I grabbed O'Rourke, said: "How did you guys get here?"

O'Rourke shrugged his shoulders. "Nelson," he said. "I
warned you about him, Race. That's why I stuck close to him.
Somehow he got word that you were going to Mount Vernon, for
we overtook you on the Parkway up above Woodlawn. There,
don't ask me how he knew. Against the law or not against the law, I
think he tapped your phone. We followed you here, but were
delayed in finding a phone and reaching the local police."

My eyes widened. Of course Nelson had tapped in on my talk
with Jerry.

The lieutenant of the local police stood in the doorway looking
important, slightly indignant, and somewhat curious. The two
cops had crowded into the room and edging over stood flat-footed
against the wall, near the outer door.

I gave O'Rourke the spiel about the Flame being blackmailed
and her getting word to me.

O'Rourke cut me short. He was very serious. "I'm thinking of
you, Race," he said. "Do you know what Inspector Nelson is
telling Gentle Jim Corrigan right now? Listen." His hand fell on
my shoulder, his words were rapid, his voice hardly more than a
whisper.

"Nelson doesn't like me because I'm a sergeant and in certain
things give him orders because I work straight from the commissioner. You know and I know and Nelson knows that Gentle Jim
Corrigan is wanted for plenty, but nothing can be proven. Nelson
hates your guts—you hate his. He brought me with him tonight
because I'm your friend. Nelson is a damned clever man. He told
me the details coming up in the car. He wants something on you—

your cracks about him—the time you left him bound and gagged in the coal bin—the laughing-stock you made of him.

"Well, he was after Corrigan, but he tried a new system. He didn't go after Corrigan for any suspected crime. He went into his past, as I told you before. Now I think he has the proof and I think it's murder. And I think he's telling Corrigan now that if Corrigan can hitch you up in anything he'll forget what he found out. Look at Corrigan's face."

I did look, and I guess I went a bit pale myself. Nelson, my worst enemy. And me—the Morse girl—the Flame. That Corrigan had kidnaped the Morse girl and attempted to kill her could not be proven, except by witnesses who had concealed from the state the death by violence of several men I had killed. My God, it was bad! I had really nothing on Jim Corrigan but the dope business—no killing I could prove. Yep, Jim could make it look like we were all hooked up together in the thing. Mary Morse, because she wanted to save her business, allowed her place to be used to receive and conceal narcotics—her stepfather, too. Me—well, I had kept my mouth closed for nine thousand dollars given to me by Mary Morse.

Sure, Jim would talk and go free, or get a suspended sentence. And all because Nelson would keep to himself the thing in Jim's past that, from the fear in Jim's eyes now, must be murder.

And Jim was talking—talking for us all to hear. "Can I talk—talk about Williams and others?" His voice was loud and clear now. "You want to know about men he killed, eh? Well—I can tell you and—"

O'Rourke crossed the room, said to Nelson: "He'd better keep it, Inspector." And when Nelson grinned evilly at him, for he knew O'Rourke was my friend, "If he talks here the local police may—"

"Correct," Nelson snapped in on him. He didn't want things going out of his hands. As for me, I said with an easy air—or what I hoped sounded like an easy air: "The man's half delirious with pain. What about lads I killed? There's no secret in that. You've read all about it in the papers."

I slid quickly in front of Gentle Jim Corrigan, leaned down over him, whispered viciously like any ten-cent villain. "I know about that old-time murder also," I lied. "Everything about it. If Nelson keeps his face closed I won't, and O'Rourke who just told me won't."

Corrigan opened his mouth once to speak, but said nothing. His eyes widened, brightened. His right hand shot over his knees, his knees closed quickly. Nelson grabbed me by the shoulder and swung me around.

"What did you say to him? And what's this talk about his being delirious?" He was rough, too—damned rough.

I don't like coppers manhandling me as a rule. But this time I rather liked it. It took Nelson's attention from Gentle Jim—the attention of the others from Jim too. For I cracked up my left arm and knocked Nelson's hand from my shoulder.

I said: "Just because a punk hood squawks he knows things about me means nothing. You make your pinch and make your charge. Everybody knows you dislike me—hate my guts. So you'd better go easy. That yellow-livered rat is taking advantage of you. Besides, there're guys in that other room, guys that got away by now."

I guess everybody moved at once. Except the lieutenant in the doorway. He sent his men to the other door at which I pointed, but stood watching me as I faced him.

I heard O'Rourke say something about Jim Corrigan—and Nelson answered that he had searched him thoroughly. I was sideways to Jim—and nothing happened. So I took the chance. I turned my back directly on Gentle Jim and walked toward the local lieutenant, spread my shoulder out too, so I would be between him and Jim Corrigan. My hands were hanging at my sides. I believe it was one of the most dangerous moments of my life. I was inviting death.

And it happened.

Jim Corrigan's voice rang out loud and clear. "Reach for the ceiling, gentlemen. As for you, Williams—"

My right hand shot beneath my left armpit as I started to turn. A gun roared. Lead pounded into my back—high up near the shoulder. Did it floor me? It did not. It helped swing me. Swing me just as Jim closed a finger again and laid a hunk of lead in my left side—close to my heart.

Close to, but not quite in my heart. At least I don't think so, for I wasn't dead. I was staggering though, going back when my finger closed. I was still going back when the hole appeared in the center of Jim's forehead, and I heard a voice saying: "Two shots, Jim. You had two free shots. No man could ask for more than that." The voice was mine.

Then I leaned against the wall and saw the huge body sink slowly, hang so with knees bent, then fold up like an accordion and finally stretch itself out on the floor.

Was he dead? He was so cold you could go ice skating on his chest.

The Flame stood in the corner. Nelson had turned and was looking questioningly at me—at Jim, the dead Jim. O'Rourke had a gun in his hand. The two harness bulls stood as they had been when the first shot rang out, as if a moving picture had suddenly turned to a still. The lieutenant in the doorway had my arm—half supporting me.

Inspector Iron-Man Nelson crossed the room quickly, knelt beside Gentle Jim Corrigan. Nelson said, and his voice sounded down in his stomach: "He's dead—he's dead." And wrenching the gun from Jim's lifeless fingers and coming to his feet with it, "I searched him. Now where did he get this rod. A forty-four revolver—not many of them in use today. It's—it's— By God, it's your gun, Race Williams!" And he crossed the room, tore open my coat. Both my holsters were empty. I had only one gun in one hand.

I tried to stay on my feet. I wasn't dying or anything like that— not me. It didn't pain either. I just felt lousy. But I got out the words: "My gun—my gun! It can't be. Damn it, Jim must have been clever—must have reached up and snatched it from my shoulder harness. Or maybe it fell out. Imagine that happening to me."

"Yeah, imagine it!" Nelson was in a rage. "By God, Race, you gave it to him. It—it was murder."

I looked toward O'Rourke for help, but he didn't need to give me any. It was the Mount Vernon lieutenant of police. He left me there against the wall, stepped before me, pushed Nelson. Yep, he actually pushed his fist against Nelson's chest.

"You're out of your head, Inspector," he said and his voice rang. "And you can't bring any of your personal likes or dislikes up into this city with you. By God, you can't! I never saw such a piece of heroism, downright courage—and fine shooting. We have respect for men like that in this town whether they are paid by the city or not."

Things were going funny on me, but I liked it. I grinned at Nelson. Maybe I did let that gun drop on Jim's knees. I'm often careless with firearms. But no one could call it murder. Jim had his chance—two chances for that matter. No, it was more like attempted suicide on my part. But I had told Jim he might make one more attempt on my life. Told him that he mustn't fail or else— It was just that the "or else" had happened to him.

Any way you look at it, Mary Morse was free. The Flame was free—and I was free. The only trouble with the whole business— everything was free. But Jim was dead and I still retained my amateur standing.

The lieutenant was still talking. He said: "I have heard of Gentle Jim Corrigan and the crimes that he has committed and the corruptions which he has practiced at will in the city of New York. And I have heard of Race Williams and the things he has done to eliminate crime. I am glad that he is alive and that Corrigan is dead." He turned to a cop. "Get the ambulance, George. Here is a man that our city is proud to take care of. We don't want Corrigan or his kind here. We have a welcome for the man who drives them out even if it is by death."

I was out and I wasn't out. The Flame had reached me now, her arm under mine. The lieutenant turned, said to me: "You will be well cared for, Race Williams. Two shots at you and from that short distance! I saw it all. Why, Corrigan's face went white, his eyes popped when you swung and faced him. There was terror in his face and—and by God, after his bullet sent you staggering back you shot him. Shot him just once—straight between the eyes!"

I sank then, but just before I passed out of the picture I got my speech in. "Thank you, Lieutenant," I said. "When better corpses are made, Race Williams will make them."

# JUST ANOTHER STIFF

■

*Dope! Rivers of it, to flood the nation! That was the tide of evil Race Williams had to stem in his final battle for Mary Morse and the Flame. He hadn't made a thin dime out of the fight to date either, so it looked like a sweet set-up for the other side. The only thing those wise babies forgot was that easy-to-dumbfound dick's knack for blasting things into shape with lead, and cashing in at the last minute on the corpse-total.*

# ONE

# A CORPSE ON ME

■

The door of my private office crashed back, and the man hurled himself in. Jerry, my assistant, was following him, grabbing at his right arm. Then followed the prettiest bit of gun-work you'd want to look at.

Both the man's hands moved at once; both of them held guns. The left one was trained on me. The right one crashed with a thud against bone, and I saw the blood on Jerry's forehead start to trickle down before he sank to the floor and lay quietly there. My visitor's foot moved too, and the door was kicked closed.

Some entrance!

I was caught with my coat off—and that's no figure of speech. It was warm. My shoulder holster was sporting a gun, but it was over on the bookcase. A bad set-up for a guy who fancies himself with heavy hardware and should be ready day and night? I don't know. I had a gun fastened beneath my desk that was handy enough. Well, nearly enough.

But I was getting a good look at this smart duck. He was high class on the outside—that is if expensive scenery makes for high class. Spats, a ninety-buck suit, a twelve-dollar hat. Things had happened to his face. Someone must have taken a sledgehammer and knocked his nose flat into the middle of it.

My hands went up and he spoke. "You don't have to play any Hold-Up-Your-Hands game with me, Race Williams. If you have any wish to use a gun, why go ahead and use it. How's that?"

I nodded and said that was fine. I wondered what he'd do if I slipped one hand under the desk, let my gun drop into it. Then I wondered what I'd do. I'd have to raise my hand to shoot; he only had to press a finger on a trigger—either trigger. So I waited—and lived on.

"So you're Williams. The wise dick, Race Williams—smartest gunman in the racket. You didn't think a guy could come from across the pond and put the finger on you—lay you right on the spot."

"Across the Atlantic?" I tried.

He shook his head. "The Orient. Don't know my face, eh?"

"Well—" I looked at that thick-lipped, flattened puss of his and said: "Maybe I knew it before you had it renovated."

He didn't get that last crack, and maybe it was just as well. He didn't look like a guy who'd take a joke, and I was in a pretty position to take a face full of forty-fives.

There was my own forty-four sprung nicely beneath my desk. Just an outward thrust, an upward jerk, and the pressure of a finger. I've done it before and gotten away with it, and I'd have done it then. But this guy could do things with guns and the best I could hope for was a double death. Besides he looked like a man who wanted to talk. And if he wanted to talk, I wanted to listen; he wouldn't be the first lad who'd talked himself to death.

"Brother," he said, "you've got a chance to live if you do exactly what I tell you. Don't go around with the wrong people. You understand that?"

"Sure"—I looked straight into his eyes—"sure, I understand that. What's the show?"

"The show is dope. Millions of dollars' worth of narcotics coming into the country through Morse and Lee, Fifth Avenue jewelers. Coming in easily until you killed Frank Morse, saved Conklyn Lee's life after he had discovered the racket Frank Morse was running. Then you even wised up the real owner of the firm—

the girl, Mary Morse—and for the time being put the easy money out of business."

"Anything else I did you didn't like?"

"Yes," he said. "The killing of Gentle Jim Corrigan, the man who started to take Frank Morse's place—that's why I came."

"You were a long time coming." I stopped and looked toward Jerry. "How about putting the boy on the couch." And when he only grinned, "He may come to and bother you."

He laughed—a very assured laugh. "He won't come to for a bit, and if he does, he won't bother me." For a fraction of a second his head jerked toward Jerry, his eyes rolled. And I took the chance. My right arm shot slightly forward, my fingers touched metal, and a forty-four dropped into my hand.

Did he see me? I knew that he didn't, for his guns never changed— nor did either of his fingers tighten. He went on talking.

"Certainly, we were a long time coming. A long time figuring out the set-up, and making new plans. You see, we figured that after the first shooting you would be out of the case, because Mary Morse didn't have any money—and wouldn't have until she was twenty-one. So she couldn't hire you. But somehow you fell for her blue eyes, and took a hand in things. And now—"

He went for his inner jacket pocket. He simply crossed his left arm, tucked the gun under his right armpit—never took his right-hand gun off me—and pulled out a long folded piece of paper. He tossed it on the desk before me. I had to move my gun into my left hand as I leaned forward to reach it. I didn't dare come up shooting then, for he was leaning far over the desk.

"Look that over," he said.

He waited while I read it. It was hot stuff—a written statement of everything that had taken place in the dope-smuggling game. My protection of Mary Morse; her own knowledge of what was going on; the fact that her stepfather, Conklyn Lee, also knew; and that I, too, had kept such information from the government. It was all there right up to the shooting of Frank Morse. It looked like a confession that awaited only my signature.

Where did he get his information? Mary Morse wouldn't talk and ruin the Morse business, to say nothing of being accused of helping her uncle. Conklyn Lee wouldn't tell for the same reason. Then it must be—

"Where did you get this information?" I asked Flat-Face.

From his indifference, I knew I was never supposed to live to repeat his answer. He said simply, and without hesitation: "The little lady known as the Flame supplied the information. But take a sheet of paper, copy that document there in your own handwriting. That will assure us that in the future, you'll stay out of this case— stay away from Mary Morse."

It wasn't the time to laugh, so I didn't. Up to date, the Morse case had not only paid me nothing, but had actually been a loss. I had thought it was over. Oh, she had buzzed me a few times on the phone, tried to see me, and then—like that—a dead silence. Which suited me, I guess.

I looked at Flat-Face's gun, thought, "Now is the time for it," pulled up my right hand and started to reach for the pen. The left with the gun in it was ready to follow, when he leaned far forward and killed that motion. "Get paper! What's the matter with your left hand? Are you a cripple?"

I dropped my gun onto my knees, and brought up my left hand. And I was right. If black had showed against the white of my hand I would have been dead, for his eyes were glued on that left.

For a moment I was glad I hadn't chanced death—I mean chanced his death, for mine would have been sure. Then I wasn't so glad. I was beginning to copy the paper. Hell, I know it's the proper thing for a real hero to throw out his chest, tell the guy that the sweet child, Mary Morse, came first and die like a man. But the hard thing to do is live like a man—if you're in a position like I was. I wanted to see a turn of his head, a second's lowering of that gun—and I wouldn't bore him with any more conversation. But I guess the main reason I was exercising my penmanship was because I was simply writing, *Now is the time for all good men to come to the aid of the party.*

After watching my moving fingers a while, he said: "You're making good time, Williams. Turn the paper around so I can see what you wrote."

I breathed easier. This was the break. He'd have to look down at that paper, and when he did— Simple? Sure. It's just playing a waiting game, having a bit of patience. I swung the paper around, slid my left hand back to the edge of the desk.

"There you are. Just what you—"

His eyes never lowered. They stayed right on my hands. He said simply: "Put both your hands in the air—both of them."

I did, and he looked down at the paper—just a quick glance. Then his right hand moved with incredible speed. I felt more than saw that the gun turned in his hand as he gun-whipped me. Sure— he just tore a thin line down the side of my face, dug backwards, and gouged out a hunk of flesh almost beneath my ear. Mad? Of course I was. This lad's technique was perfect.

His voice never raised as he said simply: "Take another sheet of paper and try again." And when both my hands were once more on that desk, and a fresh sheet ready, "Listen, Williams, the cops know I'm in town. They're looking for me. You write it and sign it and I'll pass down the back stairs and be safely hidden away. They can't possibly suspect I'm here at your office. Don't write it—and I'll blast your head off or maybe simply cut your throat."

He parked a gun then; his left hand shot beneath his jacket and out again. Silver streaked in the light—and there was a long-bladed knife sticking in my desk.

He said: "That might as well have been in your chest—or in your throat!" And his crooked mouth twisting, "Though I like cutting throats from behind—it isn't such a mess. I mean for the cutter."

Now, as I wrote, he leaned forward and picked up the knife. He was trying to see, but no matter how he bent, the writing was still upside down. So he pulled a fast one.

"Keep on writing word for word, Williams. A mistake, and I'll let the whole thing go. To be perfectly honest with you, I didn't like the looks of a couple of men outside your office building. They looked copper, and they smelled copper." He was moving around the desk as he spoke.

"Look here"—I kept my right hand on the desk, but let my left slide naturally off it and onto my knees as I turned and faced him— "how do I know that you won't kill me after it's written?"

"You don't know—only that I tell you and that my gun would make too much noise."

The knife! I thought of the knife then, and I knew what he intended to do, just as if he had told me himself. Once the final word was written, once my signature was there, it would be a single stretch of his arm behind my back, a sharp twist of his wrist and he'd cut my throat.

Then what? Why, they'd have that girl, Mary Morse, under their thumbs, have her money, the cellar of her great store to keep their dope in. The famous house of Morse and Lee that was beyond suspicion would become a huge central receiving and distributing point for the narcotics trade. And I signed that paper—with all the threats, intimidation, blackmail and extortion that were contained therein.

The killer—with the knife in his left hand, the gun in his right— was coming around the end of the desk. He was going to pass almost in full view of me. Would he see the gun? Would he see it before his body was directly in the line of my fire? Of course he would. I wouldn't dare move the hand that held it; I wouldn't dare move the arm or the shoulder that controlled that hand. Suddenly he moved forward, was directly before my gun—and he saw it.

Sure he saw the gun! He couldn't help see it. It was spewing orange-blue flame as soon as enough of his body was visible. It wasn't a nice shot; it wasn't a clean shot. But then it wasn't meant to be. It spun him as if he were a top. His own gun exploded, tore into the bookcase behind me. For a moment he swung back toward me and his gun was stretched out in his hand. And that was all of that. I squeezed lead once more and made a hole where his flat nose had been.

He was further away this time, but he was dead—dead right there on his feet. I saw it in his eyes, saw the light go out of them as if you'd switched off an electric blub, just before he collapsed there between the desk and the window.

A voice said: "Nice work, boss. You don't often let me in on the kill." It was Jerry, half up on one knee.

"*He* let you in on it and—" I paused, picked up the original paper and the copy I was making and started to tear them up. A door slammed. Heavy feet beat across the outer office and once again my private door burst open. I slipped my gun into my pocket as a face appeared in the doorway—the hard, weather-beaten face of my worst enemy on the police force. Yep, you guessed his name. It was Iron-Man Nelson. All the things I had pulled on him and taken my laugh at, at the time, didn't seem quite so funny to me now with those papers clutched in my left hand.

Inspector Nelson saw Jerry who was getting slowly to his feet; saw the deep cut in his forehead, the blood beginning to dry on

Jerry's face, and for the first time in his life Nelson was solicitous. Evidently he thought I had been knocking Jerry around and he was going to make the most of it. Apparently Iron-Man Nelson hadn't heard those shots. He'd come in for some other reason. Of course, he wasn't in a position to see the body of Flat-Face.

"What did this man, Williams, do to you, son?" Iron-Man had an arm around Jerry, and the "son" sounded as though a couple of other words were missing. "He smacked you with a gun, eh? Well that's a pastime of Williams'."

"Mr. Williams was showing me a new gun-twist," Jerry lied easily, though I knew his head was near busting as he bathed it at the water-cooler. Before Nelson could blow up he added: "Then I tried it on him and—"

I dropped the papers into the ashtray, lit a butt, and tossed the match in after them.

Nelson's eyes were wide as he looked at my face, the thin line of red down it, the dig behind the ear, for I turned my head so he could see it. Then he saw the sudden blaze in the tray, said: "What the hell! Want to burn up the place?" He stepped forward and reached for that ashtray, but I was before him and had awkwardly knocked it from the desk.

Jerry dropped to his knees, was picking up the white sheets, grinding in the partly burnt edges—and I had a real break. Sergeant O'Rourke stamped into the room, stood there in the doorway with a couple of city dicks behind him as Jerry walked by him with the papers. Good old Jerry! Walking out with a bit of writing that would have given Nelson the happiest moment of his life, and O'Rourke—well, friend or no friend, I'd have been in plenty of trouble. But the cops were ready for an argument between themselves. Nelson always was. O'Rourke gave him the chance this time.

"Now look here, Nelson"—O'Rourke worked close to the commissioner and didn't have to take guff from any cop, not even an inspector—"I tipped you to this lay, and you go in the back way alone."

"What lay?" I cut in as Nelson said something about O'Rourke being too friendly with a "private dick" and making those two words stink to high heaven.

O'Rourke began to explain then. "Why—Spats Willis. Wanted here ten or twelve years ago for murder, went to the Orient—

Singapore last time we heard of him—and mixed up in some dope-smuggling. We think he's Raftner's man—Nick Raftner."

"Who's Raftner?" I wanted to know.

"Who knows?" said Nelson. "No one has ever seen him. However, he's real. Sits pretty in the Malay States and has a big idea about filling America with dope."

"Yeah?" I said. "But why would he come here? I mean this other bloke—Spats Willis."

"We don't know, Race." And when I just stared at him, "It's not a hunch or anything like that. We had a call Willis would be found here at your office, and to come up right after one o'clock. No suspicion of you—nothing like that, Race."

"No? That's just O'Rourke's opinion," Nelson sneered. "We got a good description of Willis. He was seen entering this building, and it's fairly well established that he came to this floor. He's got a face that isn't hard to place."

I shrugged. "Who told you he was here?"

"We don't know. You didn't anyway!" Nelson blasted. "What's that got to do with it? We got to search the place—maybe take you down for a little questioning."

I looked at O'Rourke. He looked back very soberly, said: "He's wanted for at least one murder we can lay on him. It's serious business, Race, if you let him come and go."

"What would you do with him?"

Though I spoke to O'Rourke I got the answer where I hoped I'd get it—from Nelson. "We'd fry him. Or better still lay a couple of slugs in his head."

"Oh, you want him dead." I tried putting on a child-like wonder which I knew always infuriated Nelson.

"Of course, we want him dead. If Raftner's money's behind him it'll take a couple of years to get a conviction—if we get one even then. Now, Race, what do you know about—"

He stopped, followed the direction of my jerking thumb—first with his eyes, then with his head, and finally with his moving feet. His bellow of surprise as he spotted the body was pleasant to my ears. Then O'Rourke was on his knees beside him and I saw them swing the dead head around.

"It's Spats Willis all right. I remember him years back," Nelson said, and I liked the awe in his voice. "And what a mess!"

"That's right—a mess," I told him. "Get him out of here. He's all yours."

Nelson came to his feet, turned to me viciously. He accused me of everything right up to the murder of a poor unfortunate traveler named Willis, who had returned to his native shores after these many years. Maybe those weren't his exact words, but they're close enough. And they made me mad; damned good and mad. I let him have it.

"By God!" I said. "You pound in here hollering for Willis's death. And me—am I paid to sit around and wait until someone you happen to approve of knocks over your wanted man? Then you give me abuse, accuse me of about everything in the calendar." And going to the cooler and taking a drink, "Look at my rug! That's the thanks I get for spilling a public enemy's guts all over it. He's yours. Take him out of here. I'll complain to the commissioner that you got word I was to be shot to death and waited until you thought the job was done."

Nelson started toward me as I turned to leave the room, but O'Rourke reached me first. "All right. All right. How did it happen, Race?"

"How did it happen!" I flared back. "Why, he just talked himself to death." And I banged on into the outer office.

Mad? Well, not now. I went to the rear of the room and laughed for a good five minutes.

O'Rourke came out and stood looking at me. He shook his head. "I can't understand you, Race. I've been twenty-five years in this business—and I have never yet been able to see anything funny in death."

"Funny!" I told him. "Of course, it's funny. Damn it, O'Rourke! If you couldn't get an occasional laugh in this business, you'd go nuts. But I've got to go out and eat. Haven't had lunch yet."

I swung back into my private office, hopped over the late lamented Mr. Spats Willis, swung both my shoulder holsters into place and put on my jacket.

"Don't scowl like that, Nelson." I winked at the sour-pussed inspector. "They don't come much deader than that one. I'll expect the city to pay for the rug at the cleaner's. There, there—not a word of thanks. That corpse is on me."

# T W O

# TABLE FOR THREE

■

I hit my favorite restaurant, ready for a thick steak, and I saw the girl; the woman, if you like—for the Flame could be either one—a sort of flesh-and-blood Doctor Jekyll and Miss Hyde, if you get what I mean. There were times when she was young and lovely, the sparkle of youth in her eyes—and times, too, when she was hard, cold, cruel, a woman of the night. Beautiful—sure, but in a sinister way.

I couldn't tell which she was now, as I walked down the room. She was tapping a cigarette on the table, looking toward the door, and suddenly she saw me. Her eyes brightened, her head moved slightly, and I went toward her. What a coincidence finding the Flame occupying my special booth in my special restaurant? Well, if you're young and in love you might look on it like that. But the Flame has no coincidence in her life—and I have none in mine. I knew she was waiting for me.

She didn't show surprise and neither did I as she started to move over to make room for me beside her. My surprise came when I saw that the seat across from her was occupied. Long, slender,

224

neatly manicured fingers lay upon the whiteness of the tablecloth. Sleek black hair, soft oily skin—I don't have to tell you. It was Armin Loring—One Man Armin—the most dangerous man in the city of New York.

The Flame moved further into the booth. Armin just looked at me, smiled pleasantly enough when I sat down beside her.

I didn't let the Flame talk first. I said: "I suppose you wish me to sit down—right?"

"Right. Would you believe me, Race, if I said I'm surprised to see you—but delighted?"

"Maybe you are surprised to see me—alive, but I rather doubt the delighted part."

"And you may well doubt that, Williams." Armin Loring showed more of his even, white teeth, watched the Flame open her purse. He took the five hundred-dollar bills she stretched across to him. "Will we tell Williams about the bet, honey?" And when the Flame stiffened, "It's too good to keep. You see, Race, Florence bet me those five centuries that I'd never see you alive again." And twisting up his lips as he pocketed the money, "Even money, too, Race. You must be slipping."

Graceful shoulders went up and down. The Flame turned, blew a smoke ring at me, said: "You always did let me down, Race. Seriously, Armin, you're not really jealous because Race was once madly in love with me?" She looked at me steadily. "Sometimes I think he still is."

"That's the way it goes." Armin beckoned a waiter and I ordered. And then, "They say that once a man loves the Flame he always loves her."

I said: "And they say also that to love the Flame is to die."

"Yet," said Armin, "you and I are both alive. There, Williams, you can be the first to congratulate me. Florence and I have given up the racket, discovered that underneath it all we are both very conventional people. We are going to be married—and sail away on our honeymoon."

"Not to Singapore by any chance?" I asked.

Armin Loring jerked erect. I had hit him a wallop all right. He showed it and knew that he showed it. "What do you mean by that?" he demanded.

"Well"—I stuck my tongue in my cheek—"I had a visitor from Singapore today. He said you sent him."

* * *

Armin Loring looked straight at me. He seemed puzzled. I knew he spoke the truth when he said: "I never sent anyone." He looked at the Flame; back to me.

"Race"—he spoke very slowly, very distinctly, and without any dramatics—"you have never really crossed me yet." He scowled. "Except for that one time when you took Miss Morse from the Royal Hotel. Forget me—forget Singapore. I haven't got an enemy in the world—a dangerous enemy—that is, a live one. Don't make me think I have." He leaned forward now and I believe he meant every word he said. "You've walked up and down the Avenue for years, Race. Lads fear you because they fear death. They recognize you as one of their own kind. A man who has no interest in courts of justice, no interest in stupidly gathering evidence that won't stand up. You're a killer, just like—"

"Just like you're a killer," I finished for him.

"No." He was deadly serious. "Speed with a gun like speed in everything else is only relative. You don't know it, don't believe it, but I can draw and shoot in less than one second."

"Yeah?" I said. "Right now."

"Right now—one second. What do you say to that?"

I said: "Armin, you'd be exactly one-half second too late."

And Armin did it. I had heard about his speed and was interested to see it operate. Now I did. He just swept the handkerchief from his outside jacket pocket and I saw plainly the nose of the thin gun beneath it.

"By God!" Armin said, and I didn't like his eyes. "I've a good mind to do it here." And his eyes shifting up and down the room, "I will, too—unless you give me your word that you will never mention my name and Singapore. Poor sap, you never even raised a hand to save yourself."

I said easily: "Be your age, Armin. You don't think I go around letting guys pull guns on me—at least twice in one day. Put that handkerchief away or comes a sudden pain in your stomach."

His eyes narrowed. His thin lips tightened. I saw the Flame half rise in the booth.

I said: "There's a gun covering you under the table, Armin." And when doubt came into his eyes I added lightly: "A nice conventional guy like you wouldn't want a lot of strangers to know what you had for lunch."

"I don't believe you." Those were Armin Loring's words, but he did believe me just the same. And he was right. Why, a gun fell into my hand almost the moment I sat down.

I shrugged my shoulders and told him what was on my chest. "We sat like this once before, Armin. Remember? I do. Only that time both our guns were under the table. But have it your own way. Press the trigger of that toy gun—" I leaned forward suddenly, spat the words at him. "Park that gun, Armin; park it damn quick or I'll blow hell out of your insides!"

Armin's eyes brightened to twin beads of fire. For a moment I thought he was going to do his stuff and my finger tightened on the trigger. I could feel the hammer of my forty-four slipping back.

Armin smiled suddenly and said his well-known line. "No fooling, Race?"

"No fooling, Armin," I answered.

Three things happened. His handkerchief twirled back into his pocket. My gun slipped back into its holster. The waiter brought my steak. And—I'm not sure—but I think the Flame opened the bag that lay on her lap and slipped something stubby and black into it. Was I ungentlemanly enough to think it was a gun? Yeah, I guess I was. But the steak was good and I was hungry.

There were several minutes of silence then—that is, conversational silence. I like my steak and I don't care who hears it.

After a while the Flame said: "You run along if you want, Armin. I'd like to talk to Race—of our old love." And damn it, she put a hand across the table and patted the back of his.

He took a dumb look and pulled his hand away—but he liked it. He said: "All right, kitten. Just a word with Race first." And to me, "Now about this Mary Morse case and the unfortunate fact that unscrupulous people have been using her jewelry firm for dishonest acts." He grinned at his own cleverness in the wording. "You haven't made a nickel on the deal. I have been offered a big fee—a very big fee to keep you out of this case. Because of your old friendship with Florence, my future wife, and my dislike for trouble just before our honeymoon, I'll give you half of this fee to stay out of your own accord."

"The laugh's on you, Armin," I told him. "I am out of it."

"Certain?"

"As certain as a man can be." I shrugged. "I have no intention of seeing Mary Morse."

"That's a promise—your word?"

"That's nothing to you," I told him flat. "It simply means that I don't want to see her—don't want to go to her if she sends for me. But I would go in a minute if I felt like it. Threat from you—or no threat from you."

The Flame clapped her hands. "Waving the old flag, eh Race? You have to understand him, Armin. He's free, white and twenty-one, and he just won't be threatened."

"Threatened, hell!" Armin drew a small case from his pocket, flipped it open, tossed a cigarette into his mouth and popped a match to the end of it. "This, Race, is a plain statement of the facts. You never bluff; I never bluff. If you're seen with Mary Morse again—so much as talk to her in a hotel or restaurant—you'll be shot to death at once."

"By you?" was all I asked.

"By me the second time."

"You expect to kill me twice, eh?"

"I expect to kill you if the first attempt fails, though I can hardly see failure." He was tossing his napkin on the table now. "This man I have in mind would shoot you even in a crowded restaurant."

"Restaurant, eh?" I rubbed my chin as he pulled that "restaurant" line the second time, watched him start to slide out of the booth. I looked at the check for the meal beside his plate, said quickly: "It's you who are going to marry the girl, Armin. I'm damned if I'll pay the check."

It was strange to see the sudden color come into Armin's face, but he fished out a five-spot and tossed it on the table. I turned over the check, took a squint and nodded, said: "The Flame must be trying to reduce. On your way. Nothing else I should know, is there?"

Armin didn't like my light banter. His teeth showed when he leaned over and spoke to me, but there was nothing of a smile on his face—just the baring of his teeth which was anything but pleasant. "I'm going to pay you a great compliment, Race," he said. "I'm going to steal your line. If you so much as see or speak to Mary Morse again and live—then I'll shoot you to death the first time we meet."

I shook my head, smiled and filled in the missing words for him. He had left my favorite line out. "Any place, any time—at Forty-second Street and Broadway during the lunch hour. That's what you mean, isn't it, Armin?"

"That," said Armin, "is exactly what I mean." Without another word he turned and left the table. I watched him walk slowly down the length of the room toward the door. Then I turned to the Flame.

For a long moment I looked steadily into those brown eyes. They looked steadily back, didn't even blink slightly. I tried: "Too bad about the bet you lost, Florence. So you sent Spats Willis to kill me."

"To kill the man I used to love—do love?" She leaned forward.

"You bet Armin he'd never see me alive again. And Willis was fast with a gun."

"So"—arched eyebrows went up—"you admit that others can be fast with a gun. Willis— What happened to him?"

"In this hot weather they'll bury him quickly."

Red ran in and out of her face; her right hand tapped the table. If that was emotion, it was all she showed. She said simply: "It's part of the price men must pay who want to make money—a lot of money."

"And women, too," I told her.

"Mary Morse, for instance." She pretended to miss my crack. And then, "How do you know I sent him—to kill you?" And after a pause, "Maybe I sent him for you to kill."

"But why—why?" I'd had that thought, too. But I was never sure that it was an honest thought or a wish—something I wanted to believe, yet really didn't.

"I saved your life once, and you believed that I did it because I was more anxious for someone else to die. Perhaps I sent Willis to you that you might kill him."

"Yeah." I looked at her. "You've lined up with a dope outfit so you can set guys up for me to shoot down. Let me tell you something. This Willis boy very nearly got your intentions mixed and gave me the dose. After this when you set a lad up for me, give me a ring he's coming. Hell, Florence, you wouldn't expect a child to believe that!"

"I'm not expecting you to believe anything; certainly not as much as a child. A child has a clean, honest mind." And suddenly sticking out a hand and gripping mine tightly; gripping it while her fingers against my skin went colder and colder, "Let's chuck it all, Race. Let's go away together—"

I jerked my hand away, put hard eyes on her—then lowered them slightly. Damn it, the woman was a marvel of—well, maybe deceit. I could have sworn her eyes were wet and warm. But I said: "I thought you were going to marry Armin Loring."

She shrugged. "You told me once that I would make a charming widow."

I let that slide and spoke what was on my mind. "They wish to keep me away from Mary Morse. Why? She doesn't want me, doesn't need me now."

"She needs you more than she ever needed you. Armin would like an excuse to kill you. Someone watches over Mary day and night. Someone who came from the Orient. Someone who could shoot you to death right in a public place and wield enough influence—what with your reputation for shooting—to escape punishment. If you want to live don't go near Mary Morse."

I didn't get it, but I drew in my knees and let the Flame slide from the booth. Certainly, I admitted, she was a gorgeous woman, but if I were Armin, I'd have her searched upon her wedding night.

She turned her lithe, feline body there at the end of the booth and said: "There are a million tiny cells in every human brain, Race. Try using just one of them. Remember, the police arrived in time. They might have been late."

That they had been late was my only thought as she swung down the room.

A minute later I picked up my check and saw the small envelope under it. I drew out of the oblong bit of cardboard about as big as a visiting-card. It was from the Flame, of course. But it wasn't. It read simply—

Race—Race, don't come to the Green Room. Don't come to my table. It means your death. Don't come no matter what I say—how I plead. It's a trap to kill you—I won't mean it.

Mary Morse.

# THREE

# CHAMPAGNE SUPPER

■

I stalled around a bit before going back to my office. When I got there the body was gone. O'Rourke wanted to hear my story again. Nelson wanted to hear it again. The D.A. wanted to hear it and so did the commissioner of police. Also a dozen or more reporters wanted to hear it.

By that time I didn't want to hear it and had boiled it down to a few words. I simply said: "His name, the cops say, was Willis. Why he tried to kill me I don't know. He fired and missed. I fired and didn't miss." After all, there wasn't a hell of a lot more to it.

One reporter said: "You killed him." And when he saw the expressions on the faces of boys who had been around and knew my record, added hastily, "Of course."

I shrugged my shoulders. "If I didn't kill him, you've got a great story. 'Cops Bury Man Alive.'"

You just can't go around the city shooting people to death, nor are you even allowed to pull off promiscuous killings in your own office. But it was routine to me. I knew all the answers, and if I didn't, I had a damn good lawyer who did. Spats Willis was wanted for murder. It was easier to find reasons for killing him than it was to find reasons for not killing him. Everybody was pleased—even Nelson.

After I went downtown and traded dirty words with the D.A., O'Rourke got me alone in his room and talked straight out. We liked each other, O'Rourke and me.

"Race," he said, "there's a new angle to this case. You see, we got word that Spats Willis was coming to America, also that Raftner was coming. Now, Spats was known, but no one has ever seen Raftner. Raftner is also supposed to be here in New York. He's the biggest narcotics agent in the world. Yet, if he walked into police headquarters this minute no one could arrest him. You know—that knowledge-without-the-evidence stuff. Wanted in England, Germany, France, Italy—"

"I know." I nodded. "But what of that? He's in New York now."

"Yeah, that's right." O'Rourke eyed me shrewdly. "We were tipped off he was coming by the G-men. They could have dragged in Spats Willis any time they wanted to; they've been following him ever since he landed. Lost him last week—and we wanted him for murder here. But the G-men have been following someone else longer than they have been following Willis."

"Who—Raftner?"

"No. Take another guess."

"I'm not good at riddles."

"You," said O'Rourke. "You, Race."

"Hell! I should have known it. There's been a dozen or more lads playing lamb to my little Mary." And suddenly, "How long? What did they find?"

O'Rourke grinned. "You seem excited, Race. They drew a blank on you, passed you up over a week ago. Gave you a clean bill of health."

I breathed easier, said: "What put me into their heads? They didn't suspect I was in the racket?"

"I don't know what they suspected; or how they picked up your trail. But they knew drugs had entered the country and that a big man handled it. Gentle Jim Corrigan was wanted, but they weren't sure he headed the dope-ring. They only had to read the newspapers to know that you shot Corrigan to death smack in front

of Nelson and myself. So they figured some place along the line
you had a client in the racket—and they sat down on your tail."

"Well"—I looked straight at O'Rourke—"I haven't got a
client, in or out of the racket."

"Have you met the Flame lately?"

"Haven't seen her in three or four months." My attitude was
one of total indifference.

"You mean since lunchtime today." O'Rourke tossed his bomb
as casually.

"My God!" I cried out. "You—spying on me like that. How did
you find that out?"

O'Rourke chided me lightly. "Now, now. You've been seeing too
many movies with dumb cops in them, Race. You shot a man to
death and walked out for your lunch. The police were interested in
whom you met. You won't argue with me, Race, when I say that
the Flame is the most beautiful and the most dangerous woman in
New York. And today she was with the most dangerous man in
New York—Armin Loring. That's a combination a single man
can't beat. No, not even a single man like you. Women are
dangerous to men in the racket. Armin never had a woman
before—and such a woman."

"The Flame is not—" I started, but O'Rourke cut in.

"I know. I know." A long pause and then, "He'd think nothing
of having you killed. And Armin can think fast."

"Fast with his brain as well as with his gun," I thought half
aloud.

"Correct," O'Rourke agreed. "Just fast with a gun won't keep a
man from being shot in the back of the head." And with a smile,
"Your being alive sort of disproves that theory, eh Race?"

"Yeah," was the best I could do.

O'Rourke laid a hand on my shoulder. "You have something
that none of them have, boy. You've got instinct. You feel danger
before you see it. That's what keeps you alive."

"What about these federal men. Are they going to question
me?"

"No. In fact, they've decided to drop you as useless to them."

"Even though I killed Willis?"

"Even though you killed Willis. They didn't make me promise
not to tell you about them, but I think a demand for such a promise

was coming when we were interrupted. Now, Race, those are my cards. I want yours."

"Mine? I have none. You don't think Armin is in the dope racket? As for the Flame—" I stopped there. Sure, she was in it.

O'Rourke went on and his voice was low. "I never pushed you, Race. I won't push you now. You worked with the G-men once— they owe you something now. It would be a great feather in my hat if we beat them to the pinch." And after a moment, "I'd stretch a point for your client, too."

"O'Rourke!" I looked indignant. "You don't think I'd help anyone who—"

"Never mind what I think. Will you play ball with me when the big moment comes? I don't want our city to be flooded openly with dope. I'd like to think that I was the guy—even through you—who helped prevent that." And suddenly, "Did you know that Armin has been to Singapore?"

"No, but I know he intends to go."

"And for some reason or other he intends to have you killed. That's a fact, Race. It's common gossip in the underworld. Do you know why?"

I grinned broadly, thought of Mary Morse and grinned more. "Is it about a woman?" I asked innocently.

"A woman?" O'Rourke seemed surprised so I switched that. "Well—I don't know just who Mr. Armin Loring will get to alibi him in my death."

O'Rourke said rather sadly: "The lad who knocks you over won't even need a lawyer. Any self-defense plea will save the man who kills you. With your record any judge, any jury will feel that if you didn't try to kill the man first it was simply an oversight on your part."

I took a bow. "I won't worry about the lad who does me in." And in sudden thought, "Now, O'Rourke, you think Armin is going to kill me. Armin, perhaps, thinks the same thing. Just how would you feel if I—well, prevented Armin from killing me?"

"What do you mean?"

"I mean that if he wasn't alive, why he couldn't kill anyone."

"You mean that you'd murder him?"

My shoulders went up and down. "Why make a nasty word out of it?"

"I'm telling you now that he can shoot circles around you."

"That'll be fine." I grinned. "If I'm standing in the middle of that circle while he's doing his act, then good-bye, Mr. Armin Loring. Suppose"—I leaned forward—"suppose seriously, O'Rourke, because I have a great respect for Armin and his gun, that it was kill or be killed. Just one bullet from one gun—whichever lad fired first. How would you like it if Armin took the dose?"

"Personally," said O'Rourke, "I'd like it fine."

"All right." I turned toward the door. "I'll see what I can do for you—personally."

"Personally—" He started suddenly, stopped, then blurted it out. "You said it was a woman. Good God, it's not the Flame!"

"Good God—it's not." I had the door half open and O'Rourke had his mouth half open. I knew what he was going to say; what he always said. His personal opinion had nothing to do with that of the department, so I didn't give him a chance to say it. I just closed the door and took it on the run down the hall. If anything happened to Armin now, I'd tell O'Rourke I thought he wanted it that way. And truth is truth—I think he did.

I went whistling out of the building and grabbed the subway uptown. Oh, I know taxis are the thing for private investigators. You can't very well say to subway motormen: "Follow that man." But then I had no man to follow—and more to the point, no client to pay for the taxi.

When I reached my own apartment I dropped into an easy chair, picked up the evening papers. I liked the streamers on a couple of the papers. *Wanted Murderer Shot To Death* and *Hoodlum Killed As He Threatens Death*. But one sheet did its stuff and wouldn't hurt my business any. Yep, the blazing banner I liked best read—*Race Williams Does It Again*.

On the second page I took a laugh. The photograph was good; the wording under it better. There was a picture of Iron-Man Nelson leaning over the body of Spats Willis in my office. And the caption read—*Inspector Nelson First to Find the Dead Body*. Get it? Of course, you do—and so would Nelson. He had been making it a habit lately of finding bodies—after I laid those bodies out for him.

The phone rang. It was Mary Morse and she was crying. There was terror in her voice. She had hard work in getting her words out over the phone, and I had a sight harder work understanding them. Then she cleared up.

"Race," she said finally, very slowly and distinctly, "I need you more than I have ever needed you. I am at the Green Room of the Hotel York Terrace. There is a man with me called Raftner. He is controlling my every move, because—well, you know why."

I didn't get the idea, but I said simply: "Sure, Mary. I'll come around and have a talk with you."

"But this man—he'll kill you if you come!"

"Nonsense." I put it lightly. "I'll stick you for the supper check."

"But this Raftner—he's here with me."

"Then we'll stick him for the check," I chuckled.

Her voice lowered. Someone muttered beside her. Mary Morse pulled an aside in a hoarse whisper. "I won't. I won't. He's coming." A pause and then, "Close the door of the booth. Wait on the outside, and I will— Oh, I will!"

I didn't cut in on the little comedy—or tragedy—that took place in that booth. I just listened. I heard a single step, a soft swish which sounded like the telephone-booth door closing, then Mary Morse's voice.

"They are making me do this. Raftner is making me. They want me to plead with you to come. They want to find out if you would come. Race, Race! I've caused you enough danger. Don't come— don't come. This Raftner is different; has influence. He's—he's bad."

"He's kidding you, Mary. I'll just trot over to the York Terrace and see how bad he really is."

"No—no!" Her voice wasn't low now. "Don't come! He'll kill you right here at—"

There was a slight thud, a stifled scream, the click of the receiver—and I dropped my own phone back in its cradle.

I whistled softly as I adjusted my shoulder holster, slipped into my jacket, picked up my hat. Armin Loring had warned me not to see Mary Morse again. The Flame had told me not to see her again. Mary Morse herself had told me not to come—both on that card and over the phone. And a lad called Raftner—so bad that he admitted it himself—threatened my death if I visited the Green Room of the Hotel York Terrace.

There was only one answer to that.

The York Terrace is a rather classy, high-priced hotel, and the Green Room some parsnips in the nightlife of a great city. Yet, I didn't get into evening clothes. I can wear the boiled shirt as well as the next fellow and talk so I won't be taken for a waiter. But a shoulder holster isn't so good with a tux, unless you sport a small gun. Me—I don't like twenty-twos. When I put a hole in a guy I don't embarrass half a dozen doctors who try to find it. My motto is: There isn't much sense in shooting the same guy over and over.

The exclusive Hotel York Terrace was having something put over on it. I spotted him as soon as I entered the lobby. He was all decked out in fish-and-soup and leaning against a pillar—a bad boy of the night. He had the size to look down at you, and the twisted kisser to scare people to death. Now he grabbed my arm and started to work on me as soon as I reached the pillar.

"Listen, Williams," he said, and despite my six feet, I had to raise my head slightly to look at him, "I'm working for Armin— Armin Loring. You're not to go in that Green Room. You're to beat it from the hotel now before I—"

I stopped him there. I knew why he repeated Armin's name. It was like whistling in the dark. His heart wasn't in his threat. I said simply: "Take your hand off me, Sam, before I shoot your arm away at the shoulder." And when he dropped his hand as if he was gripping a hot iron, "Now—tell me what you'll do. And if I don't like it—you'll be surprised."

His face got a bit white. "Well—" He hedged trying to get us a little back from the entrance of the Green Room, which made me turn my head and see Mr. Armin Loring sitting at a table by the door with the Flame. His face was sideways to us. "Well," Sam tried again, "I was just to say it wouldn't be healthy for you." And as I carelessly crossed my right hand to my left armpit, "God, Mr. Williams! It was just a message I had to give and—and—"

I watched him back away then, fade to the left and out of sight of the crowd in the Green Room. He didn't speak again. When he got far enough away he turned sideways and did a little ballet dance toward the main entrance. And he was right. I don't take talk from guys like him; never did; never will.

I spun on my heel and entered the Green Room. Armin turned his head and saw me just as I saw Mary Morse—frightened, white-faced little Mary Morse who had gone through so much with her head up—and the gent beside her. Big shoulders, big neck, big head—and so help me God!—nose-glasses with a wide black ribbon running down from them and half twisted about the huge cigar that decorated his thick-lipped puss. They were far down in a corner of that room.

"Hello, Armin." I leaned on Armin's table and smiled at him; smiled just as the lights dimmed, a spotlight flashed, and a dame started to sing. "Is Raftner still tough? Is he the guy with the crape on his glasses?"

Armin said very slowly: "That is Raftner—and he'll shoot you to death right at the table. So don't go near Mary Morse."

I smiled cheerfully over at the Flame. She wasn't the young girl now. She was the hard, calculating woman of the night. It was in her eyes, her face, her tight lips—in the very movement she made pulling the high-priced fur piece over her bare right shoulder.

I said to Armin above the singer who had hit her stride and was raising hell all over the room: "And if Raftner isn't as bad as you think, then you'll—"

He almost snarled as he cut in. "Any time and place."

"Fine." I patted Armin—the dangerous Armin—on the back. "Get ready for the fireworks."

"You fool!" Armin clutched at my arm, looked at me as if he were figuring out if I were drunk or not. "Don't try anything here. I tell you this man will kill you."

"You asked for it, brother," I told him and then almost viciously as I jerked my arm free, "If Raftner's half the man you think he is, we'll give the Green Room a floor-show that will be entirely different."

I moved around the edge of the dance floor, cut across it on the fringe of the light, nearly lost an eardrum as the singing girl, feeling that she was not annoying enough people, began to circle around.

I went straight down the lane of light toward those wide, staring terror-stricken eyes of Mary Morse. I saw Raftner, too. He was half turned now. One arm—his left—hung over the side of his chair. His right hand was holding a glass of chamgagne. The silver ice-bucket was plainly visible beside him.

I got a good look at his face. He wasn't any gunman—that is a gunman as we picture one. He was smiling at me and his bulging, fish-like eyes had a film over them; a film that seemed to magnify instead of dim them through the lenses of his glasses.

He never changed his position as I reached the table—just smiled and said very low: "You're Race Williams, of course. I have seen your picture. I have come to this country for the purpose of looking at you—just once."

"That's fine," I said, and since his voice was not unpleasant, I tried to keep mine the same, though I daresay I didn't make much of a go of it. "You're Mr. Raftner. Well, I've got some bad news for you. Your very charming companion is coming along with me."

"That is not the truth," he said very solemnly. "She will not go. She will remain here with me. It is her preference—her privilege— and her comfort." And very slowly, "She is used to every luxury of life. Prison cells are cold and damp."

"Hell!" I didn't like this backing and filling. "I thought you were dynamite. Armin gave me the idea that this was the table of death."

"You could, of course, make Armin's words come true." Those great shoulders hunched. His left hand still hung over the chair; his right still held the almost full glass of champagne.

"Come on, Mary," I said. "Your fat friend has proved a bust. You and I are going places."

Mary started to her feet. Raftner spoke. "The dear child has a cold on her chest, Mr. Williams. She will be escorted home carefully so that the night air will not hurt her. Then she will place her feet in a hot bath." He paused a long moment, turned his head and looked directly at the girl. "Sit down, child," he said, and his voice was like fingernails drawn along a wall. "I knew a young girl once who found the hot bath so severe that she never walked again." He made a queer noise in his throat. "Both her feet were amputated."

So that was it. Here was a guy who was supposed to be good with a gun making cracks with certainly more than a hint of torture. Mary Morse put one hand to her throat; the other stretched limply toward me as she fell rather than slipped back in the chair.

"Go, Race," she said. "Go—I'll—I'll stay with him. I've got to. I've got to."

"Nonsense," I told her and as my voice rose a little I took a quick look-see around. Tables on either side of us were vacant;

people beyond were looking from the semi-darkness beneath the balcony into the light, and watching the singer. I went on: "Don't mind this big bust, Mary. You heard what was going to happen to me if I came here. Now what? A lot of wind. Why, this big stiff couldn't—"

The big stiff did. He just moved his right hand back and tossed it up again. The 'insult direct' or something like that in the book of etiquette, I guess. For his cigar puffed, smoke blew straight into my face the moment the champagne splashed all over my map.

Mad? Of course I was mad. So would you be. I just can't shoot lads to death unless there is some reason for it. Though you and I may think a face full of champagne is sufficient reason—twelve beer-drinking men on a jury might not.

Anyway, I didn't like it. His eyes were watching my right hand. Hard eyes and cold; no fish now, but steel through his glasses. And his right hand was ready to cross as soon as mine. Oh, I won't believe any man is quicker than I am, and—

I don't go in for light humor often, but I did now. I stretched out my right hand, pulled the cigar out of his wide, surprised mouth, then shoved it back into his face again. That I turned it around and shoved in the wrong end of the cigar—that is, the wrong end from his point of view—is what caused the trouble. But if he wanted to play—why, so did I.

If you have ever pushed the lighted end of a cigar in your own mouth during a fast evening, you'll know the sensation of surprise. But you'll probably have to guess how it feels when someone else does it—then screws it in like a cork in a bottle.

No, I don't know how dangerous Mr. Raftner was, but I do know what he did. He spit bits of cigar, ashes, and fire, and jumped up and down like a maniac. Sure, he stopped the show. He had half a dozen waiters around, poured glasses and glasses of water into his mouth, and just made a mess of himself as the waiters tried to stop him. He tried to talk, but didn't make much of a go of it.

To the first waiter I said: "He's drunk."

The headwaiter was disturbed—greatly disturbed. He said sort of awed: "He's the Baron from Antwerp, is he not? It is most regrettable, Miss Morse—this head of a great jewelry firm." And when I put a bug in his ear, "But certainly, *monsieur*. Miss Morse need not be further embarrassed. The door there—through the kitchen. No, no—no one knows him by name, and few saw—and none, I believe, recognized Miss Morse.''

I wasn't mad any more when a captain led the girl and me to the little door and into the kitchen. Of course, Mary was well known in the best places. For some time now she had been the actual head of Morse and Lee. Poor kid—trying to stimulate the jewelry trade by appearing in fashionable places.

I was careful as we left that dining-room. No fear that Mr. Raftner, alias the Baron, would stick a bullet in my back. Like Mount Vesuvius, he was having another eruption. It was Armin I was watching. I saw him come to his feet and start across the dining-room toward the vanishing figure of Raftner who was being pushed more than just escorted between red curtains in one corner of the room. Then Armin hesitated, hurried back to the Flame who was quickly leaving the room.

Yes, I was chuckling. But we can't have our little joke without paying for it. That's life, I suppose. The captain who saw us to the side entrance and sent for a taxi was very polite. He said quite close to my ear: "*Monsieur le Baron* was rather too clever with the champagne. But you, *monsieur,* with the revolving cigar were superb.''

So just as I was about to help Mary Morse into the taxi I parted with a ten-spot. Another donation to a cause that had paid no dividends. But I shook my head. After all, where could I have gone and had so much fun for ten bucks? Mr. Raftner had taken it, and wasn't likely to go around and tell people what had happened. I frowned. Nothing to worry me, maybe. But what of Mary Morse?

That had been my mental question. Now as I turned and started to climb into the taxi it became a physical one. Mary Morse was not in the taxi. Mary Morse was gone. She was nowhere on that side street. By the time I reached the corner Mary Morse was not on the main thoroughfare either.

## FOUR

# ON THE KILL

■

I climbed into the taxi and gave the address of my apartment. Then I did a little thinking. My main thought was that Raftner was flooding the city with narcotics and the place he would use to distribute the drugs from would be Mary Morse's jewelry shop—one of the most respected establishments in the city. The last place to suspect, it had never even come under observation when her dear Uncle Frank Morse had hidden drugs in the basement. He'd kept the stuff in vases that sold for prices that would amaze you—did me, not having an eye for Ming's Dynasty or any other guy's dynasty for that matter. Now Raftner was threatening Mary Morse with exposure of her dead uncle's activities, the fact that she'd kept her knowledge of them from the police. Also threatening to expose the bit of killing I'd pulled off in her interest.

One thing they did wish to make sure of—and that was that I was out of the picture, and out of it quickly. If I were willing to fade myself they'd let it go at that. If I weren't, they wanted to find it out right away and knock me over.

Anyway, I couldn't get the truth out of Mary Morse—at least at once—since I didn't know where she was. Then who could talk? And I had it. Her stepfather, Conklyn Lee. He had managed that firm since Mary's grandfather's death.

I'm not a sentimental fool. Anyone who knows me knows that. Oh, if it comes to a show-down, I'll die for a cause, but I'd much rather kill the cause and live for another one. And I'm not a guy who got his knowledge of drugs and the vicious part they play in the life and death of a great city by reading articles in the magazines. I have seen the real thing. Criminals turned into mad dogs by dope, murders and tortures, decent women leaving their husbands and children and walking the streets because of it. Young lives ruined, old lives taken by a jump from a window.

Of course I couldn't let lugs like Armin or Raftner tell me where to get off but when I reached Conklyn Lee's old brownstone front, I like to think there was something else besides that urging me— something of the crusader if you want to go DeMille on me. Lee let me in himself and I followed him down the hall to the library. He may have been hot stuff in the jewelry business and made quite a front, but then I guess he didn't go walking about the great floor of the shop with his nightshirt flapping out from under his bathrobe.

He had more things to do before he could get settled than a bride getting ready for her wedding. He had to get his glasses, mix himself a whisky and soda without hardly enough whisky to kill the taste of the soda. He kept walking around offering me cigarettes and lighting one himself every time I shook my head, until he had two in the ashtray and one in his hand—all lit. And all the time he kept saying: "Mary—where is Mary? No cigarette, Mr. Williams, no whisky? Some tea then?"

"I never eat or drink or smoke in a place I'm not sure of," I told him flat. "I lost some good friends that way." And when his face grew blank, I explained simply, "Poison."

"Good gracious," he said, and if the words themselves seemed trite, old-fashioned and childish, he put enough expression into them to make them sound almost profane.

I didn't waste time; I gave him straight talk. I said bluntly, and as if I knew every word of it to be gospel: "The shop is being used again to store and ship narcotics."

"The idea"—he puffed and blew a bit—"is impossible."

"Have you met the Baron from Antwerp?" I chucked at him.

"Baron Von Stutz? Yes."

"And Armin Loring?"

"Armin Loring? No."

"Maybe not under that name." I shook my head. "Now, Mr. Lee, we're getting too deep into this thing to go on with it. I may have trouble explaining my knowledge of the former use of your store for narcotics, and those men I shot up in Mount Vernon. And it may ruin the Morse firm, may give you and Mary a jolt up the river. I've got to hear talk from you—real words—or I'm going to blow the works. You're opening up a passage that will make the almost uncontrollable crime situation in the country get out of hand entirely."

He got up, paced the room, said: "I don't know. I hope not. I— God, Williams! I've thought of it day and night and have been tempted to go right to the government officials. It's Mary—just Mary. But there are times when I thought it would be best for her if I should talk to you. After all you have done it would seem so unfair—such ingratitude—to let you pay the penalty for your loyalty and help. Yes, I think I will go straight to the police with the whole truth."

So we reversed positions. It was he who threatened to go to the cops, and now I who talked him out of it. I told him all that had happened tonight. Of Mary's fear, of my attempt to help her, of the threats against my life. I watched his face while I talked. Then I watched his face while he talked, and I'm used to reading faces. His was an honest one; so honest it stood out. I'd have bet my last dollar on that—but what the hell! I've bet my last dollar on a lot of things and lost. But he gave me the story.

"Mary has taken an active part in the business lately. Even built it up considerably. After Gentle Jim Corrigan's death we felt that we had nothing more to fear. Mary tried to see you then—thank you. The past seemed so definitely the past. Then it became the present—a deadly horrible present."

He paused and I helped by saying: "Let's have it."

"Mary began to be worried. Began to spend much of her time in the basement below the store. Then she introduced me to Baron Von Stutz, who was interested in vases. Then out of a clear sky she told me that the Baron would take charge for a while of the buying and selling of vases to private collectors. He would come and go by the rear entrance to the basement itself. No one but men he selected would handle the shipments of vases. There was such a fear in her eyes, such a plea, such a—I—" His hands spread far apart. "So she asked for the key to the heavy steel door that led to the basement, and the next morning"—with great emphasis on the single word, *next*—"I gave it to her, and for the first time in the history of the shop the basement on that side was shut off from the shop itself."

"Why do you say—*next* morning?" I asked him.

He coughed, looked me straight in the eyes and finally said: "We had but the one key which I kept in a drawer in the safe. I had a duplicate made."

"You were suspicious, then?" The old boy had his good points.

"Suspicious!" His voice rose slightly. "I was alarmed, frightened, distraught."

I liked that last word so I threw it back at him. "When you visited the basement later with that key were you still distraught?"

He didn't smile, simply nodded. "This Baron knew nothing of vases. Even in the semi-darkness and without handling them I knew that a great many pieces he'd brought in were made here in America by the thousands to be sold at cheap auction-rooms. I spoke to Mary, and she told me the truth. It was blackmail. This dark man who was often with the Baron and called himself Mr. Armitage had discovered the secret of her uncle's—Frank Morse's—death. They were using our basement for the cutting and resetting of smuggled or stolen gems. It was the price we must pay for their silence."

"Did you believe her?"

"Of course." Conklyn Lee seemed surprised, and if he were an actor he was a damned good one. "You think it's drugs. No, Mr. Williams. I thought of that, too, but after what you told Mary the first time—she'd—yes, she'd sacrifice everything—name, business—before she'd agree to that."

I shrugged my shoulders as I came to my feet. "Go on believing what you like, Mr. Lee. But it's drugs just the same."

We talked after that. And I believed in Conklyn Lee, just as Mary Morse believed in him. I believed in Mary Morse, too. Believed even now that she did not suspect the real truth. Illegal diamonds, unlike dope, could not corrupt the youth of a country. Sure, she would believe what they told her. Who wouldn't believe it? And I gulped. I didn't like the answer to that thought. The

Flame wouldn't believe it. Not be fooled a minute. And the Flame was in it. Criminal mind, eh? She must have developed a criminal stomach, too.

Before I left I made arrangements to meet Conklyn Lee at the shop the following night.

The Flame was nervous; Armin Loring was nervous; Raftner was nervous, for he had sent Spats Willis to kill me. Willis, of course, was both nervous and dead. But I recognized the signs. It affects all big crooks the same. They get fidgety, suspicious, ready to act quickly; kill quickly just before the big pay-off.

The pay-off was soon, then. The drugs must be in that basement ready to be shipped. The cheap vases gave that away. That's how the dope came there and that would be how the dope left.

What would the government, the police, give for a bit of information like that? They'd give us freedom. They'd have to. It would be a great story that Mary Morse suspected something wrong, hired me and I uncovered the greatest drug-ring that ever got ready to encircle a city—a country even. The other story about Uncle Frank Morse—my killing him—why, we'd just forget that and begin with the coming of Baron Von Stutz, alias Raftner, and Armin Loring. So I was humming as I left the house.

I wasn't humming when the taxi drew up before my apartment door. My pleasant thoughts busted like a child's balloon. We could forget it all right. But what good would that do us while Raftner and Armin Loring still remembered it and could talk about it?

As I stepped from the taxi my thought was to make them forget it. Which was impossible unless—unless— And my right hand mechanically slid under my left armpit as I swung around. Yep, I thought, imagination is a great thing, as I actually caressed my gun—and I was right. For that little bit of imagination saved my life, saved it right then and there in the fraction of a split second.

Sure, for I swung my face almost against the barrel of a tommy gun. I saw the steel drum which hid steady fingers, saw a face behind that tommy gun. I don't know if the man spoke, if the man threatened. I don't think so. Just narrowing eyes, a droop to the lower lip, the sudden assurance of death, and I flipped back my hand and shot that face straight out of my life—and his too, for that matter.

The City of New York may seem insufficiently policed. You can

walk the streets at night and not see a cop; you'd think you didn't have any protection. But try shooting a man to death and see how quickly the boys turn up and want to know why. Yep, they were on their way before I skipped over the corpse and stepped into my apartment house.

I bumped into Frosty, the night-man. His eyes popped; he dropped the paper he had been reading on the floor, mouthed the words: "Lord, Mr. Williams, sah! I just read it in the paper and—and you ain't gone an' done it again?"

"That's right, Frosty. I gone an' done it again." I handed him a five-spot. "Tell the cops I'm upstairs and pay the taxi-man if he squawks." Without losing my stride I entered the automatic lift and started up. One thing was certain. The boys in the dope racket meant business.

I reached my apartment in time to get O'Rourke out of bed and tell him to hop over—there might be trouble with the police. O'Rourke was half asleep, but he came to quick enough when he realized a dead guy was lying out front.

"What the hell!" I cut in on his sermon. "I'm a citizen and I want some police protection. I want it pretty damn quick, too, or these cops will drag me downtown and keep me from shooting a guy who—"

"Another one?"

"Yeah—another one." I stopped. The bell of my apartment was ringing, and someone was trying to kick the door in at the same time. "Wait, O'Rourke. Don't go back to sleep." I put the phone down on the table leaving the connection open and went to the door, flung it wide. A sergeant was there and a couple of harness cops behind him.

The sergeant was fat, officious and had been used to scaring pickpockets and milk-bottle thieves half to death by glaring at them. I knew him and he knew me.

"Hello, Halorhan." I pushed him in the stomach. "The commissioner has let the ropes down, and you're filling up the waistline, eh?"

"Now look here, Williams." Sergeant Halorhan came into the room as if he expected guys to pull guns on him from behind every chair. "You can't be doing this, you know—not so steadily on the public streets. I've got to—"

"You've got to talk to O'Rourke." I managed to roll him across to the phone, even lifted it and put it in his hand. The talk was one-sided. It went like this—

"That's right, O'Rourke. . . . No, I guess Williams admits the killing. . . . There was a tommy gun in this hood's hand. . . . Recognize him! Why, he hasn't got any face."

There was more, but I wasn't listening. I invited in the cops who stood in the doorway. Jerry was around by now and I had him get them a drink and saw Halorhan looking at the glasses and hurrying his talk with O'Rourke. At last he hung up the phone and when I didn't say anything, asked point-blank for a "snort." He was a "one-drink man" when on duty, but he made that drink go a long ways. It knocked the hell out of a bottle.

Now he rubbed the back of his hand across his mouth, smacked his lips and said partly sarcastic, partly humorous: "I wonder, Mr. Race Williams, if it would be asking too much to ask just how it happened. Sergeant O'Rourke seems to think that you're too busy killing people to talk about it."

"No trouble at all." I was affable. "I stepped out of a cab. This lad put a tommy gun against my head, and I shot him."

"Then?" said Halorhan, falling into the trap.

"Why, then he died," I told him.

The cops laughed, stopped at once as Halorhan moved toward the door. Then they were gone.

The phone rang and it was Mary Morse. She talked before I could get started. "Race—you're alive then! You're all right? Armin Loring swore he'd kill you if I so much as talked to you. That's why I ran away from you tonight. I thought they'd know, understand. I telephoned Armin that I'd never see you again if he spared you and—"

"Spared me! That grease ball! Listen here, Mary—" And I damn near choked over the words. I thought I'd shown her enough to let her know I didn't need any nursemaid. "Wherever did you get such an idea? You saw how I handled Raftner."

"I was told, Race—yes, told by your friend—to warn you to keep out of this affair, never to see me again or you'd be killed by Armin who can"—yes, her very words were—"who can shoot circles all around you. Don't you see, Race—don't you understand! It was your own assistant who told me."

"My assistant—Jerry?" I fairly gasped, before the truth struck me.

"No, that woman. The one who helped you and me when we were prisoners. The woman with the queer name—the Flame."

The Flame. Sure, I saw what she meant then. The Flame had told her she was my assistant and I had never told Mary any different. At the time I'd kept silent, perhaps to protect the Flame. Later there was no need. Now—I just gasped, let the thing go, and asked her: "Where are you—home?"

"No, I've been walking the streets. I don't know what to do. I've got to see Armin or he'll kill you."

Dumb? For a bright girl she was certainly dumb. Poor kid. No, she wasn't dumb—except in one thing. How anyone above the age of seven who had seen me in action could think for a moment that Armin Loring would take away my appetite, I don't know. But I told her simply: "Let me run things for a day or two. Go to some hotel, register under another name and—"

"But I can't. I telephoned Armin. I must go over and see him in half an hour. He said I must. I saw your assistant with him in the Green Room tonight. Does that mean—"

I cut her off. "What's Armin's telephone number?" And when she hesitated, "I want to ring him up and tell him I won't bother with you any more"—I gulped—"then he won't want to kill me."

She gave me his telephone number at once. So her dumbness served me some purpose that time. But when I started to talk to her like a Dutch uncle she hung up on me.

Mad? I was fit to be tied. Why should I wait around for Armin to have first shot at me? Wait to let Armin set the time and the place—murder by his watch? Just wait until he was ready—then try my luck against his. No, I had had enough of that. Two could play his game.

I snapped up the phone and buzzed Armin's number. It was early in the morning, yet he answered the phone almost at once. His voice was low and expectant—expectant of another voice maybe, a girl's voice—but he got exactly what was on my mind.

"Williams calling, Armin," I told him. "You've broken that one-man record. There was an attempt on my life a few minutes ago. Friend of yours—nice boy."

"Yes?" There was interest in Armin's voice, anxiety too, I thought. "What happened?"

"He's dead," I said. "Spread all over the sidewalk, and I'll have to talk to the District Attorney early in the morning."

"I'm sorry you have to get up early, Race, but I'm sure the D.A. will be pleased."

"I won't have to get up early," I told him. "At least, I don't think I will. I'll already be up."

"Insomnia—conscience?" He laughed. "I don't quite understand."

"Listen, Armin—about that promise of yours—or was it a threat? You know—any place, any time. Does it still go?"

His laugh was light. "It got under your skin, eh Race? Well, when I talk like that and something like that machine-gun business comes off, it is unnerving. Yes, it still goes—maybe quicker than you think."

"That's right." I was very serious now. "Maybe quicker—much quicker—than even you think. I'm giving you a chance to withdraw that threat, Armin. I know you don't bluff, and it does bother me."

"Any time, any place—the five-o'clock rush hour on Forty-second Street. Do I make myself clear enough?"

"O.K." I got down to the point. "I'll be leaving here in five minutes and I'm coming directly to your apartment. If you're to make good on that threat, you've got to make good on it within the next twenty minutes."

"What do you mean by that?" I think he was a bit startled.

"I mean," I said, "some people have an idea that you're faster with a gun than I am. In twenty minutes one of us will find out—but only one of us."

"Hell," he said. "You can't try that, not tonight."

"Listen, Armin. When you open your door, open it shooting or you're never going to shoot again. I'm on the kill."

"No fooling, Race?" And something had gone out of his voice.

"No fooling, Armin," I said and hung up the phone. And I wasn't fooling when I put on my hat and walked out the door. I know it doesn't sound nice; doesn't look nice in black and white. But it was the truth. Armin Loring had to make good within the next twenty minutes or I'd shoot him to death.

# FIVE

# THE FLAME

■

I won't say it was exactly pleasant walking up the stairs to Armin's top-floor apartment, but I didn't think he'd had time enough to call in any friends, and I didn't think he'd show the yellow streak anyway—at least not to those friends.

Nothing happened as I reached the fifth floor, went down the corridor, and stood there in the dim hall-light right smack before his door. Then I lifted both my guns from their holsters, shoved one against the bell-button and trained the other on the door.

But the door didn't open. Didn't open, though I heard feet—a sort of soft pressure as if a body leaned against that door, maybe with an ear cocked to listen. I tapped lightly with my gun, moved the gun close to the lock, half tightened my finger on the trigger, then looked up and down the hall.

I shrugged and shook my head. That wouldn't do at all. This was no secret mission on my part but still— I looked toward the flight of stairs that led to the roof, jerked back my gun and sped up them. No tricks there, no lock to shoot. I simply slipped the hook off the door and walked out onto the flat roof. I didn't need the light in the window below to tell me which fire-escape led to Armin's apartment.

I don't like to loiter and pussy-foot around. In less than two minutes after I left that apartment door, I was crouching on the fire-escape by the window. And what's more the window was open a bit. A look-see under the shade did me no good. There was a window seat, and beyond that heavy curtains. Well, I was there on business. I pushed the window quietly up, slipped onto that window seat and parting the drapes, peered through just as the doorbell to the apartment rang. There was another visitor, then. Perhaps half a dozen of them. Armin wasn't taking chances.

I sat down on the window seat behind those curtains, made sure that they were long enough to hide my feet, held a gun in each hand and waited; waited as I looked between those curtains at the man who stood in the center of that room. He stood there with a gun hanging in his hand, fear in his eyes, uncertainty in his manner, as he turned from the ringing bell to the curtains behind which I sat.

It was my boy friend, Sam, of the Hotel York Terrace—the big mutton who had started out to be a tough guy and turned into a ballet dancer. The bell rang once more. Sam stiffened and listened as he backed toward me. I took a silent laugh. He was backing to that window to escape me at the door! So Armin had run out on me.

But I was listening just as Sam was listening. His hand was on the curtain when the key turned in the lock and the door to the apartment opened and closed. Feet came down the hall—light, tapping feet—the feet of a woman. Mary Morse, of course.

And I was wrong. So wrong I damn near fell off the window seat. Sam shot his gun into his shoulder holster and sighed with relief. It was the Flame, and if she had ever been the laughing happy young girl, you wouldn't know it now. Her face was hard, set; her brown eyes, twin balls of ice. She squeezed her green handbag close in her two slender, ungloved hands and popped right out with, "Where's Armin?"

"He's out. Got a message from this Williams guy and beat it along." Sam shook his head. "This cheap dick was coming down to have it out with Armin. Armin hated to leave, but couldn't afford a shoot-up here with things ready to move."

The Flame nodded, said: "Is it tonight?" And shaking her head,

"It's too early in the morning for that. Is the stuff to move tomorrow night, Sam?"

I could see the man's eyes narrow. "Don't you know? You're going to marry Armin and you don't—"

The Flame raised her head, sniffed at the air, said: "Where's the woman? Did he leave her here?"

"Why, there ain't no woman here, Florence."

"Miss Drummond," she snapped back at him. "Armin's got an eye on that Morse girl for more than just the money in it. She's been writing him letters."

"Naw." Sam let his broad thick lips part. "And what of it, Florence? You're a knock-out when you're mad. Armin was always One Man Armin—not One Woman Armin." He put a hand around her shoulders, drew her to him. "Let him run out with the dame if he wants. I'll be around to make it up to you." And suddenly grabbing her to him with both his arms, "Hell—the Flame—that's the name for you."

Did I step out to protect the frail little body of the Flame from this giant? I did not. And I didn't need to. Her arms moved like twin pistons, the hands on the ends of those arms flashing white. Just the crack, and the marks of fingers upon the man's face. A curse as sharp pointed toes pounded against his legs.

He dropped her, stepped back, muttered: "And I seen you going through Armin's desk looking for letters from some moll and never peeped. He'd strangle you for that. You want to play rough, well I'll play rough. You can't talk—can't tell Armin afterwards—or I'll talk. There, don't run. It won't do you any good."

The Flame wasn't running. She didn't even step back, didn't give an inch—just stood there clutching her green bag. This time as his hand shot out, her right had came up and down. I saw the tiny gun, saw it turn in her hand, saw its sight rip down his face and the blood come. He raised his hand to his face, staggered slightly.

The Flame watched him—calm. Her voice was even, steady, when she spoke. "Don't be a fool, Sam," she said. "I could have emptied the twenty-twos in this rod down your throat. There, that's better. I'm giving orders here. Where's that dame?"

The man eyed her, lifted his hands twice, let them fall to his sides again, said finally: "I'm sorry. It won't happen again. I swear it."

"There's nothing to apologize for," she said bluntly. "You keep your mouth closed and so will I." Her smile was not pleasant. "And it can happen again any time you want to be a fool. I always take care of myself." As if dismissing the subject, she stretched up a hand, grabbed at the lapel of his coat. "Was Williams here?"

"He was at the door and left." Sam was willing to forgive and forget, too. There was a nasty dig in his face. "I begged Armin to let me meet Williams. I'd have killed him right there in the doorway as soon as—"

The Flame laughed. "Race Williams would have shot your head right off your shoulders before you had time to tell him what a real dangerous man you are, Sam. About this dame, Mary Morse. Did she go with Armin or—"

The Flame stopped; both listened. Someone was at the door. There was the click of metal against metal as if that someone were having trouble placing a key in the lock.

"That's the girl—the Morse girl." The Flame just breathed the words. "Keep your face closed, Sam, or I'll tell Armin the trouble you have with your hands. I'll get her to go with me—say Williams sent me."

"You—you'd kill her?" He shrugged. "Well, it would save Armin the trouble."

"He was going to kill her tonight?"

"Maybe. She knows too much. Armin's afraid she'll blow to Williams. He—"

The door had opened and closed again. This time the feet were anything but steady. Mary Morse wobbled slightly as she stood in the doorway. Then she was speaking.

"Armin sent for me—and I came. I can't go through with it. I— I—" Her blue eyes grew even wider; the fear went out of them as they turned from Sam to the Flame. "You—you—Race's assistant. Oh, God, I wish I had your courage now!" She ran to the Flame, clung to her sobbing. I saw the Flame look up over her shoulder, wink at Sam.

I was tempted to step out then, but I didn't. Here was a chance to get an earful. It didn't seem like Armin was coming back.

The Flame was saying: "Armin had to leave, my dear. I'm going to take you along with me."

"You— Yes, I can go any place with you. But I must see Mr. Williams—Race Williams. I must tell him everything. I know the truth. It mustn't happen—mustn't—"

"I understand," the Flame said quietly as she patted the girl's head. "There, don't cry. Race Williams will make things come out all right for you; he always has. Don't shake like that—let me hold you."

If I wasn't on to the show I would have believed it myself. Just an older woman who had seen a lot of life comforting a younger one who hadn't. Yes, I'd have trusted the Flame, and I didn't blame Mary Morse for trusting her. Besides, there was that time when Mary had taken the Flame for my assistant and I had let her believe it. I should have told her the truth. And suddenly she did know the truth.

It was the ballet dancer, good old tactful Sam, who made his ugliest face when he spoke. "Why feed the kid baloney, sister? I think Armin may want her to live for a few days until he's sure."

Mary Morse screamed as she jumped back from the Flame. "That man—what is he doing here?" And there was recognition in her eyes, followed by terror. "He's going to kill me—kill me before I can right my wrong."

She was running for the hall when Sam grabbed her and swung her back. She was screaming, too, but her words were clear until Sam clapped a hand over her mouth. "It's narcotics—drugs—not diamonds! I know it now!"

The man's left hand went over her face, tore her head back against his chest. His right hand shot awkwardly behind him, jerked a blackjack from a hip pocket. He was staggering under her weight, straightening, trying to regain his balance, his back almost against the curtain. Then his hand went up, the blackjack started down, and I parted the curtains slightly and struck—viciously, brutally. My gun bounced hard against his head—damn good and hard.

Ballet dancer or not, Sam didn't trip the light fantastic this time. He just dropped his arm from around Mary Morse's throat and hit the floor.

As for me, I merely stepped over his body in time to strike with my gun again and knock the twenty-two from the Flame's hand. I wasn't any too gentle. Involuntarily her right hand went to her mouth, sucking suddenly at those fingers.

"I'm sorry, Florence, if I hurt your fingers." My apology was meant to be the height of sarcasm. "But it was that or shoot you to death."

She was a remarkable woman all right. If she were surprised she gave no sign. Certainly, she was not struck with any terror. She said simply and as if she meant it: "It's too bad I didn't lift the gun. I'd like to know if you'd have—" And looking at the curtains behind me, "Well, throw out the body. I suppose Armin's lying dead there."

"No such luck." I shook my head as I helped Mary Morse to her feet. "You were playing the game pretty low on the kid here. Was it money or jealousy?" And as her brown eyes flashed, "It was money, then. You wouldn't recognize jealousy. You wouldn't recognize any other woman's chance against you."

"That's right." She looked from me to Mary Morse, sobbing on my arm, and back to me. "Not even with you, Race. Your trouble is that you're too sensational. Let her go, Race."

But I wasn't going to let Mary Morse go this time. I started after her as she ran toward the hall door. Then I stopped, swung quickly around and said to the Flame: "Don't touch it!"

She shrugged her shoulders and straightened from the gun.

"O.K., Race," she cut in when I would have spoken. "I know your line. 'There is no sex in crime,' you were going to say. Then gallantly spare my life by shooting three fingers off my right hand." And biting her lips, "I am very proud of my hands. I wouldn't want to live without the fingers that make them so clever."

"I wonder," I said, "why you want to live at all." This as the door slammed and I picked up the Flame's gun. No, I didn't follow Mary Morse. I might have caught her, probably would, but the Flame still had the little green bag in her hand and I didn't know what all was in it. I might very easily catch a bullet in the back.

"I live simply for you, dear." Her smile was rather unpleasant. "Is Sam dead?"

"I'm not a doctor," I told her gruffly. "If his head is as thick as the thoughts that come out of it, he won't have much more than a dent."

She shook her head at me, smiled. "They couldn't arrest you for killing Sam. It would just be one of those mercy killings."

Not a bad crack at all, but I didn't feel in a light humor. Damn it! I had loved the Flame, had— And she was putting those eyes on me now, with a brightness, yes, a sparkle of youth in them. And— And I snapped out of it.

I said when I reached the door: "Has Armin Loring got much money, Florence?"

"Enough. Why?"

"Because if you want to inherit as the widow you'd better marry him at once. He hasn't much longer to live."

I started to turn, but didn't. I felt almost as if she were laughing at me as I backed through that doorway to the hall. Well, after all, I'd rather have her laughing at me than be dead. Did I mean that the Flame might kill me? Truth is truth—that is exactly what I meant.

# SIX

# AN EARFUL OF MURDER

■

Jerry and I hopped out of the taxi and hustled into the Morse and Lee jewelry shop the following night. Though the weather was warm we were both sporting topcoats—Jerry's, a somber blue, mine a light, unnoticeable brown. What's more, we had our coat collars turned up. If anyone watched us enter or not, I don't know. I didn't see anyone; didn't expect anyone, but I like to do things as if the whole town were watching.

Conklyn Lee was nervous as a mother hen when we stepped into his private office and fumbled with the key at least a full minute before he got that door locked. He finally said: "Why is that young man with you, Mr. Williams? And why are you wearing coats this time of year."

"We forgot to look at the calendar." I gave him a dig in the ribs. "You have your assistant manager in the other room there?" I jerked a thumb toward the door to the right. "About my size you said on the phone."

"Yes—but I don't understand."

"Fine, fine. If you don't understand, then others won't. No word from Mary?"

"No, not a word. You think they're keeping her prisoner until they finish their work below? But if they kill you, then—"

"Never mind about my life. I've taken care of it for years. And I intend to live to dance on the graves of Armin Loring, Baron Von Stutz, et al. You'd better think about her life and your own and do everything I asked you to do."

He had a first-class chill right away. Maybe I didn't hear his bones rattle, but I heard the change in his pocket.

Jerry remained behind and I got a slant at the assistant manager, standing in the room beyond when we passed through it. He was about my height and build, but not weight. He'd have to do something about that stomach of his first. And his face—well, I'm not so hot-looking I can complain. But his walk, as he opened the far door for us, bothered me. And the way he moved his hands looked as if he might break into Mendelssohn's *Spring Song* any moment. A couple of minutes later Conklyn Lee and I stood before the steel door in the back of the shop.

"I don't think anyone is down there now," he jittered. "But I don't know—I couldn't know. They come and go by the entrance on the alley."

"Open her up," I told him. "They wouldn't be around this early, and if they are—that suits me, too."

He got the key working and we went down to the basement. There was no one there—we covered it thoroughly. It wasn't such a big room—that is, as cellars go.

Just a little way from the foot of the stairs and beneath a green-shaded lamp was a stretch of carpet, a flat desk, and two comfortable chairs. There were no windows in the room, but tiny ventilators up near the ceiling.

Conklyn Lee lost his nervousness as he began to show me rare vases—far back in the dimness. He lifted them, held them as if they were a king's firstborn and looked childishly hurt when I told him flat they didn't look any better than five-buck ones to me. I was interested in those cheap ones he'd been telling me about. The ones Raftner, alias the Baron, had brought in.

We found them at once—and Conklyn Lee gasped. They were

all close to the wide steel door which led to the alley. They were all small and packed six to a partly opened crate.

"These are the ones?" I asked him. "Crated just like this? Why"—I went down the line and counted the crates, one upon the other—"there are enough here to flood the whole country with dope." I stretched a hand between the slats, had difficulty feeling inside of one, turned the crate over and slipped in my flashlight. Every vase was empty.

"There's nothing in them," Lee told me. "I have looked into every one. But if you're thinking of drugs—well, those vases are just a cheap pottery. The drug could be placed right in the mold. Do you want to break one and see?"

"No. The stuff might be in only one vase in ten. Besides, they'd notice a broken one, and I don't want to rouse suspicion."

"But if the drug is there why not—"

I cut in on him: "But I don't know it's there. They may bring the stuff with them later—tonight even—place it in the vases then take them away in a truck. A crate sent here and there—all open and above-board; just drop half a dozen vases at second-hand shops throughout the city. Nice distribution. I'll wait and see."

"Wait—and see. What do you mean?"

I didn't answer that one then. I was looking at two immense vases. Boy, they were big! Over six feet tall each one of them. If some of these small ones were worth dough why these must have been worth a cool fortune. They were both off the rug—just in the shadows away from that single overhead light. Still you could see animals and dragons dancing all over them. They were class. I told Lee so.

Conklyn Lee laughed. "Monstrosities," he said. "Valueless— sickening."

"How come you have them then?" They looked hot stuff to me.

"We give exhibitions above occasionally. A salesman on the road picked these up when the Chicago World's Fair closed. Had some fool idea that they would look nice on either side of the entrance to our little display of rare pieces."

He seemed disgusted at the thought and maybe a little disappointed that I didn't give him a chance to tell me about how they fired that salesman. I was pulling a chair over, looking at the short wide neck, trying to see things in the blackness of one of the vases.

"A man could get in there—hide in there," I said.

"Can and did." Lee smiled. "A burglar hid in one all night at the Fair, robbed the place, climbed back into the vase and the next morning mixed with the crowd and was never caught."

"A man about my size?" I was examining that opening.

"About—" Conklyn Lee nodded. "Maybe not so broad of shoulder. Good God, Mr. Williams! You weren't thinking of hiding in there. Why—these are desperate men. One of them could look down from the top and shoot you to death."

"If that one didn't lose his head."

Conklyn Lee pondered a moment. "They are very level-headed men," he said seriously.

I didn't explain how the guy who looked in would lose his head. I just took Conklyn Lee by the arm, led him to the stairs. I had seen the telephone that stood on the desk. He sat beside me on those steel steps as if his last ounce of dignity had left him.

"Mr. Lee," I said, "how far would you go for Mary?"

He said without hesitation: "I would give my life—everything for that child."

"O.K.," I told him. "There's a phone on that desk. Go to your home. Stay awake. Mary Morse is missing. They won't harm her until after the stuff is safe away from here—if it's here—or if they intend to bring it here and carry it away in those vases. You have let things go too far and so have I. I'd have the feds in here now if it weren't for the danger to Mary. I'm going to blow the works tonight—come what may. But I'm going to find out where Mary is first."

"But they won't tell you where she is. And they will kill her later."

"Mr. Lee," I said very seriously, and meant it, "if they don't tell me they won't be alive to kill her later. Now—go home. I have your number. If I don't telephone you before twelve, call this number." I handed him a card. "Ask for Sergeant O'Rourke. Tell him to come here. Then skip yourself and tell it all to a good lawyer. You'll need one."

"But what of you?"

"Oh, I'll have missed out."

"You'll be dead."

"That's right. But get O'Rourke here, tell him about the vases.

No matter what happens to me that dope must not get into the city." And after a pause, "You're not worth it. The firm is not worth it—Mary is not worth it. No, and by God, I'm not worth it!"

I dropped his hand quickly when I found I was holding it like a leading-man in a cheap road-show. Sure, that's right. I was even beginning to feel sorry for myself, and the sacrifice I was making for my fellow citizens.

I snapped out of that, said: "Jerry, my boy upstairs, will walk out to your car with your assistant manager, who will wear my brown coat, and my slouch hat. He'll turn the collar of my coat up high. If anyone is watching they'll think I've left."

Conklyn Lee preceded me up the steps to the closed door. "Mr. Williams," he said and his voice was husky, "I have read enough about you, seen enough of you to understand that this is—well, part of your business, part of your life—maybe routine with you. But it is the most fearful night of my whole life. Is there anything else I can do?"

I smiled at him. "Brother," I said. "I have a feeling it is going to be the most fearful of my life, too." And just before he closed the door, "Yeah, there is one thing you can do. Make your assistant manager keep his hands in my overcoat pocket when he leaves the store." I was thinking of the airy-fairy way he used those hands. If I was to die—well, there might be people outside who would take that lad for me, and I didn't want to be remembered doing any Spring Dance.

After Conklyn Lee left I took a look-see over that cellar again. The boys had to come in that sliding door which led to the alley. It would be simple to stick each one up and wait for the next. I looked at those huge vases, too. They'd be swell places to dump a stray body or two if a lad felt like tossing a few corpses around.

I felt I had lots of time. No one would show up until late; until the side-street would be deserted. I went over to those crates of vases and examined them again. The Morse and Lee name was printed in great black letters on wide slats. Respectability that— keen thinking. And the vases weren't completely boxed. All the world could see what was being carried. And I saw it—or thought I did.

I took out my flash and examined the boards of a crate; then another and another. By, God, the stuff must be in them! I'm not an expert carpenter; I didn't need to be. One or two boards on every crate had been hammered up far enough to remove the vases, then nailed down again. Did that mean the stuff was in them, hidden away in a secret place in those vases? Little movable parts in the bottom, perhaps, put there for that very purpose.

Should I bust hell out of them? Stand at the door afterwards and knock everyone for a loop that came in? Should I call O'Rourke and— But Mary Morse came first. But hell, she didn't come first— not before an entire city!

I went to the desk, looked at the telephone on it. The telephone! And I thought back to a mistake I had made in my younger days. Forgetting a telephone, caving in a guy's head who was supposed to use that phone to tell others the coast was clear. So it might be tonight.

My eyes raised and rested on one of those huge vases. A place to hide—a damn good place to hide. Plenty of room for a crouching man inside, and one of those vases had held "a man about my size"! Would they look inside the vase? Would the first man who came look inside it? Well, he couldn't see anything unless he stuck a light in. And if he stuck a light in, he'd never see anything again. I'd shoot his head right off his shoulders and damn near through the ceiling.

The vase was the place, obviously. I couldn't see once I was in there, but I could hear, wait, pop out with a couple of guns and do my stuff if the boys wanted it that way. No more fooling around, then. Into the vase I'd have to go.

Trouble? Of course there was trouble. First, I had to turn out the light. Second, I had to use my flash in the deep blackness. Third, I had to put the flash in my pocket while I scrambled up. And I made it—at least I was lying on my stomach on top of it. Getting inside was another thing. One leg at a time didn't seem to work, but I finally managed to get on my feet, straddling with one foot on either side of the thick circular rim around the top of the neck.

Why so fancy? Well, I wanted another chance to look inside that vase, with the flash directed straight in. I felt for my flash; the vase wobbled. I regained my balance, breathed a sigh of relief, then stuck my feet together and dropped right into that vase. It was dark and my judgment wasn't so good. My shoulders caught for a moment in the neck, slipped through and I landed bent up like a jackknife inside that vase.

Why did I pull that quick drop? Well, a bolt had clicked; a heavy iron bar was removed from the alley door. I'd heard it distinctly, as even now I heard the door beginning to slide back. But I was safe inside.

The door opened and closed. Groping feet crossed the stone floor, the feet of a lone man. Then the feet left the stone and settled on the rug. A light flashed and after a moment or two the feet moved again upon stone, passed close to the vase, hesitated. I looked up and raised my gun. My position was certainly good. If he looked in I'd simply have to decide whether he saw me or not. And on my decision would rest his life. What could be fairer than that?

After a bit the dial on the phone clicked several times. A husky voice said: "O.K., boss. All quiet here. I think you're wise to move the stuff early. . . . What . . . ? Yeah, I'd like to see Williams come here, too. He bounced a gun off my head last night."

So it was Sam. Poor dumb Sam. And the Flame had wondered if he were dead. His very next words made me feel that perhaps after all Sam wasn't so dumb.

"What?" he said. "The Flame's turned Armin's head? I don't know about that. But I tell you she's a wildcat, Raftner. See you in an hour then."

An hour. That was not so good. That vase was built funny, maybe thicker than I thought. Anyway I couldn't stand up and I couldn't sit down; I had to crouch like a guy playing squat-tag. I could turn, but I had to be careful of noise; had to be careful that neither one of the two guns I clutched in my hands pounded against the sides of the vase and rang out like chimes. How did I know they would ring out like chimes? I didn't. I didn't know what that vase was made of. But I did feel that the burglar who'd robbed the World's Fair was entitled to all he got if he spent the most of the night in that crouched position.

There was little sound after the phone was hung up. Just the pounding of Sam's heels on the desk where he sat and waited. And I just crouched and waited.

An hour passed and there was a knock, followed by Sam's feet beating across the hard stone, then the opening door.

This time more than one pair of feet crossed the floor. Each sound, each word came to me hollowly.

Armin Loring's voice snapped: "We don't need Sam here, Raftner. The trucks will be along any minute now—we'll want to get rolling."

The door closed and I guess Sam left.

Raftner said: "Sure, sure, Armin." And his voice changing to a harsh note, "Sit down. Yes—that thing in your back is a gun."

"God, are you mad!" Armin said and his breath whistled in his throat. It was a regular radio play for me from then on with sound effects and all. I saw nothing; heard everything. And I heard plenty.

Raftner was speaking and his voice was soft, pleasant. "I heard about you, Armin—One Man Armin. Yes, one man—running a great racket; building up for this great racket until you became head of it. I thought Frank Morse was at the top. When he died I thought Gentle Jim Corrigan was head of it, and when he died—I knew the real head. The last man to be suspected because you built up the one-man idea, the working-alone idea. You've been head of it all along—and neither Frank Morse nor Corrigan even suspected it."

"Well," said Armin, "why the gun in my back? What the hell? You knew you had a boss—now you know who he is. I had to come out in the open sometime—at least to you."

"Well," said Raftner, "it goes like this. Frank Morse got onto the Flame. She was shoving herself in, getting into his papers. He didn't kill her; he wrote me he wasn't going to kill her. He felt pretty cocky in having that brilliant criminal mind working for him. And he died—she planned his death."

"Hell, you're crazy," said Armin.

"There was Jim Corrigan," Raftner went on. "She played him along. He got wise, wrote me exactly how Morse died, then died himself. And *his* death was planned by the Flame. She was there in the house with Corrigan when Williams killed him. Williams didn't expose her then. He didn't expose her because she'd set Corrigan up for Williams to kill."

"Williams didn't expose her because they were once—well, to know the Flame is—"

"To love the Flame is to die," Raftner snapped in. "That went for all the others. It's going for you tonight, too."

"You mean—you're going to kill me?"

"I'm not going to have the Flame set me up for death."

"You're out of your head, man," Armin said. "It was just a coincidence."

"All right"—Raftner didn't argue—"have it your way. I'm not going to die by coincidence. But you—"

I could hear Armin's quick breath, felt that Raftner must have shoved his gun tighter against him. Armin's voice was hoarse when he spoke. "What—what do you want me to do?"

"I want you to pick up that phone, tell the Flame to come here—now."

"Then what?"

"I'm going to prevent any more coincidences. I'm going to kill her."

Armin laughed. "And you think I'd bring her here for that."

"I think—just that."

Armin spoke out like a man. I always thought he had it in him, but I had always thought also, and always believed and so stated, that all murderers were yellow inside; would do any rotten act, right up to tossing a knife into their best friend's back, if it would save their own skin. Now Armin made me out a liar.

"Raftner," he said, "I have always played the game without a woman. That's where I got the name, One Man Armin. Now—this is something new in my life. I'm taking on a wife not a woman. If you were to cut me to ribbons I wouldn't lift that phone from its cradle."

Raftner said very seriously: "I'm not going to cut you to ribbons. I'm simply going to shoot you to death."

"Go ahead and shoot then." Armin raised his voice. "I love that girl and—and— What are you going to do?"

"Count five and shoot."

"Why, the Flame means more to me than life."

"One—"

"Death would mean nothing and—"

"Two."

"You can't bluff me by—"

"Three."

"I tell you I'd die a hundred times before—" And Armin's voice had raised to an almost hysterical shriek.

"Four," said Raftner.

A sudden cry from Armin. A dead silence. Then a clicking noise. After a few minutes I heard the voice of Armin say: "This is Armin, gorgeous. I'm at the den. Come over at once. . . . Wrong? No, everything is fine. . . . Right away then. Good. . . . Sure, I have good news for you."

"That," said Raftner, "is more like it."

"That," I said to myself, "is more like what I expected also." No, there was nothing yellow about Armin but his soul.

# SEVEN

# UP POPPED THE DEVIL

■

They talked low after that—very low—Armin trying to convince Raftner, Raftner on his guard. Then I heard them cross the room, heard muffled conversation, and Armin curse and exclaim: "The vases—the one I marked with X. Look—the ones that had the stuff in them!"

"Yeah, I see. No tricks now, Armin. They still have the X on them."

"Yes, but they are not the same vases, not the same design or color even. Look there! Remember? And the crate. By God, it's been opened and nailed up again!"

Loud talk then. Plenty of cursing, the pound of something heavy, and smashing crockery. More pounding, more smashing crockery—and Armin cried out: "Millions—and it's gone! Someone has taken it away."

"Who? Who— Williams!" Raftner shouted and then, "Don't go near that door! Only you could have—"

"Me!" The door was opening, Armin was calling low now: "Sam, come here." Feet then, and the closing door and Armin's,

"You were wrong about the Flame, Raftner. She was not building me up; she's building up herself or—or— By God, she's working for—"

Mumbled words; quick questions. The voice of Sam, stupid, slow, unexcited. I damned near popped out of the vase, but didn't.

Sam was saying: "The Flame gave me money when I found her going through your desk. I thought it was love-letters, Armin. She always seemed jealous about you. I thought nothing of her looking through your things and—"

"The book," said Raftner. "The list of where the stuff was to go. What have you told her, Armin?"

"The book is in my pocket. I told her nothing—very little. Yes, she knew it was dope; didn't know I was head of the organization. She wanted me to make money. She had a key to the door here. I— I— Take that gun off me, Raftner. She made a fool of me. I'll attend to her when she gets here."

Yep, it was just like a good radio program. I could feel Raftner looking at Armin, reading the truth in that cold, cruel face of his.

It was after they chased Sam outside again that Raftner said: "All right, Armin. But I'll make her tell where she put the stuff."

"No," said Armin very slowly, "I'll make her tell. I'll cut tiny pieces from every last inch of her beautiful body—"

"You'll kill her too soon—before she can talk."

"No," said Armin, "I won't kill her too soon. I won't even kill her after she talks. I'll promise her death just as she promised me life on that trip abroad." And after a long pause, "But I'll make it a most horrible death. Yes, I'll make her tell."

That was my cue. Just to pop up with a couple of guns before the Flame even entered the place. I was happy, too, for the first time since I had met the Flame months back and believed she was in this, the rottenest of all rackets. Then I had another thought. Perhaps they were wrong and the Flame was working just for herself.

I'm of a suspicious nature and so I didn't pop up. Perhaps I would hear more when the Flame came. Maybe she'd talk. Maybe they'd talk. Maybe I'd hear where the drugs were hidden. But I was listening to other pleasant conversation.

"About this Mary Morse"—it was Raftner's voice—"she's apt to gum up the works any time. She's safe?"

Armin laughed. It was like static. "Another cute bag of tricks. I missed her going into my apartment because of Williams last night. But I caught her coming out. Yes, she was ready to holler the business from the house tops. She's tied up on the thirty-seventh floor of the Hampton Hotel." He paused for a moment. Then, "It would be just like her to jump from the window, toss herself to the street below."

"God!" said Raftner. "You haven't done that."

"Not yet. I was afraid the police might find some way of identifying her body. That'd mean an investigation and cops and government men here in the shop. Williams will have to die first. The fool nearly forced me into shooting it out with him at my apartment. It's the first time I ever ran from any man, but I couldn't chance the investigation at this time. With Williams dead—and he will be dead—there is no one to know the truth. Conklyn Lee hardly counts. He doesn't know your real identity and he doesn't know mine. I might even keep the girl alive." And talking rapidly and excitedly as if he had just had the thought, "With Williams dead—we might let Mary Morse live. She gets money—plenty of it. If Conklyn Lee knew I had her and would kill her unless she—"

"No, no," Raftner said quietly. "There's more than a million in this for us. You said you had laid the foundation for the next distribution from a house in Brooklyn. The home of a respected lawyer with a big name—slated to be senator—who killed a man twenty years ago. No, Armin. This place will be too hot after tonight. I think your idea of Mary Morse jumping from the window must stand."

I heard Armin's feet move, heard his hand come down upon the desk. I imagined his eyes narrowing and his lips tightening. "O.K.," he said. "The Flame must talk. You've got the men outside. There's no danger from anyone but Williams—"

"Yes." I didn't need to see Raftner's face; the hate was in his words. He spat as if he still tasted that cigar. "There are two men with machine guns in the alley. I had hoped to be well away in the truck before Williams could act and now—"

A sudden silence. I heard the opening door, Sam's voice, then the closing door again and a single pair of feet across that hard floor. Quick steps, woman's steps; steps that stopped before they reached the rug. Then a voice said: "What's up, Armin? You and

Raftner look white as ghosts. Anything wrong?" The voice was the voice of the Flame.

Feet went toward her, I guess. Armin spoke softly. "Why nothing, beautiful. What could be wrong with us?" Then, "To love the Flame is to die. To rat out on Armin Loring is—" A half scream, a muffled curse, a dull thud and a falling body.

Raftner spoke. "You fool, Armin! What did you hit her for? She must talk, must—"

"I couldn't help it—the two-timing little tart. Besides—her purse. Look at that gun. She'd use it, too."

I damned near popped out then, but I didn't. I waited and guessed what was going on outside. Moving feet, low voices; something knocked against the side of the desk, I think. Raftner was saying something about making the Flame trap me much as Armin had trapped her.

It was hard waiting till she came to five minutes later—maybe ten. Anyway it seemed a long time before they were hammering questions at her and she was answering defiantly.

Finally she said: "That's right, boys. I got the filthy stuff you wanted to flood the city with. You'll never find it now. Armin, you're a fool. One Man Armin—taken in by a woman. Now you'd torture the woman. Well—see how that woman takes it."

"You worked with Williams, didn't you?" Raftner shot the words through his teeth. "Race Williams—that was it, wasn't it? By God, you were the woman to fool Armin—to fool men! But Williams was clever."

The Flame laughed. It wasn't a nice laugh. "Clever? Williams is dumb. He couldn't have fooled you two for a minute. He wouldn't have let me try. No, I wasn't working with him. I was working for him—but without him knowing it. It was I who made you clever men threaten him. Mary Morse couldn't have brought him back by pleading with him. I couldn't have brought him into it again by pleading with him. He's built backward. You forced him back by threats he wouldn't take, and they were at my suggestion. Mary Morse told him not to come, fearing for his life—and I put that fear into her head. You attempted to kill him—I put the attempt into your heads. And it was an attempt that nearly suceeded when Armin kept me, so that I failed to warn him. Yes, Race is a stupid, gun-toting fool. Yet he's worth a dozen of either of you because he wins out through his lack of fear—his very conceit."

Maybe I turned slightly red in that tight-fitting vase, but Raftner said: "And just why did you do this—risk your life for Race Williams?"

"Because he saw no good in me. Because he saw only bad. Because he never believed in me. Because I wanted him to believe me—and want me. Not because I'm the Flame who can make any man love her—including the great One Man Armin. No, I wanted Race to like the girl he once thought me to be. I know I'm going to die."

There was passion in Armin's voice, a passion that he could not control. He said: "But you don't know how you're going to die."

"I didn't fail." There was a proud ring in the Flame's voice. "The drugs are gone, hidden far away where you'll never find them. I don't care what you do—no, not even if you cut me to ribbons."

"What a coincidence," said Armin Loring. "My dear, that is exactly what we are going to do. Cut you to ribbons."

"Unless," said Raftner, "you tell us where the drugs are."

"And," added Armin, "trap Race Williams for us."

"Trap him!" she said. "The only man I ever loved! Why—"

She didn't scream exactly. It was more a quick breath, a sucking sort of breath.

And the show was over. The curtain was to ring down on the final act. I felt good way down inside me. The thing was so simple, too. These men were busy with the girl. Feared, desperate killers both of them. Yet, I had nothing to do but pop out of that vase like a jack-in-the-box, throw a couple of guns over the rim and give them both the dose if they preferred it that way.

Dramatic? Sure it was dramatic. I knew that when the Flame winced again—yes, an audible wince if you understand what I mean. So I took my cue. I gripped both my guns firmly, straightened my body as best I could, braced my feet and started my body upward.

My head went up into the neck of that vase, but my shoulders didn't. They stuck; stuck there in that neck just as my head came out over the top. And I knew the truth—the horrible truth. I had gotten into the vase through the very force of my falling body. Now—I could not get out!

# EIGHT

# BLAST-OUT

■

The Flame cried out and I made another desperate effort, felt the vase rock slightly, nearly got my shoulders wedged so that I could go neither up nor down. What if my head stuck out with my arms pinned down at my sides? What if the vase should turn over and—and—I couldn't save the Flame then. Good God! I could kill them afterward, of course—sometime, someplace. I shuddered. Kill them after the Flame was dead; after I had crouched there helpless while they tortured her to death!

Minutes must have passed since my brain went dead. Things must have changed outside. The Flame was saying: "Telephone Race?" Her laugh was high-pitched, but determined just the same. "Trap him to his death—to watch you torture him so I will tell you where the rotten stuff is. No, no, no! I want him to live—live to kill you! I left a note to be delivered to him if I was murdered. I wanted him to know the truth about me then. He'll kill you—both of you. Good old stupid Race. He'd like it that way. He'd— What are you going to do with that knife! My mouth!"

Armin said very slowly: "You wish to laugh at us, Florence. I wish to make your mouth wider so that you may better enjoy that laugh. So we, too, can enjoy that laugh. Like this—"

God! I couldn't see. I didn't know what was happening. There was a struggle. I heard that and—

A hole in the vase would mean a chance to see; a second, a chance to shoot. I placed my guns against the side of that vase, one above the other. Two holes—or would there be any holes? What was the damned vase made of? It might be steel; it might be copper. The lead might strike, ricochet and—and— No, I couldn't live to get them then. I couldn't live to get them anyway, once I fired that gun. No chance at all. A single bullet-hole—two holes. With the best of luck—the greatest of luck, I might hit one man. But the shots would be heard and the other man— No, I didn't dare shoot.

"All right, Raftner." Armin's voice was high now, gloating as he said: "Hold her so. The left side first. That pretty mouth slit close to the left ear before we crop that ear. Hold her steady— steady. That's it."

Both my fingers closed. My body stiffened, tightened. The roar was terrific!

God! What had happened? I was choked with smoke and burned powder. The entire room had collapsed around me, not on me, for I was there; there in the center of the room, crouched low, blinking in the light; blinking straight up into the surprised eyes of Raftner. Raftner who had turned from the Flame; turned from the back of the chair in which he held her while Armin—

I knew then. The vase was gone, smashed into a thousand pieces. And Raftner hurled his huge body toward me—over me. He was crashing down upon me, both arms out, both hands grasping for my throat.

Then I heard Armin Loring's voice. "On top of him, Raftner! Pin him to the floor. I've got—"

That's all I heard then. I fired twice—just an upward flip of both guns and a split second between the shots. Did he fall dead on me pinning me to the floor? Not him—not a guy with forty-fours pounding into his chest. He picked himself up like an acrobat in the circus. Yes, picked himself up and went out on his back. I never saw or heard a man hit the floor harder with his head.

\* \* \*

My head still rang with those first two shots and the smashing vase. I staggered to my feet and shouted the words above the din in my head. "I'm on the kill, Armin!" I bellowed out like a madman. "On the kill!"

Whether it was the busting vase, the crashing body of Raftner or my shouting voice, I don't know. But Armin lost his head. He gave me a chance to rise and face him as he rushed to the Flame, raised his knife and yelled: "Drop the guns, Race, or she takes the—"

I lowered one gun and shot at the only part of his body I could see as he crouched there before the Flame, huddled in the chair. It was his leg—just below the knee. Did I hit it? Hell—you know me. I don't shoot at things I don't hit.

Armin regained his head then. I saw him step back and I saw that famous draw of his—that double draw—just both hands across his chest. You couldn't tell if they went under his coat or not, but they were both holding guns, both blazing as mine were blazing.

I had a sort of numb feeling as if I were going to drop. Then a sudden stab of pain in my cheek—sharp, quick pain that cleared that numb feeling.

There was blood on Armin's face—on mine, too, I guess. Warm—I felt it. But the blood was in Armin's eyes. He fired again before I did. I'll give him credit for that. But he either fired too soon or the blood blocked his vision. But he saw enough. Saw death and threw himself toward the Flame there in the chair for protection. I pushed out both my arms, twisted my guns in and fired twice.

Maybe Armin intended to kill the Flame then. Maybe he thought more of killing the Flame than of killing me; maybe it wasn't protection he sought after all—only vengeance. But I had fired directly—and surely—and calmly. Armin Loring was hurled backward. He half sank, straightened, crashed against the desk behind him. Then we hit it off together. Just crashing lead. If a tommy gun had opened up in that cellar, the staccato notes of spitting steel couldn't have been closer together.

Wildly, blindly we fired? Well, maybe Armin did. I didn't. My lead spun him from the desk, turned him completely around. I took a slug in the right side just above the hip bone.

And I did it. Two shots into his stomach, another one into his chest. He was spinning like a top now, firing as he spun, and I got him—just as clean as I ever got any man.

Eyes that were bright and hateful dimmed, faded and went blank. A small hole started to widen in his forehead, turn from black to blue, then a dull sort of red with tiny bubbles in it.

He didn't pound to the floor—not Armin. He sank very slowly to his knees, stayed there a moment, then twisted grotesquely and rolled over on his back. I wasn't any too steady myself now as I stood above him. I was nodding my head, saying over and over: "No fooling, Armin. No fooling."

The Flame! She had been in the chair. Now she was close to me, under my arm, holding me there. Had they done it? Had Armin done it? Had he ripped that knife across her face and—and—

"Florence," I said. "Your mouth—your mouth."

"Yes, Race, yes," was all she said as she pulled down my head and put her mouth hard against mine.

I had never really known if I loved the Flame. I didn't know then. But I stretched out my arms, pulled her to me, felt the guns still tight in my hands and— Suddenly I turned and faced the door that was opening. The machine-gunners—the men Raftner had there! I had saved the Flame. We were alive. I wanted to live and now—

The door slid wider. Figures were there in the gloom. I felt the Flame grab at my arms, but I was aiming straight at those figures as the trigger fingers of both my hands closed tightly.

*Click, click.* No more. Both my guns were empty, and—and Sergeant O'Rourke was pounding flat-footed toward me. There was Nelson, too. A couple of harness bulls and some plainclothesmen. And sneaking along on the side I saw the trembling figure of Conklyn Lee.

I guess Lee was talking to me. Anyway he was saying: "Mary was gone—no word from her. You were here—no word from you. I—I telephoned Sergeant O'Rourke and here I am. I—I had to."

I said to Conklyn Lee: "What did you tell him—tell the sergeant—these others?" I saw things going after all.

"He didn't tell us anything, Race," O'Rourke said. "He met us before the shop. There were guys with tommy guns outside. But they dropped them and ran when they saw us. Flannigan and his men will get them on the block behind. Suppose you tell us."

"Suppose I tell you, Sergeant—and you, too, Inspector." The Flame was as serene now as if nothing had happened. "You never believed in me, Sergeant, but Race did; kept it from you, but believed in me. These men here—one, Raftner, whom you've wanted for a long time—were blackmailing Mary Morse for something her Uncle Frank Morse, who disappeared, had done. They made use of her store. She came straight to Race. We advised her to pretend to submit to the blackmail, once Race suspected it was the narcotics crowd. You nearly spoiled it a couple of times, Sergeant—the government men, too. You see, I had to pose as a friend of Armin Loring."

Now you've got to admit that was a good story. I couldn't have told a better one myself—maybe not so good a one.

I added my bit by saying that Mary Morse was safe. I didn't say where; she might speak out of turn. I wanted to see her first—regardless of the lead in me.

"And the narcotics?" It was Nelson who shot that one in as he nearly stumbled over Armin's outstretched legs.

"In the vases over there—the real ones in the back," the Flame said almost indifferently. "Race and I moved them away from the other vases to be sure nothing would go wrong if Race were killed. Race is hurt, Inspector. He'll have to have treatment. No hospital—I'll take care of him." And looking at me, "And what's more, Race, you've got an assistant who'll see that you collect this time from the Mary Morse fund or there'll be a surrogate shot around here." And when I started to ask her what of Mary Morse she whispered, "I'll set her free when I have you home in bed and a good surgeon digging into you."

O'Rourke, with the help of Conklyn Lee, had found the drugs. Nelson was looking at the body of Armin Loring—bending closer. He straightened finally and paid me a compliment. Oh, maybe he didn't mean to, but it was in his voice more than his words.

"You, Race—" he said. "You shot it out man to man with—with Armin Loring. Why he was the most feared man in the city. No one—"

I cut in waving my hand deprecatingly as the Flame took my arm, supporting my slightly sagging body. But I got my final crack in before she sat me in a chair. I said: "It was really nothing, Nelson. Armin Loring. Nothing to me, Inspector—just another stiff."

# CITY OF BLOOD

■

*A thousand dollars a day—that was the fee
Race got for acting as public executioner
in Redmond City. And he hardly thought the
job was worth it at that—till he met the
D.A.'s daughter and arranged a one-gun-
against-gunocracy deal that netted him a
week's salary and quick curtains for the little
group of enterprising citizens who had
signed a petition with lead slugs to change
the first half of their town's name to "Blood."*

# ONE

# A THOUSAND DOLLARS A DAY

■

Action, eh? For once I got my fill of it. I was doing lunch at Rostoff's place. There was a portly gent a bit out from my table and a lad with him, who, though dressed up in high-priced clothes, looked like a thug just the same.

His nose had gone flat, but his mouth hadn't. He could talk all over his face, and his conversation was about me. He was slipping it to his companion, as if he got the words out of a dirty book.

"Race Williams, huh? If this punk, Williams, wants shooting, I'll nail him down to the sidewalk with lead so hard it will take a dozen undertakers to lift him up."

There wasn't anyone but me to hear, and I stood for it as I read my evening paper.

New York seemed a quiet town considering what was going on down in Redmond City, a spot with over two hundred thousand bodies—and not all dead bodies, though the boys were passing out fast enough.

Yep, the set-up was grand. The mayor was almost openly linked with crime. The D.A. had been elected on a drive-out-crime ticket, and the best citizens had formed their own vigilance committees, but did not know just what to do except to pay for protection and try to dodge occasional bullets. It's a well-known fact, of course, that a person is murdered every hour in the dear old U.S.A. But Redmond City, which the papers had renamed just Red City, seemed to be going out to better that record all by itself.

Criminals were deputy sheriffs. Shady birds had been put on the police force, and more than a dozen imported private detectives from well-known detective agencies, called down there by the D.A., had been shot to death within the month.

Detectives? You know the kind. Tough, honest, dumb guys who were riddled in the back while they were leaning over to pick up a bit of evidence—or climbing through the window of a politician's house and killed "while attempting robbery."

Yes, Red City was making the headlines all over the country—with first one house bombed, then another, and twice the attempted abduction of the D.A.'s daughter.

I read the editorial in the *Globe*. They weren't riding me exactly—rather, riding our own D.A., Walter Gargan, who had been landing heavily on me lately. The *Globe* wondered why I didn't go down to Redmond City, turn the dump inside out, get myself shot and so out of the hair of New York City's district attorney. I'm a private investigator who always shot sort of loosely—and didn't want the D.A.'s attention called to it so much.

And Big Mouth at the next table grew a bit louder. It was all about me. Others must have heard him. I grinned. These were respectable citizens who might make good witnesses later, if there were trouble over a corpse.

I looked directly at Big Mouth and got a surprise. He had a gun on his knees beneath the table. I didn't see it, but I knew it was there just the same. He was moving his empty left hand about too easily and trying to make it do the work of two hands.

Here was a cheap punk with a gun in his hand, trying to get my goat so as he'd have a chance to kill me. Mind you—kill me when I was sporting two guns!

Had the portly gent hired this bird to kill me? But the portly gent looked like he had some sense. Yet this guy had murder in his face, in his heart—but most of all in the right hand beneath the table.

I didn't know the answer then—didn't know it when I slipped a bill under the lunch check and came slowly to my feet. I was watching Big Mouth out of one eye. He was pulling threatening faces, and probably scaring a couple of dear old ladies from New England who were seeing the town.

I turned from my table, with just one thought. The scowl would have gone off Big Mouth's puss if he had known that thought. I was thinking, "Will I give him the dose now and make sure?" If I had actually seen that gun in his right hand, I'd have popped him over where I stood and pointed to his gun for an excuse.

But why make trouble for yourself? I don't shoot lads just for the fun of it.

So I swung easily toward the hatcheck girl, my right hand brushing back my hair and my left one swinging at my side. As I reached his chair, he looked directly up at me, spat a dirty name and started to his feet. He shot up his right hand—and there was a gun in it.

By God, he meant business. And, by God, he got business!

He stuck his chin out, but never fully got to his feet. I brought my left hand up from my knee—back and up. The gun in it cracked him with terrific force right on the end of that chin he fancied was tough.

Did he fire? He did not. I never suspected for a moment that he would. My blow was particularly vicious. I thought I had knocked his head clear off his shoulders. But I hadn't, for his entire body followed his head into the air—high over the back of the chair— and only stopped when his head cracked on the marble floor.

The portly gentleman sat stiff and straight. Others were on their feet. Somewhere a whistle blew, and I was explaining to the manager and a headquarters dick who had been eating there.

"This gentleman, here"—I tossed a hand toward the portly guy—"was in danger of his life. I happened to hear the man's talk, recognized the fact that he was full of dope—then saw the gun." My shoulders shrugged. "Naturally, I saved the gentleman's life."

The portly gent was rubbing a handkerchief across his forehead, sputtering out his words.

"What this gentleman says is quite correct. This—that man there on the floor—the one they're lifting now—sat at the table beside me. Threatened me with a gun, and—good gracious, I owe this gentleman my life!"

I leaned over, patted him on the back, wisecracked loud and

heartily: "Really, it isn't worth mentioning." Bending over close to his ear so that the others did not hear, I whispered: "Give me a wide berth, brother. The next time I see you, comes it five bullets right in the breadbasket."

Then I straightened, grinned at the police lieutenant who came in, and walked quickly toward the door. He didn't stop me—just looked after me. You had to have an open-and-shut case to drag Race Williams in—and hold him.

The next morning I had my talk with the D.A. He rapped his pencil on the desk and looked at me. "Well," I told him, "the lad had a gun in his hand—and meant to use it. Didn't you get a statement from him in the hospital?"

The D.A. smiled grimly.

"He hasn't made any statement."

"Won't talk, eh? Tough guy." I shook my head.

"Can't talk." The D.A. got up and paced the room. Suddenly he said: "God in Heaven, Race, why must you be so brutal about these things!" Then he added: "Did you see the morning papers? Yes, I mean about Redmond City, and them sending for you. But the police commissioner and mayor said they would not tolerate any outsider or—" He glanced at the paper on the desk. " 'Hoodlum' is the word they used for you." He smiled broadly and pressed a button on the desk.

I jarred up and waited. It was the star reporter of the *Globe*. The D.A. grinned, as Tommy Rafferty fired questions at me.

"Any word, Williams? One of the papers in Redmond City is for your coming in. The other one's against it. Then there's Frankie Spontz. You know—former big Chicago killer—ace man now for Johnny Vernon. Vernon ran all the gambling houses and other dives in Red City before Edward T. Martin, the new district attorney of Redmond County, started his clean-up. Johnny Vernon is running the mayor and everything now. He won't let a plum like that be taken from him."

"What are you giving me," I said, "a history of that town? Don't I have enough trouble right here with him?" I shot a finger toward New York's district attorney.

"But this Frankie Spontz—he's supposedly a special investigator for the mayor, but, in reality, is Johnny Vernon's killer. He's bad—none worse unless it's Johnny Vernon himself. But Vernon doesn't need to go into action while he has Spontz. Look at the private dicks who died down there. Look at the war on between Martin and Pendleton, the mayor. Between it all, the honest citizen is robbed and often killed."

"You lads fill your papers with wind. Make up a lot of stuff."

"But Frankie Spontz's statement about you coming down?" And before I could answer that one, not knowing what the statement was, Tommy Rafferty went on: "And look here." He tapped the folded newspaper in his hand. "Latest report is that Edward Martin, the district attorney of Redmond County, which consists mostly of Redmond City, has taken a plane to fly on here and hire you. Every paper has that story."

"That's just more wind," I said. "He wouldn't do that, and, if he did, he'd come to see me."

"He would—and he has."

I turned, faced the man. Slim, delicate build, but the face of a fighter—somewhere under fifty. "Who the hell are you?" I said, without thinking.

"I am Edward T. Martin, district attorney of Redmond County. I have come to hire your services." The gray-haired man looked at me.

"You"—I guess I sort of patted myself on the back—"you want me to clear up that war alone? Is that what you mean?"

"That is exactly what I mean." Martin nodded.

"I told him," said our D.A. rather stiffly, "that you were a man who was without fear, without heart or without soul, and made a business of killing men." The D.A. paused. "Yes, damn near made a habit of it."

"He did!" I said to Martin. "He told you that? I've never killed unless it was to save a client's life—or my life."

"That is exactly what I want." Mr. Martin nodded gravely. "I want you to come there with the purpose of saving your own life." He raised a hand when I would have spoken. "I will make you a law officer—a detective assigned to the district attorney's office, responsible only to me. I will back everything you do—stand squarely behind you. I will keep you out of jail. I only ask that you keep yourself alive. You will apparently be brought to Redmond City to protect my daughter."

"And you expect one man to restore law and order—one man to save Redmond City?"

"I did not at first, but I do now," Edward T. Martin said very steadily. "My daughter, Margie, said to me, 'It took only one man—Johnny Vernon—to wreck law and order. It took only one man to ruin the entire city. If a man like Johnny Vernon can ruin it, a man like Race Williams can save it.'"

That sounded nice—damned nice—and maybe I puffed out my chest a bit. But I didn't know if a dozen or more other dicks hadn't heard the same line and gone down to Red City and gotten their ears shot off for listening to a pretty girl's flattery.

One man against a hundred—against a thousand, maybe ten thousand. I started to shake my head, then stopped. The girl was right. It would be one man against one man—and that one man was Johnny Vernon. Of course, he'd be after my hide as soon as I hit Red City, but then I'd be after his, too. I started to talk, stopped, rubbed my chin.

"It's a dangerous job. You admit that?"

"Very dangerous—almost sure death. I not only admit it, I want you to know how thoroughly I appreciate it."

"So at last we found something that frightens you, Race," Gargan horned in. "At least you value your life."

"Sure," I told him. "Everything has a commercial value—even my life. The odds are heavy against me." I ran a tongue around in my cheek and gave it straight to Martin. "Danger, death—sudden and violent—I always reckon in hard cash. The job would be worth plenty."

Martin nodded.

"A rich man is paying for your services—a good citizen of Redmond City. My daughter has set the price that should be paid to you. I have only one offer, Mr. Williams. All expenses and one thousand dollars a day."

It jarred me back on my heels.

A thousand berries a day! A seven-day week. Why, I'd be getting paid like a movie star. And the job would be a couple of guns to use as I pleased. The hunting of human vultures. The killing, perhaps, of the very men who had shot to death, or ordered shot to death, those private dicks. The district attorney behind every move—no chance of prison. Sure, I smiled. Sure, I shook hands with Martin—and heard Tommy Rafferty of the *Globe* saying: "We want a statement. Nothing you said to Mr. Martin here will be used. But are you going—and what answer do you make to Frankie Spontz's threat of what will happen to you if you reach Red City?"

"And what," I finally got around to that, "was Frankie Spontz's threat?"

"Frankie Spontz's threat is that, as a deputy sheriff of Red City, he would permit no hired killer—whether hired by Mr. Martin or not—to leave the train at Red City. He stated that he would push a gun in your stomach and—"

"And what?" I was bristling a bit. I wanted to know.

"And either take you to jail or close a finger on the trigger. That was for public consumption. Privately, he said he'd claim you tried to draw a gun and he'll kill you."

I lit a butt, stuck my thumbs in the armholes of my vest.

"You can print this," I said. "If Frankie Spontz sticks a gun in my stomach, I'll shoot all his teeth down his throat before he ever has a chance to press the trigger."

There was more talk after that. The D.A. gave me the layout and told me that the train I was to take the next afternoon would arrive at Redmond City at exactly five o'clock the following afternoon. He would have the station well guarded, as he feared a demonstration, and I was to shoot at the least provocation.

Our D.A. laughed out loud.

"You'll have the dead lying in the streets," he said.

"Well"—I was feeling pretty good—"for a thousand dollars a day Mr. Martin's entitled to a few stiffs. What's more, he'll get them." Pounding a finger against Martin's chest, and cutting out the kidding, I went on: "Listen, Mr. Martin. You're paying one thousand dollars a day for services. That's a lot of jack, even for me. Call it conceit if you want, but there isn't one man in a million who can put a gun on me—and use it."

"Yes, yes." There was doubt in his voice. "That's what my daughter, Margie, said. She was at us for months to come to you." He lifted a book of typewritten sheets from his briefcase. "She sent you these—everything she knows or I know—about Redmond City. The murderers, their records—everything."

I took the bundle, nodded my head. I was thinking that Margie wasn't so bad at that. She had a lot of sense. I'd even have gone to Redmond City and protected her for nothing. Well, maybe not for nothing—but certainly for nine hundred or nine hundred and fifty a day.

# T W O

# A GLUTTON FOR GUNS

■

Things were all fixed for my departure, next day. Train tickets, drawing-room and all the rest. That night I spent reading an account of the activities of Redmond City. It would have made nice reading for a lad interested in death upon the public streets, disappearing or unwilling and lying witnesses, a grand jury that was too crooked or too scared to indict. The prosecutor, Edward T. Martin, was so honest he was tripping over his own feet. Certainly, Margie Martin, his daughter, had an eye for detail in her book of facts.

I wasn't interested in the past of Red City. I was interested in its present and future. I was interested in Spontz and Vernon, their deeds or misdeeds, tortures or murders. But there was one case of arson credited entirely to Johnny Vernon—a hotel fire that had burned seventeen women and children to death. That turned over in my stomach a bit.

Unbelievable? Of course not. The same thing happens all over the country. Redmond City was just having it out in the open. It's boiled over in cities before, with gunmen right in the statehouse.

Jerry, my boy, was packing the bags, enjoying the idea of a trip.

The phone rang. It was the house phone to the lobby. I took the earful and admit my surprise.

"There's a Mr. Vernon to see you," the boy on the phone said. "He's got two friends with him. He says it's business, and he wants to be sure you know what the two friends are for before he comes up."

"Sure," I told the boy. "Tell Mr. Vernon to bring them right up." Vernon, the great Johnny Vernon, the terror of Red City—and he brought a bodyguard. But I liked it; it showed respect.

I gave Jerry quick orders, helped him get the bags out of the library, adjusted my shoulder harness, tapped the two forty-fours for luck, then slipped into my jacket.

Vernon was an eyeful—not simply a high-priced clothes rack. Plain blue suit, white shirt, somber, blue tie—and a cane over his arm. It was just the yellow gloves and the edge of the handkerchief that gave him color. His eyes were a little too close to his nose. His lips were too thin, but Vernon looked like a man who had gone places and intended to go more places. He would, too, if he crossed lead with me.

The two muggs with him were a bit loud. I suppose they were as loud as Vernon would stand for. But they had *heel* written all over them. They were the usual tall and short men, in the ordinary witness's description of a killing. But they didn't have their hands in their pockets, so I followed them toward my library.

"Really, Mr. Williams, your hospitality overwhelms me," Vernon said easily. "I know you have not heard well of me—indeed, quite the contrary. As you say, my business is with you, and these men simply—"

I cut in there.

"If the big one shoves that right hand in his pocket, he isn't going to take it out again." This as we reached the library. "There—the couch. The three of you on it. Hands on knees. That's fine. You wouldn't want to lose any of the boys."

Vernon sat on the couch, the two gunmen on either side of him. Not a gun showed. Not a gun was going to show, either—at least in the hand of a live man.

Johnny Vernon leaned back and laughed. "Young, impetuous and a killer. I'm glad to meet you, Race. I'm here to make you a business proposition. Someone thinks rather highly of you in Redmond City. Ever since that reporter got shot, the papers are playing it up. Redmond City is the same as any other city. It's just getting publicity with this new district attorney, Martin. He's a worried sort of chap who—"

"You haven't come here to tell me that." Then I had to toss out another warning. "If your little rat on the right continues with the straightening of his lapel, I'll pin his hand across his chest."

"You heard what the gentleman said, Shorty," Vernon chirped and his words rasped. "Keep your hands on your knees—like mine. Let Mr. Williams see we are on a peaceful mission." He said to me: "It's like this, Race. People like to play a bit. The boys like to furnish the places for them to play in. Things were peaceful in Redmond City, until Martin came in. Martin kicked up a fuss and—well, people got hurt. Some took things seriously and got killed—and that made the front pages." He raised his left hand slowly, pushed back the lapel of his coat showing an empty holster, and, after saying, "Permit me," produced a long black wallet and threw it on the table.

"Twenty-five grand in cash, Race—right on the line." He stuck his cane between his knees and snapped his fingers. "It's yours, boy. Just to stay out of Redmond City—a town you have never seen."

"That's a lot of jack," I told him. "So you're afraid of me."

He looked directly at me and shook his head.

"The mayor is getting things under control. I'm helping him. In another month—two or three at the most—Redmond City will be a model town. Mayor Pendleton and the district attorney will not be at odds and"—he leaned forward—"I'll be putting a small fortune away for my retirement. No, I'm not afraid of you, Williams—not in the least. It's just that if you should get by the reception committee of Frankie Spontz, you'll raise hell all over that city and slow up things. It's sure death for you, but it will delay business. We know your methods, don't want to have to dispose of you as a martyr, so offer you that money."

"And if I don't take it?"

Johnny Vernon grinned.

"I've never met you, Race. I've never even traded a bit of lead with you. But I'm as quick as I ever was with a gun. You know you

can't lick a thousand organized men turned loose in the city. You
know you can't stand with your back to the wall and shoot them
down. You know that would mean death to you, just as it did to
those other dicks. So I figured out why you took the job—and how
you'll work.''

"How?" I was a good listener.

"Well"—Vernon smiled pleasantly and stroked his chin—
"you'll figure that you'll start work at the top instead of the
bottom. You figure you'll find me the first chance you get and put a
bullet in my back. Understand, I'm not criticizing you. But that's
your figuring, isn't it?" He couldn't keep the eagerness out of his
voice, nor maybe a touch of fear, for his lips moved spasmodically.

"You guessed it, Johnny," I said simply.

"You go in for murder, then?"

"If you want to call it that." I spread my hands apart. "You
control a thousand men—maybe more. I wouldn't let you send
them all out to have a shot at me. I'm glad you came tonight,
Johnny. I always like a guy to know just where he stands. You've
got it right. If Spontz makes his try when I enter Red City, be sure
he doesn't miss. For if he misses, he'll be deader than hell."

"So what?"

I moved my shoulders a bit.

"He's your man. You sent him. I won't stand around like the
others boys you had shot to death. I'll hunt you up, Johnny
Vernon, and give you the dose."

"Yeah?" Johnny came to his feet, snatched up his wallet and
stuck it in his pocket. "And what do you think I'll be doing while
you're looking for me?"

"If you're wise, Johnny, you'll be putting miles between
Redmond City and yourself. The D.A.'s men—the hired detectives
from New York—spent their time trying to find the lad who shot at
them or killed their pals. Not me. I'll be figuring that every shot
that comes my way—comes directly from you. So I'm going to
shoot the man the orders come from, through the chest or through
the back. I'm no hero, Johnny. It will all depend on which way
you're facing when I see you."

Johnny Vernon leaned forward. His two men had also come to
their feet. They were half bent toward the table behind which I

stood. "I can do a few things with a gun myself," Johnny said. "You're not meeting any punk now."

"No? That's only one man's opinion, Johnny." And, when eyes blazed and his hands moved up dangerously toward his coat, his bodyguards also letting their fingers rise a bit, I banged both my empty hands down on the desk, leaned forward and struck my face almost against Johnny Vernon's face. If he wanted action, he could have it. I'm not fussy where guns explode. I gave him what was on my mind.

"You killed those women and you burnt those kids to death just because the cheap grocer on the ground floor wouldn't kick in." Maybe I snarled the words, but certainly I meant them. "Now, both my hands are empty. There's you and the two punks. If you can do anything with a gun, let's settle it right now."

Maybe I didn't mean to call for a showdown when I started. But once I got wound up, I was ready to go. If he could do things with a gun, I wanted to see him do it.

For a good fifteen seconds we faced each other. Then I lifted my hands and crossed them over my chest. So we stood, my two guns against their three surprised looks.

Fair is fair. I'm no freer from temptation than the next fellow. My fingers were doing tricks with the triggers of both guns, and, if I had known then what I knew later, maybe I'd have closed those fingers. Not heroic that? Not good ethics that? Well, perhaps not, but it would be good common sense, and I never was one to favor pampering the criminal.

But Johnny was moving sideways from the couch toward the door. His two bodyguards slid with him. It wasn't a case of seeing the whites of their eyes, but they all showed the whites of their hands. Johnny sneered his words.

"Big guy, eh? I suppose you've got a dozen men behind curtains ready to shoot. The offer I made you is off. I wouldn't let you live now if you got down on your knees and begged for it." At the door, he said: "You had your chance and you didn't take it."

"That's right," I half murmured aloud. "I had my chance but I didn't take it."

Johnny Vernon grinned just before the door closed behind the three of them. But I don't think he knew exactly what my words meant. They had nothing to do with the money Vernon had offered me. It was the chance to kill him I was thinking about. Yep, the chance to plug him right between the eyes.

But we all have our weaknesses. I let it ride—me who had been talking about not coddling criminals.

# THREE

# AIR AMBUSH

■

The next afternoon the train pulled rapidly out of New York, and Jerry and I were on the way to Redmond City, alias Red City. I locked our drawing-room door and gave the eager Jerry the office. Jerry was the boy I had picked up in the city years ago.

"It's like this, kid," I told him as I opened our bags and lifted out a couple of extra guns. "There will be times when the two rods I carry won't be enough. So wear your overcoat. I don't care how hot it is. Carry a couple of shoulder rods and a couple in the overcoat pockets. I'll want you close to me and—"

I came to my feet, let a rod slip into my mitt, and, stepping back, nodded at the door from which the knocking came.

The porter was shaking, when Jerry let him in. He had heard my name and knew my business. The note he delivered was from Edward Martin, the district attorney, and read—

Race Williams:

Our plans have changed. I want you to leave the train at (and he named a big city). The train will arrive there at

8:00 A.M.. Take a taxi directly to the airport and catch the 8:30 plane to Redmond City.

My daughter may be aboard that plane. I have reason to believe that a trip she made is known, and an attempt to harm her may be made during her return. If she is on that plane, make yourself known to her. If she is not, take the plane, anyway. I have arranged with the air-transport company to show her every consideration and for them to reserve a seat on that plane for you under the name of "Jackson Travers."

I dared not wire you. So I telephoned a friend who will write you my message directly as I dictated it and see that the porter delivers it promptly.

I am sorry your arrival by train cannot take place, but I have every reason to believe my daughter Margie's life is in peril—perhaps deadly peril.

Edward T. Martin

So Jerry and I left the train, slipped silently from the rear platform and into the shadows of the freight yard. The timing was great. The plane was about ready to leave, though we walked leisurely across the field, after I received the ticket held for Jackson Travers, and gave Jerry his final instructions.

"Hop the next plane, which leaves an hour from now," I told him. I thought back through that mess of sheets the girl had written and finally said: "Trot up to the Redmond Ritz Hotel, grab yourself a room and wait around for me." I turned toward the plane. "See you soon, Jerry."

The plane was carrying six people and a big enough load for that time of the morning. The hostess was young, easy to look at and nervous as hell.

Two men—one reading a paper and the other dozing off—were up near the pilot. A fat gent, already fast asleep, was in the seat just ahead of me. A middle-aged lady, twisting at her handkerchief—evidently her first flight and evidently an emergency one—sat straight and stiff, determined to go through with it. Then there was a young guy who didn't know what to do with his hat, received no help from the nervous or inexperienced hostess, and did everything to pretend he wasn't having his first flight.

As for me, I jerked down my cap and sat tight in the last chair. There was still a draft and I didn't have any manners, anyway.

The girl wasn't aboard, after all. Without any additional customers, the plane glided over the concrete and slipped into the air.

I shrugged my shoulders and asked the hostess for a drink of water, drank what her trembling hand left in the cup and did my good deed for that day.

"Listen, sister," I told her. "If it's your first run, buck up and put on an act. No one need be onto you. If you got troubles that bother you, the same tonic goes." I looked her over good now. "You're a swell-looking girl—a knock-out in that uniform. The men won't notice anything wrong. The dame across the aisle has her own worries. Me, I'm for you one hundred percent."

"That's very kind of you." Her voice trembled slightly. "My brother was hurt in a crash today, and it's taken something out of me."

The young man finally got used to the air. The two men in front switched positions. The one on the right now read the newspaper, and the one on the left slept. The fat gent had awakened and was pointing out to himself spots of interest below. The middle-aged woman sat tight. It was a fine day, and I sat back to enjoy the trip. For another half hour the picture remained the same.

Then things changed—changed completely.

The man reading the newspaper came to his feet, turned suddenly and stretched an arm into the pilot's compartment. The side of his head was plainly visible. The lad asleep woke up and, turning, leaned over the seat and looked dreamily at the passengers. Then he lifted his two hands above the seat. The hands held two heavy revolvers. His words were rough, even to me.

"We have a passenger with us we don't like," he said. "Someone with guts—or he claims to have them. Someone who would clean up Redmond City. Someone who would give up their life for the people of Redmond City." A long pause there, and my eyes widened. Was the man talking about me? Was the man a fool or was he mad? Why, I was holding a gun against the side of my seat and had been from the moment he turned his puss around. What's more, the heavy man, who was pointing out the scenery to himself, blocked me from being shot.

Yes, I could have killed him. Why didn't I? Because of the lad close to the pilot. I couldn't get a good line on him, at the moment. If he were a nervous lad, heard my shot or saw his companion burnt down, he might kill the pilots—both of them.

But the lad wasn't talking about me.

"It's a young lady," he said, "rather cleverly disguised if we did not know her. Friends"—he liked the sound of his own voice— "the little lady in the company's uniform makes a charming picture. It's her first job and her last. If you look closely you can see her own dress beneath the uniform. She really is Miss Margie Martin, daughter of Edward Martin, district attorney of Redmond County and champion cleaner-upper of bad men. We'll give him something to clean up." He almost snarled. "There's the door in the rear, Miss Martin. Open it and step out." Before the middle-aged lady could get her scream out, he said: "That's right, Miss Martin. Open it and step out into space. For every minute you delay, a person in this plane will die."

The girl stood there paralyzed with fear. The man's lips twisted.

"Why, Miss Martin, I'm surprised at you! You spoke and wrote that you would gladly give up your life for Redmond City and the people of Redmond City. Now, you'll sacrifice the lives of these others for a few more seconds of your own life."

The girl never moved.

"All right. We'll pick *your* first victim while you're waiting, have him stand up while I count seven—seven is my lucky number, Miss Martin—and, if by seven you haven't jumped, then I'll shoot him to death before your eyes."

The girl just stood still. Her hands clutched at her chest, fingers twisted. Horror, more than terror was upon her face. Not fear of her own death, I don't think, but horror of the deaths of others that she was powerless to prevent.

Tragic? Sure, it was tragic until Sour Pan brought the comedy into it. That's right—he pulled the best line of his piece in an awe-inspiring voice.

"You—near the door in the back," he said, "you are her first victim. You with the cap, stand up."

"You with the cap." Get the point? That was me. I stood up, set my teeth grimly against the smile I feared was coming.

He was counting, looking straight at me, pointing his gun at me and slipping the words out of the side of his mouth.

"Four—five—six—seven."

The girl cried out for him not to shoot. And he didn't shoot. He had made a mistake. Seven was not his lucky number—not by a damned sight it wasn't. For he didn't have the seven out of his mouth before I put a bullet into it. Miss? I couldn't miss. Not at that distance. Why, the minute that lad asked me to stand up he was digging his own grave.

Brutal? I suppose you've got your way of looking at things, and so have I. I guess I can shoot a gun out of a lad's hand as well as anyone else. But a wounded rat fights back—a dead one, never. Other people were on that plane and entitled to protection. They got it.

The man with the gun in the pilot's cabin turned and faced me. That was his error. Pilots on the big ships are not exactly soft. One of them opened up the back of his head with a wrench and flattened him.

"Nice work, boys," I shouted, and, to the girl who clung to the back of a seat: "Nothing to worry about, Miss Martin. My name is Williams—Race Williams."

The pilots talked about landing at the nearest field. Margie Martin pleaded with them. The little, middle-aged lady begged and threatened and spoke of her sister sick in a Redmond City hospital. And me—I told them the truth.

"If you took orders from those guys because of a gun, you'd better take them from me. We go to Redmond City."

I grinned, and the boys grinned. They were willing to be forced into it.

"Of course, you forbid us from using the radio: Is that right?" one of them said. And, when I nodded, he added: "Of course, you make us pretend that everything is O.K. when messages come through, so the cops—the wrong kind of cops—won't be on the field when we land."

"And, of course, we dash to the car the moment we land?" Margie Martin smiled. "My father will attend to everything." She looked down at the man we had trussed up on the floor. "Charles Bordon," she whispered to me. "Johnny Vernon's closest personal friend."

After that, we talked.

Margie Martin explained things in Red City.

"My father was elected by the very men who desert him now," she said. "The citizens stood behind him in the beginning, ceased paying protection to Vernon's men. Then Frankie Spontz, through Vernon, imported hoodlums from other cities. Somehow, they got the names of the men who backed Father—and it was at them they struck. They were afraid. Only a handful are left now. Father won't quit. Politics cut off his money, but he got money from one wealthy man. This man wanted you, as I wanted you. He's paying your salary and the salary of others. But Vernon bought some of them over. You saw what they would do today. They would break my father by hurling my body from this plane."

She slipped her uniform from over her sports clothes, and talked. She was a beautiful young girl with a single thought, a single purpose—Redmond City. She was fighting tooth and nail for it. It was she who had raised the money to hire me.

"Mr. Williams—Race—" She clung to my arm, let soft hair brush my cheek. I didn't mind. But I wasn't conceited—I was just Redmond City to her, then. "You saved my life—you'll save the city. Please don't go down to the station when the train comes in."

"But I must," I told her flat. "That's my big show. I'm tough. I'm hard. I'm a killer. People are expecting things. My first impression upon the real people may mean something—everything."

"You want to make your entrance big, great and—"

"Colossal," I grinned as I looked down at the dead body and the trussed-up one of Charlie Bordon and got the pilot's nod that we were nearing Redmond City. He was going to land close to the district attorney's car on the edge of the field. Those arrangements had been made by radio.

The girl clutched my head, pulled it down, my right ear close to her mouth, and she talked. God, how she talked! My eyes widened, my mouth opened.

"Do you realize that you are suggesting murder?"

"Murder?" Her laugh was not pleasant, nor was she any longer the frightened girl. When she got wound up on Redmond City, the red got in her eyes and in her face. Damn it, she knew what she wanted done and she knew her Redmond City.

The plane was circling, when she finished talking. The dead man shifted slightly and brushed against her feet, but she didn't know it.

"So that's how you'd like it," I said simply, "the Redmond Ritz Grill?"

"That," she repeated, "is how I'd like it—the Ritz Grill."

And the Ritz Grill it was.

# FOUR

# SPONTZ DOES HIS STUFF

■

There is little use in going into our dash from the plane, the meeting between the district attorney and his daughter or the trouble I had getting the D.A. to take the strapped-up Bordon in his own car to some police station where he could trust all the boys. If Bordon was a close friend of Vernon, he might be valuable later.

After settling the Bordon question, I still had plenty trouble with the D.A. He couldn't understand my leaving him and going off with Margie in the taxi. But that was her idea, and I couldn't tell him.

"Watch over Margie," he said. "She has implicit faith in you, and—"

The taxi was gone. Margie clutched my arm. There was a desperate purpose in her face. She leaned forward and said to the driver: "The Ritz Hotel—grill side," and to me in a lower voice, "I have eaten lunch there—twice, sometimes three times a week— ever since Father was elected. Many times Spontz has come to my table and insulted me before my escort—before the entire room."

"Why did you continue to go there?" It didn't make sense. Then it did make sense.

"We've lived a long time in Redmond City," she said. "Please don't call it Red City any longer. The people are my friends. I have raised money for hospitals. I have worked among the poor. Big men lunch at the grill. Big men come there during the afternoon. I thought it would make them help Father to see how his daughter was treated—a girl who grew up with their daughters."

"It must have been tough on your escort." I shook my head. "This time, lady, there will be no insults. If you're right, it will hurt Frankie Spontz no end. There's nothing starts a bad man going downhill faster than being laughed at."

"Laughed at!" She looked straight up at me. "I thought—"

But what she thought never came out then. The taxi had pulled to the curb. We were at the grill entrance to the Redmond Ritz Hotel—Frankie Spontz's favorite spot.

The girl had to plot and plan. She finally induced the headwaiter to give us one of the booths not far down from the bar where Frankie Spontz generally filled himself with liquor.

The manager was nervous. The headwaiter was also, but a captain of waiters, who looked as if he had some backbone, did the trick. Twenty bucks, and he led us around through the kitchen, slipped us into a booth just about the end of the bar. The girl did the talking. I held my head low and wore huge sun glasses. I'm not much on the disguise business—whiskers or what have you. But dark glasses often do the trick.

The girl sat so she could see the length of the bar and see Spontz come in.

The captain set the silverware and said: "It's a shame, Miss Martin. But you know how that—what Spontz is." He drew back a bit there, explaining he wouldn't speak like that to anyone else. "He'll see you and start using—er—foul language."

The girl ordered a cocktail—took another while I was waiting for my steak, then watched me go to it with a couple of cups of coffee. I was hungry. The steak was good. I did another cup of coffee, smoked over it.

The girl put on a regular front. But her laugh was nervous when she said: "Coffee for you, Race? I thought all big strong he-men drank nothing but hard liquor."

"Not while they want to remain big strong he-men," I smiled.

"Besides, I don't need any false courage that comes out of a bottle. I'll admit that drugs and alcohol make lads get hard and start shooting. But it doesn't help you to hit what you're shooting at. The other lad, having forgotten to load up with liquor, may shoot the top of your head off before—"

She slid back close to the wall.

"Is that Spontz?" I asked.

"Yes," she whispered across the table and her hands trembled. "I'm afraid, Race—not for myself, but for you. I shouldn't have—but he didn't see me and he's there—at the bar—talking."

By this time, the grill had filled up a bit. Voices that were chattering stopped when Spontz leaned against the bar. The girl jerked her head back, went white and said: "He saw me. He turned his head. I'm sure he knows I'm here."

He did. His gruff voice grew louder. His curses turned to foul words and then to back-alley—sewer—talk.

They were pretty tough even for me to stomach. But that was my cue. I pressed the button, prayed that our captain of waiters wouldn't go back on us. He didn't. His walk was not so steady, and his face was pasty, but he came.

"There are quite a few people here—some prominent citizens," he said.

"Buck up, boy," I whispered. "Miss Martin has told me how kind you have always been to her." With a grin at the girl whose suggestion was paying all the expenses, I said: "Here's a hundred-dollar note," and, when he nodded, added: "It'll be orders straight from me—a customer. Afterwards—well, go climb under the building. Ready?"

He nodded, and I shot the works. My voice was loud, affected, important—a young smart-aleck who knew his way around.

"Waiter," I said, "if that foul-mouthed beast is drunk, ask his companion to remove him. If he's sober—but at all events, he must stop his talk at once. There is a lady with me."

I got Spontz all right. There was no laughter when the waiter turned and left the table, but there was when he repeated my words, softening them slightly. Everybody in the grill must have been in on the show.

Spontz laughed, said gruffly: "What do you mean 'a lady'? There ain't been any ladies along this bar since the D.A.'s girl started pushing her face in here and attracting the riffraff of the city." And, after a bit, he asked: "Who's her boy friend—the sap with the high-pitched voice?"

"I don't know, sir." The waiter was very apologetic. "But since you heard what he said, anyway—well, he was quite insistent."

"He was, eh?" Spontz seemed quite jolly. "Joe, drag him out of that booth and—never mind, Joe. I'll speak to this wise guy myself."

Spontz came. I leaned far down over the table, but I eased my eyes up and saw him. My first impression was a good one. There was certainly a lot of him to shoot at. As for his face and head— not much to say about that. It was just a load of dough slapped onto his shoulders with features stuck into it by a bum artist. There was some hair on top of the dough.

"Young fellow," Spontz said. "You're in damn bad company. Come on—get up and beat it." He leaned against the booth, let his coat fall back showing his gun. He held a large beer in his right hand, let it slip over on Margie Martin's shoulder, down her dress.

I was tempted then. But I didn't fall. I didn't look up. I simply said: "So you're the foul-mouthed creature? Well, forget the incident and take your friends to some saloon more fitting your class—if they come that low. Come, come—move on, my good fellow."

The white of his face turned to red. There was death in his voice. He leaned over the table. He liked to show off and did then.

"O.K., little feller," he spat the words. "I said 'get out.' Now, we'll drag you out. Know who you're speaking to? Spontz— Frankie Spontz. Come on, lift that head of yours and let me see your face. You—"

I tore off my glasses, jerked up my head and came to my feet. He didn't know at first—and then he did. His face quit doing the heavy villain. He didn't move. He couldn't move. He couldn't get his feet into action. He was a very much surprised man.

I spoke my piece.

"So you're the cheap hood, Frankie Spontz, eh?" I snatched the beer glass out of his hand and chucked it in his face—glass and all.

I was out on the floor now—plenty of foot room, and plenty of talk, since he liked talk. And, what's more, I had him between me and the others when I cracked my knuckles across his mouth. "The name," I said, "is Williams—Race Williams. You know, the lad you were going to kill." I shot out my hand, and he put up his arms to protect his face—then I flopped a knee into his stomach.

"Why, you dirty, yellow, loud-mouthed four-flusher." I was giving it to him straight as I had him against the bar now and was smacking him around. "You got a gun there, under your arm. You got friends at the bar. They're all armed. Look!" I held out an empty hand before I pushed it into his face and nearly bent him backward over the bar. "Come on, Spontz. Show your stuff—if you have any stuff."

I stepped back, slammed him one that took the white out of his face and put yellow into it. His eyes whirled in his head, enlarged like a fish in a bowl, and nothing happened—that is, nothing happened to me. Were his friends waiting for an order from Spontz, or didn't they have the guts? I guess it was both. But there's few lads want any part of me when I'm set for action.

I turned to the girl, but kept an eye on the bar, saw, too, the startled, white faces of people sitting dumbfounded at their tables—some with drinks half raised.

I nodded to the girl, saw her slide from the booth and back to the kitchen door. But she didn't disappear, as arranged. Her white face was watching in the dimness.

I backed along the bar, said to the regular people at tables: "You're just suckers here in Red City. Cheap crooks, who pretend to be gunmen, scare you half to death. Now, I'm paid well to chase them out for you. Mr. Spontz is the first to go. Don't be suckers any longer. Make one out of him. Good afternoon." I turned my back completely on Frankie Spontz and walked indifferently toward the door.

But my eyes were not on the door. They were on a face at a table close to it—a face with intense eyes. We had nodded and understood each other, just after I got up from the table. It wasn't the first time Jerry and I had pulled this little stunt—and I didn't expect it was going to be the last. Of course, he had come on the following plane, and, going straight to the hotel, wandered into the grill. Now, his eyes weren't on me. They were behind me—on Frankie Spontz, the man who was playing the people for suckers.

A woman shrieked, a man at a table yelled. I paid no attention. I walked on. Slow, even, sauntering steps of pretended indifference. Maybe they would turn out to be my last steps. I counted them.

Fifteen steps as my eyes focused unwaveringly on Jerry's head. Sixteen, seventeen—

And two things happened at once. Jerry's head moved quickly down. I dropped to one knee as I swung. Close? Sure, it was close. Spontz's gun was smoking in his hand, glass crashed behind me, fell to the sidewalk outside. Here was my game—here was action.

Spontz didn't fire again. He had had his one shot—all any man is entitled to. He jerked up his gun, and I had him.

"Sucker," I cried. "Sucker Spontz." And I let him have it. There was a hole where his nose had been—and a customer less at the Ritz bar.

His pals were nervous. Their fingers were running up inside their jackets. One pal had a gun in his hand. I squeezed lead and burnt him over.

"I wasn't expecting that, boys," I told them as I put my back to a pillar. "This little affair was just between Spontz and myself. I don't know you fellows. I don't know how many of you there are. But if any of you thinks that I didn't do right by your Nell, why let him— No?"

I backed out the door and turned in time to face three policemen— no fakes, these—in harness. But I didn't drop my guns at once. Not me. I was trying to think what I'd heard about the cops in Red City.

People were coming from the grill, gathering about the police. I lowered my guns from view. A man cried: "That's Race Williams!" Another: "By God, he should have a medal and not be arrested." Angry voices shouted: "Knocked Spontz all around. Killed him after Spontz fired at his back. The finest piece of courage I ever saw."

"We know you, Williams," one of the cops said. "Keep your guns if you want. But Spontz has friends—inside and out. There's a taxi. Come on. Kids and women will get hurt like on Essex Street."

I didn't know where Essex Street was, and I didn't care. Then I saw a face across the street. I saw the heavy overcoat the man was wearing despite the hot weather.

"O.K., boys." I helped them push through the crowd to the taxi and climbed in with them, heard the orders, "To the Sixth Precinct on Essex Street."

"I understand it was Spontz and he's dead," a cop said.

"Someone sent for the police," another cop said. "I saw the end of it through the door. Spontz's bullet near cracked me. You shoot fast, Williams, but it won't help you much in this town. Things are bad. The boys are bad."

"Spontz isn't," I told them. "He won't be unless you keep him around too long."

The youngest cop looked sort of defiantly at the two older ones and said to me: "My name's Davis—Joe Davis. You can count on me, Mr. Williams. And these boys—"

The oldest one spoke.

"I've got a wife and family. We're paid by the man who runs the city. The chief is hired or fired by him. The mayor gives the orders. We must believe they are good orders."

"O.K. by me," I told them. "But pretty soon the mayor won't be giving orders. Johnny Vernon won't be paying him off. Then—well, Mr. Edward T. Martin will be interested in cops that didn't believe they were good orders."

The three cops turned, as we climbed from the taxi and went up the steps of the police station. They looked at the two apartment houses across the street, the lot between them, the broken stone wall before that lot, and the trash strewn around it. I looked, too. As we passed into the cop house, the youngest cop spoke to me. His voice was a hoarse whisper.

"By God, they wouldn't dare!" I answered.

"It's a fact," he said. "It's been done before. That's exactly how the reporter for the News Service died."

I snapped my fingers.

"History never repeats itself." I took a good look at his somber, but honest pan.

He spoke and he wasn't kidding. He said: "But murder repeats itself over and over again in Red City—the City of Blood—human blood."

# FIVE

# RED CITY RODS

■

We entered the police station, as a taxi whizzed by with a single passenger—a passenger who wore a heavy coat. Yes, that's right. Jerry, the boy detective, was on the job. I took a chance, whispered to the youngest cop, saw his face blanch, heard him mutter, "God in Heaven!" then with a determination I liked, "I'll do it. I can get out and back without anyone seeing me."

I stepped up to the desk and nodded my head at the lieutenant behind it.

A lad with a small mustache, and a cane over his arm, came up and shook me by the hand.

"I'm Hamilton Lawrence, Mr. Williams. Chief assistant district attorney to Mr. Martin." He grinned like a boy and added: "My father's a prominent man in town. I have plenty of money, so I can't be bribed—and my death would be hard for even the mayor to swallow. Honesty, influence, and a determination to rid Redmond City of crooks like Mayor Pendleton and Johnny Vernon, murderer, are my only assets."

The lieutenant on the bench looked slightly uncomfortable.

"I wouldn't speak so freely, Mr. Lawrence," and, when Lawrence gave him that influential look, father and all, "I'm thinking of you. Mr. Williams has just shot a man to death and wounded another, probably fatally."

"Mr. Williams is a detective assigned to our office." Lawrence spoke up like a little boy who generally got what he wanted.

There was trouble. Oh, they listened to Lawrence into whose custody the lieutenant was glad to place me. And they all agreed on everything except my right to carry a gun.

There was a city ordinance, and you had to have a license. The lieutenant shook his head, said: "It's orders directly from the commissioner and is worth my job. I'm doing more than I should for you, Mr. Lawrence. But he can't go out of here with any guns."

"Why?" Lawrence was indignant. "You'll send him straight to his death."

"I'm not arguing that point." The lieutenant didn't like his job one bit. "He's welcome to stay here, be kept in a cell even until he has a license." He looked squarely at me, said: "I understand you are still armed, Mr. Williams. Give me your gun—er—or guns— or whatever firearms you carry."

I crossed my arms and recrossed them, and he had two guns on the desk before him.

He pushed them aside as he looked at me.

"You're free to go with Mr. Lawrence, Williams." This after I was carefully searched. "But my advice to you is to stay here. Men like you—at least men in your profession—have been killed on the streets of the city."

"I'll chance the street," I said, and, looking out, "There's a taxi down the block I can get. O.K., boys." I stepped out the door and saw Jerry almost at the foot of the stone steps. "I want you to know that I'm on business—real business."

Kill, or be killed, was the motto of Red City. It suited me exactly. I saw the young cop, Davis's, white face, caught his nod and thrust young Hamilton Lawrence back so suddenly that he sat down.

Things happened like clockwork. The taxi moved up before the steps and across from the vacant lot. Jerry dug both hands in his pockets, as I passed him. I entered the taxi door the driver opened. Yep, there are no two ways about it. Red City furnished action, and I was set to kill.

So these guys went in for killing and murder? Why, they even went in for slaughter, because that was what they had planned for me. I just plunged through that taxi—in one door and out the other. The gun in my left hand squeezed lead and shot the machine gunner, crouching by the broken stone wall, to death before his gun started a racket or even a whisper.

The other lad turned. Yep, he turned and ran with a gun right in his hand—guns in both hands. He was weaving his way across that lot, in and out of the refuse. Once he turned and let a gun go off. If he hit anyone with it, no one complained.

Windows were opening, children were dashing down the street, crossing between the fleeing gunman and myself. The protectors of law and order stood on the steps. The man turned again, raised his gun, and I put a bullet in his chest. I could have killed him, I suppose, even at that distance. But the children were traveling fast—at least five of them, confused, wondering, frightened and pleasantly excited little boys—and I didn't have the time for careful shooting.

Lawrence was running down the steps. The lieutenant was striding through the door. Others stood stunned by the quickness of events, but one cop and one detective got up from the sidewalk and started dusting themselves off. Yep, those two, at least, had expected a run of machine-gun bullets that would riddle me and the cab and the driver just as we pulled away.

I shoved Lawrence into the cab, held the door open for Jerry to dive in beside us, and the taxi driver did his stuff. He just jumped from the curb and smashed the car into second gear.

Lawrence clutched at my arm, gasped: "How did you do it? It was like a rehearsal—as if you knew how it was going to happen all the time and were all set for it, waiting."

"I did know," I told him gravely. "Jerry, here, was carting plenty death. He gave me the guns when I came down the steps, fixed it with the taxi driver, though I doubt if Jerry told the man there was a machine gun across the street."

"And where did you get this information? Also, how did you get it to Jerry?"

I hesitated, then said: "A young cop—Joe Davis, who deserves a reward and a damned good promotion when things are cleaned up—he told me."

"You really expect to clean them up? Spontz's death was a start. He was Vernon's right-hand man and only close associate in the criminal world. But you can't shoot all those men to death."

I smacked my lips, sat back and took a hearty laugh.

"It would take time," I said. "But at a thousand bucks a day I'd make plenty." Then I shook my head. "I don't rob clients. Besides, the law of averages would be against me." I finished: "No, I guess the next on the list should be Johnny Vernon."

"You'd—just shoot him?"

"Sure, why not? I gave him his warning. He knows what to expect."

Hamilton Lawrence looked at me in amazement, then he said: "By Jove, Williams, I believe you mean it! I envy you for the courage it takes to even think like that. But to carry it out!" He shuddered and then, "Johnny Vernon is a big man—controls the mayor absolutely." He shook his head. "You won't be able to see Vernon—not even know where he is. All his orders came through Spontz."

"And Spontz is dead," I said. "From what I understand, he has no one else he can trust with big orders. He'll have to come out in the open."

Hamilton Lawrence shook his head again.

"Not while there is trouble. And there is lots of trouble, now, since you reached town. No, we'll have to wait for things to quiet down, before Johnny Vernon will appear."

"Wait?" I gave it to him straight. "Why, we'll set off the fireworks right under his nose. The D.A. can raid, get indictments, clean up the joints while Vernon waits. But he won't wait. He'll have to see the mayor. No, Vernon isn't the sort of man to wait—just because I'm in the city and a few of his pets took the bumps. He'll have to come out and give orders to kill me—orders the boys won't like."

We were well outside the business section now, slowing up before a large, rambling house. I told Jerry to keep the taxi and for him to wait for me on the porch.

"Edward Martin's place," Lawrence said, as we climbed from

the car. "I'll get his endorsement and then drive straight over to old Judge Wheatley and get your gun permit. We must have things according to law and order."

"Sure," I said as we marched up the D.A.'s steps. "We got to do things by law and order."

# SIX

# OVER THE WIRE

■

Edward Martin was pacing his library. He shook my hand in welcome and talked unpleasantly at the same time. I had expected some pats on the back. Instead he was saying: "Five men dead already. My phone buzzing continually, the papers about it on the street any minute now. Spontz—his friend—at the Ritz Bar. Two men directly before the police station—one a detective, the other a notorious gunman indicted in the vice racket, but never brought to trial." He grabbed at his head and walked a little faster. "Another shot to death in a plane, and Charlie Bordon, a—well, hardly known to Spontz, but a close friend of Vernon's."

I was a little annoyed—take it any way you want. I had been hired to kill—or at least to save my own life.

"Not satisfied, Mr. Martin?" I said. "Well, I'll admit a thousand dollars a day is pretty high pay. But a stiff an hour is not bad—not bad at all."

"But, Williams," he said, "it was all so open—the Ritz Bar, the street, in the air. Good God, the mayor will issue a statement against my—er—methods. Vernon will come out, abhorring such

314

violence." He shook his head. "Vernon is a big man. Few people know that he actually heads things, and those few don't dare talk. Vernon will—"

"Don't you worry about Vernon." I got this in, a little hot under the collar. "He won't be expressing any opinion if you'll give me a few more hours."

"You—you mean—you'll kill him?"

"Just that." I nodded. "I'm no man's target for long. As soon as he sticks his head out of his hole—just like that—I'll shoot it off his shoulders for him."

"Good Lord!" The D.A. was actually stunned—no fake about that. "Do you think I'd countenance such an act—a brutal killing, a—"

"You mean you won't pay for it?" I jumped in on him. "You expect me to shoot Vernon to death on my own time?" I stopped.

I had sized up the district attorney, his whole staff, his friends who had elected him. They wanted to do things for Redmond City, wanted to clean it up. But when the time came, they just didn't know what to do. So, instead of cursing Martin out, I gave him straight talk.

"You brought me down here, promised me a thousand bucks a day, promised that you would stand behind me," I said. "Anything I did was to be O.K. with you. No, you didn't put it in writing, but you're a man of your word. I'm here to earn my money." Then I gave Martin a detailed description of events, told him everything that had happened and about Davis, the cop, while Lawrence went off to get my permit to carry a gun.

I tried to put the D.A. back on his feet. Oh, his determination was still there, but things had been moving too fast for him. Things he hadn't expected to happen for months—if ever. He felt he was fighting with his back to the wall. I jarred him out of that mood, talking fast.

"It's Vernon we've got with his back to the wall. Now, he'll have to fight out of it. You're striking, and they're defending. We've got them on the jump. Let's keep them that way. If the mayor makes a statement to the press, why—"

"The mayor will do, or say, whatever Vernon orders him. Poor Pendleton. I don't know what came over him. Greed, I suppose. It will be Vernon's statement."

"No matter," I told him. "We'll snap back with a fast one. Just state that the rats must go one way or another, and that the head rat will be next. Oh, you don't need to say who he is, but—"

Martin turned quickly, snatched at the evening papers that the maid brought in. He read first the headlines of one, then the other, shook his head, looked bewildered. He handed me a paper.

"The Redmond *News*," he coughed. "Our paper—the citizens' paper." He held it toward me. "And the *Sentinel* will be against us, of course." He went on reading his paper, and I looked over the headlines of the one he had handed me.

I liked it. No New York paper could do me more justice—at least none ever had. But the flaming banner on sheet one was hot stuff—

## WHIRLWIND OF DEATH FOR
## SCORES STRIKES THE CITY

Vicious Gunmen Ruthlessly
Shot to Death by
Race Williams, Notorious Private Investigator

Maybe I would have preferred "famous" to "notorious," but just the same it was good stuff for me, if not for Edward Martin. There was a line about "Spineless District Attorney Finally Goes To Work."

"Pretty good," I said to Martin. "Now, for the bad news in the *Sentinel*."

Edward Martin shook his head.

"But it isn't bad news—isn't at all. I can't understand it. The mayor condones your acts, hopes to meet you personally and says he is glad that at last he has the active and aggressive support of the district attorney, his fellow citizen. He adds that he feels certain all the influential people of the town will stand behind him, and that Mr. John Vernon, the city's leading realtor and philanthropist, feels that Mr. Williams has struck a terrific blow against crime and for law and order. And listen to this, Williams. Vernon thinks you should be rewarded. Clever, eh? They intend to kill you quietly."

"Oh, I'll be killed some day—any day." I grinned, maybe sort of grimly. "But certainly it won't be quietly. You can kiss the Book on that."

And, damn it, while we were thinking that over, the little maid walked in and tossed a bombshell.

"Miss Margie on the phone, Mr. Martin," she said. "Will you take the call here?"

"Margie?" Edward Martin looked from the phone to me. "But I thought she was with you, Williams."

"Me?" I tossed back. "Why, she was to slip out through the kitchen of the Ritz grill and come straight home."

"She didn't." He walked to the phone. "But she's all right if she can telephone me."

Was she? I had sudden doubts—you know the kind. They hit you abruptly right down in the bottom of your stomach. She wasn't safe. There were no two ways about that. I half caught, half held Martin as he staggered from the phone, and turned wide eyes at me.

"It's Margie. They've got her."

I didn't have to ask Martin any questions when I picked up the phone. Maybe I hadn't been so damned bright, after all. But I did my job. I lifted the phone, heard a low voice muttering, "Dad—Dad—"

"It's Race Williams, kid," I said. "Let me have it."

And she did—in a burst of words that would have made Floyd Gibbons, our rapid-speaking champion, sound like a lad who drawled.

"Don't leave, Race. Don't do as they ask. They intend to—"

A sudden whistling sound, a scream and a voice I recognized. It was Johnny Vernon.

"Hello, Race." His voice had an attempted laugh in it, but not a very good one. His passion, his hate must have damn near melted the wires. But he went on: "We won't discuss the past, for it might make me butcher the girl now. She was going to tell you that you were not to believe I would let her go if you left Redmond City. And she was right—and you would know she was right, for trains and planes that leave Redmond City return to it. There, we won't talk about your word or my word. We'll be two very sensible people. Are you listening?"

"Sure, I'm listening." I didn't say any more. I couldn't say any more. Johnny Vernon wasn't the only one burning with hate.

"Well, we have a little plan. We'll return the girl, if you take her place. For a month—perhaps longer. But I want you out of

Redmond City until I can reestablish things. It will take some time."

My curse changed to words. I pressed the phone closer to my ear so Martin, bending over my shoulder, could not hear Vernon's voice.

"Some time?" I said. "You mean a lifetime—my life. No, Johnny, I'm not sentimental that way. You're up the wrong alley."

"O.K. The girl dies, then—rather horribly, Race."

"You're throwing up any chance you ever had of returning to Redmond City." I forgot about Martin behind me and gave it straight to Johnny. "If anything happens to that girl, I'll pop you off with a hunk of lead the very moment I see you."

"Wouldn't you, anyway?"

"Well, we might make some deal with you." I was thinking. "We might give you a chance to leave town and promise not to prosecute if the girl was returned alive and unhurt."

"My way's better." Johnny laughed. Probably hearing my "Wait!" and Martin's insistence that he listen, Johnny raised his voice. "Martin, your boss, will have you off the case and out of town in twenty-four hours—no, twelve hours—or the girl will be delivered, her body mangled and—"

Martin dragged the phone from my hand. At first he threatened, then he pleaded. The perspiration formed on his forehead and ran down over his eyes and nose. For some time he listened. At the end, he begged to hear the girl's voice—did—a voice that ended in a shriek of pain.

Martin turned to me, opened his mouth to speak, collapsed into a chair, and finally said: "It's you, Williams—you. You have caused me this trouble. Now, they want you to die for her?" Yes, there was a question in his voice. He looked at me rather hopefully.

There was no use to fool him. I told him calmly enough, "That's out," and, when he seemed surprised, "If I died to save every father's daughter whose death was threatened, your girl would have been hurled from a plane. What else did Vernon say?"

He looked at me kind of stunned, cleared his throat, let the tirade about me slip by and gave me the worst.

"He said I was to discharge you at once. Then, since he and the mayor had both agreed that I was doing good work as district attorney, that we would all three work together. That, when things were working right, I'd see my daughter again. He said we'd all work together, but he would give the orders."

"So what?"

"It's my daughter. Johnny Vernon said something about burying her alive—he had the place for it." When I didn't speak, he moaned: "I can't let her die like that."

"You've got to," I told him, and shot in quick when he wanted to cry all over the place: "That is, you've got to chance it. If he kills her, and we can prove it—or I can even see him—he's a dead duck. As for his letting her return after he got control again, that's bunk. He may keep her alive for a few days so you can talk to her. But he'd have to kill her then, or she'd talk. She's not like you. She's got guts. She loves this city, would be glad to die to save it. He can't win if he kills her, and I stay in town. He can't win if he lets her live, and I leave—she'd give him the rap. The people would believe her."

"It's my daughter that counts," he said over and over.

"That's right," I said. "I'll never see you again, so I don't matter. Probably your daughter will die without ever knowing that you ratted out on your friends—on her."

"No—no." He came to his feet now. "I'll fight on. I'll make a statement to the papers. I'll—"

He looked noble enough and, I suppose, felt noble enough. But, after all, I was there to protect that daughter. His qualification for district attorney wasn't much better than young Lawrence's except that he was better known and more trusted. So I gave him a little experience that came out of the book of life.

"We'll act fast," I said. "He's got a hostage. We'll get one. We'll get the mayor to tell us where he's holding the girl."

"But the mayor—you couldn't do that. He's guarded too closely to kidnap."

"Hell." I gave him facts. "I don't intend to kidnap him. I'll just visit him to shake his hand. He invited that in his cracks in the paper. Then I'll get alone in a room with him—what if there are a hundred armed men outside? I'll ask him where Vernon has the girl, and tell him if he doesn't answer, I'll shove my gun down his throat and—"

"Not with Pendleton." Martin shook his head. "You couldn't fool him with any threats like that."

"Fool him?" I gasped. "God, man, I won't be fooling!"

"But the mayor!"

I shrugged my shoulders.

"Lead won't rest any easier in his belly than it does in the belly of a common gunman."

Edward Martin's face went from a sudden white to pasty yellow—then almost a cream-colored.

"I believe you mean it," he choked the words.

I nodded in satisfaction.

"And so will the mayor. Let's pay him a visit—now."

# THE SCREAM OF A WOMAN

■

We didn't pay the mayor a visit. A telephone call advised us that the mayor had left town on urgent business. The phone rang a lot after that. Politicians, soft-spoken lads, who were ready to drop from under and sell Vernon out for their own safety. Guys were getting ready to turn state's evidence so fast that it would not only be turning, but spinning like a top by morning.

Hamilton Lawrence came back, then, and the cop, Davis, walked in with a list of bulls who knew things. Those few shots of mine had blown the dome right off the city hall.

So there was the layout. Guys ready to talk, and Martin afraid to listen—afraid because his daughter was to die.

Yes, Vernon had moved quickly. He knew better than we did how near his whole structure was to collapse. Nothing would save it now, but the D.A. working in with him. Once the political boys found they couldn't get in touch with Vernon—once they felt he had lammed on them—good-night, Vernon. They'd talk any words Martin wanted to take out of the dictionary.

Only the greatest enemy of Vernon, and his rotten gang, could save Vernon. That was Edward Martin, and the price of Vernon's power was the life of the girl.

The City of Redmond was saved! There were no two ways about that. Its future lay in the hands of Edward Martin, and I saw the rest of it in his eyes before he spoke to me.

"Go down to the Ritz, Mr. Williams," he said and his voice was stiff. "I'll have another telephone call shortly. I'll have a lot to do. But stay there until you hear from me."

There were Lawrence and Davis in the room. I didn't speak, though I could have said plenty. I just walked toward the door. But Martin spoke to me, and I knew what was on his mind. He was selling out the town.

"We're all very grateful to you, Mr. Williams," he said. "It seems that your services may not be needed longer. If that is so, I'll have a check to you for"—he hesitated—"for twenty-five thousand dollars."

I spoke, then. I couldn't help it. I gave it to him straight.

"You hired me for one thousand dollars a day. Though I didn't really do a day's work, I always charge for a full day. I'll send you the bill for one grand."

I swung on my heel and walked through the hall, out the door. Gunmen laying for me, then? No. I half wished they were. I'd have shot them for nothing. What a town! The mayor was crooked, his backer, a murderer—and the district attorney a damn fool.

I was just beckoning to Jerry when Hamilton Lawrence followed me to the porch, clutched my shoulders, sputtered: "Something has gone wrong—terribly wrong. What is it?"

I chucked a thumb back over my shoulder. "Ask him—the D.A."

"It's Margie. You've got to tell me, Williams. By God, you've got to or I'll"—and damn it, he shook a fist in my face—"yes, I'll thrash it out of you."

He was a big, strapping, husky, clean-cut lad, but I don't like hands on me, nor fists in my face, and I wasn't in a good humor, anyway. I knocked his left hand from my shoulder and his right fist from before my face so hard that he fell toward me. Then I pushed a palm in his mush and if he had not missed the big pillar by inches, he might have fractured his skull. Nothing against the boy, understand. After all, he was an amateur. I'm a professional at any kind of physical violence, from a little face-pushing to a back-room brawl.

"What the hell?" I said. "You must be mad!"

He raised both his hands, dropped them again almost at once, and spoke.

"My apologies, Mr. Williams. I love Margie. She's going to marry me—if the city is clean again. That's why I'm assistant district attorney. That's why my father put up the money to—"

"O.K., boy," I interrupted him. "It's Margie. They've got her. The D.A. wants to sell out the city for her. They'll kill her, anyway."

"Yes, they'll—" He paused. "Can't you save her?" Suddenly, he said: "She wouldn't want to live like that. She couldn't live like that. Martin doesn't know his own daughter. But he loves her, too."

Suddenly it hit me. His father had put up the dough—the one thousand a day. Her father had offered me twenty-five thousand dollars to walk out and keep quiet.

Lawrence read my thoughts—or maybe I spoke my thoughts out loud—about the twenty-five grand. Anyway, he said: "Don't leave, Mr. Williams. I'll give you the money. I'll pay you what you ask, to just try and—"

"Boy," I told him, "she's in bad hands. I won't kid you about that. Vernon and the mayor are hanging on a thread between a run-out and a comeback. If it's a run-out, the girl will be dead tonight. If it's a comeback, they may keep her alive a few days—enough for her father to hear her voice—until they are back in power, and the guys who would have talked, can't. I'll gamble with you. Twenty-five thousand dollars for the girl alive—and to hell with Redmond City."

He gripped my hand.

"Done," he said, "and to hell with Redmond City."

A moment later, Lawrence said to me: "Stay at the hotel. I'll come down and see you."

I walked across the stoop and followed Jerry to the taxi. Once I stopped and turned back, but I let it slide. Sure, it was the permit to carry a gun. But I didn't worry about that now. From all reports, I was the big shot in Redmond City. Those who were likely to ask me to show a permit to carry a gun weren't likely to be alive to look at it. Maybe I had lost the district attorney and maybe I hadn't, after Lawrence had a talk with him. Anyway, I had the assistant behind me, and his father—the heavy dough of the whole parade.

I walked straight across the Ritz lobby, leaned over the desk and asked for a suite—two bedrooms and a sitting-room.

The clerk swung the register. I hesitated, then scratched *Race Williams* over four lines of the page. If guys wanted to find me, they were entitled to know where I was.

The clerk made a grimace of disgust at my scrawl and swung the register around. Then the scowl went off his puss, as if you'd wiped a rag over it. His glasses snapped off his nose; his mouth hung open.

"Good God! Race Williams!" he said and tore the page smack out of the book. But he apologized and probably for the first time in years actually stuttered.

"Really, Mr. Williams—that seems dangerous. In the hotel, too. Of course, anyone who asks for you—anyone you expect. But like that, sir. Your name for anyone to see. There's a bad element in town who—"

"You leave my name there, and I'll decorate your hotel with the bad element." Then, realizing I didn't want to have reporters on my neck, I told him: "If the district attorney, Mr. Martin, or his assistant, Mr. Lawrence, ask for me, I'll see them."

"Yes, sir." He looked toward the elevator as if he'd like to get rid of me. "No one else, of course."

"No." I started to follow the boy toward the elevator, stopped and turned back. "Oh, yes," I said, "one other. If Mr. Vernon— Mr. Johnny Vernon—should call, send him right up." When his pan opened up a gap like the Holland Tunnel I added: "Don't worry—I'll take care of the body."

I left him, then.

# EIGHT

# THIRD-DEGREE TRICK

∎

Jerry was hungry, and I was hungry. We made monkeys out of a plank steak that it would take six ordinary men to kill. We sat back, and Jerry picked his teeth with a match and gave me the dope.

"I come on the next plane, parked the suitcase full of lead downstairs and—"

"You didn't take a room as I told you?"

"Nix." He shook his head. "I took the bag to the washroom first and loaded up with artillery. You see, I threw a couple of beers into me at the bar, heard that Spontz came in every afternoon, thought maybe there'd be a break like there was, and five bucks would have been lost in a room I'd never use. After that—well, I saw you had seen me when you was knocking Spontz around and knew when you turned your back on him it was the old game. Queer, too." Jerry tossed away the match and started on another. "Right through the nose on his face. He twisted like a corkscrew. I never seen a guy die funnier."

"Saw," I corrected him, leaned back and grabbed up a match of my own.

The steak was good, things settled pleasantly, and I did a bit of thinking. I'm a guy who'll wait just so long for a bit of action—then go after it myself.

If Margie Martin didn't show up alive—well, no matter how long I was back in New York, I'd make a point of slipping down to Redmond City some night and giving Vernon the works.

Understand, that's not vengeance—though I didn't like him. It's pride in my work. I don't like unfinished business.

Vernon would know that. He wouldn't show his face in town until I was dead. And he was right. Apparently, I had both the newspapers, the mayor and Vernon behind me, as well as the D.A. The thing was for Vernon to get me killed. But here I was in a suite of rooms with a suitcase full of artillery.

Vernon would try to trap me. Right in the middle of that thought, the phone rang—and Vernon did his stuff again.

He talked good. He didn't threaten. He just laid things nice and honestly before me. At least they sounded nice, and he said they were honest. He said: "I've talked to Martin again, Williams. He feels you sort of stand in the way. A word from you, and he'll come across." I liked that. Martin hadn't busted yet. "Now," Vernon went on, "after all, it's simply a question of power. I want that. Martin wants the girl alive, and you work for money. Oh, Miss Martin has come around to seeing it my way. She wants to live because she wants to get married. We'll put the town on a paying basis, let Martin put his hands in the sugar or resign as he sees fit. And you—name a figure, and I mean real money, for I'm a fair-minded man, and we'll pay it to you." A pause and then he shot the works: "You can see and talk to the girl, Race."

"Oh"—I put on an indifference—"I've got a new client now. We're not overly interested in the girl. Don't tell me about her horrible death," I cut in as he started to talk the heavy melodrama. "I read about such things in the paper every day."

I heard Vernon call to someone behind him.

"Drag that damn girl to the phone and—"

She screamed, as I heard the blow strike her. A pause, and she screamed again—not with terror, not even with fear, but with pain.

"Tell her father about that," Vernon said. "Tell young Lawrence about that." Then, the scream again—the horrible scream of a woman in torture.

I raised my head, saw Jerry reach for a gun as the man at the door struck him with such terrific force that he hit the wall and slid to the floor.

I snapped the receiver back on the hook, hollered for Jerry not to shoot, ducked under the vicious right swing as the left hand, followed by a flying body, grabbed at that phone. Then I struck— just one fist up. But that fist came clean from below my knee. Hamilton Lawrence was at it again. He was sitting there on the floor, staring at me.

"What the hell now?" I said.

"It was Margie. They're torturing her. I could hear it at the door—her scream of agony. They're going to kill her slowly, horribly."

"Easy does it, boy," I said as I pushed him back to a sitting position when he tried to rise. "You couldn't have heard all that over the phone."

"Not over the phone. At the police station. They're giving him the third degree. But he laughs at them, admits he knows where the girl is, where they would take her, where Vernon and the mayor meet. But he won't tell. We've given him the third degree."

There was no way to stop Lawrence, so I let him blow off steam. I found out the lad was Charlie Bordon, the tough guy we carried from the plane and hid away in a cop house so he wouldn't talk then.

"You think, Bordon knows?" And, when he gulped and nodded, I asked: "You offered him freedom? You offered him money, and he wouldn't tell?"

"No, he wouldn't tell. He's an old pal of Vernon's, the closest to him—personally, I mean. But he'll talk if we give him ten thousand dollars cash and let him leave town."

"Why, it's worth that!" My eyes widened.

"But we are not sure he'll tell the truth."

"That doesn't matter. If he lies, give him a little more of that third degree."

"That's the trouble," Lawrence gasped. "He wants the money first, wants to leave town first, then telephone us from some place else and tell just where Margie is."

The phone was ringing again.

This time it was Edward Martin and he wanted to talk to Lawrence. He wasn't exactly unpleasant to me, but he was excited. I let Lawrence get his wind.

A minute later, Lawrence turned to me.

"Mr. Martin thinks it's best to let him go. It's a hope, anyway. Why wouldn't he tell if he had the money?"

"Why would he?" I took the phone from Lawrence and talked into it.

"Listen, Mr. Martin," I told the D.A., "I'm working for Hamilton Lawrence now. Oh, never mind what interest that is to you. Don't let Bordon go. I'll come right over with Lawrence. Put him through some more third degree. What will I do if you can't get him to talk? Well, I'll look him straight in the eye and advise you if I think he'll tell after he's free."

Jerry, Lawrence and myself rode downtown to the old police station.

It appeared that Vernon had sent word right to Edward Martin that if Charlie Bordon wasn't found and produced at once, it would be just too bad for Margie. So they didn't have much time to waste.

"Be sensible, boy," I told Lawrence as we went down the damp stone steps and he insisted on releasing Bordon—even if it were a hundred-to-one shot.

"Why, it isn't even a thousand-to-one shot!" I said. "He'll have both his freedom and the dough. Why should he give you the information? He expects Vernon back soon, and he'll be sitting pretty again. But the real crime you're committing—yes, it's a crime—is letting the man go who really knows where the girl is."

I held Lawrence back and put my fingers to my lips at the policeman who stood before the cell door. It was a huge, square stone pen, probably used to keep a number of prisoners ready for their day in court. So we looked in and saw the third degree in action.

There was Charlie Bordon—tough Charlie Bordon—sitting on a stool under a powerful lamp, and they were all talking to him at once. Two big cops, Edward Martin, himself, and young Davis, the cop I had recommended. Threats? Sure, they threatened him. Anywhere from life imprisonment to the chair. There was immunity offered him, money promised him—and once Davis smacked him a crack in the kisser and was admonished by the D.A.

"Really, boys, it's more than I can stand," Bordon lisped. "Give me some water, a cigarette and I'll tell all."

They gave him the water and the cigarette and he drank and smoked, spat on the floor, finally said: "I was just a little child of five when my father—"

The D.A. turned red. Davis knocked the cigarette from his mouth. Bordon sneered and said: "You got my last word. I'm not half as tired as you fellows are. Ten grand in cash, a free ticket to wherever I choose to go, and I'll telephone in where the girl is and how to reach her."

"Well, I suppose—" The D.A. rubbed his forehead, young Davis cursed, and I stepped before the barred door.

Lawrence had the man open it. The D.A. looked at me, shook his head. A cop said: "He won't talk—there ain't no use."

I looked toward young Davis. His chin was set tight; he didn't speak. Bordon said: "Mr. Williams to join the party, eh? Give me another butt."

I stuck the cigarette in his mouth, lit it for him—and shoved it down his throat. He was coughing a bit, when I spoke my piece. Yep, I stood there flat-footed and told Edward Martin, the D.A., the truth.

"Third degree, eh? You must have taken a correspondence course. You're nothing but children at play."

Bordon cursed and laughed, and I swung suddenly.

I turned the gun in my hand as I brought it down across his face, the sight ripping an ugly, jagged gash from his forehead down over his nose and chin. My second blow was a side swipe that knocked him off the chair and slammed his curse into a cry of pain.

I said to the two big cops who looked absolutely amazed: "Lift the big bum up on the chair, and we'll find out just how tough he is."

But it was Davis who got him onto the stool. Bordon didn't look so good now. He said: "The girl will die horribly when Vernon hears of this."

"Who's to tell him?" I barely looked at Bordon.

The D.A. said: "We never permit physical violence. And we've found, Mr. Williams, and the penologists agree with us, that it does not pay. An experienced criminal will confess to anything under rough treatment."

"Sure, sure." I nodded. "Such a confession never stands up before twelve men in a jury box. But we're not trying this man for anything. Get a doctor."

"Yeah, I know where the girl is," Bordon sneered. "I know where Vernon planned to take her before. But I wouldn't talk if you cut me to ribbons."

I turned and looked squarely into those muddy, narrow eyes.

"You're a good guesser, anyway, Bordon. That's exactly what I'm going to do—cut you to ribbons. Come on, Martin." I cut out the 'mister' stuff. "This man boasts that he knows where your daughter is. Get that doctor."

"A doctor—why a doctor?" Martin seemed stunned.

"You don't want Bordon to die before he talks, do you?"

Bordon laughed. "I've heard that before." But his voice had lost some of its humor.

I looked at Davis, and he looked at me. Then I got the D.A. and the two cops to stand outside the cell—even lock the door and hand me in the key. I slipped it into my pocket, looked at Davis again.

Davis set his jaw. I said: "About you, Davis—can you take it?"

"Yes," he said. "Yes." And, after a gulp, "She's a swell girl."

Bordon was sitting straight on the stool, sneering and telling me just what would happen to the girl—something about burying her alive—Vernon's hate for Martin and for the girl who had stirred the town to action against him.

"That's fine, Bordon." I stood directly before him. "She's a young girl—she's a lovely girl. She'll die in agony for Redmond City. I like her, Bordon. I'm paid twenty-five thousand dollars to find her. That's a lot of jack." And, leaning very close, "Just one man stands between that jack and me—just one man stands between that girl's dying in terrible agony or being saved. You're the man, Bordon. You'll finally talk."

He started in to tell me the kind of tough guy he was. Then I let him have it. Bordon was tough all right, but a girl's life hung in the balance. It wasn't pleasant. I didn't like it when he got at the crawling stage. Once Davis was sick—and then came an interruption.

Yep, from Edward Martin.

"God—God, Williams! No—no! I'll order an officer to shoot—shoot you in the leg."

I turned and looked at him. I saw the steel door inside that barred gate. I moved quickly, closed the door, blocking off Martin's view—blocking off any possible chance of hysterical bullets. But I said, and plenty loud through the tiny crack in the steel: "If you're built like that, Martin—to hell with the doctor. He talks, or I kill him."

I turned back to Charlie Bordon.

"O.K., Charlie, you're tougher than I thought you were. Vernon will win out, but you're not going to be alive to tell him what happened to you."

Mud-colored slits widened, stared.

"That's right, Charlie," I said as I bit my lower lip. "You got the guts for it. I'm going to beat you to death."

I was soaked from head to foot in perspiration when I opened the steel door three minutes later, unlocked the barred one, and, leaning against the stone, said to the white-faced Martin: "Fetch a doctor you can trust, at once. Your girl is hidden in an abandoned cemetery a few miles out of town—a vault owned by the mayor's family years ago. Give me a drink of water."

"Yes, yes"—Martin had the doctor there and let him in—"we must go at once. I know the place. It was used during Prohibition for smuggling liquor. Fred—Harris—" He was calling to a couple of cops when I stopped him.

"I'll run this show from now on. Damn it—fetch me that water."

I got water. Yep, the D.A. brought it to me himself.

# NINE

# ONE-WAY TICKET TO HELL

■

The doctor wanted to shoot his head off. He did, for a few lines. He said: "This is a most atrocious assault. The man will live, of course. It was as if the one who administered this brutal beating wanted his victim to live."

They all jumped on me, then, with a barrage of words. But I stood against the wall and waited. Edward Martin knew I meant it when I said Bordon could be placed on a cot there, but I wouldn't let him be moved out of that cell until the girl was safe.

"Good boy, Davis." I patted the young cop on the back. "And you, too, Lawrence. It's not pleasant work." As Lawrence stared at me in horror, and they lifted Bordon to a cot, I let myself go. "By God!" I said to Lawrence. "I did a job for the girl you weren't man enough to do yourself. And—"

"Easy does it, Race." He put an arm around my shoulders. "I understand. It was terrible. I know no money could pay you for what you did—no money would. Don't let yourself go now—don't blow up."

"Me?" I laughed. It sounded weird, hysterical. Others were

looking at me. I turned and lit a butt, swaggered over to a corner of the cell and leaned against it. I think I shook slightly, but then the place was damp. Truth is truth. I wouldn't have gone through that job again for a million dollars. No, it wasn't for money. It wasn't for hatred of Johnny Vernon. It was for the scream of a woman—a woman who had more guts than anyone in that room.

Sure, they all took my orders, yet they seemed to avoid me as I walked across the floor and stood above Charlie Bordon. He didn't look so bad now—patched up by the doctor—merely like a lad who had fallen out of an airplane.

To hell with the lot of them, I thought, as Jerry, noticing my face—maybe the whiteness of it—came in and stuck his arm through mine. But I spoke my piece.

"I'm sorry, Charlie," I said stiffly. "But it's just one of those things. I had to win. I'm built that way."

"Win what?" He looked from the doctor to the others standing around and said: "The vault is guarded by a dozen men. You'll get them with force, but they'll kill the girl."

"You wouldn't want the girl killed after all you went through to save her, would you?" As I thought of the girl, I began to burn up again. I snapped out my watch, said: "This is my assistant, Charlie. It's now nine-thirty. If I don't get back by one o'clock, he's going to shoot you to death."

Charlie nearly jarred out of bed.

"And if you do get back?" Charlie spoke through swollen lips. "Then what?"

"If the girl is dead, I'll shoot you myself. I'm not kidding, Charlie." I shrugged my shoulders, watched the others leave the cell. Then I locked the barred door and shoved the key through to Jerry.

"One o'clock, Jerry," I piped. "Then let him have it."

"Can't I give it to him now and go along with you?" Jerry came to the door and pleaded. "He ain't much account, boss."

I shook my head. Lawrence clutched my arm. He said, and I think his words squeaked high enough to reach the man on the bed: "Do you think he'll fall for your bluff?"

I looked straight at Lawrence, straight at Martin behind him, said simply: "I never bluff."

And Bordon broke. He cried out frantically for me to come

back. Jerry opened the door, and I stood above Borden's bed, looking down at his terror-filled eyes.

"Listen, Charlie," I told him. "Suppose you work this out your own way. Just how you'd save the girl if you were in my place. It will not only save your life, but Lawrence there will give you the ten thousand you asked for—and Mr. Martin, the freedom you requested." I turned to the two men. "Right, gentlemen?"

"Right," they answered as one man.

"There's a chance," Bordon said. "Oh, not for any other man, but for you a chance. That old vault was used for storing liquor. I told Vernon about it, and he used to meet the mayor there. But there's an underground passage to it from a smaller vault down near the river bank. That's how we got the liquor."

"That's talking." I rubbed my hands, bent low so that the others couldn't hear him. "Give it to me—all of it, Charlie."

This time when I turned toward the door, Charlie spoke differently.

"You think you can make it, Williams? Vernon will be in the big vault. Think you—"

"I'll take a crack at it, Charlie." I nodded. "Your life and mine hang together tonight. Same orders, Jerry." And, just before I left, "Long life to both of us, Charlie."

Edward Martin, Hamilton Lawrence, and even Davis all knew about the old vault. They were out for organizing a bunch of picked men and raiding the place. That a dozen or more men guarded it, meant nothing to them. They could get twenty-five or even fifty picked men in no time. Sure, they were all for action when it was the wrong kind.

"I've got to get inside that vault alone," I told them flat. "You can gather all the men you want outside, but no shooting until the girl is safe. The entrance to the tunnel is guarded by two men. Any shooting, any attack, any alarm, and the girl dies—dies long before you could get into the vault—but not before Vernon could escape. Since I'm not familiar with the place, Davis can come with me."

"But you'll be killed!" Lawrence put that one.

"That," I said, "will save you just twenty-five thousand dollars. If anything should happen to me and Vernon tries to escape by the river, Davis will fire a shot and you and your men can go to work. But I'll want fifteen minutes after I enter that smaller vault."

So much for that. There was a lot of talk. There always is. But I was the guy who had to pop my head up through the trap in that huge vault and maybe get it shot off. The thing, as Bordon explained it, was more difficult than you would imagine.

We finally left the D.A. and Hamilton Lawrence, who stood by the D.A.'s car watching us intently, and wanting like the devil to come and give up his life for the girl. But it was my life he might give up—so he stayed behind.

After we started off in the car, I gave Davis the lay, and it took the breath right out of him.

"The tunnel entrance to the big vault," I said, "is guarded by two men stationed outside the smaller vault. There is a buzzer with which they can give an alarm. That buzzer spells 'death' to the girl, and safety to Vernon if he's there. It closes a stone trap door. If that happens, Vernon will know that his river entrance has been discovered. He will leave by the heavy door in front of the vault and escape under fire of his own men. Bordon doesn't know where it is, but he knows that a plane is ready, day and night, for Vernon. He might kill the girl or take her with them."

"You believe what Bordon told you?"

"You were there in the room, Davis. What do you think?"

He nodded solemnly.

"It was terrible, Mr. Williams, but I admire you for it. Now, I wouldn't know what to do, except—well, just find that entrance and demand—"

"That they throw up their hands?" I chuckled. "No, they'd simply kill you, set off the alarm, and all hell would break loose. That would be fine if we could chance a dozen cops, or a hundred, but lone workers have to strike first."

Davis knew his ground all right. He knew where to get a boat. I had him put me ashore about a hundred yards down from the big vault that stood perhaps one hundred feet back from the river. The little vault was in a thick, grove-like marsh, about five yards from the river.

"O.K., Davis," I said before we parted—Davis for the river, me to travel the rest of the way by land. "Put your boat right up to that spot before the small vault and leave the light on it. One man will go down to investigate, then I'll get the other. Shove off, lying flat in the boat. When that lad comes back, I'll get him. Remember, I must enter one vault to get into the passage to the other. We must have absolute silence. Under no circumstances shoot."

"Under—no circumstances?" There was a question in his voice.

"A shot will mean the girl's death," I said. "So do as you think best, but keep out of any mess. This is my party. I've got two forty-fours." I stepped out of the boat, shoved it into the stream for him, heard the soft stroke of his oars, then I crept along the river bank.

Now, as Bordon gave it to me, the guard only surrounded the main vault. Those men didn't even know of the existence of the tunnel. Johnny Vernon didn't trust too many men too much. So I went forward along the marsh, hidden from the moonlight.

I saw the large vault, standing there, dismal, gloomy when I pushed my head from the thick growth. Water lapped at my feet, hiding sound. I raised myself, and, shielded by a dead tree trunk, tried to spot the figures that surrounded that vault. Once or twice I thought I saw a man move, but the grass was high, and I could only picture, as Bordon had pictured for me, the men who lay flat on their stomachs.

Then I saw the tiny vault that was more a huge, cave-like rock— a worn, dilapidated bit of structure buried in grass and—

I stopped dead. A man suddenly arose from a stone, walked straight toward me. The white blotch of a face was clearly there before me. He spoke to me.

"Well, who was down by the river, Laval? Was it—" His words stopped. For the first time he knew that I was not his pal. A white hand with something black in it came up—as I struck, saw the red on the white, and stepped quickly forward to let his body sink slowly to the ground. No noise, as I let the body down gently.

I jarred erect, crouched again almost at once, found the stone the lad I had bounced a gun on had been using, and sat down on it. A figure was coming straight up from the water.

A lucky break? Sure. Davis had rowed too fast. I had just made it. Then I saw the face approaching me. It was Davis. I started to my feet, dropped back on the rock again and let my face be swallowed in the shadows of the small vault. For Davis was walking with his hands above his head. It was the figure behind him who spoke—the man called Laval.

"Look what I got, Pinky." The man addressed me in the blackness. "A copper—Davis. The good and honest and faithful servant of the people. I was sitting right by the water, when he pulled in. I don't think he knows anything, for he was making too much noise, but I stuck a gun in his back and brought him along."

I came slowly to my feet, backed around where the trees still kept me in the shadows. Then, getting in the right position, I stuck a gun in Laval's ribs, saying: "Look what I got. Maybe you'd like to hear it pop."

When he just grew rigid, and I thought he was going to close a finger on the trigger of the gun in Davis' back—and so give the warning—I added: "Drop your gun, smart boy. Race Williams talking."

The "Race Williams" got him. The gun fell from his right hand. Davis started to explain.

"He was at the water when I came down and—good God, what was that?"

"That," I said, "is the lad who took advantage of you down by the river. There's another one just behind me." I was hunting for the door to the little vault, and, as I found it, "Shoot anyone who comes out of here—if it isn't me."

# T E N

# GUN FOR GUN

■

I stepped into the small vault, closing the door behind me. Sure, I
let loose with my flashlight. There was an open trap with wooden
steps down it. Did I douse my light? I did not. I shot it ahead of me
and went down those steps. The tunnel below was long and
straight—at least fairly straight—and it was braced by long two-
by-fours, the wood rotten and eaten.

I dimmed my flash for a second and nodded my satisfaction. A
glimmer of light showed far down. That would be the trap I'd go
up. Maybe I thought of what would happen if anything went wrong
with the mechanics of those slabs of stone—the one I passed
down, the one I would pass up. Yep, I was in the pathway of the
dead. I set my lips grimly.

The going was a bit rough, but I didn't show a light any more.
Ahead was that dim light, ever brightening, to guide me. The
ground was rough, and the timbers beneath had shoved themselves
up a bit. Part of the time, I went along like a drunken sailor. But if
anyone were coming the other way, why I'd rather see his light and
shoot before he saw mine and shot.

But no one was coming the other way, and I reached the end of the narrow passage. The light shone down from a square hole above, and a ladder was stretched up to that light. Voices, too—anyway one voice—as I started up that ladder.

Then a voice thrilled me. No, not a woman's voice—not Margie's. It was the voice of Johnny Vernon. He was saying: "I tell you I can't get Martin nor Lawrence nor Williams on this phone. What are you moaning about, Clarence? It's your life or the girl's. She's got to die."

I guess Clarence spoke.

"That's so. It's terrible, but someone has to kill her."

"Sure, you've had many murdered," Vernon answered. And I took a chance and stuck my head up just as Vernon said: "No one will hear the shot from in here."

Yes, I stuck my head up, and a gun or two with it, but I couldn't see anything—that is, any people. There was the cold dampness of a large vault—but a pillar of marble between me and the speaker. There were great doors to my right, and, across them, a huge bolt that was new—a long, heavy bar that could lock them by sliding it into place.

I climbed from that trap, stood erect and slipped along the cold stone. Now, I could see the light, the back of Vernon and the figure on the floor—the kneeling figure of a man with a gun in his hand, and the bound girl at his feet. The girl faced me, eyes burning straight into mine in the bright light of the electric bulb.

I nodded my head at Margie Martin, slid a bit further, held a gun forward in my right hand, and slipped my left hand behind my back. I didn't want to be interrupted now by Vernon's friends outside.

My left hand felt the long strong bar, gripped it. Very slowly, I pushed it, felt it slide silently along as oil got on my fingers. Then it clicked home with a sudden, metallic snap.

Both men swung their heads. The girl cried out: "Race—Race—I knew it!"

I said, viciously and with meaning, for I had nearly beaten a man to death for this moment: "How is it for some lead in the belly, Mr. Johnny Q. Wise Guy Vernon?"

I was looking at Vernon and the man who knelt on the floor and held his gun so close against Margie Martin's head.

Vernon was no Spontz when the big moment came. He said, and

his voice was fairly steady: "Drop both your guns, Williams, or my friend will simply close a finger and kill the girl. It won't matter then. She's caused all this and she'll be dead. So drop them now. All right, Clarence, let her—"

I didn't know Clarence's intentions, and I didn't feel I had a right to ask them. I closed my finger once. There was a hole in the side of Clarence's head, or should have been unless he just pretended to be dead. Anyway, he sort of bent over the girl, then rolled slightly and lay on his side. I'm no medical examiner, but my own private opinion was that they didn't come much deader than Clarence.

"Dead men don't close fingers on the gun triggers, Vernon," I said. "You made me kill him. Now, remember my promise to you?" I repeated: "How is it for some lead in your belly?"

I waited a moment. So he was just a yellow rat. I'd have to turn him over to Martin. I listened. Shots outside—many of them.

The girl cried out. Then hatred, fear and passion collided and broke inside Johnny Vernon. He swung and fired. Things went dizzy. I shot toward the ceiling, hit my back against the door and started to sink slowly.

Johnny Vernon laughed. I couldn't see him—things were just blurred. But his laugh was a mistake. I didn't see him, but I heard him and I set both my guns to blazing. Yes, that's right. I was shooting at a sound—shooting at a laugh. But the laugh didn't shoot back. The laugh screamed once, then thudded upon the floor, and I raised my eyes and brushed blood from them. I shook my head, too, and staggered to my feet. Guns were blazing all over the damned place now before I realized that those shots came from outside—and that men pounded upon the door and tried frantically to get in.

Then things cleared just as suddenly as they had blurred. I cut the girl loose, got her to her feet and was surprised to find no hysteria. And then—just when I began to admire her as the super-woman—she went and collapsed in my arms.

Things had gone good outside. I listened at the door and finally decided that it was Edward Martin, the D.A., hollering.

I slipped back the bar of steel, and let Hamilton Lawrence take over the girl. I leaned against the wall, sort of tired, and watched the show. Martin gave orders, as if he knew what he were talking about. The doctor finally saw me, came over, examined my head and said: "You must have been bending, my man. A heavy-caliber bullet left a furrow right across the top of your skull." He wiped the blood from my face. "The slightest fraction of an inch deeper and—hello, you're the man who beat Bordon so viciously! This is the result. So the girl might live."

"That's the ticket." I stuck a finger into his chest. "Better give her some medical attention."

The doctor smiled, said: "Young Lawrence is giving her all the attention she'll ever need."

I turned my head slowly and looked toward the wide-open doors, and the man who was slipping through them. I whipped out my gun, sprang forward. He was the portly gent I had first seen in that New York restaurant.

It was Martin who grabbed my arm. Hamilton Lawrence cried out: "Father—what are you doing here?"

"Watson Lawrence," Martin whispered in my ear. "Been working on this case in his own way, for a long time. Said he was going to New York, take a hoodlum from here with him—just to test you out. But he never does half the things he sets out to do. Rather eccentric, you know."

"Eccentric!" I gasped. "You don't mean cracked?" Suddenly disturbed now that things were over, I said: "His check for twenty-five thousand—it would be good, wouldn't it?"

"It would be good for ten times that amount. He's rich and influential." Edward Martin frowned. "You killed Vernon and—do you know the other man you shot to death?" His eyes were wide, troubled.

"No, I don't," I told him. "But we can find out, I guess. Had a hell of a first name—Clarence."

The portly gent spoke behind me.

"And a hell of a last one too, Mr. Williams. He is Clarence Pendleton—Mayor Pendleton." He smiled right in Edward Martin's serious face. "My boy tells me you have a check coming to you. I hope you will permit me to give it to you before those five bullets come right in my breadbasket," he repeated my threat of the Rostoff Restaurant.

Was that the end of Red City as far as I was concerned? Just about. But I was appointed police commissioner for one week—and at the salary of one thousand dollars a day which wasn't so bad after I had found the portly gent's check good the following morning.

Commissioner of police, eh? Me—Race Williams. I had always wanted a job like that, even for one day. I felt I could do real business.

The next day I gave my orders to the cops. I gave my statement to the papers. It was simple and direct.

"Redmond City has been held in a state of siege by the criminal. Every one of these criminals is known to me. Any one of them found in Redmond City on Monday, the eighth of the month, will be shot dead upon the public streets."

There. Laugh that off. Did it clean things up? Well, no man can be absolutely certain of anything. But the railroad company sold more one-way tickets out of Redmond City in the next couple of days than ever before in the history of the railroad.

The Mysterious Library offers enduring works of reference, biography, and fiction covering the entire spectrum of crime and suspense literature.

### Eric Ambler: HERE LIES: AN AUTOBIOGRAPHY
The Edgar Award-winning autobiography of the man Graham Greene called "our greatest thriller writer." ILLUSTRATED.
$8.95

### Robert Barnard: A TALENT TO DECEIVE: AN APPRECIATION OF AGATHA CHRISTIE
The definitive critical study and celebration of the lady whose name is synonymous with mystery, by the distinguished mystery author.
$8.95

### Raymond Chandler: RAYMOND CHANDLER'S UNKNOWN THRILLER: THE SCREENPLAY OF "PLAYBACK"
An entirely new story—in the form of a never-produced screenplay—by one of the 20th century's most influential authors.
$9.95

### Carroll John Daly: THE ADVENTURES OF SATAN HALL (A *Dime Detective Book*)
A series of 1930s novellas featuring "The Man Police and Gangdom Alike Feared," by the most popular writer of pulp detective stories.
$8.95

### Norbert Davis: THE ADVENTURES OF MAX LATIN (A *Dime Detective Book*)
Novellas from the 1930s and '40s featuring a most unusual private eye, by one of the most talented of the pulp writers. With an introduction by John D. MacDonald.
$8.95

### Patricia Highsmith: THE ANIMAL-LOVER'S BOOK OF BEASTLY MURDER
A series of extraordinary murder tales, each featuring a protagonist who is not man but beast.
$8.95